My Secret Billionaire

FRAYDUN MANOCHERIAN

For all my readers, with thanks.

PROLOGUE

HE WAS A MAN WITHOUT a home and a man without an identity, and at the moment, he was also a man with no concept of time, of place. He was floating in the air, metaphorically, and soon, literally. For this man, the sensation of taking flight was the same as he'd always known, but the perspective was totally wrong. Just like his current life.

As the giant 767 jet barreled down the runway, its tires hitting every bump and groove of the black tarmac, the man found himself mindlessly staring out the window, watching the world rush past as though it had forgotten him. Was the plane trying to catch up to the outside world, or was it running away, shooting into the sky as a way to divorce itself from reality? Were the several hundred people on board doing much the same, flying, going, running, avoiding, or in his case, rediscovering?

The engines whirred and whistled, and after one final thump of the tires, the mighty jet lifted off the ground and headed upwards toward the clouds. He enjoyed the rush of excitement as they left the earth—both the heightened danger and the powerless feeling that boiled in his blood. He always felt this ascension was a test of life's tenuous nature, though he usually saw it from the perspective of pilot, less so as a passenger. But for him, right now, all the details were changing, just as quickly as the plane was gaining altitude, and though it would level off at a cruising level of some 37,000 feet, he knew his life wouldn't be settled for a much longer period.

Several minutes passed before the cautious ding of a bell sounded throughout the cabin. An announcement was made that they had cleared 10,000 feet and that people were free to use approved electronic devices. A bustle of activity erupted in the cabin. All around him went on ear buds and headphones, phones, iPads and laptops, tucking themselves into their own digital worlds despite the cramped quarters. But he had no such distraction with him, and so he contented himself by continuing to gaze out his window to the world below. He shifted restlessly, unaccustomed to sitting still for too long. He was usually a man of action, one who used every waking moment to his full advantage. Never a dull moment, wasn't that his creed? Things were different now. He was different now.

He knew he didn't like it.

He also knew he had no choice in the matter.

He'd made a promise.

He would keep it. He was that kind of man. Honor meant everything to him.

The jet bounced along the swift currents, then bounced again. *Air pockets*, he reminded himself, but that still did not stop him from instinctively clutching the armrest. He had clocked hundreds of thousands of miles in the air during his life, and he knew how durable airplanes were, how a simple jostle had so little impact on the steel fuselage, on the roaring engines. People still looked about, nervous expressions on their faces as they realized their vulnerability, their mortality. Usually, he thought these folks were fools, so afraid of things beyond his control. Today he felt one with them, as though being out of sync with his normal life had affected his confidence. He wanted nothing more than for the flight to be over; hell, for this involuntary adventure to be over as well.

He had a long flight ahead of him.

And a long road.

Only this morning, he'd been the internationally renowned businessman Ferro Olivetti. Rich, powerful, not without influence all over the world, destined for greatness. Hours later, he was a stranger in his own body, a new destiny attached to his identity. He even had a new name attached to himself, one that sounded strange on his tongue.

Out the window, clouds gave way to an amazing burst of golden sunshine. All around him was a brilliant blue sky that seemed like something only a painter could create, with broad, bold strokes of azure. He was truly lost in time, far removed from all he knew, from the world that kept him cocooned, protected. He was on his own now.

How did I reach this point? He asked himself.

His seat companion said nothing. Just as he'd done when he boarded and when they'd taken off, his nose stuck in a book. The man formerly known as Ferro was surrounded by dozens of people and yet was truly alone. Was that the opening gambit of his new adventure, feeling the fear of abandonment, of being dependent on yourself and no one else? Was this how you started your life over again? For a fleeing moment, he wasn't sure he could do this.

It wasn't the dream's fault.

His subconscious had given birth to it.

And life had made it a reality.

What he wouldn't give to change the last few weeks.

What he wouldn't give to not be facing this adventure now.

He had hundreds of millions of dollars in banks all over the world, he had luxurious homes and fancy cars and wealthy and untold women, but even those lavish trinkets weren't enough to save him. In fact, they were at the heart of the problem. They were all just things…possessions. Who did he have in his life to share such privilege? The answer was simple, and sad. No one. This very moment, he knew it all came down to one thing:

the will of his father, and he knew deep in his soul it was the one thing that could never be altered. For there was nothing more important to him than adhering to the wishes of his recently deceased father.

The plan continued to soar over the air. He watched, he waited, for whatever unforeseen turbulence could be coming his way. Because he knew there would be. Life had betrayed him, suddenly, unexpectedly, and it had all begun with the dream….

PART ONE

FERRO'S GAMBIT

CHAPTER ONE

THE PICTURES WERE BLURRY, *with no definable images visible. There were perhaps the contours of a face, maybe two, but it was as though they were cloaked in murky darkness. Gradually a light emerged from behind them, silhouetting the images against the frame. An older man, a young boy…yes, and between them…a game? Pieces on a board, figures. People, knights, royalty. Was this the past he saw, or perhaps something still to come, alive only in his subconscious mind? His eyes adjusted to the growing light, a faint yellow glow widening the scope of the scene unfolding before him, And then, suddenly, the picture was there.*

With the quick, confident motion of a trained professional, the older man moved his game piece. It was the king's pawn, stepping forward two squares. He smiled broadly, as though he knew the game was his for the taking, even with such a simple initial move. He'd made his opening gambit, and he had a sense that his opponent would take the tempting bait.

A smaller set of hands now, taking hold of his own king's pawn, moving it ahead one tentative square. Ha, *thought the senior of the two players,* always lacking the initiative to take life by the horns. *Nuance and subtlety were one thing; aggression was quite another, and it was the latter that won you favors in the game. In life, too. That was the lesson.*

The older man made his next, cunning move. The queen, standing proud, now sliding across three squares. She moved with the elegance of a huntress, a sleek Diana, unexpectedly deceptive for such a regal woman. With that bold move, he eyed his opponent and watched as the boy's brow furrowed over this curious dilemma. He was cautious about an attack from all angles, but somehow failed to see a recognizable pattern, as though they had never before played out this scenario. The boy's fingers touched upon his bishop, but then he paused.

"Hesitation is not the game face you wish to project, my son."

"Yes, Papa—but distracting my thoughts with the sound of your voice is a cheap shot by an opponent afraid of a well-executed challenge."

Bene. *Good. The older man nodded his approval. Still, he waited.*

The once-blurry figure was that of his father, Signor Alberto Olivetti, and he studied his lone son, still a boy, just nine years old he was, but already sharp with his wit, handsome with his looks, and defiantly ambitious in his ways. The game of chess was theirs, and theirs alone in their house, played on a game board carved from African ivory. A third figure emerged, breaking through afternoon sunlight, their concentration, too; it was Mama, shaking her head. Never did Mama partake of a game she found "a foolish exercise. All that wasted time thinking." She preferred to stay in the kitchen, stirring the pot that filled their villa with the seductive scents of sauce and spice as her two precious "men" tried valiantly to outmaneuver each other. She had often told her husband that as much as she denounced this competitiveness between father and son, it was precious to her seeing the two of them spending such quality time together.

Of course it was Sunday, the only day Alberto Olivetti allowed himself complete, uninterrupted time with his treasured family. Other days were consumed with his work, an obsession he held toward building a fortune that enabled them to live in a style and comfort the elder Olivetti had missed out on during his own childhood. As a young boy, he had struggled on the crowded streets of

Rome, darting from the crumbling arches of the Colosseum to the bustling crowds of the Piazza Navona and nearby Trevi Fountain, ably scoring spare lira from unsuspecting tourists. Nowadays, he had more euros than he'd ever dreamed possible, and he also had something else he always wanted that money could not possibly buy: a son to carry on the Olivetti name. But only a son who could compete in the real world, one who would succeed because he'd learned at an early age the sour taste of defeat.

Just then young Ferro made his move. King's rook moves one, no, two squares. From there, the game went all too predictably, and quickly. Signor Olivetti acted fast, his hands working faster than his clever mind. Queen forward two more squares, staring down his opponent's king's knight's pawn.

"Checkmate," Signor Olivetti stated.

"But, Papa!"

"Ha ha, Ferro, my boy. I made a fair move, a classic move, and now your king is mine in just four simple moves."

"Shall we play another?"

"What, so I can then beat you in three moves?"

"One of these days, Papa, I will defeat you. In fact, I bet I could beat you in the very next battle."

"My son, that is my most treasured desire," he said, "but much like a lawyer should not ask a question he does not know the answer to, one shouldn't bet so unwisely, not unless they know they are assured of winning." And with that he ruffled the boy's thick dark locks, watching as this action lit up the boy's eager, smiling face. Oh yes, a game was one thing, but life, that was another, *thought Signor Olivetti,* and in that you have already defeated me, you won me over the moment you were born. *There was nothing that he wouldn't do for his son. He could teach him about life, and he would teach him about winning.*

Ultimately, though, he would teach young Ferro Olivetti the most important thing in life. Something stronger than wealth, bigger than power. Not to discount the importance of such desirable trimmings, certainly not, but those were nothing compared to the enveloping happiness that comes from a full stomach and the sweet embrace of the one woman who stands by your side.

"Come, my beautiful men," said Signora Olivetti in her sing-song voice, "before supper grows cold and I grow stern."

Signor Olivetti took hold of his son's hand, and together they walked to the table to join Mama. To be a family, and to partake of their bounty.

Mama, setting a steaming plate of pasta before them, said, "And do I even need to ask who won your silly game?"

Ferro waited for his father to proudly proclaim his easy win. Instead, what came out was another of his father's lessons, and this one had the ability to stick with him. For what his father said was, "Always remember Ferro—victory is empty without humility, respect, and charity." Then Signor Olivetti turned to his beloved wife and said, "Our boy, there will be many days ahead that he will succeed. He just has to be mindful at times. Or he could lose it all."

The second to last word he heard was mindful.

Then that awful word: Lose.

Young Ferro did not want to lose. Not anything.

"Promise me you'll never leave me, Papa."

But in this fuzzy reality, there came no answer. The image faded, leaving Ferro standing alone, adrift, not even sure where he was.

And then the image blurred again, and the only sounds he heard came from a swirling wind.

*   *   *

"Never leave," came a disembodied whisper.

He jolted awake, the voice inside his head forcing open his tired eyes. He gazed about the darkened room, momentarily distracted by his unfamiliar surroundings. A quick check of his iPhone, strategically positioned bedside on the night table, indicated the time was 3:30 in the morning. A glance showed there were seventeen new emails awaiting his attention, all of which he presently ignored. There were more troubling matters than business floating inside his head.

Pictures, blurry at first, clear, then blurry again, as though the images were fading in and out of some other realm, all of them beyond his control. That's when he realized he'd dreamed that same troubling dream again, he and his father innocently playing chess while enjoying their precious Sundays together. Not exactly one particular memory, the dream was more of a composite of his times with his father, the man's challenges and lessons—all meant to send a young and confident Ferro out in the world. Looming success was imprinted on those lessons; he took them with him everywhere. But usually, those lessons lay dormant deep inside, part of his instincts. He was aware of them, always, but it had been some time since he'd heeded his father's words. Ferro Olivetti had his own style now, one the press had dubbed "brash, bold, and biting." Still, why now did the dream come to him? It had begun just a few weeks ago, coming to him in the wee hours of night with no discernable pattern. Still, the dream never failed to wake him from a supposed deep slumber. He always awoke bathed in sweat.

He slipped out from beneath the protective covers, felt the cool chill of the room against the heat of his body. Careful not to wake the woman who slumbered in his bed, he stared back at her as he stretched his body. His reaction to seeing her was not one of love, nor at the moment one of lust. She was just there. A comfort, yes, a warm touch. Her soft, blonde hair splayed against the pillow, her skin pale like porcelain, noticeable from the glow of the moon bathing the room. No denying she was beautiful. But weren't they all, Ferro thought.

He padded his naked self across the carpeted floor to the window, where he noticed on the nearby table the remnants of their passionate night together, an empty champagne bottle and two crystal flutes, one of them rimmed with scarlet lipstick. A sip of bubbly remained in the other glass, and he reached for it now, gulping down the flat liquid gold with one swig. Then he shook off the cold that rippled throughout his system. Damn, how could he feel sweat on his brow, and a chill up his spine?

The dream, his mind said.

Ferro stared out the window at the gorgeous view afforded by this mountain retreat deep in the mountains of Colorado. The snow was pure and fresh, and new flakes drifted down from the sky like magic dust, covering the tiny town of Telluride. They had spent the last few days here, skiing down dangerous hills, snowboarding off ice-hardened ramps, indulging in cold champagne and hot fires, making powerful love when their passions overwhelmed them. If anything marred these perfect last days of his vacation, it was the recurring dream. Why was his father's presence such a part of his subconscious thought? What did his childhood have to do with anything dominating his life now? Despite the month-long pleasures in which he'd indulged, business called to him, a major deal that would assure him a place among the power brokers of the world. Taking his millions and edging him close to billionaire status. Tomorrow, he returned to strike the next blow that would secure the deal, hopefully bringing ruin to whoever dared to thwart him. Or, at least, attempt to. Was this it? His desire for revenge for the person who dared challenge him. Was the dream a message, his father warning him that emotion had no place in business?

When he returned back home, he would call Papa, and of course Mama. She was not without her own lessons, less overt as they were. He reminded himself to tell them he loved them.

An empty feeling dropped into the pit of his stomach. He felt his head spin.

Could this be what other people call stress? Was the juggling act that was his crazy lifestyle finally catching up to him? Is that why he had prolonged his time away from Olivetti Enterprises? For the past several weeks he had been all over the planet, playing and partying in the world's top capitals and destinations, worrying about nothing but having a good time.

Was that another message his dream-state Papa was trying to get across to him? Ferro had a lot riding on business now, but he hadn't wanted to problem-solve lately. That's what he had people for, and why he paid them a fortune.

Didn't having buckets of money mean you could pay others to handle your stress for you?

Just then he felt a cool touch on his shoulder, causing him to nearly jump out of his skin. As he turned, anger written across his face, he found the woman from the bed standing behind him.

"I'm sorry, Ferro, to disturb you. Come back to bed. I'm lonely."

"Aren't we all," he said without thought, the words as cryptic to him as to her. He looked away, again focusing on the snow falling outside. The wind had picked up again, the drifts were deep as mounds of snow backed up against the walls of the cabin. It was as though the outside winds were encroaching on their safety, threatening to encase them in a block of ice, chilling them while holding them hostage. He knew he had to make a move, not unlike the game of chess he'd played with his Papa in that dream. Trouble was, he'd lost that game. He'd lost so many of them.

Before he could protest, he felt the woman's arms encircle him, her cheek resting on his back. "The dream again, Ferro?"

Why had he ever told her about his dreams? The last thing he wanted to discuss was what ailed him. How could he talk when he didn't understand it himself? A man of power never revealed his weaknesses. But not even Ferro Olivetti was impervious to fear. The night was not picky when it came to choosing its victims. It knew when to haunt, and who.

"Yes, the dream came to me again."

"I'll make everything right."

He wasn't so sure she could accomplish that. No woman had ever been able to penetrate his heart deep enough to make any lasting impact, not since…he pushed her name from his mind, then thought of his long-suffering Mama, truly the only woman who understood him. Mama hadn't yet given up hope of grandchildren, but she had ceased bringing it up in conversation whenever Ferro phoned. The woman with him today, tonight, she was a delectable distraction. She had certainly proved that each night and each morning. He doubted she would be the one to provide those desired grandchildren.

She too was naked, her curvaceous body and generous breasts causing his body to stir. He set aside his troubles and concentrated on the lovely sight before him. He marveled at her beauty, the way her smile could intoxicate him the way no champagne ever could. An image flashed in his mind of her face when they made love, the way she gazed into his eyes and let him know how amazing he made her feel. Taking hold of her hand, Ferro led her back to their king-sized bed, where the two of them lost themselves in each other, in their embrace and in their kisses. With his muscular body atop her, her fingers gliding across his muscular, lightly hairy chest, he could smell her sweetness and taste the lingering effects of the bubbly. He felt himself growing with anticipation of what was soon to happen.

"Ferro, make love to me," she said. "Now, make it sweet, make it gentle."

Ferro's eyes blurred. He wouldn't admit to shedding a tear. He shut out the reasons why. Gone were the images of his father, his mother, his long-ago youth in Italy, the innocent he once was, all of it faded and what was left was the powerful and ambitious Ferro Olivetti, the man who was unstoppable, both in business…and in bed. Passion fueled through his loins. Something took over inside him; the fear was gone. Ferro the animal had returned.

He quickly slid open her long legs and thrust inside her with his thick, engorged cock. She cried out with surprise at the suddenness of his entrance.

"Oh, Ferro, wait…"

He didn't. He thrust again, and seconds later the protests transformed into generous moans, signaling her absolute pleasure, a total submission to his passionate whims. He pushed and pushed more, crying out each time like an unleashed beast, filling her while fulfilling himself. They were miles from civilization, secured in this cabin, surrounded by mounds of snow, and connected only by technology they could easily avoid. Their lovemaking was loud, intense, focused on the here and now. Nothing else mattered but their mutual pleasure. For the moment the dream was gone, there was no past and certainly no future. The worries about what the dream meant had already receded in his memory.

When at last he climaxed deep inside her, he felt a flood of tension leave him, and he waited to catch his breath. But he kept going, he needed more, and he knew she needed more. He penetrated her again, and this time she let out cries of delight. Waves of desire came over her, not one, not two, but more than she could count. Ferro knew how to love a woman, even if it wasn't a love that came from the heart. He had satisfied them both, and at last he fell back against the pillows, once again lying in his own sweat. But this time it was for an altogether different reason. He was physically spent; their acrobatic sex had been just what he needed.

"Tomorrow," she said, sidling in next to him. "In the light of day, all will be better."

But Ferro wasn't convinced of that. He turned away from her, not wanting to hear any false platitudes she conjured. Lightness would not, could not, fix what ailed him. And strangely, darkness did nothing to cover it.

Still, tomorrow held some sort of promise. Because tomorrow he returned home, to face what an already generous life would afford him next. He had all he'd ever desired: the wealth, the looks, the power, the reputation as a man not to be messed with. Tomorrow he would begin to take his company to greater heights. Even in a moment of vulnerability, he had the strength to snap out of it and take charge, just as he had moments ago with…

Shit, what the hell was her name? He came up blank.

But couldn't he ask the same of himself? Who was he, really? Sure, he knew his name, but he meant something far deeper. Sometimes, like now, lying in the pitch darkness when it seemed the night would never end, he wondered just who was this creature named Ferro Olivetti. He dared not close his eyes again.

Dreams were messages.

Dreams were the future. They were the past.

Dreams also went by another name. Nightmares.

*   *   *

For a man suddenly plagued by inner doubts, Ferro Olivetti still had it all. He was easily a man to be envied by some, scorned by many, and gossiped about endlessly. When you have money and looks, somehow the press thinks you are fair game. Ferro, though, was resourceful, and he afforded the *paparazzi* little chance of snapping his photo and plastering his image all over the tabloids. One of those ways? To fly his own plane as much as possible.

The silver-colored car dropped both Ferro and Cassandra at the small airport in Telluride, where his Gulfstream V had already been cleared for takeoff. If any press was present to snap a photo, good luck. The car had tinted windows, the Gulfstream was hidden inside a hangar, and it only took moments for the couple to make the transfer from one form of transportation to another. Cass looked at the luxury afforded by the plane and stared at Ferro.

"I still can't believe you know how to fly this."

"Cass, this plane is my most prized possession. Other than internationally, it's all I ever fly. You will sit back and enjoy the ride, yes?"

"What does gambit mean?" she asked, noticing the name of the fuselage.

"It is my name for her. Gambit One. An opening move. Hopefully she is the first in a fleet," he explained, for a moment remembering the dream. Named more for the way his father played the game than anything else.

"You are very good at opening moves," she said, "remember it well, at the gaming tables in Monte."

Ferro smiled at the recent memory, then let it go just as quickly. Business awaited him, and there could be no more delays, no matter how much he enjoyed the kind of delays that Cass afforded him. Ferro escorted his luscious blonde date inside, told her to get comfortable in the cabin while he set about the controls.

"Am I really coming with you, Ferro? Not just to San Francisco, but to your home?"

Ferro paused, a look of consternation suddenly crossing his face. "I have to check all the instruments. We will talk later when we're in the air."

"In the air? Aren't you the pilot? Don't you have to, uh, fly it?"

"Cass, in the short time you've known me, have I not proven myself of handling many things, all at the same time?"

She grinned back. She knew he was right.

And he had expertly changed the subject.

Ferro, dressed warmly for the cold weather that had settled over the mountains during this late stretch of March, shed his coat when he entered the small cockpit. He dropped into his seat, affixed the seatbelt, and immediately put on his headgear to get in contact with the tower. Instructions were handed out, tests were run for the preflight check, and before long Ferro pronounced the plane fit to fly. Frankly, he couldn't wait to take off. The world was never more beautiful to him than when he looked down upon it, the snow-capped mountains here in Colorado, or the wondrous calm that was the Golden Gate

Bridge on final approach. He was headed home. Ferro took a moment to breathe.

From behind, a hand snaked inside his sweater. He felt a kiss on his neck, both tender and tingling. Ferro eased back and closed his eyes, a smile broadening his face as Cassandra worked her magic. The first thing she did was unclasp the seat-belt. The second thing she did was find the zipper. It was always good to fly relaxed. She would help him achieve that level of Zen which so enlivened his flying. Hardened, excited, he ran a hand through her platinum blonde hair, helping her with her up and down motions.

"Meeting you, Cass, you have no idea how you've helped me," he said, and then with a laugh, added, "how you're helping me now."

Cass said nothing. Her mother had taught her it wasn't polite to talk with your mouth full.

Just then a crackling sound came over the headset. He thought it was the sizzle between them.

'Gambit One, come in, please."

Then another crackle of static.

Ferro's eyes jerked open, and he realized the tower was trying to reach him.

"Gambit One," he heard, this time more insistently. "Mr. Olivetti, is everything all right? You've been cleared for take-off, and frankly sir, there are two other planes awaiting departure this frosty morning. Shall I give one of them their clearance?"

"Sorry, sorry, guys. I allowed a distraction, my apologies."

He stared down at Cass, who wasn't yet finished.

"Yes, indeed, Mr. Olivetti, we were having trouble reaching you. Is there a problem with your communications system?"

"No, everything's just fine."

"We could send someone down there right now to dou-ble-check," the traffic controller said. "You don't want to fly without the ability to keep in touch with air traffic. That leads to all sorts of trouble up in the sky."

Interference from the grounds crew was the last thing Ferro needed. "No need to send reinforcements," he cautioned. "I'm in good hands, fear not. Sorry for not getting back to you when you first called, all this preflight preparation, something, uh, came up. Gambit One out."

Ferro removed the headset. "You're terrible, Cass. Getting me in trouble with them."

"Is that a complaint?"

"Hardly."

"Besides, I thought you were the boss. Don't they answer to you?"

"In life, Cass, you must remember to treat the little people well. You never know when you may need assistance when you're down on your luck."

"I can't see that happening to you. You make your own luck."

"Indeed, I do," he said. "Now, buckle us both. We're ready to fly."

"I'll go back to the cabin."

"Stay with me in the cockpit. What you will see from the sky will amaze you."

Words he lived by. Ferro Olivetti, for all his toys and indulgences, loved nothing more than flying. He had taken lessons in his late teens, received his pilot's license after his twenty-first birthday, and after he'd made his first ten million, he'd followed through on a promise to himself: He bought his own airplane. When he had made his first one hundred million, he upgraded to this current plane, a Gulfstream V, sleek and sexy. His ability to fly gave him that much more of a sense of control. That's what made getting to his destination half the fun: the rush of the jet down the runway, the whoosh of the engines as the plane shot forth into the sky, the near-climactic moment when you realized the earth could no longer hold you in its clutch. *God*, he thought, rife with anticipation for the oncoming high, i*t was almost better than sex.*

Another look at Cass, and he thought: almost.

"All set?" Ferro asked, an unmistakable grin spreading over his face, highlighting the dimples that jumped out from his freshly shaven cheeks.

"You know, until I met you, I'd never been seated in anything but coach," she said. "Now look at me, a virtual co-pilot. I like being inside your cockpit."

Ferro laughed at her decidedly racy comment. He liked the way her tongue played with the language.

"Okay, put your headset on," he instructed her, and then, once he was settled, he contacted the tower and announced he was finally ready.

"As are we," said a weary voice. Ferro chose to ignore the sarcasm laced inside those words. "Just remember to stay focused, Mr. Olivetti. Flying may be an art, but it's a potentially deadly one if you're not focused."

Ferro took the man's point well. He also knew they'd seen Cassandra's name on the flight manifest.

"Understood. And appreciated."

"You are now cleared for take-off."

Ferro felt a familiar tightening in his groin; from the sight of Cassandra or from the notion that he would soon be shooting into the sky, he couldn't be sure. But he took full advantage of the thrill. He acknowledged the tower, and then he maneuvered the plane onto the faded blacktop of the runway. Sunshine found its way inside the narrow windows, making both Ferro and Cassandra slip Versace sunglasses down over their eyes. Seconds later, the whir from the engines overtook all other noise, so Ferro smiled and gave his new lady the thumbs-up. Then he increased the speed, and when he reached a delicious, head-rushing velocity, he thrust the controls forward, and the mighty craft parted ways with the ground, floating on smooth currents of air as they climbed and climbed to their approved cruising altitude. Telluride to San Francisco—it would be a short flight.

"Ferro, do you really know what all these controls do?"

"I better," he said. "It's not like I brought along a spare pilot."

"It looks like a video game," she said, "with all those buttons and dials."

"All you need to concern yourself with," Ferro said, "is the joystick."

See, he could play with the vagaries of the English language, too. Not bad, considering his Italian heritage.

"You're an animal."

Still, that didn't stop Cassandra's hand from finding its hardened target once again. "Now, where were we?"

"You're insatiable," he said, drawing in his breath.

"Would you have it any other way?"

This time, they were both at a loss for words.

Ferro set the plane to automatic pilot, and instead concentrated on one of the rare, intense pleasures of life—delivered by a woman who knew the perfect way to show her appreciation for a week's worth of luxuries. The fact that they were twenty-thousand feet above the earth notwithstanding, Ferro couldn't wait for the moment when she brought him to climax. Correction, he could wait a bit.

My God, he thought, *he had to be the luckiest man in the world.*

Life, though, was not unlike the sleek airplane that would take Ferro to his desired destination. Because as high as it took you, as attractive as things looked on the surface, there was that inevitable moment when you could no longer hide in the sky from the problems that awaited you. What went up, according to conventional wisdom, would come down eventually. They would soon return to solid footing, the safety of the ground. Better than the alternative: crashing and burning.

"Uhhhh…"

"Oh Ferro," Cassandra suddenly said in surprise.

San Francisco, here we come.

*　　*　　*

My God, Ferro, look at that magnificent view."

"That's why I live to fly, to soar like a bird and see what it sees."

"Why, Ferro Olivetti, you didn't tell me you were such a poet," Cassandra said.

"I am a man of many interests."

"And appetites."

"Later," he said, patting her supple leg but not taking an eye off the horizon stretched out before him. "For now, we must prepare to land. It's the most delicate aspect of flying."

In the distance, Ferro and Cassandra could make out the delineation between land and sea, where California's precarious coast met up with the cascading waves of the Pacific Ocean. Where the magnificent Golden Gate Bridge seemingly floated in the low-lying clouds, where the TransAmerica Pyramid and other towers both steel and concrete jutted up from hill upon hill like spires on an ancient castle. As Ferro banked the plane to the left, the glare of the sun was behind them, offering up a clear sight of blue skies and blue water, mingled slightly with the overhanging fog he'd been told to expect by the tower at San Francisco International. He wasn't surprised; the City by the Bay not being enshrouded in a hazy fog was like trying to permanently rid the city of the poor; it just wasn't going to happen.

Dispensing for the moment with Cassandra, Ferro focused all his attention on the matter of landing. This was the most complicated part of the trip, keeping control of the plane as you descended through the sky. He felt the bump of resistance of fuselage to sky as he hit the one-thousand-feet level; he passed through a series of clouds, and when they emerged into a cloud-free, sun-drenched sky, he could see they were that much closer to the runways of SFO. In the near distance he could make out Oracle Park, home of the Giants, and the bustling waters of McCovey Cove. He called in again to the tower.

"Gambit One, you are cleared for landing. Welcome home, Mr. Olivetti."

"Thank you, it's good to be here."

Ferro banked the plane once more, and suddenly the runway appeared straight ahead. His chocolate brown eyes became wide with an unmatched excitement. Like with the final lap of the Daytona 500, he knew to let the rush of adrenaline flow throughout his system as he steered them toward a victorious approach. He could see nothing but his target, and so when he suddenly felt a hand on his arm he jerked with surprise. The plane swerved in mid-air, the result of an unsteady hand.

"What the hell?" he yelled, trying to right the direction of the plane.

"Ferro, I'm sorry," said Cassandra, pulling her hand away quickly. "I was just caught up in the moment."

"Not now," he demanded.

"Gambit One, is everything all right up there?" came a concerned voice from the tower.

"Yes, it's fine," Ferro replied, anger coursing through this voice.

Anger was not a good emotion to carry with you in such a precarious situation as landing an airplane. He tried to swallow his fury as he finally leveled the plane and made the final approach again to the airport. Hitting the runway a bit harder than he had planned—Ferro had already envisioned in his mind a landing as smooth as their flight—and the fact that the wheels skidded and bumped hard on the ground only served to feed the anger already fueling him.

As the plane came to a rest, Cassandra tried her best to assuage her newfound lover by planting kisses on his face and telling him what a wonderful pilot he was. He ignored her as he tossed aside the headset and found his way out of the tight confines of the cockpit. He needed to stretch, he needed some air. *My God*, he thought, *I need to be alone for a moment.*

Inside the small plane's cabin, he shed himself of his winter garments and withdrew a pair of slacks and a silk blue shirt from a closet. He affixed cufflinks to the French cuffs of the shirt, and then checked his appearance in the mirror. He did not like the sour expression on his face; this was not the way he'd wanted to return home. He had much to accomplish, and to be in a foul mood was not good for him or his employees, and certainly not for his enemies.

He turned and saw Cassandra standing in the space between cockpit and cabin. With her still dressed like a snow bunny and he like a modern-day businessman, he couldn't help but realize the chasm of differences between them. What had he been thinking, inviting her back to join him in his everyday world?

"Ferro, I said I was sorry."

"Change into street clothes, Cass. I'm already late for a meeting at my office."

"I'll be quick."

He gave her credit there; they were ready to go two minutes later.

Opening the door, he breathed in the warm, fresh California air. Immediately he felt better. Taking a deep breath and then exhaling, it was like excoriating the pent-up emotions he'd been feeling inside the cockpit, especially after the slight mishap in the air. He even beckoned Cassandra to join him. The disagreement between them momentarily forgotten, he escorted the leggy beauty down the few steps of the *Gambit One*, As their feet touched solid ground, a gleaming black limousine pulled up beside the airplane, as though appearing from nowhere. The driver's side door quickly opened, and a tall, lanky gentleman emerged.

"Mr. Olivetti, welcome home."

"Thank you, Claude."

Claude, fully dressed in chauffeur-black, tipped his hat at Cassandra. "Ma'am."

Cassandra did a double take as she looked from Claude the chauffeur to Ferro the businessman, and back again. Not twins, not exactly. Claude had a harder edge to his face, less elegant in design. But still, there was a similarity to them that could make them, if not brothers, cousins. As it was, Cassandra would have to be left wondering whether there was something more to Claude than met the eye. Ferro did not bother with explanations.

Escorted into the rear of the limo, Ferro sat opposite Cassandra and immediately withdrew his iPhone from his jacket pocket. Claude closed the door behind them, and soon he assumed his dutiful position behind the steering wheel. The limo drove off, leaving the Gulfstream behind them, and seemingly along with it all the fun and frivolity of the past week. It was as though, with landing, Ferro had transformed from one person to another. No longer the insatiable lover with a passion for wantonness and its willing women, he had become cold and distant, a businessman who was used to getting his way. His brow furrowed as he spoke into the phone.

"Lawrence, it's me," Ferro said. "My ETA is perhaps thirty minutes, barring any traffic snarls. Be waiting for me in my office. And I want the very latest on the Vodell deal we've got brewing—and I mean the latest. Information that fool Dunbar couldn't possibly be aware of." Then he smiled, mostly to himself. "Time to strike while the iron's hot."

"It's good to have you back, Ferro," spoke his trusted aide.

"It's good to be back," Ferro said, closing his phone.

For the remainder of the ride, no words were exchanged between Ferro and Cass, as Ferro stared out the tinted windows at the rolling hills, the cable cars, the masses of pedestrians who called this city home. For Ferro, this was a city that most reminded him of Italy. It wasn't Los Angeles by any stretch, a town he loathed, and it wasn't New York, a city he considered all too brutal in its appeal. There was a muted elegance to the City by the Bay, rich in culture and food, a city that knew its past, knew its place in the world. Like Rome, without the beauty of language. For a moment Ferro thought of home, of his parents, and again remembered that dream. Taking out his phone, he had just started to scroll his parents' phone number when Claude announced they had reached their destination.

The limousine arrived before the gleaming, twenty-five-floor building that was known simply as the Olivetti Building, located in the heart of the city, on Market Street. Ferro liked things simple; his name adorned all he owned, the *Gambit One* excepted. Olivetti Enterprises, The Olivetti Building. His villa up in Napa, simply was Villa Olivetti. For the past week, those tabloids which attempted to track his romantic entrails had even dubbed Cassandra "Olivetti's woman." Possessions, all of them.

Claude again opened the door, and with a motion as quick as a jaguar, Ferro exited and began to make his way toward the entrance.

A voice called out to him. It was of course Cassandra.

"But what about me, Ferro? What am I do? I don't know a soul in San Francisco."

Ferro had the look of someone who couldn't be bothered with such details. But then his mind quickly flashed to memories of their time just spent; skiing and gambling, making love before roaring fires, the way she had comforted him last night after the haunting nature of his dream.

"Claude will take you home," he said, and then realized Cassandra was far from any place she might call home. He wasn't even sure where she hailed from. He addressed his loyal chauffeur. "Claude, er, take Cass to my villa. I will see her at my return party later."

"Very good, sir."

And with nary another look at Cassandra, Ferro disappeared within the confines of the glass tower he called home more so than he did his Napa Valley estate. Some might think the fun was over for Ferro Olivetti.

But business to him was more than fun—it was a powerful aphrodisiac. And it would wait no further.

CHAPTER TWO

EIGHT ELEVATORS SERVICED THE entire building, but only one of them had been exclusively designed as an express lift, traveling only from the ground floor lobby to the executive offices on the top floor, the twenty-fifth. When Ferro swung through the revolving doors into the expansive marble-clad lobby, an attentive guard in uniform sprang into action and summoned the private elevator. Fortunately, he'd been given advanced word from the executives above to expect Mr. Olivetti, and so after the push of the button the doors opened just in time for Ferro to slide right inside with barely a break in his eager stride. Like a choreographed routine, all of them synched.

"Nicely done, Nick," Ferro said.

"Doing my job, sir," the guard said. "Welcome home."

Home. Yes, the office was more than a place of business—it was, if not his soul, at the very least, his beating heart. Right now, his heart swelled from the pride in his relationship with his employees, from the highest executive to the people who truly kept Olivetti Enterprises running. There was something to be said for "the little people," those who made daily decisions that impacted their tiny lives. They were much more real, honest, than the entitled so-called country club set. Ferro was not a fan of exclusivity.

"Wife good? Charlie likes his new school?"

"All good, sir."

"Wonderful to hear."

Both men nodded as the doors closed. No more small talk. Still, Ferro made it a point to know details about everyone who worked for him.

He pressed the button for the top floor, and soon he was rushing back into the sky, the thrill not quite that of the *Gambit One* taking off but still pretty good. He enjoyed the short ride, though, not only for the excitement but for the brief moment of solitude. Gave him a chance to focus, to breathe, to find within himself that killer instinct that served him so well in business. Because once those doors opened, it would be like someone switched life into overdrive.

The elevator pinged, and the doors opened onto the twenty-fifth floor of the Olivetti Tower, and Ferro quickly rushed out of it.

"Welcome back, Mr. Olivetti," stated a lusciously dressed receptionist, her blonde hair teased, and her long nails lacquered as though they'd just seconds before been painted. Ferro noticed everything, including the fact that things at the office were a bit more relaxed when he went off on one of his pleasure junkets.

"Lucy, looking good. New hairdo?" Ferro asked, briefly acknowledging the receptionist and not really caring that she was rushing to put away her manicure kit. The woman smiled and waved. He barely saw the wave. His mind was suddenly focused in on the business awaiting him, but it was always like that once he got a taste of the atmosphere at his privately held multimillion dollar corporation. It was as though shooting his way up the elevator immediately transformed him from ordinary mortal to indestructible corporate mogul. Like Batman, going back up the batpole to become Bruce Wayne. Pity the joker who tried to laugh in his way.

Ferro had barely turned a sharp corner to his office when he was met directly by his trusted number one, Lawrence

Henderson. Lawrence looked very much the opposite of Ferro—dark suit, rep-tie, and a crisp white shirt, which contrasted nicely against his chocolate-colored skin. He was the epitome of a professional who had never heard the term "casual Friday," much less the concept of the weekend. He joined Ferro, and together this long-standing team walked and talked.

The niceties came first. "How was your trip?"

"Fine," Ferro said, his one-word answer curt and clipped, as though saying "Let's move on."

"Some of the other employees saw photos of your activities in the newspapers and the tabloids and online. Of course, none of them were particularly good shots—uh, if you know what I mean. You always seem to put your hand up at the wrong time, your face always blurred or behind some obstacle. Usually a woman." Lawrence said all of this with a smile; he knew the drill, the fact that Ferro liked to keep his image from curious onlookers. And also, to know of his success in achieving such clandestine actions.

"Yes, funny how that always happens," Ferro said with pointed sarcasm.

He'd always hated to be photographed. Ever since he burst upon the San Francisco scene as a young mover and shaker, a dot.com genius who would weather the fluxes of Silicon Valley, he wasn't sure who wanted to share a bigger part of him: the women or the paparazzi. He was classically handsome, and with an accent to melt even the most frozen heart he quickly became a sought-after property on the social circuit. Ferro, though, had managed to have it his way: share as much as he liked with those clingy, lingering women, and frustrate the hell out of pushy, greedy photographers. Just because he was rich, good-looking, and enjoyed the jet-set lifestyle, that didn't give the media the right to track his every move. He wasn't royalty, and he certainly wasn't something ghastly like an actor. And as loyal as was Lawrence, he supposed he'd never understand a lot about Ferro. For his own day in the sun, Lawrence might very well sell his mother to even the lowest bidder. But then again, he was a lawyer by trade; it came naturally.

"So, the Vodell deal. I asked for the latest."

"And the latest is what I have, Ferro. Perhaps it's best I disclose this information behind closed doors," Lawrence said. Lawrence was nothing if not discreet, an appealing quality in a lawyer and a man Ferro entrusted with far too much. But you had to trust someone, didn't you?

The two of them had by now traversed the length of the floor, bypassing both open offices and tight but neatly appointed cubicles, all of them occupied by well-dressed, well-heeled, and well-compensated employees. That didn't necessarily buy their loyalty, though, and Ferro's arrival had caught all their attention. Folks at this office were not unlike people at most companies who liked to listen, to feed off gossip and rumor and business secrets as though it was all printed on the cafeteria's lunch menu. After all, if they had time to look at photographs in the tabloids, they certainly had the inclination to learn all they could about their notorious, enigmatic boss.

As much as he tried to hide his face from even those inquiring eyes, it was Ferro's turn to acknowledge the street smarts of his second in command. "Point taken, Lawrence. This matter calls for the utmost privacy. My office it is," he volleyed back.

They arrived at Ferro's luxuriously appointed corner office, where Ferro stopped to greet his secretary. "Lana—holding down the fort?"

A pretty brunette in a smart, stylish red suit flashed him a bright smile. "Always, sir. We've managed in your absence, but of course it's always great to have you back. You are the adrenaline that gives this company its energy." It wasn't a suck-up statement, but rather the truth, and that's what Ferro valued the most. People who spoke the truth. "Still," she continued, "I'm sure Lawrence is glad to you're here. Lessen those worry lines on his face."

"Lawrence is never happy unless I'm at his side."

Lawrence cleared his throat. "I am standing right here."

"As you should be," Ferro said, downplaying the joke.

Lana spoke. "Also, Mr. Olivetti, your messages are on your desk, faxes in the folder, and your email in-box has been cleared of stuff you needn't concern yourself with. I've just left the important ones. And a few personal ones about tonight's gathering at Villa Olivetti."

"You're the best, Lana," he said. From the pocket of his tailored slacks, he withdrew a small felt box. "You had a birthday when I was gone, if I remember correctly. So, here's a little something from Paris."

As Lana oohed and aahed over the gorgeous set of earrings, Lawrence and Ferro entered the office and shut the door behind them. Ferro went directly to his oversized mahogany desk and flipped through the pink message slips with only passing interest while he fired up his computer and logged online to his corporate email account. A couple of personal photographs adorned his desk, and he did his best to avoid them. Complications could come later.

Just then he looked up. Something wasn't right. Lawrence wasn't talking.

"It's awfully quiet in my office, Lawrence."

"Oh, right, sorry. Thought I'd give you a moment to review those messages."

Ferro's thick eyebrows suddenly arched with consternation. "Lawrence, when did multi-tasking suddenly become difficult? That's hardly your style—and definitely not mine either. Speak. And make it good."

"Indeed. My apologies."

Messages still grasped in his hand, Ferro let out a deep sigh. "Okay, I get it, Lawrence. I left you in the lurch and went to play for a few weeks all over the world. You, I bet you've hardly changed your tie, much less your mind. But having you here enables me to take whatever time I need. That's the problem with the American work force; even when you get generous vacation time you seldom take it all. We Europeans know when to take a breather from life; we know all of our troubles will be waiting for us upon our return. But while we are away, we are richer in life's experiences." Ferro paused. "So, take your disapproval down a notch. I'm here, I'm back, and I'm ready to problem-solve. Just tell me the problem."

"It's not good."

"That's not what I want to hear."

Lawrence actually offered up nothing in return. He just crossed his arms across his suit as a form of corporate protest.

Ferro let the messages flutter to his desk. But still, he allowed himself a smirk. He and Lawrence had an unspoken language between them that came from years of working together. It's just that Lawrence wasn't usually so garrulous in his silence. "Okay, I'm focused. No multitasking. So, the problem?"

"Right."

Ferro promised to listen to his trusted advisor, but that didn't mean he could sit still. He rounded his desk and was just now staring out the huge plate-glass window at the sights of the city laid out before him. Hundreds of feet above this land of opportunity, he imagined himself back behind the controls of his plane, flying higher into the sky and retreating to the world from where he'd come. There was this fantasy deep inside him, to give it all up and just lose himself in life's many pleasures. But as his eyes scanned the view, they came to rest upon the shelf situated just to the right of the window. More photographs, these encased in gilt-edged frames, of a young Ferro. One with his parents together, another with his beloved Mama. The third, he and his Papa, playing chess and, conversely, smiling at the camera. All of them taken at their family villa in Italy, a place that seemed as far away as could be, but also strangely close. As though what lived in the heart could never be fully distant. At the sight of the photograph of his father, Ferro somehow returned to the present, as though he was being told by his elder to focus on the here and now.

Remember the energy you felt when you stepped off the elevator, take charge again, and listen to what issues Lawrence is addressing, his father seemed to say. Ferro always listened to his father; sage were the man's words. And for another split-second Ferro realized he missed his father's voice—he reminded himself again to call his parents later.

Ferro's mind cleared, and he turned around and saw Lawrence looking at him with a curious expression.

"Sir, is everything okay?"

"Yes, perfectly. You were saying—a complication with Vodell? "

"It's Dunbar."

Richard Dunbar, a corporate raider of the old school, was a shark who circled only when he saw blood. He was no one's chum. "I see. What about him?"

"He's trying to knock us out of the Vodell deal."

Ferro laughed. "So that's who the business papers are speculating about. Dunbar hasn't got the money—or the balls. But he's a persistent son of a bitch, I'll give him that. But that's all I'll give him. Except maybe a headache for daring to take me on. Is that what's got you so worried? Some impotent move to knock us out of the biggest deal ever? And from a has-been like Dunbar to boot? Why do you think I went away, Lawrence? I wanted to see what kind of competition crawled out of the woodwork, thinking he could take advantage of the deal while I was away." Ferro grinned suddenly, an alligator about to snap up his prey after lurking just beneath the surface. In a fight, he'd pick a gator over a shark any day. It would be fun to engage in such a fierce battle. Messages, emails, intended calls to parents, all were forgotten as Ferro realized the hunt was on. "Tell me, Lawrence, what's Dunbar's move?"

Just this morning he's filed for another two hundred thousand shares. Other investors are panicking, dumping stock, and so he's scooping them up like they're confetti. The word is definitely out: Vodell Technologies is ripe for the picking.

It's in the business articles and in the Journal and FT, and so Dunbar is gathering up as much stock as he can. He knows a good deal, that's for sure."

Fool was what he was, that's what Ferro thought. Dunbar was more like one of those fish who took a shark's leftovers, picking at scraps in its teeth. "That may be so, Lawrence, but taking over Vodell was my idea. It's my deal to begin with, and damned if I'll let Dunbar get away with stealing it out from under me. Not when I've done so much prep work and spent so much money already. No doubt he's probably trying to weasel a meeting with the head of Vodell. Like she would ever be charmed by a snake like him. Son of a bitch."

Despite his feelings toward the older businessman and chief competitor, Ferro was still grinning, his smile held by either admiration or something else…something dangerous. Like Dunbar had just seen the gator slip up the bank and poked it in the eye. The chase, the hunt, it was on, and it would be fun to take Dunbar in his jaws and perform the death roll. A shark, a snake, it didn't matter what he called Dunbar. In the end, he'd conquer him.

Lawrence, unnecessarily straightening his tie, said, "Ferro, perhaps it might be a good time to re-evaluate your position on this deal. Is Vodell really all that necessary to Olivetti Enterprises? I mean, in this economic climate, should we really be spending?"

Ferro tossed Lawrence a thoughtful look. He could have lambasted him for displaying an uncommon trait of weakness, caving at the first sign of difficulty, but that's not what Lawrence was ultimately suggesting. Playing devil's advocate was what he was paid to play at, and he was paid quite well for that ability to examine all angles of a complex deal. Which only reinforced Ferro's renewed consideration of the plan he'd kept in the back of his mind. If Ferro was the impulsive one in this relationship, Lawrence was its steadying force. That's what made them work.

So, he stopped and wondered: Was the Vodell deal worth the aggravation? Worth a new fight with a known enemy as formidable as Dunbar? Ferro knew he could beat him—he'd done it before. No doubt it was one of Dunbar's motivating factors, but defeating him now would probably cost Ferro more than he had initially allocated. Was Lawrence right to be cautious in this recessed economy? Actually, he was surprised he was considering an alternative solution; he'd been looking forward to this challenge the moment he'd decided to come home. Ferro tossed that worrisome claptrap out the proverbial window. Because he knew just how to handle a man like Dunbar. And what better way than to up the ante but call the man's bluff. Literally.

He depressed the buzzer on his phone. "Lana, get me Mr. Dunbar on the phone."

Lawrence raised an eyebrow. "Venturing into the lion's den?"

"Yes, but in this case I'm the one ready to pounce."

So, metaphorically speaking, they'd left the dangerous waters and were now headed onto the plains. Big-game hunting, indeed.

*　　*　　*

Just what was Vodell, and why were two of the West Coast's biggest electronics rivals about to go head-to-head in an effort to absorb such a company into their respective empires? In the grand scheme of today's complex, corporate world, Vodell Technologies, Inc. never really had a chance to survive independently. In an era of megacompanies such as Microsoft, Google, Apple, a pesky little upstart company with a flawed product was destined to be swallowed up quickly. In operation for barely ten years, they had made their mark enough to be noticed by the big boys but not enough by the consumer for them to have any true impact on market share. When after two years they had an IPO, lots of investors stayed away. Too many. Sure, the initial offering would line the pockets of even the cheapest suit, but its long-term prospects were as suspect as a stripper in Silicon Valley.

The rumor surrounding Vodell was that it had developed a new microchip that would revolutionize the way the world communicated, enabling easier talk and text and DM features between people no matter where in the world they were. The other rumor was that it hadn't quite got the technology figured out. The idea was brilliant, but like Vodell's other products, was missing that one key element that would make them true competitors. An established corporation with the right resources, the talent pool representing the best IT people in the world, would be the ideal one to easily take over Vodell. There were two such companies that industry leaders immediately thought of, Olivetti Enterprises chief among them. But that did not discount the other: Dunbar Industries, Ltd.

Vodell's history of near-success but ultimate failure was the primary reason why a veteran businessman like Richard Dunbar had avoided anything to do with them—until he learned of a certain interest from a certain company. Or rather, a certain individual. Say what you will about a corporation like Olivetti Enterprises, its fortunes were built and destroyed not by its work force but by the vision of its owner and heartbeat: Ferro Olivetti. It would be a certain pleasure to trump him.

Dunbar, a man in his late sixties with close-cropped gray hair and a prickly goatee, stood at his own office window, pruning the leaves of his prized orchids. He examined one particular flower and decided it had to go; he snipped the head from the deadened flower. He thought of Ferro as the shears sliced through the delicate stem, and he grinned as the faded petals dropped to the floor. It joined one other flower that hadn't the strength to survive. He had named that one Vodell. This new one he called Olivetti. Such was life in the cutthroat, corporate world of mergers, acquisitions, and takeovers. The strong survive while the weak are cut off at the knees. Or the stem, as Dunbar liked to think.

Raising orchids was his passion, his way of retreating into himself. Roses might be more attractive, but the thorns, oh how they could betray you. Ferro Olivetti, he was like a thorn for sure. Fortunately, the playboy millionaire was out of town, partying overseas and gambling away his hard-earned fortune—that is, based on the intelligence reports his staff had culled from the newspapers and the web, and from the report filed by his private investigator. A foolish man was Ferro Olivetti. His play-first, work-second approach to life would be his ultimate downfall. Who knew, if Dunbar weakened Olivetti Enterprises enough, it would make Vodell's failures seem like playing Monopoly.

Dunbar's phone buzzed.

"What is it, Mabel?" he said irritably, checking the time on his diamond encrusted Rolex. Two-twenty, she probably needed to leave early, get her nails done, and pick up her bratty kid at the babysitter, Did no one believe in a full workday anymore?

A request, Mr. Dunbar, from Mr. Grayson. He needs to leave early—his wife has to be picked up at the hospital."

Grayson, he mused. Laziest VP he had ever hired, always looking for an excuse to cut out early. "Tell him I don't care if his wife has the swine flu, if he leaves before six he can leave with all his belongings."

"Mr. Dunbar, with all due respect, she's in labor."

"Then, as far as I'm concerned, his role happened months ago."

Silence on the other end as Mabel canceled the connection.

Dunbar hated tired excuses. He paid his employees extremely well, and he expected as much from them as he expected from himself, maybe more. Even as he approached his eighth decade, with more years beyond him than were before him, he still managed to be in at seven o'clock every day and didn't anticipate arriving home until well after ten in the evening. Though—and not that we would admit it ever—he had nothing to return to, no wife (swine flu or not), no newborn children, no grown children for that matter. Dunbar was synonymous with business, and business was synonymous with Dunbar.

He was born Richard Alexander Dunbar, the product of parents who dreamed of more for their only son than anything they themselves had been able to achieve. Dunbar was a self-made multimillionaire, dubbed by the press as "Dun Deal" for his penchant for closing every deal he'd ever attempted to secure, and anyone in their right mind would have been pleased with such a noted reputation. And therein lay the key. After years of living for the kill, Dunbar could hardly be what some would call in his right mind. He wouldn't be satisfied until he was either quieted by death or achieved the gross level of billionaire, and he was doing his damndest to ensure the latter happened before the inevitable former. Too many people—in business and in life—enjoyed the chase, the pursuit. Not Dunbar; he grew antsy while waiting for the close of a deal. He enjoyed counting his spoils the most. That's why he was quick to go for the jugular, and he smiled each time he imagined a geyser of blood erupting from the wounds he inflicted. Act fast, steal from beneath unsuspecting companies. Such was the way he ran his business.

His intercom buzzed again.

"What?" he asked gruffly. Could no one leave him alone? "Let me guess, Mabel, it's a boy. No, a girl. Twins? Great, that's all we'd need, two more inept Graysons in the world. I suppose you should send some flowers." He stole a look at the dead orchids on the floor of his office.

"Uh, Mr. Dunbar, it's Ferro Olivetti for you. Line six."

That certainly got Dunbar's attention. But with kids on the brain, he couldn't help but think that here was another petulant child who should never have been brought into the world. Stupid excuse for a businessman, that's all he was. All show, style over substance. Still, that didn't prevent Dunbar from grabbing the phone with fierce curiosity. In fact, he'd been waiting for such a move.

"Ah, Ferro, it's about time you called. Is this your concession speech I'm about to hear? Lost out on another one, did you? Funny, from all I've been reading about you lately I thought you might be buried under an avalanche. Of snow, or perhaps beautiful women. Hard to tell given your recent exploits." He finished with a smothering laugh.

"I didn't realize you carried a subscription to 'People' magazine, Dunbar."

"Always with a joke," he huffed. "Hiding behind humor will cause your downfall."

"When you can't take a joke, Dunbar, that means you've truly lost your edge. Remember that laughter is the best medicine, and with your advancing age you'll need all the help you can get in that department." There was a pause, and Dunbar gave him nothing. "But I will agree with you on one matter—business is never funny."

"What would you know of true business? Your little company is just play-acting for you. Why not leave the deals to the big boys and go back to playing cards."

"Last corporate report had Olivetti Enterprises with a significantly higher profit margin than Dunbar, and as such has massive cash flow—much better than the declining fortunes of your tired, weary company. And keep in mind, Olivetti Enterprises is all mine. I don't have any stock holders or investors to answer to. Can you say the same, Dunbar?"

"I think I heard you wrong, Ferro. Declining?"

"Try turning up your hearing aid."

"Cheap shot, Ferro—so unworthy of a competitor such as you," Dunbar retorted. "So let me give you some sound business advice. Don't get emotional over your deals. I assume you've heard about my aggressive move for Vodell and you're calling me the instant you got back to the office, right? It's always better to wait, let the emotions subside, and then make your call. A calm and steady hand triumphs in the end."

"That's how I succeed, my passion. But enough sparring, Dunbar. I'm a busy man; can we get down to the reason I called?"

"You want to discuss Vodell, obviously. What, are you calling to warn me away from making any further overtures, or maybe better, to make me an offer on your company? Nothing would please me more."

Ferro cut him off with a wicked laugh. "I'm calling to warn you. Vodell is mine, it's that simple. I've been working on this deal for months, and you can't just swoop in at the last minute and take what is rightfully, deservedly, mine. I won't let a thief like you—one who enjoys bankrupting widows and pick-pocketing orphans—ruin a deal he has no business even getting involved with. Why not pick on a company your own size—even Vodell, with its challenges and lack of funds—is more lucrative than your piddling interests. Are you still investing in pork bellies, crop sharing? It's all forward-thinking technology, and it's all gone way beyond you. You're a dinosaur, Dunbar, and like them you'll someday be extinct. Someday real soon."

"Overconfidence and arrogance are the undoing of most species," Dunbar stated, taking another look at the assortment of dead orchids lying on the floor of his office. They weren't even worthy of being picked up and dispensed with properly. Same with Olivetti.

"As charming as it is talking with you, Dunbar, I'm afraid I have more pressing matters."

"As do I, assuredly," Dunbar said. "Let me guess, though, on your plans. Gone nearly a month from your business concerns, no doubt you'll be celebrating your return with some self-indulgent gathering at your Napa property—the wine will flow, your guests will take advantage of your wealth, and when all is said and done, you'll be poorer for it. And alone. Shame, Ferro, that you allow such a lifestyle to dominate your existence. Enjoy the good life while you can—oh, and not to tip my hand or anything, but while you're partying, I'll be dining with none other than Ms. Constance Wilde. You are acquainted with her, right? CEO of a certain company that goes by the name Vodell?"

There was a moment's pause on the other end. "Just remember this, Dunbar. I'm back, and this time I'm not going away until Vodell is brought under the Olivetti umbrella. There's not one thing in this world that will prevent me from completing the Vodell deal. I'm back, and I'm not going anywhere until the deal is complete. If I take your company along with it, so be it."

"Strong words, my boy. Let's hope you can live up to them. Or die trying."

Dunbar laughed as he set down the phone, hoping his voice echoed over the wires long enough to taunt at Ferro Olivetti.

"Let's see him rise to this challenge," Dunbar said to his empty office.

For the remaining orchids in the vase on his desk, Dunbar opted not to cut off their heads. He would feed them with water, nurture them, give them a chance at survival. He was suddenly interested to see which of them would live, and which of them would die.

*   *   *

Back in his high-rise office across the Bay, Ferro slammed the phone down onto his teakwood desk. Lawrence, sitting on the leather sofa with the other phone line still near his ear, gave his boss a cautionary glance.

"He's right about one thing, Ferro. You're too emotionally attached."

"I just don't want anything to screw up this deal," he said. "These people like Dunbar, like Ms. Wilde, they think all I am about is partying, the good life. I know a good deal, and this is one." Ferro paused. "You know, Lawrence, when I made the decision to move from Rome to the United States, I thought long and hard about where I wanted to settle, what I wanted to achieve. Olivetti Enterprises started as a small retail shop near the Pantheon, and since then it's grown into an international conglomerate, all because of my drive, my instincts. My father listened to all my dreams and my hopes, he was always there for me, encouraging me every step of the way. He told me I could achieve anything. This Vodell deal, it's perhaps my biggest get in years. I need to prove to my father that he was right. He'll be so proud."

For a second there was respectful silence in the room as Ferro occupied himself with the photographs spread throughout this office.

Lawrence waited out the moment before he said, "So, Ferro, what are we going to do to fend off Dunbar?"

"That's what I like about you, Lawrence. You always know how to get me focused." Ferro thought for a moment before saying, "Buy another five hundred thousand shares."

Lawrence paused dramatically, surprised at not just the suddenness of the decision, but the great risk Ferro was taking. Even for cash-rich Olivetti Enterprises, a move like the one Ferro was suggesting was dicey. "Uh, you do realize how much money that will take? Approximately seventy-five million."

"So, take it from the wall safe in the back of the shop," Ferro said, and then smiled at his own joke. Lawrence knew of Ferro's long-ago distrust of banks, and that he once kept all his cash from his storefront shop in a wall safe. That had been years ago, and there had been far less money in the coffers than there was now. And thankfully, tucked safely in the bank. "Listen, Lawrence, I know how much money this Vodell deal will take. But the upside potential is just too good to pass up. It could put us in billionaire's club. Our tech guys here are chomping at the bit to get a look at Vodell's schematics. So just put in the order, we can handle it."

"Very well," Lawrence said, rising from the sofa. Quietly, he approached the desk and placed a thick folder on it. "In the meantime, these legal documents require your signature, and the gentlemen from Thompson are here for the tax meeting."

With a quick rush of his signature over the pile of documents, Ferro approved whatever was on his desk with nary a glance. At the moment he didn't have much patience for the details. That's why he paid Lawrence.

Rising from his chair, he grabbed his iPhone and headed for the door.

"Ferro, where are you going? You just got here."

"You know how much I hate tax lawyers. You handle the meeting, Lawrence. After all, you've been doing just fine without me for the past several weeks. What's another day? I have other matters to attend to."

"But Ferro," Lawrence said to a retreating figure, knowing his protests would fall on deaf ears. When a man like Ferro Olivetti made up his mind, there was no going back.

Just then Ferro stopped in his tracks and turned back. "Oh, and Lawrence, will I see you later at Villa Olivetti?"

He shook his head. "Doubt it. One of us has to work."

"Lawrence, all work and no play?"

"Keeps this company afloat."

Ferro looked wounded by not only the retort but the tone which Lawrence used.

"Lawrence, everything will work out fine. I'm in control."

"I hope so, Ferro."

And with that warning ringing in his ears, Ferro rushed out of the office and made a quick escape from the building. Once outside in the clean, fresh air of the San Francisco afternoon, he took a deep breath before exhaling. Why was he such a jumble of emotions? Angry one second, laughing the next. Nostalgic one moment, then troubled the next. Like he was on a roller coaster, and the car was tossing his insides all over the place. Was it Dunbar's taunts? The idea that his chief competitor was dining with Vodell's admired CEO? Lawrence's overwrought concerns? Or maybe the seventy-five million he had just authorized to be spent on a decidedly chancy deal? Or was something else bothering him, nagging at his insides and having nothing to do with business at all? Something he wasn't even aware of?

Was it the dream? his inner voice asked.

Ferro tossed on sunglasses, hiding himself from the world with the ease and expertise he'd long ago perfected. To hell with all that was eating at him. His friends awaited him back at Villa Olivetti.

Just then Claude pulled up in the limousine.

"Perfect timing, Claude. If there's anyone I can truly depend upon, it's you."

"Anything you ever require, sir."

With that, Ferro hopped into the back of the limo and it pulled away from the curb. As they drove over the Golden Gate Bridge and up toward the lush Napa countryside, Ferro had the strange feeling that he was forgetting something. A promise he'd made, gone now in the wake of his newfound inner fears.

CHAPTER THREE

NIGHT HAD BEGUN TO FALL early on the picturesque, verdant Napa Valley. Ferro returned to his villa later than expected, traffic out of the city worse than anticipated, and as Claude swung the limo around the circular driveway to let out his lone passenger, neither could help but notice the party was already in full swing. Soft lights bathed the expansive back lawn and patio, and the gentle buzz of happy conversation and music and popping champagne bottles could be heard from the moment Ferro stepped out from the rear of the stretch.

The two men, loyal to each other, exchanged knowing glances.

"Looks like they didn't need me to get things going, eh, Claude?"

"Indeed, sir. Your friends, perhaps they enjoy the wine and the locale a bit too much."

"Are you saying they're not really my friends?"

"Money attracts strange bedfellows."

Ferro might ordinarily find himself growing mad at such insolence coming from someone who worked for him. Had that person not been the ever-faithful Claude Reneau, that is. Even even-tempered Lawrence might have suffered some back-handed retort. There was something innate about Claude that

Ferro respected; wisdom earned from years of service, and from the many episodes of duplicity the two of them had engaged in with the media. Ferro remembered Cassandra's strange reaction upon seeing Claude, the double-take she did when seeing Ferro and his driver at the same time. Yes, there were physical similarities, and that was more by design than by mistake. Often when a photograph of the "enigmatic" Ferro Olivetti appeared in newspapers and websites, it was really Claude ducking the shutterbugs. For people of influence, it was not an uncommon practice to employ a body double. Many times, Ferro himself had donned the chauffeur's uniform, only to slip past the curious with barely a glance and enter his location of choice. It was no wonder with so much of his time spent driving Ferro around, Claude was bound to pick up on certain clues about how life really worked. Like now, the party and the fact that Ferro was an afterthought at his own welcome-home celebration.

"Thank you, Claude. For everything," Ferro noted, the implication clear. "I'll call you if you're needed. Otherwise, enjoy your evening."

"Goodnight, sir."

As Ferro walked beneath the portico and entered his spacious home, he realized he'd forgotten he had a guest staying with him. Cassandra. Was she already immersed in the goings-on in the back? He stole a quick look inside the house, bypassing the living room, where a couple of guests were admiring the art work that hung on the walls. Ferro rounded his way up a curved staircase, his feet padding lightly on the carpeted steps so as not to draw attention to his presence. Down the lengthy hallway he went to his bedroom, where he discovered Cassandra. So, she hadn't braved the party. In fact, she was waiting for him, hands on her hips and looking none too pleased.

"It's about time you showed up," she said.

"Excuse me? Did we have a prearranged time for when I was to arrive at my own home?"

"Apparently your friends thought so. They started showing up over an hour ago."

"And so why aren't you down there with them, greeting them? You knew I had business matters to attend."

"Oh, don't get me wrong, Ferro, I know how busy you are with your company, especially this being your first day back from your big holiday. But really, you can't expect me to join your friends out on the back patio and just immerse myself in their conversations while they look at me with suspicion. 'Hi,' I'll say, 'I'm the girl Ferro met in Monte, fucked in Cannes.' They don't even know me. They'll just assume I'm some easy lay, some nothing girl you picked up."

"So, you've been what? Waiting for me to escort you to the ball?"

She actually let go of her anger and grinned at such a thought, despite the taunting tone in his voice. "It has been a bit of a fairy tale the past week."

"Perhaps it's time for the carriage to revert to a pumpkin."

Cassandra's smile faltered at the meaning behind those words, and her body language slumped. "Ferro, where is the man I met over the baccarat table in Monte, the sweet-natured, high-stakes gambler who swept me off my feet. And into his bed?"

Ferro's brow furrowed; he did not like to be second-guessed. "I warned you, Cass, things would be different once I returned back to the States. Perhaps it was a mistake to invite you here to my home—into my life. But you proved to be quite a comfort to me, especially during the nights when those dreams continued haunting me. Perhaps because of that I thought we had an understanding." At the mention of the dream about his father, Ferro's irritable mood was dissipated, and once again he was that lonely boy seeking welcoming arms. His tone softened. "Look, I'm sorry I've been such a beast since landing; it's just my mind is preoccupied with a business venture that is turning out not to be the lock I thought it would be."

As he was talking, Ferro had begun to shed himself of his clothes.

"Here," Cassandra said. "Let me do that."

Cassandra approached the man who had been her lover, her confidante, for the past week, and she took hold of the buttons of his shirt. Slowly, seductively, teasingly, she revealed a chest whose strong contours she had begun to memorize. His pecs, his flat stomach, those six-pack abs. Pulling the shirt off his broad shoulders, she let it drop to the floor as her hands grazed against the hair of his chest, down farther to his waist. Taking hold of the buckle, she released it and let his pants drop down to his feet.

"Cass, really, my guests…"

"…have waited this long, surely another minute or two."

"That's just it, given what's about to happen, I anticipate it taking more than just a minute or two—and you should know that better than anyone of late."

"Now there's the Ferro I've gotten to know. Intimately."

With that, a giggling and seductive Cassandra slipped the silky white dress off her own shoulders, revealing underneath nothing but her bare, tanned skin.

Ferro took hold of her right there and then, kissing her hard, there was a hint of desperation to his kisses but also an animal hunger. She'd done her job well, enticing him easily and with such practiced precision. She found his weak spot as she kissed his chin, his neck, his nipples. Ferro grabbed her and tossed her down on the bed, where he immediately began to suckle at her generous breasts. *My God, she was beautiful*, he thought.

He couldn't hold himself back any longer. With his guests waiting downstairs and not even aware he'd returned home, pushing all other concerns aside, Ferro took Cassandra hard, perhaps harder than he had in all their time together.

"Oh, yes, Ferro…oh, now, more…"

He thrust and he thrust further, and he could feel

Cassandra's long red nails digging into his strong, muscled back, urging him further, deeper, letting the passion overwhelm any sense of propriety. Minutes clicked by aimlessly, distraction the order of the moment as the room grew darker, and the intensity between them built and built until Ferro could hold off no longer.

With cries of pleasure shaking against the walls, wafting down toward the terrace, Ferro unleashed himself with one last eager, powerful thrust. Cassandra took all of him, smiling at the satisfaction she had been able to bring to him. Suddenly he rolled off her, the passion draining from him. He didn't even slip in a kiss.

The sound of the telephone rang in the silence of the room.

Ferro went to grab for the cell phone that was practically another limb, but of course he was naked. Where was the blasted thing? Oh right, his pants pocket, the pants lying on the floor. As he reached for his pants, he nearly fell off the bed. Finally, he had the phone, just as Cassandra let out a sigh of frustration. Ferro might have gotten off, but she'd only just been on the verge of climax.

The caller ID identified who was interrupting them.

"Hello, Steve," Ferro said.

"Where the hell are you? Isn't this your party?"

"I will be right down."

"Oh, so that was you everyone heard? Man, Ferro, give it a rest and get your ass—and whoever you're with down here. Christ, we thought it was an earthquake rumbling through the valley—and then Dora says, 'No, that's just the way Ferro fucks. Loud.'"

"Ha ha," Ferro said with a disingenuous laugh, "Not that she would ever know. She'd never get the satisfaction."

In the darkness of the room, Cassandra said to anyone listening, "I can relate."

All Ferro said to Cass was, "My presence is required. Get dressed."

*   *   *

"My apologies for being late to my own party," Ferro said, standing before an attractive couple dressed in the latest trends from Milan. "May I present Ms. Cassandra Hardy. Cassandra, these are my friends, Steve Donovan and Dora Hicks. Steve is a dear friend from my early days in San Francisco, and he likes to think he has more money than me. In truth, his grandfather did, and Steve is now spending his life spending it all. As for Dora she, well, she accompanies Steve whenever there is some interesting place to go. Meaning: someplace where there is money."

"How do you do," Cassandra said nervously.

"I do quite well," Steve said, amiably, "or at least my late grandfather did, if you believe the lies Ferro is spewing." He was impossibly blond, impossibly tan, and ridiculously well-dressed. A preppy model brought to vivid, pink life. But his smile held nothing suspect, just an honest welcoming grin, which served to calm Cassandra's nerves. The same could not be said for a disapproving Dora.

"The question is, my dear, how do you do?" asked Dora. She was slim, early thirties, and dressed all in funereal black. Trying to look edgy, but without makeup she just looked like she'd come from Steve's grandfather's wake. "And really, I'm hardly the gold-digger Ferro paints me out to be. And you, Cassandra, dear, did you bring your digging implements?"

Ferro smartly intervened. "Dora, you're usually not so crass so early into a party. Come, Cass, let me get you some champagne."

The party was definitely in full swing. Despite the late-March night, the air held a thick humidity, enabling several of the guests to venture out clad only in bathing suits, the women in skimpy bikinis and the men in briefs so revealing they redefined the word. Some of them were swimming, but most were lounging around the Olympic-sized pool flirting, talking, drinking, indulging in whatever floated their boat. Music played quietly in the background, and several of the ladies swayed to the rhythm of Italo house. Ferro greeted several of them as he escorted Cass to the bar, receiving kisses on both cheeks in the process.

"Welcome home, Ferro," said a blonde.

"You promised to call me, Ferro," said a brunette. "And I'm still waiting."

"You're looking mighty fine, Ferro, and I know from mighty fine." That last comment came from a busty redhead with curves in all the right places. "Obviously your time spent away was, uh, therapeutic." This last word was said with a disparaging eye cast on Cassandra.

Cassandra gave her date a withering look. "Well, at least they know whose party they are at. They all practically had orgasms when they spoke your name. Like cats purring. Honestly, Ferro, are these type of people really your friends?"

"They are harmless."

"That's not what I asked."

"Forget them."

"And they are remarkably beautiful."

"I told you, Cass, forget about them and their petty comments. If you want to be on my arm, do not concern yourself with those who wish to be but are not. Jealously is almost worse than insecurity. Now, can we just enjoy the party? After being away for so long, it is good to come home to Villa Olivetti."

"It is beautiful," she said.

Ferro's grin widened. "See, even you agree that it is not a crime to want to be surrounded by all things beautiful, to indulge in life's finer things. Come, Cass, let me get you that glass of champagne I promised you. I remember how well you enjoy the bubbles."

Cass, assured that he only had eyes for her, happily accepted a tall crystal flute of golden champagne. Together, linked arm in arm, like they were one, they walked over to a private table far removed from the scurrilous action by the pool. Ferro's friends Steve and Dora had already settled themselves at the table with their own drinks. Empty glasses and an overturned bottle of Dom Perignon adorned the table, leaving Ferro to surmise his friends had been enjoying the party for quite a while.

With drinks replenished, Ferro noticed that Dora had moved in closer to Cass, no doubt to get as much dirt as she could. Where they met, how many times a day they did it, did he satisfy her, all the things that mattered most to Dora. *Good,* Ferro mused, *let them talk.* It gave him some quality time with the affable Steve, the very antithesis of Lawrence. One was all business, the other all play. This was how a man of Ferro's diversified interests stayed, well, interested; surrounding himself with those who enhanced the double life he'd always led.

"So, Ferro, I saw her picture in the paper," Steve said, nodding in Cassandra's direction, "and also in that same picture was what I have to assume was your hand. Well done as always, keeping those nosey photogs frustrated as hell. But really, Ferro, she doesn't look like your kind of woman—she's not an international model, she's not supported by her rich daddy."

"She is very nice. What's wrong with that?"

"Nothing. So, is she the one?"

Ferro laughed in an obvious attempt to disregard Steve's leading question. For as long as they had known each other, Steve was always trying to pin down Ferro's type. As though Ferro getting married would then give Steve permission to settle down. Until then, the bachelor boys would have their fun. Ferro, knowing the routine, sipped at his champagne. "I think you are putting far too much emphasis on Cassandra's presence here. She is fun, she is beautiful, and we have shared an amazing time together. Why must there be anything more to it than that? Like I said, she enjoys what I can give her, and I enjoy what she does for me, so if that's your definition of 'the one,' then fine, Steve, she is. Cassandra is my kind of woman."

"Okay, okay, don't get so defensive. It's just, it's not like you."

"What? To be accompanied at one of my parties by a beautiful woman? Have you not been paying attention to me all these years?"

"Yeah, all too well. Which is why I'm being suspicious. You usually let them go with a kiss and an expensive bauble whenever the vacation—or party—is over. This one you brought home."

Ferro shrugged. "Perhaps I am changing. Perhaps this place needs a woman's touch. A man must change, evolve, Steve," Ferro said, a wistful quality to his voice. "Now, may we change the subject, please? We sound like a couple of gossipy teenage girls with all this nonsense talk, and I for one have grown bored of sounding like Dora."

"I heard that," Dora said, looking up from her téte-à-téte with Cass.

She went ignored by both men.

"Fine, shifting the conversation then," Steve said. "I was reading the business section yesterday—don't laugh, okay, I stay interested in how my investments are doing—and it seems someone leaked some very valuable information about your interest in a hostile takeover of Vodell. Dunbar and his vultures must be circling. You do know that, don't you? Or were you so busy poking the pretty blonde all day and night that you allowed Dunbar to one-up you?"

"Steve, you sound like a man who is either jealous of my prowess or has not been laid in quite a while," Ferro said, eyeing Dora as he spoke his statement. "So, let's make a deal. I stay out of your personal life, and you stay clear of mine. As for that fool Dunbar, what makes you think I allowed him to do anything without my prior knowledge?"

"Hey, I may not need to work for a living, but I do keep an eye on things. Like Vodell's stock. It's been up and down so much you'd think it was a Times Square hooker. Just as outdated, too," he said with a smirk.

"You surprise me, Steve, colorful metaphors aside. Since when does the market interest you?"

"I do more than just spend money, Ferro."

"Yes, but among those things is not making more."

"What can I say? " he said with an easy shrug, "Some of us were born to spend. I was always told, when you're good at something you're supposed to embrace it. You know as well as I do that Grandfather's trust is reportedly bottomless—I'm testing that theory to its fullest."

"That's why we need people like me—to replenish the market."

"And Dunbar?" His question was like a taunt.

"Dunbar is a fool. A fool who will believe anything he reads in the papers."

With that cryptic comment circling the table, a snort suddenly escaped through Dora's nose like a prized race horse stating its disapproval. "You men and your tiresome business concerns. Can't you just relax and enjoy the night, the bubbly. and the lovely ladies in your company. Honestly, Cassandra, was Ferro like this on his holiday? Discussing big deals and the ups and downs of the stock market? Really, it can get ever so boring."

"No, Ferro was almost like a different man. Sensitive."

"Sensitive? Ferro?" Dora howled over that as she poured herself another glass.

Ferro shot Cass a dangerous look, and she instantly clammed up. Even though she was in the company of his good friends, some topics were to remain just between the two of them. Like vulnerable nights, haunting dreams, taunting fears. Steve and Dora noticed the private exchange between the new couple. They were only more intrigued.

"Oh, don't quiet the girl now, Ferro," Dora insisted. "What does she know?"

Ferro dismissed Dora's question with a simple, dismissive wave, changing the topic to the exhilarating skiing he experienced in the Alps. That got Dora off and running, gossiping about someone else, Steve nodding along and interjecting his own secret information about who was doing whom, and whose spouse didn't know, did know, and would know soon. As for Cassandra, she was rewarded for her quiet loyalty with a gentle touch of Ferro's foot against her bare leg. He traded knowing glances with her as he did so, and he saw a smile break out on her face. He was letting her know that their brief interlude upstairs in his bedroom had been a mere prelude— tonight after the party she would be his, he would be hers. Steve and Dora went silent about skiing, wondering just what had transpired between the two to cause such a shift in mood at the table, but neither Ferro nor Cass said anything; short of looking under the table, their friends would have no idea of the hanky-panky going on.

Ferro's foot slid further up her leg; it wouldn't be stopped from reaching its port.

"Anyway, you were saying about Dunbar?" Steve said.

"Oh bore," Dora said.

"I said he's a fool. That's all that matters."

"He's been quoted as saying he has you by the jugular."

"I will give Dunbar credit for one thing, and one thing only: He knows how to promote himself, to get the press to suck up to him, but it does not always work to his advantage. Soon he will go the way of the dinosaur. I told him as much today when I called him. With my help, if I'm lucky, it will happen sooner rather than later. And luck has always been on my side."

Just then Cass let out a sudden, "Ooh," and everyone turned to her.

"You okay, dear?" Dora asked, her hand on the woman's shoulder.

"Oh, yes, I'm very fine, thank you. Must have been the bubbly, makes me hiccup."

Ferro's toes had, during the flowing conversation, slipped between her legs and were now caressing her newly wet, inner softness. He worked the angle perfectly, increasing the motion and delighting Cass to the point of a shattering orgasm, the one she'd been denied when Steve had interrupted them earlier with his call. Ferro knew to deliver on his promises.

"Isn't it nice to be in love," Steve said, sarcasm dripping between them all.

Just then their party-within-a-party was interrupted by the arrival of one of Ferro's maids, a round Hispanic woman with a thick accent.

"Sorry to interrupt, Mr. Olivetti, sir. It's a phone call. From Italy."

Ferro swung around quickly, practically ripping the phone from the maid's hands. In Italy, the hour was late…no, it was very early in the morning. He had lost all track of time. Was it already tomorrow somewhere? But the fact of the call meant only one thing—there was bad news to be delivered. "Hello?" he asked with a note of caution to his voice.

From thousands of miles away, a continent away but also a world away, Ferro heard an intake of breath, and he knew at once his Mama was on the other line. Deep concern immediately afflicted his system, causing him to sit up. Worry lines creased his forehead.

"Mama?"

"My Ferro, I'm sorry to be calling you with this news."

"What's the matter?" But even as he asked the question, he knew. Somehow deep inside he knew. He'd been right, or at least, his subconscious had. The dreams had been a tease, a message for him to read.

Papa, he thought.

"Papa," he said.

"Yes. Ferro, he's asking for you. My dear, I'm sorry, he's not doing well."

"I'll be there as soon as I can, Mama," he said.

"Ferro, hurry."

Hurry. Now there was a word without much meaning right now. How was he to achieve the impossible and be there for his father, his family, when it most mattered?

Ferro let the phone slide from his grip, and the receiver clattered to the ground. He cursed aloud, and not out of sadness or despair over the situation suddenly at hand. No, he was angry with himself, because he'd known something was wrong. The dreams had told him so, and yet he hadn't done anything to react to them but seek comfort in the arms of a woman who ultimately meant nothing to him.

What mattered most was family, and he'd let them down.

But I meant to call them, he thought, and even as the thought reverberated in his mind, he knew how hollow his defense sounded. He was just back home, but something far greater called to him: the past, his real home.

Finally, he emerged from his thoughts and found a woman staring at him. "Ferro, is there anything I can do?"

"I'm sorry, uh," said, struggling suddenly to recall her name. And as he hesitated, he saw the crestfallen look on her pretty face. She knew before he even said it that whatever had existed between them was suddenly over. He knew it had been wrong to bring his vacation fling back to his real life, and now he knew why. Perhaps he'd allowed the distraction to continue this time because he didn't want to deal with what reality was bringing him. Because when it came to family, Ferro stood alone, he let no one in, not since…again, he pushed the name from his mind. He stole a look again at the woman he'd invited into his life. His body was one thing to share, his heart another. It had been that way with him for too long. Since he'd allowed it to be broken.

"I'm sorry to you all, but other matters require my attention. Goodbye," Ferro said, his voice choked with emotion. "The party is over."

*   *   *

Villa Olivetti was empty now; even the maids had been sent home. Ferro stood in the foyer, the bag from his recent trip at his side. It was still packed. The only additions were a couple of his finest silk suits, both black. He knew he would need them. Even in the face of heartbreak, he was able to find some semblance of rational thought.

Reservations had been made. Arrangements had been made. All he needed now was the light of day to crest over the horizon and the arrival of his limousine. Claude was, of course, on call at all hours, and he would be on time. Ferro was certain of that. That's when he realized there was one last detail to be taken care of.

"Lawrence," he said to the hollow room, his voice echoing in the eerie silence.

He hadn't informed Lawrence that he had to go away again. But this was no pleasure trip, this was business of the utmost, because it involved family. The thing most precious to him. How could he have forgotten about Lawrence in all this? How could Olivetti Enterprises have been so far from his mind? Hadn't he built the multimillionaire dollar corporation to make his father proud? Now, with his father at his most dire hour, what was he thinking? That was the problem. He wasn't.

He grabbed hold of his cell phone and dialed. He saw the time. Four a.m.

"Hello?" said a groggy voice on the other end.

"Lawrence, it's Ferro."

"Ferro, what time is it? Is everything okay with Vodell? Dunbar? I can be ready in fifteen minutes."

"No, nothing like that. I must return to Italy."

"Italy? Weren't you just there a couple weeks ago?"

"No, no. To Rome I must go. My mother called."

There was silence on the other end. "I think I understand."

"Yes, unfortunately. It's my Papa. He is not doing well, and they fear the end is near. My mother, she says I'm needed as soon as possible. He's asked to see me. Claude is picking me up shortly. The flight leaves early this morning."

"Of course, I'll take care of everything. Don't concern yourself."

"Listen to me, Lawrence. This Vodell deal, I can't lose it. Not now. I fear that I may already be losing too much else that I care about."

"You can depend on me, Ferro."

"Yes, Lawrence, I know that."

"Ferro, remember, you're not alone in this."

His words were supportive. Ferro always thought they reeked of hollowness. No one could possibly understand the bond he had with his Papa. "Thank you, Lawrence. I will phone when I can."

As he hung up and replaced the phone in his jacket pocket, Ferro looked around at the home he'd fashioned after an Italian villa, a near-replica of the place he'd once called home. Villa Olivetti was filled with the most beautiful things money could buy, art and antiques that were as rare as they were expensive; it had rooms to spare and could have housed half the party guests had Ferro the inclination, but even with all this before him the only thing he could hear was the sound of nothing. He had no one to share his luxuries, no one to share in his pain. Even Cassandra was gone, taken by cab to the Fairmont, and tomorrow, to a flight to wherever she wished. He'd known it wouldn't last; nothing ever did for Ferro Olivetti.

And soon, he feared he would lose one of the most important people in his life. Indeed, nothing was forever. It was a hard lesson he'd learned as a child. And now, the grown-up child wished for nothing more than to arrive home with time to spare. He thought again of those last words of the dream, "Never leave me…"

Right now, every minute counted.

CHAPTER FOUR

FLYING ACROSS THE COUNTRY, the ocean, headed for a continent he called home. Again. And unlike his previous journeys where the promise of decadence and indulgence was part of the allure, this was a trip that was not only necessary, but also long dreaded. Ferro knew his father had been diagnosed with cancer, but that had been over three years ago, and the hulking man refused to let it beat him. Ferro had always assumed his father would triumph over the disease, just as he did with everything he achieved in life. Perhaps not, perhaps the world was cruel. So here was an inevitable moment in life when a man like Ferro had to put aside all his own concerns and concentrate on those of others. His father. He sighed with frustration. My God, aren't we there yet? Of course not, they hadn't even taken off.

Just then a crackle sounded over the speaker, and then came a soothing voice.

"Ladies and gentlemen, we'd like to welcome you all aboard Alitalia Flight number 3549, with nonstop service to Paris's Charles de Gaulle Airport, with continuing service to Rome's Fiumicino Airport. We ask that you settle in for the long flight, and hope you enjoy your time in the sky with us."

The voice of the pretty flight attendant was sweet and comforting, and as she switched languages to make the same announcement in French and Italian, Ferro could almost imagine he was already back in the enveloping, welcoming arms of his loving parents. She was that good. Also, her accent was perfect, which only made him yearn more for the land he'd once called home.

He secured his seat belt as directed, then watched out the small window of his seat as the giant Airbus readied for its take-off. It was hard to imagine that only twenty-four hours ago he'd been up in this same wakening sky, piloting his own private plane. How he wished to be inside the safety of Gambit One's cockpit, his destiny in his own hands. For a transcontinental, transatlantic flight like this, flying first class was not only the quickest route to his destination, but also, for him, the safest. It went unsaid that given his fragile emotional state, taking command of an aircraft was the last thing he should be doing.

Still, with hours in the air separating him from his parents, he'd never felt such a disconnect with them. He just hoped the holdover in Paris wasn't terribly long and that he would arrive in Rome with time to spare. *My God*, he thought, *I had been so near Rome while skiing in the Alps, gambling in Monte Carlo, dancing in Parisian clubs.* He had practically flown over his family villa, never once thinking of visiting. He knew how much his parents disapproved of his jet-set, party-all-the-time lifestyle. And once he hooked up with Cass, flying to Rome was definitely out of the question. It was still his parents' fondest wish that Ferro settle down and provide them with a new generation of Olivettis to spoil. Ferro himself had no such plans in the near future.

As the great 767 roared down the runway and shot forth into the early morning sky, Ferro closed his eyes against the glare of the brilliant sun, the fluffy white clouds. He settled back and hoped for sleep. He certainly hadn't slept the night before, packing and worrying his main distractions. Before long, his wish was granted, and sleep came. But like his slumber over the last several weeks, it was peppered with dreams.

This time the dream was different.

This time the dream was a distinct, distant memory.

Back in Rome, a place he'd come to know as the Eternal City. But it was one morning when a young Ferro learned that eternal *was just a word, devoid of meaning, the more you spoke it aloud. Ironically, death had entered the impressionable boy's life, and he was as unprepared for it as he was unsuspecting of such a possibility.*

It was appropriate that the young Ferro called the seven hills of Rome home, for even at a young age he dreamed of constructing his own empire, and he envisioned he could do it any way he saw fit, through fear or intimidation, talent and drive, or a driving combination of all. Following in the footsteps of his once penniless father, now awash with riches. For this untamed boy named Ferro, all of life was as eternal as his home. Family, friends, and the citizens who plied their trade on busy streets, he knew they would always be there for his amusement and for his education, to quench his insatiable thirst for knowledge. Foremost, though, in young Ferro's mind was the unconditional love of his generous parents. They were his rock, the very foundation for all he believed. They would forever be a part of his life. He fed off their encouragement like no other. For this optimistic boy named Ferro with the sparkling eyes and wild mane of fly-away brown hair, when he roamed the bustling streets of Rome, he was poetry in motion. He darted through sidewalks flush with locals and tourists alike, through dense crowds tossing shiny coins into the sparkling blue waters of the Trevi Fountain or circling the magnificent arches of the Colosseum as though a twirling wind, running between street performers and musicians in the Piazza Navona as though it was an obstacle course, All the while he would smile and laugh with delight as local shop owners called out his name or just waved, his quick feet almost too fast for their greetings of "buon giorno" to register, That was unless someone was holding out a tasty delicacy, a gelato or sweet cannoli dipped with chocolate, filled with sugary ricotta. Only then would he stop and happily accept whatever treat came his way, chatting up the owners, advising them with this limited knowledge of the business world that free samples were a sign of desperation. People should want your product without having to sample. You should retain an air of mystery.

"Ah, but only free for you, eh Ferro, my boy?" would say his favorite shop owner, Giuseppe Santino, who worked each and every day for decades behind the counter of his family's tiny pastry shop, "Piaceri di Giuseppe" along the curving Via Veneto,

"Spero cosi, Giuseppe!" Ferro would answer before flashing his brilliant smile and dashing off again on another of his imagined adventures.

Ferro knew that the Eternal City was his, and he carried in his innocent, inquiring face a vast appreciation for his city's storied past, its history and grandiosity, certain one day he would grow up, and all of Rome would fall at his feet. That was just for starters, Soon enough the rest of the world would discover the many charms, the many dreams, the many desires, of the boy named Ferro.

It was a quiet Sunday morning that found eight-year-old Ferro Olivetti gazing into the languid waters of the Tiber, seeking out his reflection on the shimmering surface. As seen in the gentle waters, the face staring back at him wavered as it rode the currents, shifting with the motions of the river. He would smile and then frown, his ever-changing expression making him appear as someone other than himself. It was a game he liked to play, centered on the notion of being able to adapt to any situation, to be someone other than himself. It was a game he played only when alone, All the other times, he was Ferro, the boy everyone knew.

Satisfied that he'd won his little game, Ferro realized he had skipped breakfast, and his stomach grumbled. He raced off the bridge and began to run through the city, his destination clear in his mind. A gooey pastry was his goal. It wasn't long before a breathless Ferro rounded the corner and veered upwards on the Via Veneto, where he suddenly came to the front of Giuseppe's store. Except on this morning, something was different, something was wrong. The gate was closed, the lights off. Ferro looked to the sky for the position of the sun. There was no reason for the store to be closed. That's what he thought.

As he peered inside, he saw that the cases of pastries were empty. There had been no fresh baking overnight. An unknown sensation overcame the little boy, and he gazed up inquiringly, finding an elderly woman standing before him. In her hands she held a simple bouquet of purple flowers, which she gently placed before the empty shop.

"Pardon me, but why do you leave flowers like that?"

"Purple ones," she said, "to reflect rebirth. Our Lord rose, and one day too will our departed Giuseppe."

Ferro scrunched his nose. "But where has he gone?"

"He's gone home."

"That makes no sense. He should be here, at his store. He always tells me, work saves him from having to hear his wife's nagging voice."

The woman laughed. "Yes, my boy. A man's work is his salvation. But I don't mean his home like that. The Lord's home. Heaven. I'm sorry, son, did you not hear that Giuseppe passed away yesterday?"

"Passed away?"

"Yes. Died," the woman said, cupping a comforting hand beneath Ferro's chin. "Do you not know of such a thing? We will all die, someday. For me, sooner rather than later. I shall miss the sweet treats Giuseppe shared with the world. He was a true master, and a good man."

"Yes," Ferro said, "a very nice man."

But even as he spoke those words, he still didn't understand the meaning behind them, or the heaviness that weighed on his heart. A tear sprung from his eye and slid down his cheek. He thanked the old lady for her kindness, and then, with more tears streaking down his face, he ran, ran as fast as he could through the streets of Rome, not resting until he had at last reached the safety of his home.

"Mama, Papa, what is this thing called death?"

Ferro was jolted awake by several pings sounding throughout the cabin, and he realized someone's gentle touch upon his shoulder had stirred him. He'd been stretched out in his seat, in full recline, enabling him to gain a deeper sleep.

"I'm sorry to disturb you, Mr. Olivetti, but we're preparing to land in Paris," said the pretty flight attendant with an easy smile, perfect for waking up to. "I just need you to put your seat back up and secure your seatbelt again. My goodness, you slept nearly the entire flight. But fear not, we'll be back in the air shortly and on our way toward Rome. A decidedly shorter excursion, wouldn't you say?"

Ferro attempted a smile, but felt weary from the dream that had consumed him during his long flight. As he yawned, he said wistfully, "It doesn't seem I got the rest I needed." He paused, remembering what he'd dreamed. His friend, Giuseppe, his first experience with death. How he had insisted the family attend the old man's funeral, because it was the proper thing to do, to offer respect. He would not be talked out of it, and finally his parents relented. Now, he feared he was returning home for yet another goodbye. "But it will be good to put foot on Italian soil again. It's where we Olivettis came from, and again where we will find our eternal rest. I have missed my home, more than I can say."

The bewildered attendant patted him on the shoulder, then went to ready the cabin for landing. He gazed out the tiny window as the city of Paris grew before them. No wonder they called it the city of lights; golden beams swept over the land like a beacon, willing the plane to land in its welcoming embrace. The first leg of his journey was nearly complete. How he had wished for a nonstop flight, something unavailable from San Francisco; still, the flight attendant was right—the journey to Rome would be fast, with barely any layover now. He'd be home to his parents in no time. It seemed both days since his mother had called and mere minutes. Time meant nothing in the sky. Still, he was nearly there.

He wondered if he was prepared for what awaited him.

*　　*　　*

Night had fallen on Rome by the time Ferro's flight touched down, and an hour later he was immersed in the heavy traffic that swirled around the busy roads, surrounded by the city's wondrous mix of ancient treasures and modern conveniences. Ferro, in the back seat of a cab, stared out the window as though it were his first time in the city of so-called eternal life. He never tired of seeing his homeland, and only now did he realize how much he missed its culture. How could he have not planned a diversion during his recent trip, Cass notwithstanding? He could have just put her up in a hotel while he went to visit Mama and Papa. He had been so close, and yet his penchant for parties—and the ladies who joined him—had otherwise engaged Ferro. Now he was paying for that poor decision.

Once the plane had landed, Ferro had taken out his cell phone and called his mother to let her know he'd at last arrived. His father was still hanging on, calling out his name, she told him, her voice tight while she kept careful control of her emotions. He knew the moment he stepped foot inside the foyer of the family villa his mother's tears would flow like the Tiber. Checking his watch, Ferro estimated five more minutes.

The cab swung around the huge Colosseum, its crumbling façade awash in lights against the pitch-black sky. It was amazing for Ferro to see something so old to still look so alive, so vibrant. He wondered if he could say the same for his father. Had the disease devastated him? And why had his mother not informed him that his father's body was failing him so. Was she in denial as much as Ferro himself? The images in his mind had the man looking as fragile as Rome's antiquities. And yet, those were still standing, enduring.

He had to wonder the toll all of this had taken on his mother. Caring for the sick was a terrible burden, even when it was done out of love. Caregivers often went unrecognized for their noble efforts. He thought of the elegant beauty that was Helena Olivetti. She had always been there for both her husband and her lone son, born late in their marriage as a gift they thought they would never receive. Helena represented a mix of old world and new, as her dedication to her family came first, yet she still managed to exude the characteristics of the modern woman. Not an easy task in any culture, but in the Italian life it took an understanding man to know the ambitions of the strong woman who shared his life. And Helena was one such woman.

Guilt accompanied Ferro the final few roads to the family villa on the southern edge of Rome, but finally the cab pulled beside the main entrance to the place where Ferro had grown up. A place he'd loved, but also one he'd desired to escape. Again, there was that image of dueling needs, the juxtaposed emotions of comfort and drive, not unlike what fueled his mother. Being there for your family; wanting also to express your own individuality. He'd learned both traits were important, instilled at an early age by both of his parents. For the past two weeks and beyond, Ferro had lived his life as he'd seen fit, indulging in all its pleasures and riches. Now, though, the time had come for him to return to his roots, to be there for family.

Tossing a series of euros at the cabbie, Ferro emerged from the back seat with his suitcase and in that instant breathed in the sweet spring air that swirled around him. Even though darkness had settled over the city, Rome was still very much alive, and in the distance the din of laughter and music could be heard. After a seemingly endless trip, it was nice to be on the ground and stretching his lungs to capacity. He felt invigorated, ready for nearly anything. Nearly. That bit of caution was what held him back. He stole a look at the villa and at the lights brightening the various windows, and he imagined the lives that were being played out inside those rococo walls. Also, the one life that was nearing its inevitable end.

Ferro blessed himself in an attempt to prepare himself for the worst, and then knowing there was nothing but an uncertain future waiting for him inside, he stepped forward. About to enter the villa, the front door swung open, and his bustling mother came rushing at him. She embraced him like a fierce wind, an unstoppable force of nature.

"Ferro, my dear, thank the Lord God you have made it in time. The doctors are here, making your father as comfortable as possible. But still, they advise it is a matter of hours."

"Mama, I'm sorry. For everything. For not being here."

She shushed him. "Later, Ferro. Remorse is not what is needed now."

"I'm here. There is no other place I could be."

"And that is what matters. I called, you came. A boy to his mama."

After another lingering hug that spoke volumes, she pulled back and that's when Ferro took in her full appearance. Aside from the tears that streaked her cheeks, she looked strong and healthy; she looked just like the woman he expected to find. Only a hint of weariness was hidden behind her eyes. He smiled wanly at the sight of his beloved mother, wiping away a stray tear as he did so. She allowed herself a brief smile, as though she thought somehow, she was betraying her dying husband with this slight moment of pleasure. But Ferro understood, and words once again went unspoken between them. Their eyes said all they needed right now. A language all their own.

Helena Olivetti was in her late sixties, and she was as beautiful today as she was the day she married the handsome and charismatic Alberto, a self-made man who wanted nothing more than to share his life with the most alluring creature he'd ever met. Helena was still that woman, filled with laughter and a generous heart that swelled with love, and it was this inner, innate strength that Ferro depended upon now. He knew, too, he needed to be strong for her; he also knew she was thinking the exact same thing. Such was the bond between mother and son.

"Come, Ferro, it's getting cold outside."

Ferro did feel a chill, but he wasn't sure it was from the changing patterns of the weather. It was as though by crossing the threshold from the cool outside to the warming hallway of the Olivetti villa, he was passing down ghostly paths of the past.

Clinging to his arm, Helena escorted Ferro inside the familiar environs of the villa, where he was greeted by a small, assembled group of family and strangers alike. Though he had not seen some of them in several years, he saw his aunt and uncle on his father's side, who were also his parents' closest friends and confidantes. Ferro was very glad to see them, if only for their supporting his mother during this troubling time. He walked up to them and gave them both pecks on each cheek.

"Thank you both for being here."

"Where else would we be?" his uncle said. "He is my brother."

"And your mother and I, we are as close as sisters. But this time now is when a mother needs her son."

As for the remaining person standing in the foyer, he was probably his early fifties and with graying hair at the temples. He had a seasoned, educated appearance, and if Ferro had to guess, this man was one of his father's doctors. He introduced himself to the man, shaking his hand.

"Ferro, dear," his mother interjected, "this is Doctor Lazerri, who has been helping your father during these difficult days."

Ferro noticed but said nothing to the fact his mother couldn't use the phrase "final days." He swallowed his own fears, knowing he wouldn't be able to find voice to such words either. He said, "Dr. Lazerri, I appreciate all you've done to ease my father's pain. But I don't understand. The cancer, it was gone, yes? And he was recovering. Now I am to believe my father lies on his death bed?"

"The cancer was in remission, my boy. He was never fully cured, he couldn't be. In layman's terms that just means the disease was hiding—getting ready to strike again when it was strong enough again, and in this case, it came back more determined than ever. As it often does. I'm afraid there is nothing we can do for your father, strong man that he is. The cancer has worn him down and is showing little mercy."

"Is he in pain?"

"Some," Doctor Lazerri noted. "But he is on medication, which helps alleviate the worst of the pain. He is as comfortable as he can be, here at home. I had advised your mother that he really belongs in the hospital."

"No," Ferro said, "he will die with dignity. Here in the home he loves, surrounded by those he loves. My father is a man of great passion and determination. If this is truly the end, he will meet it head on, and on his terms. Just like he has lived his life. How he taught me to live mine."

The doctor nodded, then stepped aside.

Ferro turned to his mother, his hand touching upon her shoulder.

"I'm so sorry not to have been here."

"Regrets, Ferro, are for tomorrow and beyond. Let's not waste precious time on that now. Today, this moment, you are here and that's all that matters."

"I must see him. No more delays."

"Of course. Father Dominic is upstairs with him now. Shall I...?"

Helena was not able to finish her question. Ferro instantly turned and took the stairs two at a time, his boots clacking against the marble steps. My God, with a priest at his father's bedside, surely, he couldn't have run out of time already. Were last rites already given? Was the end that close? *Please*, Ferro thought with a powerlessness that felt uncomfortable in his own body, *give me this precious time with my father and I'll do anything necessary to prove my worth.*

*   *   *

Ferro was struck by the strange juxtapositions offered by this strange thing called life. Now that he stood outside his father's bedroom on the second floor of the spacious villa, the last thing he wanted to do was open the door and enter the room to witness the man he most revered at his sickly worst, but on some deeper level it was the thing he most wanted to do in this world. Summoning strength your body held only when necessary. He knew that not every person was blessed with this gift: the opportunity to say your goodbyes. This was his final chance to tell his father how much he loved him, and how much he had taught him. Things like being a man, about being a loving and loyal son. About how to create an empire yet remain grounded as to what mattered most. Ferro was thankful beyond words to have this chance with his father.

That is, if he ever stepped inside.

His hand hesitantly holding the doorknob, he took a deep breath and steeled himself for the fearful stench of encroaching death. Bedridden for days, he wondered when his father had breathed fresh air last. Did they allow the windows to be opened, for him to hear the songs of birds, the sweet sounds of the world happening all around him? Was it too much for him to bear that he preferred to be shut away from everything he'd held dear?

With the thought of his father all alone, Ferro stepped inside the darkened room, where the only sound came from a radio playing in the far corner. Ferro could not make out the music, just the dim strains of an Italian tenor performing an aria from some opera. Verdi, probably, his father's favorite. Just then he realized he wasn't alone. Of course, his mother had said Father Dominic was offering comfort, how could he have forgotten? The priest turned from the bedside, nodded quietly at him. The elderly priest, a longtime friend of the family, with his bald dome and his frame hunched with age, approached Ferro and embraced him.

"Ferro, how good to see, even under these difficult times. Your Papa, he has been asking for you, waiting for you. I will give you some time to visit with him, some privacy between father and son."

"Thank you, Father," Ferro said. "Your presence has brought him great comfort."

With a solemn nod, the priest then made his exit from the room, and for the first time in months Ferro was alone with his father. Though he knew that was not necessarily true, because he always carried his father with him. In spirit and in his dreams. Only now was the reality set before him, and Ferro could honestly say he was frightened of what lay before him. His eyes fell upon his father's frail, withering body. He could hardly believe this was the same man with the booming voice, the wall-shaking laugh, the man who had schooled him in the arts and in culture, in business and in civility. This was the man who had shaped him, and now he hovered near death, a shell of a vibrant man who had embraced all life had to offer.

"Papa." Ferro said as he approached the bedside. "It is I, your son. Ferro."

Alberto Olivetti, lying beneath a swarm of thick blankets, turned his withered face toward his only son, and for a second Ferro detected the slightest hint of a smile. No doubt even a simple move like that required the strength and energy his body no longer possessed. But for Ferro, he would try.

"My son…*bene*. Good, good."

As Ferro settled down on the edge of the bed, he smoothed away a stray lock of gray hair from his father's cool forehead. "Papa, you'll be just fine. You must be strong, like you taught me all my life." Then he bent down and took hold of his father's hand, kissed it. It, too, felt cold.

"I am glad you came," his father said, somehow finding strength in his voice.

"Where else would I be?"

This time his Papa did grin, widely. "Ah, where indeed. From all I read and see, you travel the world like it is a park for your amusement. Your mother, she tells me of your exploits. Reads me fantastical stories from the newspaper." He coughed, then paused while he struggled to find a deep breath. He indicated a series of newspapers and magazines lying on a nearby table. "Those silly rags. You know I have always watched you closely, Ferro. Even as a boy you dreamed of conquering the world. It appears nothing can stop you."

"I work hard, Papa. You taught me that."

"Yes, my son, and you also have learned to play hard," Papa said. "That…that is something you have taught yourself. The playing, it makes a man soft. Causes him to lose his focus."

Ferro bowed his head, not from shame necessarily but at hearing such words spoken by the one man he trusted. Was this what the old man wanted to tell him before he died? Was this to be their final goodbye, words of how Ferro had failed him? The fact that his father knew of his recent trip, the gambling and the yachts and the women, this sat in the pit of his stomach. It was not the image of himself he wished to project to his Papa. Which was just one of the many reasons he shunned the *paparazzi*, the press. He knew how his father disapproved.

"I am just living my life, Papa. Is that so wrong?"

"No, my son, I taught you to be independent, and that is what you've become. But too much with the women, but none that make you happy. You must be careful." He sought more air, pushing himself to impart this final lesson to his only son. Papa beckoned him closer. His breathing was growing ever shallower with each statement, and he wished not to strain himself further. "I have a request. A final request."

"Papa, please, none of this finality."

"Ferro, my boy, let us not dishonor this moment with false hope. My destiny has already been written, and time is no longer my friend. Your life is still to be, and that is what I wish to discuss with you. I have a request of you. I have been saving my strength, my voice…for this conversation. Now, you must listen."

"This request, Papa—I don't understand."

The senior Olivetti pointed to the radio. "Please, turn it down, you must hear my every word."

Ferro could hear him just fine, but he did as instructed, lowering the volume on the radio. He rejoined his father on the edge of the bed, and anxiously awaited whatever this mysterious request was. For a moment Ferro felt a chill rip through his spine. Whether he was nervous for himself or for his father, he couldn't be sure.

"You will understand only when you've truly embraced what I ask."

Ferro remembered his own promise he had made to himself, on the plane and standing before the villa and just now, outside the door to his father's room, to do anything the dying man desired. Anything to help ease his mind in these final hours.

"It will be hard for you. Very hard. Perhaps the most difficult thing you've ever had to do in life."

"Whatever it is, Papa…I will do it."

The old man leveled his eyes at Ferro. "You must go far away. Away from the decadent life that consumes you. Away from all you believe that matters. Not permanently, my son, just for a month. That is all the time you need, all that I require. It is time enough for you to see things differently, the world and yourself. Your hopes and your future, it all depends on your fulfilling my wish."

"But Papa…"

"A month, Ferro. No money, no privileges. No Olivetti name."

"My name? I cannot deny who I am, where I come from. How can I not be the son of Alberto Olivetti?"

"If you do not do as I ask, what kind of son would you be?"

Alberto looked up at his son, his eyes fierce with determination, but also with disappointment. "I know I am dying, that my time has run out. You must promise me, no less than a month. Thirty days. You must not let anyone know who you are."

"Papa, this is…" Ferro let the unspoken word drift off. He wanted to say insane, that this entire proposition was just crazy. But that's not what you said to your father, not ever, and certainly not when it most mattered. "Papa, we will talk about this later."

"No!" his father said, his voice suddenly filled with the power Ferro remembered as a boy. "There is no time for later, later does not exist for me. Your promise to me, here and now, that is what will give me my greatest comfort in the end."

Ferro, his mind swirling with so many questions he didn't know where to begin, suddenly fighting back tears and losing the battle. He continued to hold his father's hand, letting the tears slide down his cheeks. One drop fell to his own hand, mixed with his father's perspiration. As though linking them, not by water but by blood. Ferro knew what he had to do.

He nodded. "I promise you, Papa."

"Good, good. *Bene.* I know what I am doing, Ferro. The Olivetti name depends upon you doing as I ask. It is my wish, my will. Go now, Ferro, see to your Mama. She needs you more now. Sleep comes to me, as it so often does these days. And my boy, my most precious son, may God be with you on your journeys. *Arrivederci.*"

Ferro silently sat there as his father drifted off to sleep, thinking, wondering, and still crying. Emotions overwhelmed him to the point where he no longer knew what to think. What did he mean, the Olivetti future rested on this decision? Just then he felt the comforting arms of his mother surrounding him, cradling him. He hadn't even heard her come in. But there, in the growing darkness of the room, as his father slept and his mother held him, Ferro once again felt like the little boy in his dreams, needing his parents, needing the past to be the present. Remembering the death of Giuseppe, and how his parents had explained that with life came endings, and it was how you reacted to such losses that built character, made you who you were.

His mother surprised him when she whispered to him, "Your father spoke to me of his wish. Will you do it, Ferro, what your father asks of you?"

"Mama, how can I? I don't understand it."

"He started with nothing and struggled to make a good life, a beautiful home. For me, for us. His family. That is something you are missing. Lacking."

"Mama, please, I cannot think about this right now. I need time to think, to absorb all that Papa asks."

"You have given him your word?"

Ferro nodded.

"Then there is no more to think about. Honor him, you must. The Olivetti name rests on your word."

"That's what Papa said. But I don't understand."

"Once upon a time, Ferro, you found love. You were ready."

Ferro raised a hand, a defensive move against a topic he did not wish to discuss.

"Please, Mama, I don't want to hear about that. About her."

She nodded. But her eyes said she wasn't done with the conversation.

"Mama, I made a promise, and I will honor his wishes. It's just that I can't do this right now. The timing."

"You think the world revolves around your schedule, Ferro? Were that the truth, your father would not be lying in this bed, waiting to die. There is never a good time. You must embrace his request, and you must do it now."

Ferro could say nothing more. Control no longer belonged to him, he had given himself up to time and to honor, to his parents and to what was truly important: digging deep into his own soul to know the answer to what was truly important. And knowing that family was the answer.

Still, in the dim light, sitting with his beloved parents, Ferro thought about all that was missing from his life. Rome was filled with unavoidable ghosts, and now that he had returned, they were creeping back into his consciousness. As though they were sitting right beside him, reminding him of what he had lost.

CHAPTER FIVE

THE LAST OF THE OLIVETTIS. *Is that what he truly was?*

Such was Ferro's thought as he stood in a place where he never wanted to be, a place he knew was the only place he could ever be at this given moment. Graveside, with his mother at his side, and his aunt and uncle near her, the remnants of a family who defined love but that God had denied further chance at enduring. His Uncle Stefano and Aunt Giulia had been blessed early in their marriage with a daughter, yet she hadn't lived beyond seven years. Nearby was her oft-visited grave, a sight that served as a constant reminder of what they had lost, what had devastated them to the point where no further children were to be born. Ferro had been a year old when his cousin Carina Andrea had succumbed, and only years later did he learn that for the Olivetti family, its entire future rested on Ferro himself. That fact was punctuated today by the presence of his remaining family, once again, for the passing of another Olivetti

The family had lost its leader.

"Ashes to ashes, dust to dust, and from life we return our beloved Alberto from where he came," intoned a somber Father Dominic, presiding over the graveside ceremony. "May he find peace in his eternal sleep, wrapped in the love and memory of this eternal of all cities."

It was a day of brilliant sunshine, temperatures in the mid-fifties and with a swirling wind, it was almost as though his father hovered over them, blessing them with his presence even while they said their final goodbyes. And while the family huddled close, they weren't alone, certainly. Friends, neighbors, men that Alberto had done business with, drank copious amounts of wine with, had talked long into the night at the local taverns with, they were all here. Ferro knew that the ceremony had come to an end and it was time to meet, greet, and thank each and every one of them with the grace and kindness his parents had taught. Under a copse of poplar trees just yards from his father's waiting grave, Ferro stood, his eyes disguised by sunglasses to simultaneously cut the glare and mask his feelings.

There were possibly one hundred mourners, and after a while their sentiments all started to sound alike.

"Your father was so proud of you," some said.

"Your father was the best of the best," others said.

The parade of people passed by him in a blur, their words, though kind, starting to sound pat, rehearsed. He was gracious, though, especially with his mother at his side. It was only when he heard the sweet tonal quality of a woman whom he feared seeing that his emotions got the best of him. She took his hand and said, "I'm so sorry for your loss, Ferro. I know your father meant everything to you."

Ferro, whose eyes had been downshifted, gazed back up at his fellow mourner. He took off his sunglasses; to get a better view. Not that he needed one—he would always know her look, not just what she showed the world but what she kept hidden deep in her soul. He had known her that well, once upon a time. She was perhaps the loveliest creature he'd ever laid eyes on, even dressed in a smart black dress, her face nearly covered with a wide-brimmed hat. He didn't need to see her to know how beautiful she was, the voice alone could devastate him all over again. It nearly did in this instant.

"Anna Maria," he spoke, his own voice a near whisper.

"You look good, Ferro," she spoke.

"As do you. Thank you for coming. If you don't mind, I have more guests to greet," he said rather coldly, somehow finding strength within him to rebuff even the simplest of gestures, even as his resistance was at its lowest.

"Of course, Ferro. I'll extend my sympathies to your mother."

"And then go, please," he said.

She appeared visibly wounded and wouldn't surrender herself so easily to his whims. "Ferro, I know how much this day pains you. I was hoping our past would not interfere with my presence—I truly loved your father, he was such a good man, an honest man, and he was always so welcoming to me. Making me feel like your home was mine."

"And it could have been," Ferro said.

He noticed that his words hit his target directly. She wiped away a stray lock of dark hair and with an expression of sadness written over her face, she turned away from him, only to embrace the widow Olivetti. He heard his mother exclaim how lovely Anna Maria looked, and then thanked her for coming. Ferro himself had had enough of this meet-and-greet, and he wandered off without any particular place in mind. But of course his feet took him to his father's grave. The casket still hovered over the freshly dug hole in the ground; for propriety's sake, Alberto Olivetti would not be lowered into his final resting place until the family had departed. It was one thing to toss roses and recite prayers at this site, another to watch the actual interment. Ferro knew his mother would be unable to handle that, and truthfully, he felt rather weak too when it came to witnessing such finality. The vibrant man he'd called Father his entire life had been reduced to a shell of a person, lying inside this box, already unaware of the pomp surrounding his death.

Ferro looked back at the assembled guests, where, in the distance he noticed Anna Maria approaching a dark car. The passenger side opened and out stepped a small girl who appeared to be an amazing replica of the statuesque woman she ran to. Anna Maria bent down and scooped up the little girl in her arms, all the while accepting a series of kisses upon her cheek. Ferro smiled briefly, both from the scene unfolding before him and also for what might have been. He imagined the little girl calling to Anna Maria, "Mama, Mama," and then in the flash of fantasy, she was grabbing Ferro's hand and proclaiming, "Papa, isn't Mama so beautiful?" And then Ferro heard his response echo inside his mind, "Always, my sweet, Mama is very lovely, and so are you," and then the little girl would giggle with delight. A twinge of sadness overcame him as he realized he did not know the girl's name. She was not his; she was not an Olivetti. He still held that crown, the last of them.

Ferro blinked away blurry tears, then watched as Anna Maria guided the precious girl back inside the car, then she herself disappeared behind the tinted glass. The car drove away, getting lost in the crush of Rome's traffic; suddenly Anna Maria was gone from his life as quickly as she had re-entered it, and always, always, on her terms.

Just then he felt a hand upon his shoulder. He turned to find his mother's comforting presence, her gentle touch warming in the cool breeze.

"Are you okay, Ferro?"

"Yes, Mama," he said. "But there is something I must do. Perhaps you can catch a ride back to the villa with Uncle Stefano. I shall see you back there momentarily."

"Of course I can," she said. "But, Ferro, I can also help you."

"This is something I must do alone, and it cannot wait," he explained. Then he planted a kiss upon his mother's cheek. She put her hand on his cheek, held him in check. At last she released him, blowing a kiss in his direction. Smiling back at her, he pantomimed catching the kiss and then slipped past the trees where he'd earlier greeted his guests, now heading off on his own, as the crowd dissipated.

Slipping the sunglasses back on his face, Ferro contemplated the best way to get to his destination, by cab or by tram, preferring the former to the latter if only for privacy's sake. But he felt it would be good to be about the people of Rome, to soak in their sounds and scents, to know that life continued, that Rome and all its glory persevered even in the face of death. A few blocks later he came to a tram stop, where he noticed the slim vehicle approaching. He stepped on with several others, then contented himself with the back and forth rocking motion as he awaited his destination. It had been years since he'd ridden the tram, but it came back to him so easily, as though once again he was that small boy roving around the city as though he owned it. In a way, hadn't he owned it, in ways that mattered more than owning corporations and having buckets of cash at his disposal. Back in Rome, he was once again the innocent.

So it was only perfect that he wound up on the Via Veneto, which once had housed old Giuseppe's pastry shop, and then, years later, after the family had sold not only the business but the building, the first electronics retail store owned by an upstart young businessman named Ferro Olivetti. He'd been just nineteen and had only begun to tap his own potential and ambition. Standing before the small shop, Ferro felt a mix of complex emotions, wishing somehow he could go back in time to this time of self-discovery, when he'd had the support of not just his parents but of the girl of his dreams, one Anna Maria Peroni, when he announced his decision to leave college and pursue a dream only he could envision. The store had been a starting point, the location perfect, if not poetic.

For two years Ferro had purchased products and sold them—he was the staff of one—using his charisma to fuel demand for the latest gadgets, amassing as much money as he could in the safe stored in the back room, initially living back there, too until he'd saved enough to buy the apartment above the shop. Before long, he owned the building, and that's when he'd gotten serious with Anna Maria and asked her to move in with him. She agreed, and why not—she was as much in love with Ferro and he was with her. Yet something was lacking between them. And Ferro decided that to make his true mark on the world he had to leave Italy. Anna Maria wanted nothing to do with the rest of the world, and so there it was, laid out before them, a fundamental difference in their ambitions.

Ferro sold the property and the business, and, at age twenty-three moved to the United States with a decent savings and pretty much nothing else. He had no friends there, few business contacts, and definitely not Anna Maria at his side. With the only thing fueling him his own drive, he found employment with a start-up firm in Silicon Valley, invested some of his hard-won cash into the project, and when the company announced their initial public offering, Ferro was the first to line up for shares. His investment paid off. And soon after that, Ferro Olivetti was on his way toward his great fortune, as well as his reputation. And he had done it all on his terms, with himself as the boss, never once letting personal feelings, or, for that matter, another woman, interfere with his plan. Olivetti Enterprises was born, with Ferro settling his interests in San Francisco, the grand City by the Bay. All of it done in the name of his father, a father who now, was no longer at his side.

"Nothing is forever," Ferro said aloud, staring at the structure where as a boy he'd devoured sweet pastries and treats, where as a young man he had come into his own and mapped out his future, a place that now held nothing but memories. But it was almost as though life were working in a cyclical way, returning the property to a pastry shop, albeit not one owned by Giuseppe's family. Ferro smiled at the wave of memories that hit him. He had done what he wished by coming here, getting back in touch with the man he'd been before the money and indulgent life had consumed him. Is that what his father had meant with his wish? Ferro supposed he had already begun the journey that was being asked of him.

But no, his thirty days could not begin now, and certainly not in a city he knew, a city that knew one of its favorite sons. He knew what he had to do, and this time he turned and found a waiting cab. He hailed it and gave instructions to be returned to the family villa. Not even stopping to alert his mother to his return, Ferro took the stairs to the second level with as much alacrity as he'd had the night he'd arrived to say goodbye to his father, as though this second visit was just as important, maybe more so. As Ferro entered his father's bedroom once more, looking now at the freshly made bed, he tried to take in the events of the last few days. The long flight, the brief reunion with his beloved Papa, and mostly his strange request to part, even briefly, with the life he'd carved for himself. He had an idea of why it was so important to his father, emotionally, but there was a practical quality to this that made no sense. What was he supposed to ultimately again from the experience? Still, a promise was made. He would have more time to think on the flight home.

"Only for you, Papa, always," Ferro said, and with that he turned to leave. But not before he reached over to the silenced radio and flipped a switch. The lush song that played washed over the room; Ferro smiled. Verdi, again.

An hour later he ventured downstairs, his suitcase at his side. His mother heard the commotion and came bustling from the kitchen. She came to him. "Ferro, must you leave already? I will miss you."

"And I will you, Mama. I will see you again, very soon. But as you know, there is much to be done. Father has requested such a thing."

"Take one last lesson with you, Ferro, my dear. Remember today, the service, the many people there to see your father to rest. He earned the respect he got. You understand?"

"I understand, Mama."

"I hope you do, Ferro." She paused, smiled wanly at him. "I know you do."

Ferro embraced his mother one last time, kissing her cheek lovingly. Then he grabbed hold of his suitcase and made his way out the front entrance to the villa, where a cab awaited to take him back to Fiumicino. The plane would take him home, but for how long he stayed in San Francisco he couldn't be sure. Decisions needed to be made. Settled back in the cab, he stole a glance back at the villa, at his home, and at his mother, still waving to him, the tears still visible on her cheeks. In a way, he felt as though he was saying goodbye not only to his father, but to himself as well. As if with Alberto Olivetti ceasing to exist, so too did Ferro Olivetti.

The time had come to be a different man, a stronger one.

A better man.

*   *   *

"It's an intriguing report, Mr. Olivetti."

"Please, Ms. Wilde, I insist that you call me Ferro," he said into the cordless telephone, deliberately imbuing his voice with a thicker accent. He knew that to many his voice bordered on the exotic, and he often found women were suckers for the Italian lilt that came naturally to him. He hoped to use his charm to sway the cool efficiency of Vodell's chief.

"For now why don't we keep things on a formal basis," the woman replied coldly. "We don't want to get ahead of ourselves now, do we, Mr. Olivetti? How would that look, cozying up to your undeniable charms when I have interest from both you and Richard."

Richard. Inwardly, Ferro seethed, knowing she meant Dunbar, and her use of his first name was obviously done with pointed intent. She was letting Ferro know that this was purely a business decision, that she would do what was best for Vodell. She would not be swayed by a smooth-talking, handsome playboy.

"1 understand," Ferro said, hating to acquiesce.

Since his return from Rome, Ferro had worked side by side with Lawrence and his other top advisors on their proposed takeover of Vodell Industries. Now, two weeks had somehow slipped by since the passing of Ferro's father, and in all that time his son had buried himself in his work. He'd been thankful for the long nights and weekends spent readying this important document. It seemed the only way for him to fight the overwhelming sense of loss, and perhaps it was for this reason that he hadn't yet felt compelled to honor his father's last request. As though by packing up his own life for thirty days was too much to bear in the wake of his father's death; it would be a case of admitting the truth that Ferro no longer had the one person he could always depend on—the man whose telling, helpful advice had seen him through more business deals than he could count. How Ferro needed him now, especially in the wake of new developments on the Vodell deal.

Ms. Wilde continued. "Vodell Technologies, as you can well imagine, is important to me. It was my baby from the get-go, and though it hasn't developed over the years the way I had envisioned, there's still a great deal our products have to offer the marketplace. I also want to see my legacy played out in the best scenario possible. So, I will read over your proposal thoroughly, as will my top vice presidents and advisors, and we will get back to you as soon as we can. But know this, it won't be tomorrow or the day after. This is a decision that will affect the rest of my life."

Ferro was familiar with such notions. "Careful consideration is the key to any successful business venture."

"So is knowing who you should do business with," she said, "and who you should not."

"Duly noted," he said.

"I appreciate your call. Oh, and Mr. Olivetti?"

"Yes, Ms. Wilde."

"My condolences on the passing of your father," she said.

Ferro felt a lump in his throat; mixing business with personal family issues was not a card he liked to play. "My father taught me everything he knew. Business to him was not just about making money, it was building relationships that endured for decades."

"He obviously taught you well. Good day, Mr. Olivetti."

Ferro placed the phone down on his desk, his mind pensive. Invoking his father's name was a smart move on Wilde's part, she was letting him know that she respected family, even in the face of a potential fight for ownership of her company.

Despite their exchange, Ferro still found himself smiling. Olivetti Enterprises was very much in the mix, and his fingers tingled with excitement. The chase enticed him.

"Well, look at that, a smile on your face. That's something we haven't seen in a while, and it's damned good to see," said Lawrence as he opened the door to Ferro's office.

"You never swear, Lawrence."

"I do when it's needed. To make a point."

"Aha. Well, point taken, my friend."

"So, am I to assume the phone meeting with Vodell went well?"

"As well as can be expected. She's in receipt of our proposal that would ensure a smooth transition of ownership while avoiding all the unpleasantness of a hostile takeover. I know it's not what my advisors want. They want to go for the jugular, but in the end I think this is the proper approach. Still, it's going to be a couple weeks before we receive a response from Ms. Wilde and her team," Ferro said, then paused, as if a notion had suddenly occurred to him.

"Ferro, something wrong?'

A distracted Ferro looked back up at his trusted senior VP. "Hmm, oh, uh, no. All is fine. In fact, it couldn't be better. Given the current situation with Vodell, I think it's time I concentrated on something else. Lawrence, you're not going to like this," Ferro said. He'd told Lawrence nothing of his father's will, and now he was cautious about how much to reveal. "But I need to leave."

Lawrence, ever-practical, checked his watch. "It's barely three in the afternoon, do you have an appointment somewhere? I have nothing on my calendar."

"No, you misunderstand. I have to go away for a while."

"Away? I don't think I like the sound of that. And 'a while,' that makes it sound even worse. Ferro, you've only been home for two weeks, and before that you were gone nearly three weeks between your trip and your family crisis. Surely whatever you have to do can wait. At least until we have this Vodell deal wrapped up. Our lawyers, even waiting for a response, will be burning the midnight oil anticipating various scenarios. They will need to be advised."

Ferro shook his head. "I've already waited too long. I really must go."

"I'm not sure I understand, Ferro. Where are you going, and when will you be back?"

"Where am I going? That's a fine question, perfectly understandable. But Lawrence, it's not one I'm ready to answer now. Mostly because I'm not sure where I'm going. As for how long, it shouldn't be longer than thirty days." This last statement was said as a matter of fact, and yet retained an air of mystery.

"An entire month? You're kidding me, right Ferro? What about Dunbar? Vodell? What if Dunbar pulls a fast one while you're away? We're going to need you here to sort out the crisis. And that's just the tip of the iceberg. There are any number of other important deals that we are monitoring. Anything can come up at a moment's notice. We need you right here in the office."

"Lawrence, trust me, it's going to be all right. I'll be in touch."

"When? After you arrive? Where can I reach you? You have your cell, of course?"

"Lawrence, if you don't mind, I have some things to figure out."

Ferro paused, taking in the confusion and frustration worn by his friend like a heavy suit. He wished he could say more, but what he was planning was between himself and his father, a promise that called to him from the grave, had nagged at him during the day, slept with him at night. This was a request he could only respond to with action. "Lawrence, you've trusted me for years, haven't you?"

"Yes, sir," Lawrence said with deliberate formality.

"And everything has always worked out. For you, for me, and for Olivetti Enterprises. We built it from nearly nothing, and despite some upsets, we've always landed on our feet."

"Correct," he said, wiping newfound sweat on his brow. "But never before have we had so much money in flux, such a big acquisition as Vodell pending. And with you missing in action, you can bet Dunbar will strike."

"Forget the likes of Dunbar. Trust me, Lawrence, this situation is well in hand, and I promise Vodell will not slip through our fingers," Ferro said, though his confident voice caught in his throat, doubt creeping up from his gut like acid reflux. Still, he maintained the poker face that won him so many rounds at the casinos of Monte.

"I still don't understand," Lawrence said.

"Lawrence, all you need to know is that this is something my father asked of me. That's all I can say."

Suddenly Lawrence nodded. "I've known something was bothering you since you came back, not just your father's death. There was something hanging over you, distracting you."

"And I need to eliminate the distraction. Please, Lawrence, I don't wish to say anything further. I hope you understand."

"As much as I can."

"I could say the same," Ferro said enigmatically.

Lawrence departed, clearly not completely soothed by Ferro's words but giving him the respect he'd earned. Once again Ferro was left alone with his thoughts. He knew the when of his departure, now. The where, now that was the question.

He needed a place where anonymity was the key, where he wouldn't stick out. And where he wouldn't necessarily need the basics, like a car. An idea popped into his mind and suddenly he swung around in his chair and turned to his computer, where he logged onto one of those popular travel websites, the one with the yellow suitcase as its logo. He'd never used the site before, relying instead on his secretary to make travel reservations or for Claude to ready his jet. This was new territory for him, relying on himself. He had a sense this wouldn't be the first time in the coming month such would be the case. As he clicked the necessary information—dates, times, destination—into the fields, he then clicked and waited for his options.

"Ah, that looks good," he said aloud. And then he began typing the vital information, beginning with his name. He hesitated over that one, and for a split second he wondered just who would be traveling, who he would become. The answer was simple, it turned out. The idea came to him instantly, and with a conspiratorial smile, he hit the confirmation button. He felt as though the Ferro Olivetti of old had begun to drift into the past, and a new image was developing before him. He could see his reflection in the screen of the computer, and the face that looked back already looked different, changed.

"For you, Papa."

As he started out of his office, Ferro turned back, as though he were looking at it for the last time. The mahogany desk, the Tiffany lamp, the computer and phone representing a lifeline to the outside world, and finally, the photographs set in gilt-edged frames. He took a few unsteady steps back, where he reached for one of the photos. It was of himself and his father; he was a boy and he sat upon the man's lap, smiling up at him with absolute wonder written across his face. There was admiration then, just as there was now, even though his father was no longer living.

Just then Ferro's eyes darted to the shelves to the side of his office, where he saw the great chess board he and his father had played so many games on. With an outstretched hand, he took hold of the first pawn, moved it not the customary two squares but just one.

Like his new life, ready to move forward but with caution.

Still, he silently announced to his father, *I've made my opening gambit. Let's see where this new game takes me, how many wrong moves it takes to make the right one, I hope I know what I'm doing, because I feel like the rules have all changed.*

*   *   *

The next morning found Ferro leaving his villa at six A.M. The sun had not yet risen on this lush land covered with the fruit of the vine. Truth of the matter was, it was easier to begin the day on the go and not see all that he was leaving behind, his treasured house and sports cars, the marble fountain that spewed water fresh enough to drink, the rolling hills of the valley, the vines that gave this area its culture and livelihood. Instead, Ferro closed himself off from the world, hiding in the back seat of the limo behind tinted windows.

"Where to, Mr. Olivetti?"

"San Francisco International Airport, Claude."

"Very good. Another business trip?"

"No. A personal trip."

"Very good."

Unlike Lawrence, who panicked and asked questions and debated the merits of never knowing his boss's next move, Claude was rather restrained. He never needed to know plans in advance, his job was to show up with the limo at the appointed time and drive to the desired location, all without complaint or speculation. This morning was no different, Ferro noted, watching his driver's face with curiosity. Nothing caused an upset in Claude's balance—he took life as it happened. Ferro tossed that nugget of information into the back of his mind for future reference

"Claude, may I ask you a question?"

"Certainly, sir."

"How do you do it?"

"'Do it', sir? I'm not sure I understand."

"In all the years you have worked for me, you've never requested any special favors, and I cannot ever recall a complaint. You are as even-keeled as they come. Don't get me wrong, I appreciate you more than I could give voice to. But still, aren't there days you wake up and wish you were someone else—that your job was something else?"

Adjusting his cap with one hand while maintaining a steady grip on the steering wheel with the other, Claude stole a look back in the rearview mirror. "Sir, my job is to assist you in whatever you need, and you have always treated me fairly. Regular pay raises, bonuses, time off when needed, why if I have all that going for me would I think to be unhappy? I have a good life, sir, it's fulfilling to me, and in the end, if I'm content, so then should you be content with my role."

"Thank you, Claude. I'm sorry to intrude."

"Do you mind if I ask you a question?"

"Fire away."

"Are you all right?"

Ferro hesitated. Truth of the matter, he wasn't sure he could answer that question. He was physically fine; emotionally, though, he was a work in progress, still dealing with the emptiness he suffered from his father's death and the uncertainty he felt about what awaited him on the other side of his upcoming airplane ride. In the end, he gave Claude the safest answer possible: "I'm getting there, I think."

The two men grew silent as the limo wound its way to the highway and began the journey through the valley and down toward the Golden Gate Bridge. From there, they were in the home stretch of the hour-plus journey from his Napa home to the airport on the southern edge of the city. Ferro occupied his time by checking emails on his cell phone, answering those that required his immediate attention and deleting those he deemed unimportant. He sent one new email, this one to his mother, Helena, with the simple message: "My journey begins today." Then he logged off and turned the cell phone to silent. He settled back against the soft leather of the back seat and thought about that email and its implications.

At last they reached the outskirts of the airport, and that's when Claude lowered the divide between them. "Sir, which airline? Alitalia, again?"

"No, no, Claude. American. I'm staying within the states this time."

"You are not taking the Gambit One, sir?"

"Not this time."

"Very good."

Ferro grinned at his chauffeur's signature line. God, how he would miss that phrase, the words and the serious, studious voice that spoke them. For those who said you could never find good help these days, they need look no further than the reliable Claude Reneau.

Minutes later Claude had navigated the complex roads inside the airport and parked curbside at the American terminal.

"Sir, your destination. Will you be needing anything else from me?"

The moment of truth was upon Ferro, and he steeled his nerves for what would most likely sound like a strange favor. There had been uncommon requests over the years between Ferro and Claude, but this latest one was sure to be the strangest.

"Claude, I need your license."

"Pardon me, sir?"

Ferro paused, wondering how best to explain this. "I realize it's an unexpected request, but there's no other way. Your driver's license, please. Here, as a good faith gesture, you can have mine," Ferro said, reaching into his back pocket and handing over his wallet to Claude. "Driver's license, credit cards, all of my identification. My phone. I need you to hold on to them. And in return, all I ask for is your own license. Please, Claude, don't choose this moment to begin to defy my wishes."

"Such a concept never entered my mind, sir," Claude said, and without further word he passed through the divider his leather wallet. Ferro took hold of it like it was the holy grail, destined to gain him admission to the Knights of the Round Table. In fact, it stripped away any pretense of royalty, reducing the multi-million dollar playboy called Ferro Olivetti, revered by women and sought by the press, a man who could have anything or anyone at the snap of his fingers, to just an ordinary citizen.

As Ferro emerged into the sunlight of the new day, he thanked Claude once again.

But he wasn't in the clear just yet. Claude had one more question for his boss.

"Sir?

"Yes, Claude."

"If you're not you, just who are you?"

Ferro actually allowed himself a grin. "At the moment, I am you. In the future, that is still to be determined."

And with that, Ferro, dressed in casual jeans and a blue Oxford shirt, carrying a duffel bag that served as his only luggage, rushed toward the airport terminal to claim his boarding pass. He was also racing toward whatever and wherever this grand adventure was to take him. Getting the boarding pass was simple enough; what came next, he could only imagine.

"Papa, this is for you," he silently mouthed.

But in reality, Ferro knew this journey was ultimately for him. Whether that was good or bad remained to be seen. For now, the time had come to board his flight. Once again, Ferro Olivetti was taking to the sky, anticipating the adrenaline rush as the airplane cruised down the runway and shot into the sky. But he knew once he was airborne, the Ferro Olivetti the world knew would cease to exist. For the next month, he would be transformed into a simple man known as Claude Reneau. An ordinary man. Ferro didn't even know how to act, who to be. All he knew was that there was nothing waiting for him when he landed, certainly no one was going to be there to greet him.

No one who knew who he was.

And that included himself. Because at the moment, he didn't even qualify as the last of the Olivettis.

PART TWO

FERRO'S JOURNEY

CHAPTER SIX

THE THOUGHT THAT ENTERED her mind was this, and it wasn't entirely ironic: she hated all men.

Certainly, her husband, for dying on her.

Certainly, the man who had claimed to know details of how her husband had met his end, only to take advantage of her.

Certainly, the man who was making her perform this most disrespectful of tasks.

After all, she was a professional; she'd worked to get where she was in this world and had brought the company lots of money, tasteful clients, exciting properties. So why was she being denigrated in such a way?

Her name was Diane Mancini, and of all labels she'd accumulated in this world—daughter, wife, widow, real estate agent with a loyal client base, good friend to Vita and others—the one thing she never claimed to be was a chauffeur. Or was that chauffeurette? That's not what most people thought of when they saw Diane. She was naturally beautiful—that's what most people noticed first about her—with soft skin that made her somehow accessible. With flowing dark hair and an innocent smile that snuck up on her whenever she wasn't concentrating on all that had gone wrong in her life, she somehow felt that life for her, despite all she'd lost, all she'd dreamed of, was something that hadn't truly begun. Still, today, she found herself taking a new road on the journey that was living, figuratively, and certainly literally. Because she found herself behind the wheel of a gleaming Lincoln Town Car, and all she felt was missing was the proper uniform. Well that, and a customer riding in the backseat. But that would change soon enough, since she was on her way to the JFK to pick up her pig of a boss.

As she drove along the Jackie Robinson Parkway, following the signs to the airport, she couldn't help but remember her lack of luck in catching this assignment. On this Monday morning, she'd just returned to the office from showing a three-bedroom on the Upper West Side and was as happy as a lark, knowing an offer was imminent. Nothing could have ruined her day. And then the phone rang.

She was not the receptionist, she hadn't had to take the call, but the end result was that the instructions handed out landed on her desk.

"The Mrs. just called. And she wasn't happy, although when is she ever, right? Someone has to pick up Mr. Curtis from the airport, and lucky you, your number came up. His flight from San Francisco will be arriving in about two hours," said Kelly, the often times put upon secretary who somehow kept Curtis Real Estate up and running, despite the repeated absences of their leader, the company's founder and owner, Mr. Stan Curtis.

"Why me?"

"Because Mr. Curtis fired his last chauffeur before he left for his trip."

"Where's Timothy? "

"On a call."

"Where's Sandra?"

"Showing an apartment."

"And Jennifer? "

"Girl, you know I don't drive," said a person rising from a nearby cubicle. She wore a big smile, knowing her lack of a driver's license would come in handy someday. Diane tossed her a weary look.

Then Diane sighed, realizing her assignment was inescapable. She also accepted the keys. Both seemed to go hand in hand when it came to helping out Mr. Curtis.

"Of course, you need to stop at his house, that's where the car is parked."

Diane sighed again. That meant a subway ride from Manhattan to Forest Hills, not exactly a quick trip, and then she'd need to get the car, hop on the Interboro, and hopefully not encounter midday traffic on her way to the busiest airport in the world. Gee, what a plum assignment.

Turned out, traffic wasn't so bad as Diane weaved in and out of lanes, wondering why the other drivers didn't anticipate where they were going and get in the proper lanes with enough notice. She had to use the horn several times as cars tried, at the last minute, to slip into the lane ahead of her, as though it suddenly occurred to them they wanted to go the airport. A place like that, you never went voluntarily.

At last she arrived at Terminal 7, home to American Airlines. She pulled up curbside, then checked her watch. The flight was probably still in the air. She grabbed hold of her phone, punched in the website for American and checked the flight status. Another thirty minutes. Good, she thought. The last thing she wanted was to be late and to be on the receiving end of one of Mr. Curtis's rants. He ran a decent business, sure. But as an individual, Mr. Curtis was perhaps the most unpleasant man she'd ever met.

See, Diane hated all men.

Which is why, as she was waiting, she happily accepted a phone call from her friend, Vita.

"Hey, girl," her friend said.

"Hi, Vita."

"Where are you?"

"JFK. Waiting for Mr. Curtis."

"Ouch. Sorry. So, I have to meet someone for drinks later, but I shouldn't be late. Are you still coming over?"

"Are you kidding, after having to pick up Mr. Curtis, the last thing I need to endure is a night with my parents. If I can stay at your fab pad, I'd appreciate it. To be thirty years old and back living with my parents while I rebuild my life, well, you know how it goes."

"There'll be plenty of Chardonnay in the fridge."

"Vita, you're a lifesaver. So, drinks you say?" Diane said. "Got a hot date?"

"Ha. Hardly. Just business," she said. "Besides, you know men suck."

"I hate them," Diane said.

Vita laughed and then told her friend she'd see her later.

Diane hung up, smiling for the first time since she'd made that near-sale on that three-bedroom apartment. That would all change soon enough; the bombastic Mr. Curtis would be landing soon enough. For a moment Diane pitied the person who had ended up sitting next to him for six hours. At thirty-six thousand feet, escape was not exactly an option.

"Unless you want to jump," Diane said, with a laugh.

God, what had that flight been like from the start?

*   *   *

"I don't care who it is, but I expect that car to be waiting for me—not me waiting for it!" the man screamed into his cell phone. He paused barely less than a second before he added, "Yeah, you're such a supportive wife, no wonder I need to surround myself with far too many people I have to pay far too much for, since you won't do anything I ask…wait, yo…hey… miss, I'd like more champagne, and this time make sure it's cold. Why not just open a fresh bottle. What? No, not you, Hilda, Christ, I'm on an airplane all the way across the country, how the hell could you bring me a glass. Oh, never mind. Girlie, are you getting me my drink? Now, just do it."

On that last line, an amused Ferro Olivetti couldn't be sure just who the command was directed at, the poor thing named Hilda on the other end of the line or the frustrated flight attendant who probably would sooner want the plane to crash into a mountainside than deal with this ill-mannered buffoon. Still, the blowhard having two arguments—and simultaneously pissing off both recipients of his tirade--didn't seem to be having much luck. As he tossed his cell phone down, he had neither confirmation of a pick-up upon arrival, or that cold glass of champagne.

The man hadn't made any friends with the rest of his compartment mates here in first class. Everyone could tell one thing about the passenger: he was a complete and total jerk, and what it made it worse was the fact he was seated in the privileged world of first class and as such thought he had earned the right to demand whatever he desired. Next, he'd be demanding to fly the plane. And, of course, the obnoxious passenger was oblivious to anyone around him, their eyes rolling over his behavior, catty comments exchanged at his expense. He was above all that, seemingly, as though he were on a chartered flight, the only person who needed looking after. For the rest of the passengers, Ferro included, it was going to be a long flight. Longer still for the harried flight attendant who just now was bringing a refreshed bottle of champagne. She maintained a rigid stance as she went to pour the bubbly beverage into his glass.

"What, you can't bend down to do that? You don't want to spill any, right? Besides, that tight little uniform you got on, it's already showing off enough of your curves, what's wrong with displaying a bit more of that yummy cleavage my way. You got it, honey, flaunt it."

"Sorry, sir."

Her tone indicated she was anything but sorry.

That mountaintop, were they anywhere near it?

As the man drank his champagne with one hand, he immediately started dialing another number on his retrieved cell phone. But just then the pilot's voice crackled throughout the plane, and he announced they were second for take-off.

"Sir, you'll need to put that away," the flight attendant instructed the man.

He took that moment to down the final remnants of the glass. "I meant the phone."

"Goddamn rules everywhere," he said in disgust. Still, he put the phone away, actually shutting it off.

Ferro found that a curious move on the man's part. Sure, this guy could make demands all he wanted, but ultimately he was a pushover, just doing enough to make himself a nuisance without ever breaking any rules. Just enough bad behavior to not get kicked off the flight. The flight attendant would be wise to pick up on such an obvious character flaw. Ferro just tucked that little morsel away, in case of any further trouble from him during the transcontinental flight.

As the plane hit the sky and Ferro settled in for the long climb to their cruising altitude, he took a few moments to assess this flying companion. Whoever he was, he thought he was important beyond words. Probably early sixties, with a thick salt-and-pepper beard covering his cheeks and chin, and he seemed to be carrying a bit more weight than a man his age should. The beard, he supposed, covered up the man's jowl-like façade, and was no doubt supposed to lend him a distinguished air. The effect failed, and instead he looked messy and unkempt.

Just then the man looked to his left, directly at Ferro. "Something interest you?"

"Oh, just looking out your window."

"You want a window view, get a window seat," he said dismissively. Then, unbuckling his seat belt, he got up from his seat, mumbling something about "gotta see a man about a horse." Ferro watched as the man shuffled his way down the aisle and into the tight confines of the bathroom.

As Ferro gazed back, he noticed a slip of paper on the floor of the cabin. He reached down and retrieved it. It was the receipt of the man's boarding pass: Stan Curtis. The name meant nothing to Ferro, but that didn't mean much—in Ferro's lofty world there was no room for idiots such as this Curtis fellow. Still, it was nice to have a name to go with him, never knew when it might come in handy. Ferro stuffed the boarding pass into his own jacket pocket and then went back to enjoying the smooth flight. The flight attendant suddenly loomed over him.

"Sir, with all the, uh, drama I feel I've neglected you a bit. Is there something more I can get you? A refill of your seltzer? Some of that champagne to take the edge off?"

Ordinarily Ferro would not have turned up his nose at such an offer; he might have even propositioned the pretty young thing. Instead he shook his head and said, "Thank you, but no. I'm fine. Actually, come to think of it I wouldn't mind a few more packets of those pretzels. Never know when your hunger needs to be satisfied."

"That's not a problem, but do you know we'll be serving dinner shortly?"

"Yes. Still, good to have a reserve."

"Sure, I'll get those pretzels for you," she said with a smile. Then she indicated behind her. "Where's my friend?"

"I think someone pushed him out the emergency door."

She laughed, the first smile he'd seen on her harried face since Curtis had started his bellowing. "If only. And if anyone asks, my fingerprints are supposed to be on that door."

Ferro joined in her wicked laughter, then thanked her as she returned with five additional individual packages of the sourdough pretzels they'd given everyone in first class before takeoff. *No more Peanuts*, he mused, *too many people were allergic*. Ferro stuffed the bags inside his coat pocket, right next to Curtis's boarding pass.

The next hour passed without incident, as Ferro flipped through the inflight magazine and occasionally snuck a glance over at an obviously impatient Curtis. The man fiddled with his cell phone, clearly wishing he could spend the remaining few hours of the flight yelling at some lackey on the other end. Fortunately he hadn't demanded anything of late, champagne in particular. He was belligerent enough without adding alcohol to his fiery temper.

The peace was short-lived.

As dinner was being served—the flight attendant smartly serving Curtis first—Ferro couldn't help but hear the disgust in the man's tone. Seemed he wasn't pleased with his meal. "Miss, hey, miss…" he screamed out, his head poking out from his seat and down the aisle. He snapped his fingers. "What the hell is this supposed to be? This tastes like stew, not steak. I thought I ordered steak."

Groans could be heard throughout the cabin; everyone around him was getting sick and tired of this guy. Really, couldn't he be satisfied ever?

"Would the filet mignon be more to your liking?"

"That's what I ordered! This is inedible, whatever you want to call this mystery meat."

As the flight attendant switched meals, she grinned over at Ferro. Complicit in her conspiracy, Ferro knew she had given him the wrong meal on purpose. If she was going to get yelled at, which was near certainty, why not have a little fun while she was at it? Ferro liked this woman; she had gumption, and no doubt had been flying a long time. Clearly this guy wasn't the first unruly passenger she'd encountered. First class had little to with actual class.

As she turned to return to her other passengers, Curtis suddenly shrieked.

"Now what?" the woman said, her temper growing short.

"What do you call this?"

"It's the filet…"

"Not that, this poor excuse for a baked potato. One bite and you can tell it's bad. It's a bad potato."

"A bad potato you say, Mr. Curtis? Well, allow me to discipline it."

And with everyone watching her, she reached over to his tray and took hold of the baked potato. She instantly smacked it, not once but twice, then a third time, all the while saying, "Bad potato. Bad potato. Ooh, what a bad potato you've been." No doubt a pantomime of how she felt about the owner of said bad potato. Then she set it back down on the tray, splattering sauce all over his shirt. She glared at her passenger. "Now it ought to be a good potato."

Her zinger was perfectly placed, and immediately the rest of first class began to applaud as their caustic laughter filled the cabin. Ferro just glanced at Curtis and allowed himself a broad smile, Good for the attendant, Ferro thought.

"What the fuck do you find so funny?" said an irritated, humiliated Curtis.

Ferro opted to skip a reply, he was still enjoying the raucous laughter surrounding him. He had to imagine that the folks in economy must be wondering what was going on up here. Some special performance by an actor, or maybe just a better movie? Yeah, the latest sequel of *Flight Attendants Gone Wild*. It was a good one.

*   *   *

Four hours later the plane was thankfully on the ground at JFK, and unlike everyone else on board, Ferro was content to sit in his seat and watch the ridiculous game of hurry up and wait. They were barely parked at the gate when Stan Curtis took the lead from his fellow passengers and unhooked his seat belt and retrieved his carry-on luggage. Of course, his phone was turned on the second it could be, and he was dialing some unlucky soul. Curtis appeared determined to be the first one off the plane, and frankly, no one stopped him. They'd all had enough of this guy.

After a good fifteen minutes of bustling activity the cabin was cleared of all passengers, save Ferro. Thoughts raced through his mind—sure, he could easily get up from the comfort of his seat, stretch his legs, head off into the terminal with his carry-on luggage, and begin the next part of his journey. His only hesitation? He didn't know what the next part of his journey was.

"Sir?"

Ferro turned to find himself looking at the pretty flight attendant who had endured the long flight and difficult customer with charm, grace, and ultimately humiliating humor. She was smiling down at him.

"Oh, sorry, I suppose you need to get the aircraft ready for its next flight?"

"That, yes. And I'm off duty, so I need to get home and get some sleep. I've been back and forth to both coasts so much recently my body has no clue what time zone it's in. I think my mind is somewhere over Kansas still."

"I know what you mean," he said, thinking that in the past several weeks had flown twice across the Atlantic—and back—and endured several other short flights. He'd spent so much time in the air he wondered if gravity still held any pull on him. Still, he knew he had to get going, and with a rare bout of reluctance, Ferro Olivetti grabbed his small overnight bag and made his way toward the exit door. The flight attendant, accompanied by her rolling suitcase, was following close behind him.

As they exited the jetway together, Ferro turned and said, "So, are you based in New York?"

"I am. Why?"

"It's just, I wondered if I could hitch a ride into the city."

"I'm not going to Manhattan."

"Ah."

"I live in Queens, and well, my boyfriend is picking me up."

"Of course he is. I didn't mean to imply otherwise. He's a lucky man," Ferro said with a sheepish grin. Not that he was looking for sex or any kind of personal entanglement; it was just hard for Ferro not to turn on the charm for a beautiful woman. Harder still for him to hear someone turn him down. "Thanks for a great flight—the way you handled that jerk was far more entertaining than any movie you guys played."

"After a while, you figure out how to deal with guys like that."

Ferro nodded, then realized there was nothing more to be said. They parted ways, and Ferro made his way through the busy terminal, people rushing past him with bags and excited chatter, weary tourists given new enthusiasm for having reached their destination or residents simply glad to be home. Ferro fit neither of those categories, further fueling his growing sense of displacement.

He avoided baggage claim and finally found the exit doors. Once outside, he breathed in the crisp, cool March night. His watch indicated it was just after eight o'clock, a time when people were beginning to wind down from their busy days and begin to think about sleep. Sleep was the furthest thing for Ferro, since at the moment he had no clue where he would be resting his head this night, much less the next and beyond. With his wallet in the hands of Claude thousands of miles away, Ferro had no money, no prospects, and no idea what tomorrow would bring, much less the next hour.

Good thing that he'd come to New York, the city that reportedly never sleeps. It was nice to have one thing in common.

"Okay, Papa, I'm here," he said, "Now what?"

CHAPTER SEVEN

STAN CURTIS WAS NOT A HAPPY MAN, though ask his friends and family if he ever was, and you'd pretty much get the same negative response. But right now, in fact, his mood was worse than ever, although how much more foolish could he feel?

Standing curbside outside Arrivals with his bags, waiting and waiting still for his ride. While all the other passengers from his flight—and from others that had landed after his—hurried about the terminal, catching cabs, Ubers, rushing to the parking lots, gazing upwards for something called an AirTrain, grabbing drivers of prearranged pickups, all of them had the same intention: getting away from the crazy congestion that was JFK. Hadn't he told those idiots at home what time his plane was getting in? Hadn't he insisted that someone be there already, whether from home or the office, so he didn't have to wait? Christ, he'd spent the entire day on board that metal deathtrap, was it so hard for someone to drive his Town Car and pick him up?

Curtis, wiping sweat from his brow despite the cool air, was just about to give up on anyone coming to his rescue and call a ride share to take him instead, and quickly. He could pay handsomely; and then of course someone at his office would pay, too—with their measly, thankless job. That's when he peered around a bank of limos and recognized his own Town Car attempting to pull ahead of a line of cars that were jockeying for space in front of the American terminal. He waved it over, received back a blast of its horn as acknowledgment. Either that or the driver was just trying to clear a path.

Finally, the big, sleek car came to a halt in front of Curtis. The windows were, of course, tinted, so he couldn't see who was inside. That was the point, wasn't it, to keep curious gawkers from getting a look at him? Not that anyone would recognize him; he wasn't a celebrity, or a mover or shaker. Still, he was rich, and that's what people liked. Money, lots of it, or at least the illusion of wealth. But at the moment he only felt that his vehicle was guilty of betraying him, too, just like his family and employees. He was anxious to scold whoever the driver was; he was angry still, and as was his pattern, he couldn't wait to unleash his wrath.

Just then the front passenger window opened, and a face looked over at him from behind the wheel.

"Good evening, Mr. Curtis," said an attractive woman, her dark hair tied up into a tight bun, her dress conservative and reserved, her delicate hands awkwardly placed on the steering wheel. She was obviously trying to look as professional as she could behind the unwieldy car. She wasn't exactly pulling off the chauffeur look very well.

"Can I help you with anything?" she asked, attempting to remove herself from behind the wheel. "Your bags, perhaps?"

Curtis glared back, holding up a hand as he said, "Stay where you are, I'll deal with the bags. Just pop the trunk. The sooner we get out of here, the better."

The woman did as asked, fumbling with the location of the trunk release, while Curtis busied with equal parts amusement and frustration. Finally, the trunk popped, and he tossed in his luggage before clambering into the back seat of the car, slamming shut the door behind him. The partition between driver and passenger was down. Good, time for a dressing down.

"How are you, sir? "

"Skip the niceties, Ms. Mancini," he said, deliberately addressing her formally. "I'm in no mood for them. I'm tired, and the flight was one of the worst I've taken. Bumps all the way, plus a horrible staff and smart-ass passengers. So, that answer your question of how am I? Enough already. Why the hell are you so late, anyway? What's the point of being first off the plane if you're the last to leave the terminal? Time is money, and that wait just cost me plenty."

"I was here early," he heard, the voice edging on whiny. "But the airport security waved me off, said I'd been waiting too long. I had to pull away and circle the airport again. Getting back to Terminal Eight was no easy task."

"You should have left earlier."

"Mr. Curtis, like I said, I was here."

"Whatever," he said with a dismissive wave. "Excuses don't interest me."

"Sir, you asked."

"You being flip with me, Ms. Mancini?"

"Sorry, sir. I meant no disrespect."

He waved off her apology. "Why did they send you anyway?"

"Guess I was the only one available. Your wife called the office in a panic, spoke to Kelly and said something about having plans of her own, and that there was no one else at home to pick you up at the airport. What happened with your last driver, Eric? Last I knew he took you to the airport just the other day, and then your wife told me that you fired him? You let him go all the way from San Francisco?"

"No, I fired him from the airplane as soon as I knew he'd dropped the car safely back at my home. Damn kid, couldn't drive worth a lick and besides, I was almost late for my flight. Damned traffic, he should know a better way to get here. And my missing my flight would not have been good for business—my business, of which helps pay your salary. Now, speaking of bad driving, just what do you call what you're doing?"

The car wasn't moving.

"Sir, it's a red light."

"Excuses, that's all anyone ever has for me. And foolish excuses at that."

"With all due respect, Mr. Curtis, I wasn't hired to be your chauffeur. I'm a real estate agent, and a damn good one. And don't forget, most of my salary is commission."

"Yes," he said with a sneer. "Most."

This was the second woman today who had dared to admonish him. First that useless flight attendant with the bad attitude, and now one of his top agents deciding she could be disrespectful to him. But as much as Diane had spoken out of turn, she'd done so in privacy, it was just between the two of them and not in front of a plane full of jerks who enjoyed nothing more than seeing him getting their brand of come-uppance. So, he let Diane's insubordination slide, he was too tired anyway. The trip had been a bust, and so for now Curtis realized he had to hang onto the people who actually brought money into the company. Diane Mancini, she couldn't drive worth beans, that much was certain. She almost just rear-ended the yellow cab in front of them. But she was damn good her job.

Curtis Real Estate was a Manhattan-based boutique agency that dealt equally in both commercial and residential prop-erties; they managed sales and rentals for a couple high-rise towers in midtown, as well as for smaller apartment buildings throughout the city. Certainly not on the level of Corcoran or Douglas Elliman, Stan Curtis made his money from average New Yorkers looking to rent their first apartment or upgrade to something more family-oriented, or maybe lease a storefront for some start-up venture like a coffee shop or catering com-pany. There were lots of those small fish in this big aquarium called New York.

Still, despite the size of his operation, that didn't mean Curtis wasn't an ambitious businessman. His trip to San Francisco had him meeting with basically a West Coast version of himself, and the two of them were exploring the possibility of, if not merging companies completely, exploring options that would be mutually beneficial to them both. Lots of business folks these days needed to be bi-coastal; they liked having two apartments or wanted to look into opening a branch of their business in other cities. It had been a good idea, but not the right fit for Curtis. At least professionally. But the other details of his trip, he didn't wish to discuss. Some things were intended to be private, discreet.

"How was your trip, sir?"

Shit, small talk in traffic. Hadn't he just said he didn't want to talk about the trip?

"Guy was a jerk," he huffed, "I couldn't see myself in bed with a guy like that."

"Excuse me, sir?" Diane said, a startled look crossing her face as she looked in the rearview mirror.

"Get your mind out of the gutter, Ms. Mancini, that's just an expression, dear," Curtis said, even though he did turn a particular shade of red. Enough chatter. He depressed a button and watched as the partition separated him from his driver, effectively cutting off all communication. Silence at last. Only that wouldn't last long either, knowing what—*and who*—was waiting for him upon his return. Maybe there was something positive to come out of this traffic hold-up.

But the Jackie Robinson Parkway cleared soon enough, and eventually Diane made the turn onto Queens Boulevard. Once they finally reached Curtis's mock Tudor home in the exclusive enclave known as Forest Hills Gardens, his nerves still frazzled from the experience of the start-and-stop driving, he leaned in and instructed Diane to leave the car where it was parked in the turnaround.

"My advice, Diane? Take a cab home. You're a terrible driver," he said. "As it is, I think you almost clipped some poor loser a ways back. You saw him, right? Though maybe we could have scored two points, isn't that how the old joke goes? Guy was stupidly walking on the road's shoulder, I could have just opened the door and sent him flying. As it was, he could have gotten killed if you had hit him. Last thing I need is some homeless guy making life difficult for people like me." Me, not us.

"Indeed, sir, I'm not keen on driving in New York, too many crazy drivers," said Diane. "I was planning on taking the subway anyway."

Looking back askance at her, Curtis said, "The what?" with a horrified expression, as though he'd never heard of such a ridiculous thing.

Such was the clueless bubble a man like Stan Curtis lived in.

*   *   *

He was not off to a good start, what with nearly getting killed.

Ferro realized he was in unfamiliar territory and had to be careful by watching out for bad drivers. Wasn't New York notorious for them? God, of all the cities in the world, why had he picked this one, where it counted its residents as crime statistics more so than tax payers, and that was truly saying something. Where he was at this moment wasn't exactly among the safest of places, he came to surmise. On the road's shoulder about two miles from JFK, he could have sworn a fast-moving black Lincoln Town Car had come dangerously close to clipping him. Which is why he was suddenly so grateful that, during one particular stretch of slow-moving traffic, a truck honked its horn at him and the driver invited him inside the front cab.

"You trying to get yourself killed, man? Huh?"

"Just trying to get off this road," Ferro said.

"Yeah? Where you going?" asked a tough-looking man, peering through the open passenger window as best he could from his seat behind the wheel. He was probably fiftyish; his cheeks wore the thick stubble of neglect, and he was clothed in thick flannel despite the balmy weather. A thick wad of chewing tobacco stuck in the side of his cheek kept his language slightly garbled. Not exactly Ferro's brand of company this guy, but then again, he'd demonstrated better manners than had that buffoon Curtis during the five-hour flight. He took a chance.

"The city," Ferro replied.

"What part?"

Good question. "The part you're going, too, I guess."

"Fair enough, man, fair enough. Some people just don't like answering questions and as far as I'm concerned, the fewer questions I ask the fewer non-answers like that I'll get," the man said, with a booming laugh. Sounded like the voice of experience. This truck driver knew the rules of the road better than most. His genial nature Ferro could not have asked more of.

"Hop on in, man, this seat's empty," the man said. "Though the way the traffic is moving, you might get there faster on foot."

"I'll take my chances sitting in traffic," Ferro said, climbing into the cab and extending his hand. "Thanks."

"Not a problem. Even in a city as mean as this, there's people who still got to look out for each other. Name's Al."

"Fe . . . Claude."

"FeClaude, huh? I gotcha, man. Think I'll just concentrate on my driving," he said, and again laughed. "From non-answers to complicated names. My lucky night."

"Shall I get out?"

"Nah, man, settle down. You got a classy look to you, good threads. I'm sure you got a story, but that don't mean I need to hear it."

"I appreciate it."

On instinct, Ferro liked the affable Al. He seemed like a real person, no pretention, with a good sense of humor. It was hard to believe people could still act so altruistic toward their fellow man. Ferro himself had lived so long inside his gilded world, dealing with tyrants like Dunbar and idiots like that guy from the plane, he had little sense of how to interact with the "little" people. First experience with them, via Al, not so bad. They listened to a Rangers game on the radio as the truck slowly made its way to the Grand Central Expressway, and eventually, signs for the midtown tunnel appeared, as did Manhattan itself, its jutting spires and skyscrapers alight and glittering against the dark night.

"I'm headed to lower Manhattan eventually, got a couple of deliveries to make. You want me to drop you somewhere along the way? Midtown, Village. Say it, I break for it."

"Along the way somewhere is fine."

"Gee, that clears it up."

"Sorry, it's just…"

"New York ain't your town. I can tell. So, where you from?" His question was met with silence.

"See, there I go again, asking questions."

"I don't mean to be so mysterious, it's just…"

"Hey, FeClaude, no problem from this guy. Despite the fact you were hitchhiking from JFK and seemed a bit lost along the highway, you still look like you can handle yourself just fine. Look, we're almost to the city. We'll see what's a good corner for you and I'll just drop you off."

That corner turned out to be in the East Village, just east of Lafayette Street, on Bond Street. Ferro liked the name of the street. He'd done well with bonds over the course of his career, and so he took the street name as an omen and ran with it. Stock Street might have done even better, but that didn't appear to be an option.

"Thanks, uh, man," Ferro said, hopping down from the high cab as they stopped at a red light. "You have no idea how much I appreciate your help. You're a fine person, Al."

"No reason to get mushy on me. Hey man, it's not a problem. You take care. You know where you are?"

"I'll figure it out."

"Hope you figure it all out," Al said with a knowing nod.

Ferro took his meaning well.

The truck rumbled off at the change of the light, and Ferro found himself alone at last, albeit in a city of eight million people. The lay of the land on Manhattan island wasn't one of his specialties, and when he did visit for occasional business, he tended to keep to the Midtown grid, and usually by limo to boot. The easy layout was his kind of Manhattan. This funky, downtown locale was new to him, and he kept his eyes busy by keeping track of those fast-walking pedestrians that passed him by, the cabs that sped around him onto hard-to-find narrow side streets. Still, he liked the pulsing vibe of the place, even at this late hour there was plenty of action still happening. He passed by buildings in need of gentrification, and in his mind, he imagined the large real estate fortune just waiting to be had in this inevitably rediscovered neighborhood.

Ferro was so preoccupied with thoughts of increasing his already sizable fortune, he hadn't realized how far astray from the main avenue he'd wandered. The street names had given way to lettered ones. Avenue C was where he found himself, and guessing he needed to retrace his steps and find a noisier, more populated and better lit street, he turned, and that's when he saw trouble waiting for him about one hundred feet away. Three punks leaning against the side of a trash barrel, and they were all focused on the same thing: Ferro. Darting his eyes down to the sidewalk, Ferro considered his options. The last thing he wanted was any potential difficulty with these loitering hoods. He knew their kind, though, they traveled in packs and went in search of trouble, or in Ferro's case, lay in wait for him to stumble past them. His tight fist instinctively grabbed onto his overnight bag like it was glued to him.

Problem was, such a defensive move wouldn't be enough to deter them. It might even encourage them, smelling the fear coming off him. The punks—two black kids and a white kid, all of them teenagers with faces hidden behind hoodies and tattoos exposed on their arms—were no doubt experts at provoking trouble.

"Hey, man," the white kid said, "how about a cigarette."

Ferro patted the pockets of his blazer in a mock search. "Sorry, I don't smoke."

"Too bad. Guess you'll just have to buy us some smokes. Like with the money in your fat wallet."

"Sorry, I never carry my wallet."

The white kid again, apparently their leader, snorted. Gave both of his friends a look, which made both nod. Code between them. "Gee, you don't seem to have much on you, man. Seems, uh, weird, you know? What, you gonna try some sob story like you've already been cleaned out, some big thugs back on Ave B took your money and your watch and hey, maybe even your girl—or your boy, that it? You got a boy toy? You don't smoke, but you sure like fags."

The leader laughed at his pun; clearly he hadn't skipped that much school if he was able to come up with a pun like that, streetwise as it was. The others laughed, too, but Ferro detected a look on their faces like they hadn't shared in the humor. Still, Ferro managed to keep a straight face, not wanting to encourage any of them. In that instant, he tried to move past them, but found himself suddenly, expertly, encircled by the triumvirate. Like a pack of hyenas who had long ago perfected their strategy.

"Look, guys, I don't think any of us need this. Why spoil a nice night like this."

"Shut the fuck up, man. Like we give a shit about the night," said the second of the three. He was the gutsy one of them, the one Ferro sensed like to heighten the level of menace with intimidation. "Now, I think my friend asked, po-lite-ly, too, for your goddamn wallet. So, before my other friend here gets out his carving knife to make a wallet from your leather face, I think you should just fork it over. Now."

"Look, I said…"

Just then the middle punk pushed Ferro up against the side of the building and began to dig through his pockets—jacket, pants—and he wasn't exactly gentle in his search. The first punk parted Ferro's legs to keep him from making any fast, foolish moves. As for the third guy, he was now brandishing a shiny knife, its three-inch blade outstretched and gleaming in the moonlight. Ferro knew he was in his first real jam since embarking on this new journey, and as a result found himself in unfamiliar territory. Sure, he was a man of action, could handle any fight that came his way. But his defenses were down, causing him to play a rare passive role. Almost as though he really were Claude. Acting like a servant, waiting for instructions— as opposed to the man who handed down those orders, who kept tight control of matters.

You are Ferro Olivetti, an inner voice said.

And with that confidence coursing through him, Ferro grabbed the hand of the punk who was manhandling him, and with one tight squeeze he broke several bones in the kid's hand. A loud squeal of pain shook the dark street, and the sound shocked the other two from their dormant positions. Ferro's legs were suddenly free of constraint and that's when they lashed out too, Ferro's training in karate and judo taking over. The first thug was brought down faster than the flare of a match, and the third felt a kick to his ribs so unexpected it was like he was blinded. The knife went clattering to the ground.

And in response to this effective distraction, Ferro took off down the street, free from the thugs, grabbing his lone bag from the sidewalk.

But for how long would he be free of them?

Because behind him, he heard them in hot pursuit.

"Gonna slice you, mofo!" screamed one of the three.

Ferro darted down an alley, realizing at the last minute that it could be dead end. If so, he needed to find a good hiding spot, and fast. But it didn't look good, they wouldn't give up searching the dirty pathway. That's when Ferro decided that his escape was not to come from the end of the alley, and certainly not from the way from which he'd come. Nope, his escape was upwards, toward the sky.

A fire escape was in his sights. So, he'd need to climb up. Quickly.

The three thugs were closing in on him.

Sweat dripped from Ferro's brow as he began the ascent to what he hoped was safety. Because no longer were there guys just out for some trouble, for his wallet. They were out for blood. Ferro's blood.

That's when Ferro made what he considered a possibly fatal mistake.

His overnight bag slipped from his hand, and as he tried to grab at it, he almost lost his balance. Righting himself on the fire escape, he watched helplessly as the bag fell back down to the alley with a thud. Surely the wild boys heard that.

Great, now what?

Ferro was about to find out.

*　　*　　*

"Yeah, that's it, give it to me baby, yeah, go for it."

The reply, such as it was, suggested something animalistic, more a series of grunts and groans than actual words.

Ferro could only shake his head at his predicament.

Here's the situation: He'd gone from a high-tension scene in a gang-themed movie suddenly to some low-budget porno movie where both "actors" had seen better days. Ferro wondered which of them he'd rather be faced with, which was the lesser of two evils. Really, in New York just hours and he was already seeing the human race at its most desperate, most dangerous. This could hardly be what his father had wanted. But all that would have to wait, he still had to extricate himself from this conundrum. The image before him didn't help; in fact, it was anything but pleasant. Still, he watched with a mixture of fascination and disgust.

The woman had mounds of flesh forming around her middle, with huge, sagging breasts that somehow commanded his attention. The fact that she wore no clothing only revealed her gluttony that much more. As for her victim, uh, lover, the man was small and scrawny, his pale body barely visible beneath her generous flesh. Only when she pushed up did more of him emerge. Pain seemed to be streaked across his face, but that didn't stop her violent movements; anything but. As seconds clicked away into minutes, neither of the unlikely lovers seemed aware that their live show was being witnessed.

Hiding out on the fire escape four flights up, Ferro turned away, pressing himself against the side of the building as he did. He hoped that his stealth movements went undetected—by either the copulating, corpulent couple or the angry trio of thugs positioned in the alley beneath him. Between grunts he could hear his pursuers below.

Thug 1: "Where'd he go?"

Thug 2: "Fuck if I know."

Thug 3: "Loser anyway. Man, I thought we'd scored. He looked like some lost richy-rich, but when I patted him down there was nothing. Figured he'd have a wad of cash and all I felt was…well, shit, never mind, guy was packing. Know what I mean?"

"Faggot," one of them said.

"Hey, shut the fuck up."

"You two homos want to shut the fuck up. Could be the guy was telling the truth, someone else tapped his pocket before us. Why else would he be wandering around here like some homeless asshole."

"Yeah, well I still vote we track that mofo down, find out what he's doing on our turf. Make him pay."

"Or maybe his f-ing wallet's in his f-ing bag," said Thug 1.

At this point, Ferro was getting good at recognizing their voices.

"Yeah, 'cept that bag is still with him."

"Wanna rethink that one, homey?"

There was silence between them, then:

"Sweet."

"Fucking sweet."

"Yeah. Fool dropped it. Probably dropped a load, too, you know?"

They all laughed, their hyena-filled sound echoing down the alley.

Ferro thought: *Oh, shit.* In the alley were any number of discarded items, garbage and rats and other such filth you'd find in such a neglected place. So why then did they have to stumble upon his overnight bag? Because it was new and clean and therefore hard to miss, that's why. Ferro listened more, heard the zipper being undone, his belongings being rifled through.

"Shit, man, nothing but clothes. Fricking underwear."

A smashing of glass against the hard ground put an exclamation point to his words. A discarded beer bottle, bearing the brunt of their anger.

"Leave it, dude's gonna need a change of pants, the way we scared the crap out of him."

"Fuck. Let's go get some beer. We'll hit someone else later, this loser ain't worth the trouble."

And suddenly that was the end of the incident, with the three punks moving on to other targets, their wicked laughter dying off as they left the alley. Ferro wiped his moist brow, which had grown slick with sweat. What the hell was he so afraid of? He could have pounded all three of them to the ground, right? Then he remembered the knife and the scared look on the face of the kid holding it and realized he'd made the smart choice. Kid had been more afraid he would have to use it than Ferro was at the thought of it slicing his throat. Chickenshit thugs without the guts to carry through on their threats. Probably most of their victims caved in right away. Ferro was different, even when he wasn't Ferro.

He had to give credit to Claude, his new self. He liked the way he handled the situation.

"Could have been worse," he said aloud, albeit too soon.

"Ahhhh," came a scream directly behind him.

Just when he'd escaped the thugs, the lovers had discovered him. He turned fast, gazing quickly inside the apartment, where he saw that the woman was no longer in the throes of ecstasy and instead her eyes were now wide open, and what she saw apparently scared the bejesus out of her. A stranger… an intruder, right out on her fire escape, scoping out the lovers in the throes of pleasure. She clambered loudly off the bed, screaming in Spanish for the police. Ferro knew his cue. He hustled down the fire escape, and after retrieving his wayward bag, hurriedly stuffing its contents back inside, he started to flee the scene.

A slight problem cut off his exit route. As he darted to his left from the alley's mouth, he ran straight into the fender of a white and blue NYPD cruiser. Its engine was on, and its lights were flashing, and Ferro had to assume they'd been close enough to hear the woman's screams, which had pierced the otherwise quiet night. Both cops were waiting for him. Neither cop had to tell him to freeze.

Ferro knew the drill. He just put his hands in the air.

His bag dropped, once again, to the ground.

Explanations could come later.

For now, he did as instructed. The cops turned him around, patted him down, and then cuffed him.

Hell of a first night in New York.

CHAPTER EIGHT

HE WAS PLACED OUT OF SIGHT, but he could still hear what they were saying. The door had been left ajar, and this, Ferro surmised, had been done on purpose. Part of their game. Cops, they always had an agenda, even when they didn't know the full story. Hell, they'd barely asked to hear the first chapter.

Between the cops, it went like this, all staccato-like:

"What'd ya find on him?"

"Get this. Four packs of airline pretzels and a dozen condoms."

"Guess he's more horny than hungry."

"At least he practices safe burglary."

Partners like them, together too many years to count, they were the only ones in the squad room laughing at their lame jokes. Ferro wasn't laughing either. He continued to listen.

"He have any ID?"

"Patted him down. Nothing on him, and nothing in that fancy bag of his. Some designer label stuff, guy's got money, or he stole it from someone who's got money."

"He kind of looks unlikely for a thief, wouldn't you say?"

"In this economy, even the rich are down on their luck. Still, we don't know what we're really dealing with. Whether he's a thief—or just a Peeping Tom. Or at least, he's gotta be the guy, only one we saw coming out of the alley. We'll call the Big Lady down later, she can I.D. him in a line-up."

There was silence between the cops. Ferro arched his ear, trying to interpret the words not being spoken.

"What are you thinking?"

"I'm thinking there's something weird about this guy."

"Yeah, he was poking his face where he shouldn't be poking it. We call them perverts."

"No, not that."

"Look, this is New York, takes all kind of folks to fill our streets—it's what keeps the city moving and us busy. Place like this, the rich are no exception. We even had a governor who got taken down by a hooker. Money, even the appearance of it, don't mean shit."

From his seat in an interrogation room, Ferro shifted his position. The chair wasn't very comfortable—wooden, industrial, impersonal. He supposed that was the point. Let him stew while he got to listen to the by-the-script chatter between partners. But it also gave Ferro time to try and formulate some kind of plan. Or make up some story that would get him out of his ridiculous predicament. Honestly, just a few short hours ago he'd been enjoying first class service on board a huge aircraft while it shot across the country; now he was in jail. Papa, are you watching?

Okay, so things weren't that terrible. He hadn't been dumped in a cell, not yet. He'd only been here for an hour, and they hadn't booked him on anything yet. No fingerprints, no mug shot, but still cuffed. For nearly thirty minutes he'd heard only the steady buzz of the station, the ringing phone, the crackle of the dispatcher over the wire, the rumbling from other cops about working another long graveyard shift. Finally, though, the two cops who had brought him in were conferring with the desk sergeant, filling him in on the details, and that meant they were getting closer to moving this along. Ferro couldn't wait.

"Talk to him, see what his story is," the sergeant said.

"Gotcha," they both said.

Five more minutes passed. Then the door opened, and the two cops stepped into the room. They shut the door fully this time. Nothing to disturb them.

"I'm Officer Pierce, this is Officer Sanchez."

"A pleasure, I suppose I should say, though it isn't."

"See, Sanchez, this guy here has got manners even when it's not called for. I think this is a false alarm. A case of mistaken identity."

"I don't trust him," Sanchez replied.

Ferro smiled widely. "Okay, officers, I've seen your routine in many movies and on TV. One of you plays the good cop, the other the bad cop. Let's just save us all some time and trouble and get on with things. You ask questions, I'll provide honest answers. And then—hopefully—we can all go about our own business."

"Hmm, a real-take charge kind of a guy, aren't you? Okay, Mr. Whatever-Your-Name Is, wanna tell us what you were doing up on that fire escape outside Mrs. Gonzalez's place? Almost gave ol' Rosario a heart attack, looking in while she was having her fun with her downstairs neighbor. See, beat cops like us, we know the neighborhood, we know the people who live around here. And we like to look out for them."

"That's comforting to know, and how too little too late of you," Ferro said. "How I wish you'd been around when I needed your able assistance."

"Care to explain that, sir?"

"You asked what I was doing up on the fire escape? I was running from some thugs who tried to mug me, maybe worse considering the knife blade that almost made friends with my throat. I ran down the alley in an effort to escape, not realizing it was a dead end. They did, which means they gave chase. My only recourse was to climb up the fire escape to thwart them. My unfortunate discovery once I'd made the climb was pure happenstance."

"You hear this guy? Recourse? Happenstance?"

"Like he ate a dictionary for breakfast," said Sanchez.

"Okay, Mr. Smarty Mouth. How about you give us a name."

This time Ferro didn't hesitate. He was prepared. "Reneau. Claude Reneau."

"Where do you live?"

"California."

"Oh, California. That clears things up. You know the place?" Sanchez paused to exchange a short snicker with Pierce. "You got anything more specific, Mr. Reneau? California's kind of a big state."

"San Francisco."

"Better. What brings you to New York?"

"Looking for a job."

"Where? Cleaning fire escapes?"

Sanchez said that bon mot. He was the comedian of the two apparently; he laughed at his attempt at humor, the only one in the room doing so. His partner was done with the laughing, and Ferro had the growing sense that the guy named Pierce was just going through the motions here. He knew this case wasn't anything but a time waster. Must be a slow night out on the beat. Still, they hadn't released him yet, so obviously they were looking for something more.

"Gentleman. Officers. I would appreciate it if we could dispense with the sarcasm. This is clearly, as you suspected, a case of mistaken identity. Why aren't you out looking for those punks who tried to knife me?"

Just then Pierce looked at Sanchez and said, "Look at him, telling us how to do our job. Guess he hasn't watched as much TV as he claimed. Cops don't like to be told who to book, who to bust." He turned back to Ferro, but still addressed his partner. "Till we know more about this guy, book 'em. Figure out a charge, suspicion of disturbing the peace. carrying condoms without a license, for all I care."

Damn. He'd almost been free. Then he'd opened his big

mouth and out came Ferro-like arrogance, the corporate boss and raider, a trait too closely associated with him. It had won him many enemies over the years, but none ever held much power over him. The police, though, were a different matter. They were in charge by default. A man like Ferro Olivetti was nothing to them. Especially since Ferro Olivetti didn't presently exist.

*   *   *

"Excuse me, officer, aren't I allowed one phone call?"

Pierce was no longer part of the equation, and instead it was Sanchez who was walking Ferro down a long hallway past old metal file cabinets and photographs of fallen police officers. Then down a flight of stairs, where they came to a series of holding cells. Ferro's eyes balked at the thought of being held behind those iron bars. Him? Ferro Olivetti? Now considered a common criminal to be tossed inside with the likes of hardened criminals and drunks. He shuddered to think of the company he might soon be keeping. So that's when he devised this latest distraction. A delaying tactic.

"A what?"

"A phone call. You know, to my lawyer?"

"Man, you really do think this is the movies."

"I don't hear a 'no' in your reply."

"I'm not walking you all the way back to the squad room just so you can get lawyered up. Wait here," Sanchez said, taking out a bunch of loose change from his pocket. He produced two quarters and placed them in Ferro's open palm. "Use the pay phone over there. And make it fast, no fancy talk like you did in the interrogation room."

"Nothing funny, just my constitutional right."

Sanchez rolled his eyes. "I'll be listening."

"Even better," Ferro said.

The pay phone was old-fashioned, though in this modern age any pay phone would be an antique. Pretending to put the coins in, he instead pocketed them and dialed the operator, quietly asking to make a collect call. How often did anyone make those anymore? He was glad he didn't have to explain what he wanted to the operator. All she did was ask for the number.

A few clicks later, a short exchange between the operator and the party of the first part, and Ferro was connected.

"Lawrence, is that you?"

"Ferro, is that really you? My goodness, where are you? It's past midnight here. Where are you? Are you okay? A collect call? Honestly, not since my mother…"

"Lawrence, I don't have a lot of time."

"Sorry. Right. Something must be wrong."

"Forget that for now. What's going on with the Vodell deal? How did our latest stock purchase go?"

"I got the seventy-five million from Chase and Citibank, though they weren't happy to be stretched like that on such short notice. But we may need further capital to purchase more shares once Dunbar gets wind of our backend deal. Definitely if we want to gain more control, and at the same time keep Dunbar from snatching any additional shares that become available."

"There is no 'if.' But do whatever it takes. Sell treasuries if you have to, your mother, too, anything to raise the necessary capital for the deal. I know Ms. Wilde said she needed time to review our proposal, but we cannot sit and wait around on such a valuable company. Vodell cannot slip through our fingers, not now, that's for damn sure."

"Ferro, this is ridiculous. You're needed here at the office, and instead you're off on some wild goose chase. A chase where you need to rely on pay phones? I talked with Claude earlier; he came by the office, wanting to store your wallet in the safe in your office. Where are you that you don't need to prove who you are?"

"Lawrence, I explained all this before I left. It's something my father asked me to do, and the only thing that would stop me from completing the Vodell deal would be not living up to my promise. So, neither of us has any choice in the matter right now. Look, I'll be in touch later, when I can. For now, do as I say and just know that I'm fine. It's all fine, and it's going to work out even better than either of us expected."

"But Ferro…"

Ferro had hung up the phone, only to find Sanchez leaning against an ink-stained wall, inappropriate messages scrawled by inmates like graffiti poetry.

He had a look of disbelief on his face.

"You shitting me with that conversation?"

"I'm not sure I understand."

"Man, I don't know who you are or what your deal is, but the more I get to know you the more interested I become in the real story. Like I've got some secretive big-time tycoon here, Howard Hughes-like. I saw that 'Aviatar' film, and I know all rich people have a case of the crazies. I'm beginning to think you're borderline psycho, you know? First we find you hiding out on a fire escape claiming some punks wanted your wallet but you somehow evaded danger, then we take you into custody, and still there's no wallet, and there's no sign of punks either, then you use your big fancy words to try and talk your way out of a night in the cell, and now your big talk of money and stocks makes me wonder just what's really going on."

Ferro had to agree with the cop, longwinded as he may be. He wondered just what all this meant, too.

Regardless of all the intrigue surrounding Ferro at their precinct, it still didn't win him any favors from Sanchez. Because the next thing Ferro knew, he was led behind bars, the clang of the iron gate shutting behind him as deafening as any sound ever to fall upon his ears.

"Think about telling the truth, maybe you'll see the light of day," Sanchez said before departing.

Left to his own devices, Ferro turned around and noticed he wasn't alone. His cellmate, wearing an old wool coat that hadn't seen the inside of a Laundromat in years, gazed down with wild eyes from the top bunk. The bed consisted of a dingy mattress. It looked old, as did his cellmate, each of them suffering from some deathly gray pallor.

A crooked, toothless smile grinned at him. "Whatcha in for, handsome?"

Morning couldn't come soon enough.

Ferro ignored him and remained on his side of the cell, sitting on top of a toilet that didn't have a seat. It wasn't comfortable, but he was sure the bed was less so. He closed his eyes and shut out the world, praying for morning.

The night passed without incident, but sleep was evasive, as though it was the only thing that could slip through the iron bars and escape. A clock in the corner ticked away the minutes, like a form of torture, letting the inmates know how long it would be until morning. Finally, enough revolutions of the small hand had occurred, as Ferro observed the time as half past five in the morning. His stomach rumbled at the thought of breakfast. Even prison breakfast, watery coffee and all. Assuming he was entitled to food.

Suddenly footsteps echoed in the silence, and Ferro perked up at the fresh noise. Sitting up from the bunk he'd eventually moved to, he noticed it was Pierce, and he was sans partner.

"Okay, pretty boy, you're free to go."

"You talking to me?" said a sudden voice from the top bunk.

"Uh, no, sorry, Edgar. You'll have to stay a bit longer, maybe work on that beauty sleep."

"Fuckers, all of you," Edgar said, and then went quiet.

Ferro waited by the cell door as Pierce fit the key into the lock. "Care to tell me why I'm suddenly being let go?"

"You want, I can keep you longer?"

"Officer, I don't think that's called for. Given the shoddy treatment I received here, it's only fair and just—as in justice—that I know why you kept me and why you're releasing me."

"Let's just say your story checked out."

"What story?"

"About the punks. We caught up with them, roughing up some bar kids who didn't know last call meant just that. Your thugs tried to fleece these young yupster lawyers of their money, but they found a whole lot of trouble instead. We know the punks, usually just looking to cause trouble, not hurt anyone. They told us about you, laughing at how you crapped your pants."

"Not that I did, mind you," Ferro said.

"Just humoring them, deflates the situation."

"I don't know why you don't keep them in jail and keep us honest citizens far away from them."

"Honest citizen? Let's not get too high and mighty, okay? Because we both know your name is not Claude Reneau."

"How could you know something like that?"

"Your phone call from earlier? Let's just say it provided a few more clues about you than you might have wanted known. But I don't need more of a headache from you, so I don't want to get into it. Let's just say our goodbye, and you and I and the NYPD will never again have to see each other. Fair enough?"

Ferro contemplated the situation, and that's when the silence was interrupted once again by his grumbling stomach.

"Do I get breakfast?"

Pierce frowned, as though he'd reached his end. "You think this is some five star hotel? Come on, Mr. Reneau, get out of here before I book you for loitering."

Ferro had played the wrong hand once before with Pierce, and that had landed him behind bars for the night. He opted not to test the officer again.

With his bag back in his possession and his pocket rich with the fifty cents that Sanchez had given him, Ferro strode out of the police precinct and steadied himself for the early morning of New York City. The city was just garbage trucks noisily collecting the flotsam and jetsam of last night's indulgences, early morning dog walkers out for their daily constitutional, early-bird workers hoping to catch the worm along with that desired raise and promotion.

Ferro breathed the fresh air, gazed east at the rising sun.

Okay, a new day had dawned, and with it came an entirely new promise. such was the case every morning. He always knew the gift that was each morning, but for some reason Ferro found this one much richer, more important. What would his first move be? Finding food, he'd missed dinner, and the pretzels would only satisfy him for so long. And then, what next? A job? A life? A purpose?

Twenty-nine days to go.

"Okay, Papa, I'm here. Now what?"

As he strode up First Avenue, he clenched the fifty cents in his palm as though it was the last remaining money on Earth. Hey, he mused, fortunes were built on less. He'd gone from a storefront in Rome to the towering heights of corporate America. What was this but a chance to reboot? He merely needed to know the perfect place in which to invest his hard-won new savings. Somewhere deep inside him Ferro Olivetti still breathed, still thrived. Still survived.

*   *   *

For the first full day of his new life in his new city, Ferro knew he needed to earn some money, and money only came from working. So, he set about securing a job. But what was he suited to do? Mergers and acquisitions and startup dotcom's were not exactly advertising for street help, and that's where Ferro found himself at the moment, on the mean streets of Manhattan, where life in the guise of rushing pedestrians and bumper-to-bumper traffic jostled all around him. His current location? Broadway and Twenty-First Street.

The time was just after ten o'clock in the morning.

Having temporarily satiated his hunger with one of the bags of pretzels, Ferro nonetheless was attracted to the spicy aroma of pizza from a nearby pizzeria. As he crossed the street against the light, horns honking at him, he wondered if he had something with which he could barter. Or better yet, he could work for a slice, and maybe more. Because in the window of the tiny parlor was one red and black HELP WANTED signs. Pushing open the door, an Italian-looking man with a thick black mustache and arms of flour-dusted fur looked up at him.

"We're not open yet," he said, the hint of an accent to his voice.

Ferro noticed no fresh pies on the platters, the counter devoid of food. Of course, the lunch rush was a good hour away. He smelled them in the oven.

"The sign," Ferro said. "I'd like to apply for the job."

The man gave Ferro a passing glance. "We hired someone. We don't need anybody."

"Then why are you still advertising for help?"

"You think I got nothing better to do than put up and take down signs? Like I said, I don't need you."

Ferro thought he'd give it another try, and so he switched to Italian and said, "1 am good with customers, and they will like me."

"Fancy, fancy," the man responded. "Look, I don't need anyone who speaks Italiano. Espanol, eh? That would be good. For a delivery boy. You are not delivery boy material."

"Grazie," Ferro said, nodding. "Could I trouble you for a cup of water then?"

"Twenty-five cents for the cup."

The two quarters were still in his pocket. And they would remain there—he wasn't about to give up half his money for something so trivial as a paper cup. Ferro gave up, said, "Ciao," and then walked out of the pizza place, disheartened by his first attempt at securing a job. Was it his clothing, his demeanor, his accent? He supposed he was a tad overqualified for a pizza delivery boy, and, besides, bosses and owners usually took upstarts like him as a threat to their own security.

But hey, it was early in the day, and in a city this big there had to be some kind of job he could perform. He continued to walk, and as he did the numbered streets grew higher, and the traffic grew thicker as midtown gave way to uptown. Along the way he'd stopped into several stores—a deli run by Koreans, a wholesale perfumery, a women's shoe store, and always the result was the same: no job. Bemusement was the least of the reactions, outright hostility the worst. One attractive male employee—at a tiny dress shop that offered middle-budget women's dresses and tops—just gave Ferro a quick dressing down and said with mocking jealousy, "I don't think we'd have a place for you. I don't need any competition from the likes of you."

By the end of the day, Ferro was hungrier and thirstier (though he did find a water fountain inside one of the stores he stopped in and he drank generously from it), and as the sky was beginning to darken and the temperature turn cooler, he had to wonder where he would be spending the night. Actually, at the moment he didn't even know his exact location.

Looking up, he saw he was all the way on 145th and Broadway, a great distance from where he'd begun his day and if nothing else, he was getting his exercise. Still, it wasn't a neighborhood to his liking, and he caught several curious expressions from the mix of black, white, and Hispanic people who passed him by. Ferro stuck out, and the last time that had happened he'd been mugged and ended up spending the night in jail. A similar thing happening would at least give him a roof over his head, but he knew he could do better. He just had to be more resourceful.

A few raindrops began to fall from the sky, and Ferro knew he needed to seek shelter sooner rather later. That's when he noticed the subway station, a red circle and a #1 identifying which train line ran through here. He hustled down the "Downtown" side and found himself presented with a bank of hostile-looking turnstiles. With no Metrocard to gain entry—and no money to buy one—Ferro considered what he did have.

Inside the booth was a young large black man; he didn't look excited to be there. Ferro approached the booth.

"Yes?" asked the guy, a hint of suspicion in his voice.

"I wonder if you could help me out with something. I have misplaced my wallet, and I'm afraid I don't have the money for the fare. Perhaps we could work an exchange." Ferro paused, thinking about the change in his pocket and the various items in his bag. A change of clothes, some toiletries, the condoms (which looked like a ridiculous thing to have packed), and he realized he had nothing. But he tried anyway, and so he pulled out the package of condoms from his bag. "Your girlfriend, perhaps you're meeting her later tonight, you won't have time to go to the drugstore. I could help you."

"Fuck you man, you're offering me condoms for a subway ride? Man, this city, where do people like you get off, anyway? What the fuck you think this is?"

"That's a no?" Ferro asked.

The guy turned away from Ferro and started texting on his cell phone. Ferro turned away, too, and that's when he noticed an older woman standing behind him. Before he could even think, he said, "Would you be interested?"

The woman looked horrified. "I knew I should have taken the bus," she said.

Feeling absolutely humiliated, Ferro slunk away and walked back up the stairs, hearing laughter from both the clerk and the woman. This world of the everyday person, this just wasn't his arena, and so he didn't know how to deal with them. And they didn't know how to react to a man whose very appearance spoke "money." He wondered what might have happened if he had just jumped the turnstile. Would the clerk call the police or just let him go to be rid of him? At least the guy would have an amusing story to tell people. To attempt a free ride now, he'd have to go back downstairs, and Ferro was just inclined to forget the whole incident.

For a fleeting second, he wondered what poor people did, how did they survive each and every day in a city like this without a hint of promise? Even with the sun shining, did they always see the encircling clouds?

A few more days of life on the streets, and he might begin to find out the answer to that question—because no doubt he would have lost that privileged glow that currently surrounded him. The upside to that possibility was that perhaps he could fit in better. Trouble was, he didn't think he had a few days, much less the twenty-nine more required by his father's request.

It was going to be a long month.

Hell, for starters, it was going to be a long night.

By nine o'clock, after wandering, walking, thinking, returning to the safer confines of midtown, Ferro had come up with a plan that could score him food, drink, and no doubt a comfortable place to stay for the night, and quite frankly he couldn't stop grinning at the prospect. He'd spent a couple hours in Central Park giving thought to his predicament, and it was only when a pair of young lovers walked by him that he realized the easy solution to his problem. He'd been trying to get any type of menial work—at the pizza shop, deli, at the women's clothing store—but he was going about it all wrong. Even if he had to pretend to be Claude and not be the real Ferro, that didn't mean he couldn't use certain things to his advantage. For instance, there were his impeccable looks. Change his name, alter how he thought, sure, you could do all that and more. But cosmetically he was still Ferro Olivetti, and the one thing a man like he had always succeeded with was simple: women.

The setting now? Times Square. The night was pulsing with activity, the city's heartbeat in good health. Seemingly thousands of people were meeting at the crossroads of the world, and Ferro was lost among them. Though he wasn't exactly sure whom he could conceivably meet, the possibilities of places for such a transaction were certainly numerous. The rain that had threatened earlier had been just that, a threat, and now a lovely early spring night had settled over the city. Ferro felt alive for the first time since deplaning just twenty-four hours ago. He had a plan and was now moving in for the kill. Such a notion was what always got his blood bubbling, and so with all of that in mind, he settled on where to set it all in motion. A gleaming club at 47th Street and Broadway was just to his liking.

It was called Blue Fin, he noted, a street-level bar attached to one of the famed "W" hotels, and it had the right mix of crowd sitting and standing against the large plate glass windows that looked out on Father Duffy Square. Ferro checked his appearance in the glass doors, then, after smoothing down his thick black hair, he slapped on an irresistible grin and walked inside. He quickly used the bathroom to clean up before finding his way inside the bar. Guy had to look his best in a place like this.

Loud music met him first, then a flirty smile from some young woman with a pink drink in her hand. He didn't stop to say anything; the night was younger than her, and Ferro had just arrived, barely time to scope out the crowd. The mating dance never just happened immediately. Sometimes you had to get the band warmed up first. So, Ferro just allowed the woman to pass by him as he moved toward the bar, encouraged by the idea he had taken the right approach to his housing shortage.

The bar area was packed, and Ferro had to work a three-person deep crowd to secure himself a small spot to lean against. As he waited to catch the bartender's attention, his dark eyes scanned the length of the room. Couples and groups hung out at tables, and pretty young things mingled about, chatting, laughing, texting, the entire ritual of a Manhattan bar after the work day had play out. Ferro realized he was the only one without a drink, and finally he was given the opportunity to join them.

"I'm waiting for someone, so, can I just get a water?"

The bartender was fortunately too busy to complain. He just set a glass down in front of Ferro, the glass more ice than water. He actually didn't mind; it would enable him to nurse it for far longer. The guy was working hard, and Ferro felt bad, since not only couldn't he afford a drink, but he also couldn't leave a simple tip.

In front of him was a bowl of nuts and olives. Snacks for some, dinner for Ferro.

So, he gorged himself as surreptitiously as possible. He was hungry, though, from lack of food and from a bad night's sleep in a prison cell with a loon; add in all the walking he'd done, and it was amazing he could still stand. The nuts would help, all that protein giving off its natural energy. And the water cooled his parched throat. After a few minutes, Ferro started to relax. This just might work out.

As he finished the last of the olives and tossed the pit into the bowl, he saw that he was being casually observed. She was an attractive blonde who reminded him a bit of Cassandra, the woman he'd brought back home with him. For a moment he wondered what had become of her. Had he even said goodbye to her? Sort of, if putting her on a plane back home was a substitute for a passionate kiss. Cassandra was the past, though—part of Ferro's past—and this woman here represented the present.

"Hello," he said, his smile heightening the dimples at his cheeks.

"Hi yourself," the woman said.

Ferro extended a hand. "I am Claude."

"Laura," she said, giving him her own slim hand. He didn't shake it; rather he kissed the soft skin and then smiled at her. He knew the combination of his likeable smile and his Italian accent were lady killers, and he'd just brought out the dagger that would pierce her heart.

"I haven't seen you here before."

"That's because I've never been here before," he said. "How about that?"

"Let me guess, your wife threw you out."

Ferro waved his hand before her. "See, no ring. And no tan line on my finger."

"Ooh, an honest-to-goodness single man? Right before my very eyes? And good-looking, too. We're not in Vegas, but hello. jackpot."

Ferro nodded agreeably. "That's me. Honest to a fault. But no gambler."

"I adore your accent," she said, the key word sounding like two the way she pronounced it. "Are you visiting the States from Europe? Wait, let me guess…no, it's not French ooh, with that gorgeous hair, you've got to be nothing but one hundred percent Italian."

Ferro nodded, took a sip of his water. "You are very perceptive."

Just then Ferro felt her foot rubbing against his leg. She had removed her heel, leaving her standing like an ostrich. A very sexy ostrich. This made Ferro lean in further; his plan was working faster than he had imagined. His water glass was barely half empty. Of course, given how well things were going, he supposed he should perceive the glass as half full.

"So, you're here on business?"

"Sort of," Ferro said playfully.

"Sort of is sort of evasive. What happened to that honesty? Come on, what do you do?"

"A little of this," Ferro said, trying to maintain an air of mystery but not come off sounding like a player. What could he reveal about himself? Not much, He'd have to rely on charm. "Oh, and a little of that."

"Uh huh," Laura responded, not happy with the response. "Where are you staying? "

"Sometimes here. Sometimes there."

Laura's expression went from coquettish kitten to cool feline, and suddenly her foot no longer wanted anything to do with Ferro's leg. Apparently, no part of her wanted any part of Ferro. She downed the rest of her cosmo.

"Did I say something wrong?" Ferro asked.

"Only everything," she said. Then, as she grabbed her purse and began to walk away, she turned back to him and said, "I hope you have a nice stay. Wherever. Doing whatever. Or not doing whoever." And with that, she was gone, not even giving Ferro the dignity to answer his fleeting question of "Wait, what did I say?"

"I'll tell you," Ferro heard behind him.

He spun around to find himself staring at the direct contrast to the lovely woman who had just given him the cold shoulder. Probably in her thirties, she was chubby in build, with what he surmised a mother would call a "pretty face" but to Ferro was not exactly on a level with the type of woman he was accustomed to. In Ferro mode, he would have turned right back without even acknowledging her and begun to scope out the room for someone more to his liking, like Laura. In his guise as Claude, and given his situation, Ferro just gave the woman a curious look.

"You heard all that?" he asked.

"Every word."

"The music's pretty loud in here. You had to have been concentrating real hard."

"Hey, some people here treat the meet market like a game—yourself included, I might add. All that mysterious 'here and there' bullcrap? Please. A woman like me, the action here is more of a spectator sport. I have a drink, I watch the players, I comment on their play. All in all, a fun night. And you, my friend, in baseball-ese, you just struck out. And you made an error too, which is statistically impossible to do when you're batting."

"I'm not much of a sports fan."

"From where I'm sitting, the only thing you're a fan of is olives."

"Excuse me?"

The woman indicated the bowl of discarded pits.

Ferro shrugged, trying the innocent route. "Sometimes I don't even realize I'm doing it, and before you know it the whole bowl is gone."

"The nuts, too."

Another shrug.

"You don't strike me as the nervous type, Mr. Whatever-Wherever."

He smiled at her. "It's Claude."

"If you say so."

"No, really, I'm…" But he stopped, because he saw the grin on her face and realized she was kidding with him. Rather than having his leg rubbed, it was being pulled. How had she read him so well? He thought he'd tucked away his nerves the moment he'd entered the bar. Maybe his failed coup with Laura had rattled him more than he suspected, and he was wearing it better than he was his Ferragamo shoes.

"So, penny for your thoughts," the woman said.

Ferro put his hand out. "Pay up."

The woman blanched, and then with a laugh decided to play along. She opened her purse and after ruffling through the change compartment came up with a dime. She pressed it into his palm, her touch lingering more than was necessary.

"Inflation," she said with a smile that made her look like a blowfish. "What's your thought? And make it a good one, seeing that I just paid above market value for it."

"I was wondering if your eyes were really that green, or if you were wearing contacts."

The woman laughed loud enough to catch the attention of several nearby drinkers. She leaned in, said, "Okay, again, in baseball-ese, you just fouled a ball into the stands."

"I'm afraid I don't understand these analogies."

"Okay, slugger, let's cut to the chase. What are you looking for?"

Why not try the truth? It just might work.

"A place to stay tonight," he said.

"Ah, now we're getting somewhere productive. That's probably the first honest thing you've said since you walked into this joint. Imagine had you been so upfront with your little friend Laura, you might be sharing the sheets with her. Instead, you're talking with me. And might I add, we've already progressed to talk about where to spend the night and you haven't even offered to buy me a drink. Some women might question your manners. Or your wallet."

"A dime doesn't go very far in a place like this," Ferro confessed.

"Ooh, more honesty. I'm liking you more and more, Claude," she said, extending her hand in a gesture meant to seal some kind of hidden bond between them. "By the way, the name's Vita."

"Vita?"

"Yeah, Vita Banger."

"Bang her?" Ferro asked, a smile lighting up his face.

Again, she laughed, this time at her own expense, her boisterous personality somehow charming Ferro. "Funny and honest, huh. Come on, Claude, let's get you a drink before you implode. And don't worry, it's on me. I think you need one more than I do, and I know I definitely do." Then, sounding like some big mouth at a ball park, she screamed out, "Hey, barkeep, couple of beers here. You got Peroni?"

Ferro just accepted the drink and the unexpected company, and before too long he accepted her offer of a place to stay. Only one topic remained on the table, neither of them daring to bring it up: what Ferro might have to do to secure such easily obtained lodgings.

He supposed he was about to find out.

CHAPTER NINE

THE IRONICALLY NAMED VITA BANGER lived in Queens, and she confessed it was a long subway ride away, longer still given the late hour and the lack of frequent service on the N line. Thankfully they hadn't waited on the platform, and instead they had hailed a cab. As they approached her building, she gave her guest a wary glance and said, "Let me guess, I'm paying for this, too?"

"I'll pay you back," he said.

"No sweat, sweetie. I think you're already worth the investment."

Over the course of a couple of drinks (and a plate of fish tacos), Vita's smile had gone from flirty to lascivious, and Ferro knew exactly what she was expecting. He wondered if there was any way for her to not expect what she was expecting. Though he had to laugh at the irony, he'd been trying to use the stash of condoms to barter for things all day, and finally he had a chance to get some use out of them. Then he shuddered at the thought. No offense to Vita, she was kind and giving, he just wasn't sure he could reciprocate. At least, not in that way.

"Cold?" Vita asked, as they started up the stairs to her building.

"Oh, uh, yes, it's definitely gotten colder tonight."

"A heavier coat would do you wonders," she said. "A warm body even more so. And look at that, here we are, home."

Ferro found that words escaped him, so he just followed her inside the brick five-story building and down the hallway to her first-floor apartment. Pulling out her keys, she unlocked three separate locks and then waved him inside, putting her hand to her lips for him to be quiet. She hadn't turned on any lights. Which was fine, nothing on him was turned on either.

As she closed the door behind him, Ferro let his eyes adjust to the swarming darkness. When he had regained his night vision, he detected a lone figure on a nearby sofa, long dark hair splayed out against soft pillows, the body hidden beneath a rumpled pile of blankets. The gentle sounds of sleep came from the woman.

"You didn't say you had a roommate," Ferro said.

"You didn't ask."

"Perhaps I should go."

"Go where? Back to the bar, try to find that dippy blonde from earlier? Trust me, she found her prey and left long ago. I watched as the guy paid. I watched as that made her happy. So even if she was still waiting for you, you couldn't exactly pay for her, uh, services."

"She was a hooker?"

"She wasn't a nun," Vita offered. "Now, enough talk, we don't want to wake my friend."

"So, she's not your roommate?"

"Sssh, ssshh," Vita stated, "She's just a friend in need for a couple of nights."

"You're full of generosity tonight, aren't you?"

Vita grinned, and then grabbed hold of Ferro's hand and pulled him into the bedroom. She closed the door. Still, she didn't turn on the lights. There was a shadow against the far wall, where the yellow glow of a streetlight eased through the curtains. It was enough to see by, and what he saw he didn't really like.

"Make yourself comfortable," Vita said.

Ferro excused himself and went to use the bathroom. Staring at himself in the mirror, he didn't even recognize the face that looked back at him. Just where was he, and what was he doing? Or about to be doing? He thought back to a few weeks ago in Rome, sitting by his father's bedside and listening as the old man made his strange request. Get in touch with the real person that existed deep inside him. Surely this misguided trip to a strange woman's apartment wasn't what Papa had intended. Ferro's existence was hapless, going from moment to moment without knowing how or why. Was the life he had been living so bad? What harm had he done? To himself, to others? Seeking fortune and having his every desire fulfilled? He failed to see what point there was to all of this.

Then he thought about Cass, how he had so cavalierly discarded her.

He thought of Anna Maria, back in Rome, with the little girl so dependent upon her.

The two images could not have less in common, except for one thing.

His own selfishness.

And look, here was his reward. A woman named Vita Banger, a woman with whom he wanted nothing to do with. Well, sexually.

His thoughts were interrupted by the sound of Vita's voice coming through the closed door. "You all right in there?"

Ferro replied yes, then to busy himself managed to pee out the remnants of that last beer he'd drank. After flushing the toilet and splashing his face with cool water, he reluctantly returned to the small bedroom. The lamps were still off but a soft, flickering glow illuminated the room, casting shadows on the walls. She'd lit a candle, its piney scent enveloping the room. Vita herself lay across the bed, her body, her arms and legs, spread out seductively, waiting for her reward for a night on which she'd done the picking up, and all the buying. His turn to pay up.

Ferro blinked away the image of the future and proceeded to yawn. A defensive act; lame, he knew, but he was out of other options. "Those beers, plus being awake at such an early hour this morning, I think they are conspiring against me. I just need to go to bed."

"Exactly the point," she said.

"Uh, sleep," Ferro added.

"I don't think so."

With a strong, aggressive move, Vita grabbed Ferro by the belt and drew him to the bed. She pushed him down against the soft mattress and climbed atop him, her lips finding his, her hands busily finding everything else on his body. Unbuttoning his shirt, she drew nails against his chest hair as they continued their desired downward journey. Her body rubbed against his, and she let out moans of pleasure, even though she was the only one of the two of them who seemed to be partaking of the current goings-on. She finally took note when her hand slipped beneath his pants and found nothing much happening.

"Shit," she said.

"I'm sorry, Rita."

"Vee. Vee," she said. "It's Vita. It's not hard to remember," she said irritably. "Not hard. As in, just like you."

"Look, Vita, this is really embarrassing. I can't…"

"You can't what? Get it up?

Please, don't be upset.

You have no idea how much I appreciate your offer of friendship, and one day you'll realize this is the right thing not to do."

"How about fewer words, more action. And I've got the perfect antidote to your problem." Vita pushed him aside and got up from the bed, where she opened a drawer beside her bed. Withdrawing a small brown prescription bottle, she waved it in the air. "Nothing the big 'V' won't cure. And I don't mean V as in Vita. The other Big V." She laughed again as she took a pill out of the bottle and handed it to Ferro.

"Actually, no, that's not it. I'm sorry, Vita. It's not so easily, uh, fixed."

"Oh, Christ. What are you, gay?"

Okay, so there was a perfect opening. "You didn't know?

"Funny how you go from straight to gay faster than you go from Laura the whore to Vita the saint," she said. But then she just gave up and threw a pillow at him, hard. She pointed to the floor, where a thin carpet was waiting to embrace him. "Welcome to your bed, hope it gives you back cramps. Jerk."

"I'm sorry," he said, his words falling on deaf ears.

"Am I really that unattractive?" he heard,

"Vita, you are a special woman. And a special woman should not offer herself to a man just because he's available."

"Well, you've gotten better with your lines since that slut, Laura."

And that was the end of the seduction. The candlelight doused as quickly as their romantic encounter, Vita retreated to beneath her thick covers and Ferro crawled to the floor with a thin blanket that barely covered him. For now, all was quiet. Except for Ferro's mind, which was racing with thoughts of how better this scenario could have played out. Sure, he was relieved that Vita hadn't pushed any harder for sex, but he was also feeling a slight case of remorse. She'd been nothing but kind to him, and what had he done in return? Taken advantage of her—and not in the way she had wanted.

Ferro eyed the clock. Two-fifteen.

It had been a long day. Tomorrow was another day, again filled with great uncertainty. That could all wait. He closed his eyes and wished for sleep to wash over him.

Vita began snoring loud enough to wake the dead.

"Christ," he said in the darkness.

*　　*　　*

At four o'clock in the morning, Ferro gave up on getting anything resembling sleep, as Vita had added an annoying wheeze to her sleep repertoire. Looking at her sleeping figure, he decided the better part of valor would be to just leave. He was accomplishing nothing, and to wake Vita in an attempt to stop the noise wasn't fair to her. She was who she was, just as Ferro…Claude, was who he was. Why wait till first light and relieve the awkwardness? Before he decided fully, he sought to find a snack and something cold to drink.

Opening the door to the bedroom, he skulked out into the living room, nearly forgetting that Vita had more than just him for company. With the aid of the dying moonlight streaming through the window, he could see the woman more clearly than before. Even beneath the blanket he could see the woman's shapely self, a sleek leg sticking out from the warmth of the covering. It looked supple, and he imagined the skin was gentle to the touch. As she rolled over, letting out a soft moan, Ferro felt a noticeable stirring in his loins. It was a feeling that had rested quietly in Vita's bedroom, only to be awakened by this sleeping beauty.

Now why couldn't this creature have been the one to meet at the bar?

He was tempted to move in closer to further gaze on her radiant beauty, but he knew his looming presence might startle her. So, he went against his natural instinct and slipped past her, entering the kitchen, where, without the aid of the light, he felt around for the door to the refrigerator. Inside it he was met with all sorts of mouth-watering temptations—leftover Chinese cartons, half a bottle of wine, some blocks of cheeses. He could make himself a nice feast here, sit down at the small table in the corner and enjoy these simple pleasures while the two ladies slept the night away.

As he grabbed for the wine, the bottle scraped against the shelf.

A noise stirred from the living room.

Damn, his plan was interrupted before it could begin.

"Vita, is that you?"

Quietly closing the refrigerator door to the shut out the escaping light, Ferro stood silently, hoping the woman would just think she'd imagined the noise and fall back asleep. Perhaps she wasn't even aware she was awake or speaking aloud. He waited another minute, heard no further sound, and decided this was foolish, skulking around Vita's apartment like a thief. He opted to return to Vita's bedroom, wait out these lost hours of the night, and begin anew in the morning. Vita would no doubt feed him, let him shower, and best of all, introduce him to her alluring friend who slept the sleep of the angels. Ferro was halfway between kitchen and bedroom, which placed him in the middle of the living room and subsequently exposed for anyone to see.

That's when he heard, "Who the hell are you?"

Dressed only in his boxer shorts, his olive-toned skin prickled at both the cold air and the sudden voice coming from the sofa. As nonthreatening as possible, he turned to face the woman, to let her know it was all right, go to sleep, he was a friend of Vita's. That would have been the rational thing to do.

Rational thinking is never at its strong point in the predawn hours, and with a man of Ferro's appetites, he could hardly be blamed for what he did next. Right? Except he was forgetting one valuable lesson. He wasn't supposed to think or act like Ferro. He suggestively said to the woman, "A beauty such as yourself, no wonder sleep defies you. The world is just waiting for your sunshine."

From the sofa, the woman popped wide awake, the sheet covering her near-naked self slipping away to expose her slim torso for all to see. Or at the very least, for Ferro to see. He'd been correct, she was lovelier than anticipated, and nothing would have pleased him more than to be with her. He made a move toward the sofa, offering up gentle ssshing in an attempt to soothe her fears.

"What are you doing here? Who are you?"

"It is okay, miss, my name is Claude Reneau. I came home with Vita, she offered me a place to crash. I'm sorry if I disturbed you, but I couldn't sleep over all that snoring going on in there," he said, indicating Vita's bedroom. "When I saw you sleeping here, I don't know, you looked so lovely, and I wished to speak with you."

"Are you crazy? You wake me up in the middle of the night to talk to me? You don't know me, and more importantly, I don't know you."

"I didn't purposely wake you. I went to the kitchen for something to eat and drink. I suppose it was the light from the refrigerator that streaked across your her, eyes, opened them up to me." Why was he speaking with such romantic gestures? Because the setting was perfect, even if the response he was getting from the woman of his pursuits wasn't exactly garnering the desired effect.

"Vita? Vita, honey? Vita, where are you," the woman called out. "What have you done with her?"

"Done with her? Nothing. Trust me, absolutely nothing happened between us."

Just then the door to the bedroom opened and there stood the formidable presence of Vita Banger, all five foot three of her, but still somehow imposing in the door frame. Her thick arms were positioned on her round hips, an expression of displeasure etched upon her face. *Don't wake the sleeping giant*, Ferro thought.

"What the hell's going on out here?"

"I just wanted some water."

"He wanted something more than water, that's for sure," the woman said to her friend, now covered by a mass of blankets.

"No, no, she is mistaken. I merely wanted…"

Ferro looked down at himself, his body naked except for his boxers, and to the women who knew where to look, it was obvious who was mistaken.

Vita stepped forward. "Listen, Claude, I trusted you. I welcomed you into my home, and despite my generosity you rejected me flat out. Fine, I can live with that. But to then try and put the moves on my friend? A friend who didn't even know you were here and who came to me for help? I think you've overstayed your welcome. Get your stuff and get on out of here."

"No, but Vita, I didn't mean…"

"Fine. I'll get your stuff. Diane, take the bedroom while I deal with this creep."

"I am not a creep, that's unfair," Ferro said, his protests falling on deaf ears. "Please, give me a chance to explain."

Diane did as instructed, slamming the door behind her. But not before she looked at Ferro and said, "There's a phone in Vita's room. 911 is an easy call. Don't tempt me."

"You have nothing to fear."

The two of them now left alone, Ferro saw how angry Vita was. Despite Ferro's six-foot self, she came at him like a Mack truck. He started to back away from her, his feet taking him toward the apartment entrance. Vita beat him to it, did him the favor of opening the door, and with a push that no one could call playful, Ferro suddenly found himself in the hallway, the door to the apartment slamming in his face.

"But…wait."

His words hit the closed door and fell into the air, where they disappeared without effect.

Standing in the hallway with nothing on but his boxers, Ferro couldn't believe this was happening to him. What the hell was the world coming to? What was wrong with everyone in this city? Why had he suddenly lost his ability to reason with people, sway them to see reason and logic and see things his way. What was wrong with handing a woman a compliment?

Waiting a minute, hoping Vita had calmed down some, he finally had the nerve to knock on the door.

He breathed easily when the door opened, and then had to take a deep intake of breath when his body was hit full force with his clothes, the clasp of his belt leaving a sharp mark against his left side. His "ow" was lost in the sound of the door slamming shut again. This time he heard the turn of a lock, then a second. Finally, a third turn of the knob. That one sounded final, definitive.

Two mornings in New York, and twice he'd been tossed out of his lodgings.

And neither place had served him breakfast.

He really needed to get some money and find a hotel. Damn but he missed room service.

*   *   *

On the subway ride home, she replayed the strange scene from the night before, both the events with the mysterious (but undeniably handsome) man, and the explanation offered up by her friend that she'd picked up the guy because of his sad sack story (and undeniable good looks). As the R train rattled its way deeper into the borough of Queens and brought her closer to her parents' house and whatever nagging questions they might have for her now—where have you been, who have you been with for the last two nights, for starters—she couldn't deny a hint of excitement about what had happened the last few hours. For Diane Mancini, it was certainly better than driving Mr. Curtis around town.

The Grand Avenue station gave way to Stillwell; she was still several stops before her regular destination. To pass the time, she mused over the man who'd stood over her while she'd slept. Claude, he had said, some foreign-sounding last name, and Vita had confirmed both, though she'd also revealed, "I don't think that's his real name." Then they had both commented on how gorgeously attractive he was

"Did you get a look at that body?"

"Hard to miss, strutting around in his boxers."

"Like he's from Mount Olympus."

"Trust me, I tried to go for a ride on his chariot," Vita had said, and then both women had broken out into peals of laughter, safe now since the object of their desire had long since cleared out of the apartment. Sure, it was easy to laugh about the volatile situation now; but at four in the morning with a strange man walking around practically naked and peering—leering—at you the way he had, well, it was no wonder Diane had panicked. Bottom line, she didn't trust men, and she had the experience to back up such suspicion.

"Honestly, Vita, what were you thinking? How could you bring a total stranger home?"

"Hey, girl, it's not like that's my first time."

"Yeah, but all those other occasions, I wasn't sleeping on your couch."

"All those other times? What, you make me sound like a slut."

"Oh, Vita, I would never think that about you."

Vita had feigned hurt feelings but ultimately, she gave way to more bouts of laughter. "Just kidding. Hell, a girl like me, I'd take that reputation over the one I have—or don't have, as the case may be. But hey, Claude and I only had a couple of beers—which I bought, mind you—so it wasn't like I was drunk to the point of I didn't know what I was doing. Just…you saw, he was hot and he was talking to me. I'm sorry mostly, though, for not considering your feelings. I forgot you had told me you were staying a second night—next time send a reminder text, a DM, that might have helped. But no harm, no foul. I mean…seeing him hovering over you while you slept, that must have been especially scary for you."

Diane had waved the concern away, even though both knew the truth unspoken behind those words. She'd been scared witless. In the end, Diane steered the conversation away from weighty matters she didn't wish to revisit and offered up comforting words instead, with, "Vita, you'll meet the most perfect guy someday. Just not in a bar, okay?"

"You, too."

"Ha."

"Seriously."

"I'm not interested in meeting anyone," she said flatly. "Ever again."

That conversation had taken place over freshly brewed coffee, and whether it was the chatter or the caffeine, both women remained awake long into the dew-soaked morning, each of them filled with her own version of regret. Together they watched the sun rise in the eastern sky and give way to a beautiful day dawning on the blue horizon. At last, Vita yawned and said she needed to catch some more winks, since work called in a few hours.

"How 'bout you, work later?"

"Believe it or not, Mr. Curtis gave me the day off—first one in two months."

"Wow, he's feeling uncharacteristically generous?"

"Beats me. All I know is I picked him up at the airport—de facto limo driver, such as I am—and I guess he was grateful that someone seemed concerned enough about him to fetch him. The next day he calls me into his office, hands me a wad of cash to reimburse me for the cab ride from his home to mine—even though I took the subway—and then suggested I take a day off to enjoy myself. If I didn't know better, I'd think Mr. Curtis's trip to San Francisco was more than just business. There was a hint of a smile on his face, and that never happens. Man is as surly as they come. But, hey, I'm not one to gossip, I just look at the day off as a gift and simply smiled."

After that Vita had gone back to bed, and her friend had packed up her stuff and headed toward the subway.

Now, thirty minutes later, Diane broke from her reverie as the train approached her stop. She couldn't wait to get home, shower, and then relax for the remainder of the day. She just hoped her parents didn't bother her too much. It wasn't easy being a grown woman with a respectable job and decent pay and still be living at home. But for the woman whose name happened to be Diane Mancini, ace real estate agent and unfortunate widow, the only things that kept her going were her job and her family. Where would she be without them? A lost soul, searching for everything, finding nothing.

Fortunately, she was spared from answering such a haunting question as the train came to a screeching halt and the conductor announced, "Elmhurst Avenue."

Rego Park was a quiet neighborhood in Queens comprised of single and double home dwellings, as well as brick-laden apartment buildings. A mix of middle-class Americans and races of all types, it was a melting pot of mom-and-pop shops and privately-owned ethnic restaurants, as though the chain stores had yet to discover the small village's potential. These streets were all Diane had known when she was growing up, and only recently had she come back to their comforting sights. In all those years gone by it seemed nothing had changed; her parents still ordered from the same take-out places, shopped at the same five-and-dimes they had when Diane had been a child, probably still had the same furniture, covered as it was with plastic. Like they were lost in time, both oblivious to the dangers that existed in the otherwise real world of Manhattan.

As safe as she felt in their home, the streets held their own share of suspicion. Dangers lurked everywhere these days, as she reminded herself daily, and that's why when she walked topside from the subway station to the ever-busy Queens Boulevard, she kept her wits about her. True, it was a weekday, and the sidewalks were busy with people headed down into the subway toward the city and their jobs, and elderly ladies with their pushcarts went about their early morning shopping, Diane still felt a bit rattled. And she wasn't sure why. The fear of the incident with the man named Claude lingered; perhaps, too, it was the caffeine she'd consumed so early that was making her jittery.

Or maybe it was something different.

Diane turned off Queens Boulevard onto a side street, and even though she was just three blocks from her parents' quaint little home, her eyes darted about nervously. She was attuned to recognizing a couple of the homeless guys who tended to hang around the neighborhood a lot, and though they had never done anything to truly frighten her, their very presence worked her nerves. *My God*, she thoughts, *can't I even walk down my own street without thinking the worst is going to happen?*

An unfamiliar man walking across the street caught her attention. He was dressed in tattered clothes, and his skin looked as though water, much less a bath or shower, was a foreign notion to him. As he picked through the trash for discarded beer and soda cans, he suddenly turned and noticed that he was being watched.

"Whaddaya want?" he screamed at Diane.

Fear rose up in her throat to the point where she tasted the coffee all over again. She hustled down the street faster, turning back occasionally to see if she was being followed. In her mind she knew the homeless guy was lurking nearby, ready to strike at her. Truthfully, deep down she suspected he'd forgotten all about her and was busy seeking out his breakfast money by redeeming cans for cash. It was amazing to her what some people would do to survive. And then she felt bad, not about the homeless man but about the handsome Claude, too, who according to Vita was having his own string of bad luck. A looker like him, reeking of money; the fact that he needed a place to crash for the night was odd. Dining on olives and nuts—she had to wonder what the real story was.

Not that she'd ever find out. The man was gone from her life.

"Just put it out of your mind, girl," Diane said.

She would have to, anyway, wouldn't she? She was home, and her mother was standing on the stoop, giving a throw rug a good thrashing. *Better it than me*, Diane thought, as she watched the dust swirl in the air. She sneezed.

"Honey, are you all right?" her mother asked with concern

as over the top as her Queens accent. "You know, a mother can tell right off when something is wrong."

Sophia Mancini, for her sixty-plus years, could only have been one thing in her life: a doting, overly concerned mother and wife, a woman who lived to keep a clean house and prepare meals that would please (and plump) her tiny but adored family. She might as well have been sent from the files of some Hollywood version of central casting, her tongue as tart as her apple pie, and her love as expansive as the Queensboro Bridge.

As Diane walked up the steps and kissed her mother's cheek, a look of concern crossed the older woman's face.

"Hello, Mother."

"That's all I get? A peck and a hello? Diane, please won't you talk to me?"

"Oh Mother, it's nothing…really."

"Hmm. Your pauses, I can hear them better than your words. Diane, I can tell when nothing means something, and when something means everything. That's what makes me the mother. You were supposed to stay overnight at your friend, Vita's—a second night, I might add, not that I'm counting—but I am—and here you are home in time to hear the rooster crow. Did Vita toss you out?"

"No, Mother."

"What, you couldn't sleep?"

"Yes, Mother, the rooster woke me."

"There are no roosters in Queens, dear."

"Ma, sarcasm, remember that?"

"Hmmph. It's just an expression. And might I add a much cheerier one than the one you're wearing."

"Vita had to get up early to go to work, and she makes a lot of noise when she's getting ready. It was easier to just pack up and come back here."

"Here, you say it like it's a prison," Sophia Mancini said. "This place you refer to as here—it's what your father and I call home."

"I'm sorry, I just didn't sleep well."

Diane then leaned in and gave her mother a tight embrace, felt it returned in earnest. When trouble reared its meddlesome head, Diane always knew where to turn and she was grateful for the support afforded by her aging parents. Not everyone had such loving and understanding people in their lives, much less coming from those who raised them. Yet her mother and father could be frustrating, too, because as supportive as they were, their support did not come without cloying strings attached. They expected answers and explanations, her mother more so than her father. They liked to play this game of good mom, bad dad. Or vice versa.

"Leave the poor girl alone," her father could often be heard saying.

"What, I can't be concerned about my only child?"

"You smother her any more, you won't have any child."

"Blah," her mother would reply, dismissing his comments as coming from a do-nothing lay-about like him.

That's how it usually went, scripted to the letter. But not this morning. Sophia Mancini merely held her daughter's embrace for a long time, and when they parted, she wiped away a tear that had suddenly formed on her daughter's lovely face. If only Diane would let herself go, truly reveal her innermost concerns, her basest fears, those tears might wipe away remnants of a past life she no longer wished to remember. It was healthy, cleansing.

"It's not getting any easier, is it?"

"Mother, not here, on the stoop. And not now, so early in the morning. I think I need to just catch some more sleep and enjoy this day off."

"What did I say? I just want to see my baby happy again. You were such a cheerful girl, Diane, always smiling, dressing in your pretty clothes and pretending you lived a fairy-tale kind of life. It's time for us to rediscover that little girl. Your smile. And you know just how to go about that?"

"Oh, no. Mother, like I said, it's too early."

"Nothing is ever too early. It's just an excuse people use

to avoid things." Her mother paused. "You know he called again the other night, just after you left. He's such a sweet boy. Very caring."

"Mom," she said, hoping the intimate term would get across how she was feeling. "Really, not now."

"I'm just saying. He's a successful accountant, honey," she said. "Sure, he needs to shed some pounds—who doesn't? You could at least have him over for dinner."

"Great, Mom, that's the way to get him to lose weight, serve him several portions of your secret recipe lasagna. Look, I told you, I'm not interested, and it has nothing at all to do with his weight, his height, or his appearance. I'm just not ready."

"It's time you start going out," Sophia said, shaking her head.

"Actually, Mother, it's time I went in."

"What?"

Diane ignored her mother's false protestations and did as she'd said she would, went inside the two-family house, closing the front door behind her with more effect than she intended, as least, consciously. Thankfully her mother dropped the topic and resumed her battering of the dusty rug; the battering of her daughter could wait for another time.

Diane retreated to her childhood bedroom, which now served as a sanctuary of sorts for her. She lay down on the bed with her stuffed teddy bear—which had seen better days— and she settled back down to regain those lost hours of sleep. It wasn't easy given all on her mind, but finally those images faded away. The man named Claude, the strange homeless man from the street, and even her own mother. Sleep settled over her. It was safe, this sleep mode. That's when she didn't have to think about now, tomorrow, the future. It was only when she woke, that's when she had to start thinking about a new life, or at the very least, a new attitude.

She couldn't keep living with the fear.

She couldn't keep living alone.

Because she knew she wasn't really living. She was hiding.

CHAPTER TEN

THE LAW OF AVERAGES SAID something had to give. The pendulum of life had to swing back in his favor at some point, didn't it? Ferro had to hope so, especially after another fruitless day of job hunting and another day where his stomach grumbled from neglect. He still had the same sixty cents (which included Vita's dime for his thoughts), but he was now out of the pretzels from the airplane. Dry and salty, they, along with water from a fountain in Central Park, had temporarily provided some sustenance.

Frustration had been his constant companion during the day, and more times than he could count on his hands (and toes) he had considered placing a call to Lawrence back at the Olivetti offices, and even once (okay, twice) to his mother all the way in Italy. He would have requested from Lawrence that he send the private jet immediately, to return him to his regular life of making deals. Carving up failed businesses and selling off the best parts for high profits would fill his gullet. But it was thinking about the conversation with his mother that stopped all thought of placing those phone calls. Him having to again question his father's motivation for sending him on this quest, hearing the disappointment in her voice from thousands of miles away that her strong and self-sufficient son was incapable of completing his father's final request, it was too much to bear. No, he could more easily live with starvation and life on the streets for these twenty-seven more days than listen to his mother's heavy sigh on the other end when she would invariably say, "You must do what you feel is right, Ferro."

Guilt in the guise of complacency.

It actually served as a strong motivator for Ferro.

He was walking through the winding paths of Central Park on this, his third day. More than a shower, what he most desired was a luxuriant shave in the hands of a proper barber, since his beard was growing heavy and thick, the five o'clock shadow edging closer to midnight with each passing minute. He didn't want to think about his appearance—at least, not at how other people perceived him. A man wandering the city alone, looking unkempt, the way people looked askance at him made him feel bad for those who had to deal with this on a daily basis. Being rich didn't necessarily buy happiness, but it sure bought a lot of other things, all of which Ferro had before taken for granted. He was learning already.

As he neared the Alice in Wonderland statue and the pond where little boys and their fathers sent homemade sailboats adrift on its current, Ferro sat down on a bench to watch. With the weather having turned in spring's favor, a warm breeze was blowing through the air, and the small ships glided across the water's surface to the instant delight of both a small blond-haired boy and his equally blond father. The boy was like a carbon copy of his father. Ferro thought of his own Papa, and of the many games they had played together, the chess matches and stern but necessary lessons he would impart to his only child. Always instructing, always guiding, himself like a captain of a boat, his son the vessel he was attempting to steer.

Just then a stronger wind blew past, and the tiny boat in the water capsized.

The boy cried as the father made a rescue attempt.

Ferro himself thought of crying, but he hid his tears, as he did often with his emotions. The boy had no such filter, and over the brief joy the boy had experienced with his boat, and now the sudden grief over its loss, he was reduced to a confused child, suddenly wanting his mother. Ferro watched as the boy went running over to a woman sitting on a nearby bench, taking the boy into his arms. The father stood impotently by the pond, looking forlorn, like he'd lost everything.

The scene was a bit too much for Ferro right now, and thankfully the pungent smell of food was able to break him from his reverie of parents and children, losses and regrets. He noticed beyond the pond a cart that sold hot dogs, pretzels, and sodas, and the scent of the boiling franks awakened his senses. His leg shifted, and he heard the clink of the coins in his pocket. Maybe he could buy just the hot dog, forget the bun, with the sixty cents Why not, he was a man who knew how to negotiate, it was one of his many strengths, and there was no rule that he couldn't use his wits. So, nothing ventured, nothing gained. Besides, getting back to that law of averages, right, it was time for life to side with him.

Ferro waited until the food cart was clear of other customers and made his approach. The owner of the cart eyed his new patron with a wary glance. Ferro realized he must look like a walking contradiction, well-tailored clothes in need of some laundering, his scruffy face giving him a dangerous edge. The food man himself wasn't the picture of prosperity either, his salt and pepper hair belying his years.

"How much for a hot dog?" Ferro asked as casually as he could muster.

"Three dollars."

"Must be a tidy profit margin, charging that much," Ferro said. "I don't suppose you've got anything for sixty cents?"

"Maybe a small cup of mustard," the man said, and let out a jovial laugh.

When Ferro didn't respond to the supposed joke, the man scrunched his face with new consideration toward his new customer. Then he dipped the tongs into the water and withdrew

a long, slim, red-skinned frank and set it between the fold of
the bun.

"You like it plain, or with mustard?"

Ferro, suspicious of the man's actions, played along. "A little
mustard."

Was he cruel? Was he teasing him, only to pull it back at
the last minute?

The man finished dressing the dog and with a flourish presented it to Ferro, folded as such in a white napkin. Attempting
to hand over the sixty cents, the man shook his head at Ferro.
"Today, you get a new customer discount. No charge," he
said, and then with a look of sympathy, told Ferro that, "All
of us at some points are down on our luck. Once upon a time
I dreamed of owning a cart but hadn't the start-up money.
I found my dream, eventually. You know? We look out for each
other, that's how people should be."

"Thank you, that's awfully kind of you," Ferro said. "I'm
Claude. What's your name? "

"Angelo."

Ferro extended his hand, and Angelo accepted it easily.

"Are you always at this corner of the park?" Ferro asked.

Angelo nodded. "You can count on me more than the post-
man. Six days a week, ten hour days, rain, snow, sunshine. Of
course I prefer that last one a whole lot more," he said, and
again he let out his quick little laugh.

"Again, my sincere thanks."

"It's just a hot dog, Claude."

Ferro smiled. "No, it is more than that, and you know it.
Your act is a kindness to be repaid."

"The money, it is not important," Angelo said.

"There are some things in life more valuable than money,
Angelo."

They exchanged no other words, just a nod of understanding. Ferro went shuffling off, savoring each tiny bite of the
hot dog until every crumb had been consumed, every drop of

mustard had been licked clean from his fingers. He thought it was quite possibly the most delicious meal he'd ever eaten. Filet mignon for the desperate.

Ferro would never forget Angelo's generosity.

He would also never forget the lesson he'd just learned.

"So, Papa, your plan? Is it working?" Ferro asked with a hint of mist in his eyes, those spoken words caught by the swirling currents of the air, lifting them and taking them on a journey all their own. They were gone, yes, but somehow imbedded deep within him also.

*   *   *

Hours passed as a starry night fell upon an already glittering Manhattan, the towers like sparkling jewels rising up toward the heavens. Magic happened in these city streets, all of it powered by the bustling people who thrived off its energy. They were out dining or dancing, attending theater or opera, cheering good fortune with a few drinks, or inside making love with great intensity and passion. Such was New York on any given night. In stark contrast there was an underbelly to the city, where misfits and criminals fed off the darkness, people who seemed forgotten amidst all that the city had to offer. And it was Ferro who found himself in this unlikely scenario, living in the shadows while others beamed in the limelight.

Still seeking refuge deep inside Central Park, Ferro realized he had no other choice at the moment but to rest his weary feet and seek sleep on a nearby bench. He felt he'd been walking the dark paths of the park for hours. Fortunately the temperature had remained mild, and so he settled on a nearby bench, exhaling as he considered his situation. He assumed the clock had struck midnight and beyond, so now as he attempted to get comfortable—the hot dog long ago digested—Ferro's grumbling stomach betrayed his presence. A homeless woman who had made her bed on a neighboring park bench, her body buried beneath a blanket of sheets from the *Daily News*, looked up with anger and surprise. She was covered in filth to the point where not even a hard rain would have washed her clean, and her sudden appearance startled Ferro up from his own bench.

"Yeah, that's it, go on, get out of here, ya punk. This is my bench, my park, my city, my world. Go back where you came from and stay there and don't bother me no more," she yelled, her voice rising with each declaration of her possessions, each insistence that he leave.

"Look, ma'am, it's a big park," Ferro attempted as a way to quiet her. Who knew how many other people were lying about, watching them, looking for a fight or an opportunity for mayhem. That was life on the streets and in the park. "There are lots of benches, this one was empty and surely I'm not disturbing you. Surely there is a compromise."

She was having none of it. "Shirley, Shirley, Shirley, I don't know who Shirley is," she said with a witch-like cackle that resonated through the dark night. Creatures in the trees squawked back. "So, go away, I got all the company I need," and so she did, since that's when she withdrew from a rumpled brown bag a tiny pistol. Fear staked a surprise place inside Ferro's heart. He silently hoped that fear would be the only thing to pierce his heart and that she kept the bullets in the barrel. Stumbling back, Ferro tripped over a tree root and nearly fell to the hardened ground.

The woman cackled again and again, and then she started jutting the pistol forward like a poking stick, all the while exclaiming, "Bang bang bang bang."

She hadn't pulled the trigger.

And why?

The pistol was a damn toy.

Still, Ferro wasn't taking any further chances. She could have the entire park to herself, she and her wily craziness. Ferro gathered up his dirtied bag and left the woman to her wild delusions. Winding around a bend in the path, he saw the buildings of midtown emerge through the trees. He quickly made his way out of the park, glad to be free of the threats and uncertainty of the park. At Columbus Circle, the streets nearly deserted at an hour best meant for sleep and love making, Ferro had had just about enough. The gun, fake or not, had been the last straw. This quest of his had its sacrifices, but one of them wasn't going to be his very life.

He raised his arm and hailed a cab.

"Where to?" the cabbie asked as Ferro hopped in the back seat.

"Which way to the Waldorf Astoria?" Ferro asked.

"Park and Fiftieth. Come on, hop in, it's a quick trip."

"No thanks, I'll walk."

Ferro had a feeling the guy wasn't nearly as magnanimous as Angelo the hot dog seller and that in the language of New York City cab drivers there was no such thing as a free ride. They probably expected a tip for advice, directions for a fee. With a foul word tossed out at Ferro, the cab spun off, tires screeching against the road. Whatever, he could be as angry as he wanted, at least Ferro had gained the necessary information he sought. Now all it would take was a quick walk through midtown and a phone call to Lawrence, and in an hour Ferro could be sitting in the lap of luxury, well fed with caviar and cheeses and a bottle of the finest champagne at his side. Enough was enough.

"I'm very sorry, Papa," Ferro said to the night wind.

It whistled back at him, sounding a lot like disappointment.

*　　*　　*

Of course he wondered how the tide of his fortunes might have turned had he actually made it to the Waldorf Astoria Hotel that night. He might already have been on a plane back to San Francisco, back to his life and Olivetti Enterprises, but at what cost? Knowing he was an utter failure, constantly fraught over his inability to survive in the real world for barely three days, much less thirty of them. Imagine the detrimental effect such a decision could have on his psyche, on his business acumen, gnawing at him to the point where he would question himself and his ability to close deals. Vodell might simply go Dunbar's way with nary a fight, slipping through his fingers as easily as he'd given up on his quest, and again Ferro would be left feeling like a failure. All of which was unacceptable to a man who had come from Italy with nothing but ambition in his pocket.

Before heading off to the tempting luxury of the Waldorf, Ferro had planted himself on a bench just inside the park near Columbus Circle to reconsider his decision. Was he really giving up so easily? Was this the kind of adversity he couldn't rally against? Was he so pampered by the trinkets in his own life that he couldn't survive without any of them for more than a day or two? Was this the secret message his father had been trying to impart? Giving thought to the whirlwind his life had been since his return to San Francisco after two weeks of partying in the world's most exclusive playgrounds, Ferro realized he hadn't had a moment's peace.

Now, with morning breaking, inside the park even the birds were quiet with sleep. The city actually seemed to be in a slumber all its own, and Ferro felt like the only person awake. That's when his eyes finally closed. He huddled tight on the bench and welcomed what would turn out to be the most rest he'd gotten since his arrival in New York. No one disturbed him, and when he opened his eyes just before six, he was greeted by two frantic squirrels foraging for food. Survival seemed a common theme.

"I can relate," he said to his furry companions.

When one of the squirrels nabbed some unidentifiable junket and went off to enjoy his spoils, Ferro grinned and realized that if squirrels could survive in this city, so could he.

He rose from the bench, stretching his body to the welcome crack of his back. My God, he thought, what he wouldn't give for a gym where he could work out, to push his body to excess with weights and a boxing ring or a pair of nun-chucks. It would alleviate the tension he felt. But there were other matters to attend. That's when he headed out of the park, intent on the next adventure that awaited him. As he passed a trash can, he noticed an edition of the *New York Post*, and he started to reach for it, figuring it might be good to catch up on what was happening in the world.

Another hand stopped him from gaining full possession of the newspaper.

"Excuse me?" Ferro said to the person who had appeared seemingly out of nowhere.

He was an old man hidden behind gray-whiskered cheeks and torn clothes that not even a thrift shop would take. Clearly homeless, but unlike crazy Shirley (as he thought of her) from last night, this gentle soul seemed harmless. Looking at him and receiving back a gaze of bewilderment, Ferro simply let go of the hold he had on the paper. Perhaps this was part of the man's daily routine, knowing where to find items discarded by others.

The man then thrust the paper at Ferro, pressing it against his body.

"I'll find another, I always do," the man said.

"Thank you," Ferro replied, taking the paper.

The man turned to dash away when Ferro called out to him. The man found two quarters and a dime outstretched in Ferro's palm, the move a gesture of faith and good will. Hesitating, cautious—suspicious, no doubt—the grizzled man scooped up the coins and darted back from where he had emerged. Ferro watched as the man approached an underpass in the park, one that seemed to swallow him in the morning's near darkness. He sensed the man needed the change more than Ferro.

Ferro felt good about his own good deed; what did they call it? Pay it forward, like that movie. Having gotten the day off on a positive note, Ferro walked with an added spring in his step as he perused the paper's contents. Flipping quickly to the classifieds, he started to pore through sparse job listings, all while not watching where he was going. Suddenly his foot was lost in the air and it went down with an unexpected thud. He'd missed the curb and lost his balance. The paper slipped from his hands and while his body flailed he noticed what was going to break his fall: an oncoming truck.

Feeling a sudden disconnect with his own body, unable to control his body, Ferro didn't even hear the shouting of nearby pedestrians. Even so, he couldn't be sure whether they were yelling to him to watch out for the truck or for the driver of the truck to watch out for him. Thankfully the truck was slow-moving, merely backing up in an effort to park, and when the rear of the truck struck Ferro, it was with more of a gentle push than a full-on assault. Still, it was forceful enough to knock him to the ground, where he felt the rough pavement scrape the skins of his palms.

As a couple of good Samaritans came to Ferro's aid, the driver of the truck finally realized what was going on, and he too rushed to Ferro's side.

"Oh my God, are you okay, man?" he said, his voice in a panic. "I'm so sorry, I didn't see you. Should we call 911? You bleeding? Shit, my boss will kill me. Lemme get you to a hospital, get you checked out."

"No, no, that's not necessary," Ferro said, the fog lifting and his eyes focusing on the scene he'd been partly responsible for. As he saw all those eyes on him, he looked down, afraid to be recognized. That's all he needed, for the press to find him and start wondering why one of the richest young men in America was walking around New York City like a derelict. But no one said anything; Ferro's attempts at hiding his face all these years seemed to be working. "I'll be fine," he assured everyone. "I am fine, just a couple of scrapes."

"Are you sure? Nothing broken?"

"No, I missed the curb and then you bumped me, that's all that happened. How about your truck, is it okay? I've been told I can be rather hard-headed at times."

The humor dispelled any further worry over Ferro's condition, and the crowd began to disperse, leaving only Ferro and the truck driver to sort out any remaining issues. Ferro noticed the man was tall and lanky, pretty young, perhaps in his early twenties. Beneath his Yankees cap Ferro could see genuine concern on his face.

"Again, I'm really sorry," the kid said.

"Please, let's not give it another thought. It's entirely my fault anyway, I wasn't watching where I was going."

"Yeah, right into the street from the looks of it. Columbus Circle is difficult to cross even with the light in your favor, traffic swirling from so many different streets. Come on, why not take a seat in the truck, get your wits about you."

"That's really not necessary," Ferro started to say, but then changed his mind. Run with it, see where this goes. "Thank you. I'm Claude. Claude Reneau."

"It's nice to meet you, Claude. I'm Fred Evans."

"The pleasure is all mine, Fred."

The two men clambered inside the front of the truck, which was now parked just a block up on Central Park West, away from the busy sounds of Manhattan's morning traffic. Fred had offered Ferro a cup of coffee from his thermos and half a bagel with cream cheese, which Ferro accepted without protest. Silently the two of them snacked at their meal and drank from Styrofoam cups; the warm beverage helped settled Ferro's stomach. When he was done, he placed the cup between them on a pile of books.

Ferro glanced at the spines of the books. Textbooks, all of them.

"Are you sure you're okay?" Fred asked, caution still present in his voice.

"Yes. Even better now," Ferro said, raising the half bagel as a toast to his new friend's generosity. The doughy bagel and cream cheese did wonders to fill his hungry belly. "So, Fred, all these textbooks, they're yours? Studying hard, looks like. Where do you go to school?"

"NYU. Graduate school, which is expensive beyond belief. That's why I'm driving a truck in the wee hours of the morning, gotta earn a living before classes consume the rest of my day. But it'll pay off; I'm a business major and once I'm done? Bingo. Life will be sweet, and rich."

"You're ambitious, I like that," Ferro said.

"I try, that's all you can do, all anybody can do. How about you, what do you do?"

"A little of everything, but at the moment, not much of anything."

"Tough economy out there," the man said. "What kind of work are you lookin' for?"

"At the moment, anything. You'd be amazed at the basic jobs that people seem to think I can't do," Ferro said with a laugh. "I'm having what those in the business world might call a cash flow shortage."

Fred nodded, then pausing as thought to think something through. Ferro reached for his coffee again, downed the last few drops, and then started to depart when Fred spurted out, "Hey, wait, I've got an idea. Believe it or not, I know someone who's looking to hire someone. He's sort of a pain, but he pays pretty good from what I hear. Ever drive a limo?"

Ferro nearly spit out his coffee. Or was that Claude spitting out his coffee? The coincidence was unlikely, but yet, there it was. "Excuse me? Did you say drive a limo? You mean, be someone's chauffeur?"

"Well, yeah, this guy is loaded, and so I don't think he'd be doing the driving and allow you to be the passenger." Fred laughed at his little joke.

Ferro grinned, but then quickly brought the conversation back to the job. It sounded ideal. "No, no, Fred, that's not it. It's just, well, in my previous employment, that's one of the many jobs I performed. I've been a chauffeur before."

"No kidding, that's real strange. The fates must be working overtime, having you get hit by my truck and needing a job and me knowing someone who has an opening…and well, you get the picture. Actually, you sound like you'd be perfect, and what's better you could start immediately, seeing as though you're having that cash flow problem. That will probably be your strongest selling point, your availability. Look, Claude, I've got some errands I need to run first, you know, some deliveries. Got to keep that paycheck coming in. But when I'm done, we can get the ball rolling. So, you up for a little drive?"

"As they say, my dance card is clear," Ferro said. "Let's go."

Fred started up the truck's engine and pulled out into the flow of Manhattan's steadily growing traffic. The moon and stars had been put away again until nighttime, enabling the sun to emerge with its daily chance of promise. For the first time since he'd left the safety of his home, Ferro felt as though those glowing rays from the sky were meant for him. Almost as though his father was shining down on him, proud of him for not giving up.

Ferro thought, What's next? Was this meeting with Fred Evans an opportunity or something bigger than life, an elusive something that others might call destiny?

*   *   *

Four hours and several deliveries later, Fred and Ferro were finally en route to the man who was looking to hire a chauffeur.

For Ferro, he was certainly anxious about the prospect of a securing not just the job, but the interview for starters. He wasn't exactly looking his clean-cut best at the moment, but what he lacked in sartorial splendor he could make up for with his enthusiasm, because it had been a great day so far, the best since his arrival. Fred was a great companion, a real conversationalist who did most of the talking and little questioning. He had a great intuitive sense of when he was pushing too hard for answers, and Ferro, in true Claude guise, was not giving up much in the way of information. They'd even stopped for a meal along the way, a quick run at McDonald's, which, like yesterday's hot dog and this morning's bagel, ranked among his favorite foods lately. Fred had insisted on paying for the Big Macs and fries.

"Consider it thanks for helping my route go so smoothly this morning."

Ferro had insisted on buying a couple of apple pies for dessert with the two-dollar tip he'd received when he'd delivered one of Fred's packages to a lonely old woman up in Westchester County. Fred had told him to keep it.

Finally, they were in Queens and had trundled along the expressway until coming to their exit for Forest Hills. Fred obviously knew his way around the neighborhood, and Ferro just marveled at the way his new friend negotiated the congestion, the narrow streets, the double-parked trucks and cars. He wondered if he himself could handle driving in this city, and not just any kind of driving, but the awkward bulk that came with a limousine. There was only one way to find out.

Down the busy Continental Avenue they drove until Fred made a left turn into an exclusive enclave full of fancy-looking homes and spectacular foliage. Money lived here, and Ferro felt himself relaxing. He knew this crowd. This was his world.

They pulled into the circular drive of a house modeled in the Tudor fashion, and Fred switched off the engine. He'd called ahead following their last stop, so they were luckily expected. As Ferro hopped down from the cab, he looked at himself in the rearview mirror. He needed a shave badly, but he combed his hair with his fingers in an attempt to neaten those flyaway locks. As for his fingers, they were slightly dirty from the last couple of days. He could just keep them in his pocket.

Rounding the lushly attended gardens, Fred led Ferro to the back entrance, which he said was the "servant's entrance." He said those last two words with raised eyebrows. Ferro grinned.

A quick ring of the doorbell and suddenly the door was opening to reveal a small-boned woman with a feather duster in her hand.

"Ah, Mr. Fred, hello."

"Hi, Doris. Nice to see you," he said affably. "This is my new friend, Claude. I called earlier, left a message for the big boss that I'd be bringing someone by to apply for his driver's position."

"Hello, Mr. Claude, come inside please, wait here in the kitchen and I'll see if he's ready to see you."

Ferro turned to his new friend and said, "Thanks, Fred, there's no need for you to stay. I've got it from here."

"Are you sure? I could stick around."

"You've gone above and beyond—not to mention you must have a class or two this afternoon," Ferro said. "I'll be just fine."

"I do have a class to get to," he said. "Hey, good luck to you, Claude."

"And to you, too, Fred Evans."

A curious expression came over Fred's face, as though he was confused over why Ferro would speak his entire name. But for Ferro it was simple: he was again making a mental note of the name of the man who had helped him in his moment of need. He wanted to remember those who deserved to be remembered. Fred just tipped the brim of his Yankees cap, and with that he departed, leaving Ferro in the kitchen of this stranger's home.

"Hang on here, Claude," Doris said. "I'll get Mr. Curtis for you."

A chill ran up Ferro's spine, settling at the nape of his neck. "Curtis?" he asked. With sudden remembrance, he patted the inside pocket of his jacket, came up with what he was looking for. Why he had kept it, he couldn't say. Maybe as a reminder that, as tough as things were to get in these thirty days, to never turn into a beast such as the man from the airplane. Through all Ferro's trials and tribulations, his encounters with thugs, police, homeless people, only one thing had survived this entire adventure: the airline boarding pass of a rude, nasty blowhard who went by the name Stan Curtis.

It couldn't possibly be the same man, right?

Could life really be that small?

Could Ferro really work for this guy?

He braced himself for his meeting with Curtis, wondering if he would take one look at Ferro and throw him out of his house.

CHAPTER ELEVEN

ACTUALLY, NOT ONLY COULD IT BE the same man from the airplane, but it *was* the same man. How did Ferro know without even having come face to face with him yet? Real simple: that voice. That bellowing, belligerent, bombastic tone that echoed in the tight confines of the first-class cabin (and probably in economy, too) now vibrated throughout the house. And from the conversation Curtis was having, clearly it wasn't a good time to have come looking for a job.

"Listen, woman, you can't just go spending money like it's made from water. God, if I let this go on much longer I'll be drowning in debt!"

Give him credit for keeping his analogy consistent in the heat of the moment.

"You don't want me using the credit cards you gave me?"

"I don't see why you need to have them all maxed out," he boomed. "Christ, the clerks must smell you coming a mile away. Speaking of that, stop buying that expensive perfume, the more it smells the more it costs, and right now you reek, woman."

"Better than smelling like Ben Gay," the woman replied. "Besides, if you don't want me using your precious credit cards, you shouldn't have given them to me. And if you think you're using this as one more excuse to get rid of me, think again.

You're going to have to pay up—and big time, you freak. You don't get rid of this girl that easily."

"The prenup says otherwise."

"That piece of trash isn't worth the paper it's written on. No judge would uphold that in any court."

"You signed it, bitch. That's good enough for any judge."

"Yeah, any judge who lives up your ass, that is."

A beat of silence fell between the two, and for Ferro, stuck in the kitchen hearing but not seeing any of the action, he could only imagine what was taking place between spouses who'd obviously seen the love slip away. He snuck over to the swinging door that separated the kitchen from the rest of the house, and as he inched the door open, he saw both man and wife (soon-to-be ex?) staring at each other, their breathing making them look like two-thirds of the little pigs, all huffing and puffing, neither ready to blow the house down but both getting ready. They looked to be at a stalemate, and neither wanted to give in, or seemingly speak the next declarative word. Divorce.

"Get out of my face, woman," Curtis finally said with a wave of his hand.

"Yeah, give me what I want, and I'll be out of your face and out of your home and your goddamn life in a week."

"If only it were that easy," he screamed.

The wife named Hilda stormed away in one direction, Curtis headed another way. The living room was suddenly clear of victims, and only the residual effect of their fight remained, like a toxic cloud hovering over the house. Ferro eased the door closed and returned to the center part of the kitchen, where he contemplated his next move. There was no way he could work for this guy. He'd seen him in action on the plane, and now he'd seen him within the sanctity of his own home. No matter where he was, he was down and out just an asshole.

But that wasn't Ferro's true concern. No, there still was the possibility that Curtis would recognize him from the airplane, and who knows where that could lead. Why would some scruffy-looking guy who had poked fun at him on a transcontinental flight be willing to work for him, and besides, if you're so desperate for a job, what the hell were you doing enjoying the luxuries of first class? Ferro considered leaving right there, but then two things stopped him: first of all, this was the first true lead he'd had on a job, and damned if he didn't need it. And second of all, he was stuck. Doris had just returned and said, "Mr. Curtis will see you now."

"Oh, goody," Ferro said, his voice tinged with sarcasm. "I sure do have great timing."

"Oh, that," Doris said. "We get those about once a week, though I will admit this one was worse than previous bouts. They rarely bring up the prenup, gets the Mrs. all riled. Who knows what's really going on between those two, you never know. Still, it sure makes the job interesting." And then with a wink, she said, "Welcome to the family."

"I don't have the job yet," Ferro said.

"Oh, I have a feeling Mr. Curtis will like you just fine."

With that enigmatic statement wafting away into the ether, Ferro was escorted into the living room and left to wait for his prospective employer. He took a moment to take in his surroundings. The place was decorated with a noticeable lack of taste or restraint, a room straight out of Vegas, with leopard-skin prints and plastic coverings on the dated furniture. Ferro looked around for a bust of Elvis but came up empty—even Elvis was smart enough to leave the building.

Ferro should probably do the same.

But it was too late to back out now, as he heard the sound of heavy footsteps approaching. Ferro steeled himself for whatever was about to occur, wondering if, in his guise as Claude, he could handle the abuse that regularly came out of this guy's mouth without tossing in a few of his own comebacks. Ferro wasn't accustomed to being subservient. Time sure would tell.

Curtis blasted into the room like a wave of negative energy and had Ferro any lingering doubt about who this man was, it was instantly dispensed with. Oh yeah, he was the "buffoon" from the plane who'd screamed his way across America, only to be humiliated in front of everyone by a flight attendant—and potato—who had had just about enough. Ferro reminded himself of his own experience with the man, and of what Doris the housekeeper said: His bark is worse than his bite. A bully who never followed through on his threats.

"So, you're looking for a job," Curtis said, not even bothering to introduce himself.

"Yes, sir."

"Fred Evans recommends you."

"Yes."

"How do you know Fred?'

"We met recently, had some business interests in common. He's a good kid."

"I suppose," Curtis said, his voice sounding as though he'd never considered it before. "You got a name?"

"Claude. Claude Reneau," Ferro said without hesitation. He supposed he was getting used to being someone other than himself. Given the events of the past few days, he sure didn't feel like Ferro Olivetti.

Out of the corner of his eyes Ferro saw Curtis's wife Hilda sneak into the corner, watching the interview unfold. Ferro looked her way, getting his first real glance at her. She was late twenties, awfully young for the sixty-something Curtis, and even in a trashy, overly made-up way she was far too pretty for the chubby, balding man. Now he saw where the Vegas-lounge-act living room came from. All Hilda was missing was a pole to dance with. Her sense of fashion was lacy, tawdry, but expensive. All Victoria, with no secrets left to the imagination.

"Hire him, Curtis."

"Hilda, go away. This is a job interview."

"Oh, please, you'd hire the devil if he showed up."

"No, apparently I'd marry her," Curtis said, and gave Ferro a devilish smile all his own, clearly pleased with himself at his lame joke. Ferro grinned for the sake of keeping the peace. For the sake of securing a job.

"No, I'm serious, Curtis, I think he's got potential."

"Yeah, potential to get in your pants."

"Um, excuse me," Ferro began, but to no avail. Curtis shushed him.

"You ever drive for someone before?"

"Yes, I was a personal driver for a wealthy executive back in California."

"Really. Care to tell me who?"

"Mr. Ferro Olivetti."

"Ooh, baby, I've heard of him, he's dreamy looking, and has got money Trump probably dreams about," Hilda said. "Some of the gossip rags I read at the beauty salon have articles about him. Not a lot of pictures but based on his exploits he's got to be one of the best-looking guys on the planet."

Ferro smirked. Avoiding the paparazzi, it had its benefits.

"Big deal, Hilda, looks ain't everything. Look at you," Curtis said, again amused by himself at his wife's expense. "So, this Olivetti guy had you driving his limo, no kidding. Care to tell me why you're no longer behind his wheel?"

"Simple. I moved. Kind of hard to drive his car when I'm here on the opposite coast."

"Good point, I like that. You're good, you think on your feet."

"Yeah, a lot better than you, he just made fun of you, you jerk," Hilda said. "That's what happens when you're so busy sitting on your brain, can't think clearly."

"Hilda. Shut. Up."

"Oh, all right, have it your way," Hilda said, satisfied to have gotten in a couple of good digs at her husband's expense. As she began to slink out of the room, a smile of triumph plastered on her plastic face, she turned back to Ferro and said, "I'm looking forward to getting to know you better, Claude. You're not so bad looking yourself." With that, she was gone from the room, and at last the men could get down to business.

"What'd he pay you?"

Ferro thought fast. "Uh, one thousand a week." He paused. "Cash."

Curtis nodded. "You got references? Can I call this Olivetti character?"

"You could try, he's hard to pin down. Always traveling."

"Okay, I see how it is. Don't worry, I'm not going to push for the details. Look, I need someone immediately, so I'll forego all those references and pay you eight hundred a week. That comes with room and board—if you don't mind a bedroom that's little more than a closet on the third floor. Oh, and they'll be assorted other duties, as required."

Ferro stood there, nearly dumbfounded at how quickly the process had gone. He realized he hadn't said anything since Curtis had made his offer and he struggled to find the words.

"Yeah, I know, you're surprised. Such a generous offer doesn't come by every week, even if I do say so myself," Curtis said, his eyebrow raised, suddenly eager for an answer. "So, you're interested?"

This time there was no hesitation. "Yes."

"Welcome to Curtis Enterprises," Curtis said. "We've got only one rule: Do as I say, don't piss me off, and we'll get along just fine."

Ferro merely nodded his acquiescence. For him to succeed in this job, he'd have to hold his tongue a lot. Still, how bad could it be? Maybe in the confines of the limo, Curtis was different, more introspective, not always trying to prove to everyone around him what a powerful man he was. Ferro supposed he would find out rather quickly. Still, it was only Day Four of his quest, and finally he'd found employment, been given a roof over his head, and in minutes he imagined himself beneath the stinging spray of a long, hot shower. The price for all of this? Putting up with a man he'd wanted to toss out of an airplane. In mid-air.

* * *

Better than sex, better than fresh Maine lobster dripping with real melted butter, better than the finest black caviar from the Caspian Sea—that's how much Ferro thought of the shower and subsequent shave he'd treated his body to. Not to mention the simple ham and Swiss cheese sandwich and glass of milk Doris had brought up to his tiny attic nook of a bedroom. For the first time in days, he felt renewed and refreshed. Dare he say it: he felt human.

Though he was posing as Claude and denying his true self to others, given this alone time he stole a moment to gaze at himself in the mirror, wondering what, if any, ill effect the experiences of late had done to him. Other than dark circles under his eyes, there was little difference in his face. His olive skin still held its radiant health, and his body remained the picture of fitness. Not that he expected it to be any different. He had always been diligent in his eating habits and workouts. A few days off his routine shouldn't matter.

Pleased with what he saw, Ferro smiled at himself. His grin was a knockout and had won him many favors over the years. All he had to do was flash his pearly whites, and the woman of his choice could be his, like Cass back in Monte Carlo all those weeks ago. He thought of the snowy cabin, the crazy sex and skiing, the indulgence he'd allowed himself. How things had changed. He wondered how his charm would fare in this seemingly crazy household, Curtis and Hilda and whoever else might live under its roof. Wrapping a towel around his waist, Ferro padded back into the tiny room, and that's when he discovered he wasn't alone.

"I had to check you out," he heard.

"Excuse me?"

"That shrew downstairs, she was practically salivating at the mere mention of you."

"Me?"

"Uh-huh. Gotta say, for once that hag and I agree."

"That…hag…shrew," Ferro said, finally realizing that the person he was talking with was a young woman, perhaps a teenager. "Uh, wouldn't she be your mother?"

"Hah! As if. First of all, she'd make the world's worst mother. I'd even buy her a mug that said so, but she wouldn't even allow herself to get pregnant in the first place. Second of all, she's my stepmother, and trust me, that's what I'd like to do to her—step on my mother."

"So, you are Curtis's daughter?"

"Ooh, you're smart, too," the girl said.

"Do you have a name?"

"Does it matter?" the girl asked, moving suggestively toward Ferro.

For each step she took forward, he took two backwards. At least it gave Ferro a chance to truly take in the sight before him. If Curtis had a horrible personality, he'd seemingly passed it along—and a few other repugnant traits—to his offspring. She was short, probably five-two or three, and she was plump all around. She tried to hide her weight issues with billowing clothing and lots of make-up, but it gave off the effect of a spoiled child who'd raided her mother's closet. With that baby fat still hugging her sides, she could have been as young as fifteen but perhaps as old as eighteen.

She certainly acted older.

"You've got a nice body, Claude. You work out a lot?"

"Aha, so you know my name. Still not fair, me not knowing yours."

"I like to retain an air of mystery," she said huskily, sounding like she'd read that line in a trashy romance book—or some bad television movie. He doubted she really knew what retain meant.

Their private moment was mercifully interrupted by the arrival of Doris, who didn't appear in the least bit shocked by the girl's presence. Instead, she just looked at Ferro and said,

"Mr. Curtis would like to see you downstairs. And as for you Miss Nancy, I suggest you not let your father catch you up here."

"Why? I'm legal."

"In some states," Doris said, standing in the doorway, but leaving enough room for the girl to pass.

Nancy, though, wasn't done yet with her newfound prey. "See you around, Claude." Again, that exaggerated husky voice of hers filled the room, nearly bringing him to hearty laughter.

"Goodbye, Nancy," Ferro said.

The girl gave her housekeeper a withering look, as though saying she'd ruined it all.

"Thanks, Doris. Tell Mr. Curtis I'll be down in a minute, I just need to get dressed."

"Yes, in this household, that would be recommended."

They exchanged conspiratorial smiles, and then Doris left Ferro to get ready.

Five minutes later Ferro was back downstairs, having changed into the spare outfit he'd brought, despite the fact that a chauffeur's uniform hung in the closet of his room. He wasn't sure just what he was needed for, driving his new boss or for one of those "other" jobs which might be required of him. He stood at attention in the Vegas room (as he had come to think of it) and awaited Curtis.

Turned out, more than just Curtis arrived. In tow was Hilda, and behind her, Nancy.

"Daddy, you're not listening to me, hello? I said I need money."

"That's all you ever say, all you ever need," Hilda retorted.

"Hello? I'm not talking to you."

"She's got a point, my peach. You're always wanting money."

"But Daddy, I have nothing hot to wear for the party tonight."

"The finest couture wouldn't make you 'hot'," Hilda sneered.

"Bitch," Nancy said.

"Hey, we'll have none of that language," Curtis said.

Ferro just stood there at attention, keeping his mouth shut. He wondered if this family drama came with commercials.

"Daddy, you tell that woman you married to shut up. She's not my mother."

"I'm right here, dear, tell it to my face."

"Shrew! " Nancy screamed at her stepmother.

"Why you little…"

"Wait, wait, wait," Curtis said, stopping this before it got worse. "Peaches, how much do you need? "

"Five hundred will do nicely."

"If it buys me a moment's peace between you two, it's well worth it," Curtis said, and from his pocket he withdrew a roll of cash. He easily counted off five bills and handed them to his daughter, but not before he said, "Spend it wisely—unlike this one." And he indicated his own wife.

No wonder Nancy had no respect for her stepmother.

With a winning sneer at Hilda and a kiss on the cheek to her father, Nancy went dashing out of the house, the door slamming behind her. Hilda just looked at her husband in disgust, as though saying he was a total wuss when it came to his daughter. No backbone. If Hilda wasn't thinking it, Ferro certainly was. That wasn't the way to indulge a child, pay her off to shut her up. God, these three were horrible people. What had he gotten himself into? He was beginning to wonder if Fred had done him a favor. But he knew it wasn't Fred to blame, not really.

Curtis then turned to his new employee. "Ah, Claude. We'll be requiring your services tonight."

"I'm at your disposal, sir," Ferro said, swallowing the bile that came up when he spoke each word. Subservience was not a trait he did well with, less so in the presence of a man who deserved no respect.

"We're having a bit of a gathering tonight here at the house—as you may have guessed from that…uh, conversation. You ever bartend?"

"No."

"Think you can?"

"Pouring champagne and wine into glasses? I think I can handle it."

"Might be some mixed drinks."

"I'll figure it out."

"Any questions on how to make something, ask her," he said, and again he pointed to his wife. "She's been known to knock back every drink known to man, surely she must know what goes in them."

With the plans established for the coming night, Curtis dismissed Ferro. But before he could make his desired exit, Hilda made her own, and she did not go quietly into the afternoon. She, too, slammed the doors behind her. Curtis sure had a way of clearing a room.

Just as he would have cleared a plane, had they not been 36,000 feet in the air.

*　　*　　*

With a few hours remaining before the party, Ferro decided to busy himself. As a man who took pride in his work no matter the job he was hired to do, he took one look at Curtis's limo—actually, a mere Town Car—and immediately set about giving it a good cleaning, a buff shine with a waxy paste. By everyday standards, it was a nice enough car and would be noticed on the streets, given its tinted windows, but it was also a model from a couple of years ago, and it wasn't kept in the best condition. It was a stark contrast to the sleek BMW machine that the real Claude escorted Ferro around town in.

As Ferro eagerly soaped down the car in the driveway, the spring sunshine waned to the welcome light of dusk. With the hose in one hand, he gave the limo a healthy spray of water and in doing so wasn't fully watching behind him. A car swerved into the driveway and came to a sudden halt just a couple of feet from him. He jumped back, hearing a slight giggle come from the driver of a battered-looking Jaguar.

It was the spoiled brat Nancy, arriving back from her shopping spree. With bags in hand, she smiled at Ferro.

"Did I scare ya?"

"Less this time than you did in my bedroom."

"Aw, don't be frightened of little me," she said, a wicked grin crossing her face that made her look more pathetic than sexy. "But watch out for the Missus—she should live in the tool shed."

"Why is that?"

"Because she likes to screw drivers."

"Very funny," Ferro said, surprised at her wit.

"No really, you're our third chauffeur this year."

"What happened to the other two?"

"Duh. Daddy fired them.

"You paint a vivid picture, Nancy," he said.

"I love the way you say my name—that accent of yours makes me wet." Ferro blanched at the girl's brazenness. He didn't know what to say.

"Are you married, Claude?

"No."

"Good."

"Why is that?"

"I don't like complications. Trust me, I've been through that before."

Poor girl, where was her actual mother?

"Before you get any ideas—let me tell you I've entered a period of celibacy in my life."

She frowned at that comment. "Uh, that means you don't have sex, right?"

Ferro nodded, trying his best to hide his growing grin.

"Kind of a waste, if you ask me. But if that's how you're going to act, well, then you're just the hired help, and you can call me Ms. Curtis," she said, piling on sudden attitude. "And to think, I bought the sexiest outfit I could find, all the time thinking of you. Guess I'll have to rope some other guest at the party tonight. Girl needs some, you know?"

Ferro wondered if perhaps he should be hosing down the daughter rather than the limo.

*   *   *

Nighttime at the Curtis residence, and the outside lawn of the Tudor home was bathed in soft white light, an unexpected flourish of taste in an evening of tastelessness and crass vulgarity. The party had been in full swing for close to two hours and seemed to consist of people doing something that looked like dancing but more closely could be called dry humping, all of them grooving to something that resembled music but couldn't quite win Grammys. So many drinks had been consumed by the guests they were practically getting sick in front of each other. Ferro knew how they felt.

Ferro was situated in the Vegas room behind a makeshift bar surrounded by bottles and glasses both clean and dirty, as well as discarded paper plates and dirtied forks; seemed people thought they could leave their trash anywhere they felt. As though Ferro was a mere "employee" (meaning something less than human) and not subject to maintaining a clean work station. He was constantly tossing items into a nearby trash can, rolling his eyes at the debauchery around him.

He supposed there were about thirty people in attendance, though the way the doorbell rang and the front door opened and closed, it wasn't necessarily the same thirty people; this was a party filled with transients, and from what he could gather there was no purpose to the party other than for people to pour booze down their throats and grope each other. Making business contacts was the furthest thing from anyone's mind, and for a moment Ferro was reminded of that last party he had thrown at Villa Olivetti, the one which had ended abruptly with the call from his mother, Was his party similar to this? Was it filled with people who were only taking advantage of the free stuff and who didn't really give a rat's ass about the host?

Ferro shuddered to think his life was anything like Curtis's.

"Hey, barkeep, are you working or modeling?"

Ferro snapped out of his thoughts and saw a familiar face before him. He didn't know the guy's name, but he knew the face. He'd been up to the bar far more times than any other guest, and his frequent trips were beginning to show their glassy-eyed effect. He might have gotten that full sentence off, but it was not without some slurring.

"What'll it be?" Ferro asked.

"You don't remember? Geez, the number of times I've been served by you, you'd think you could do me the courtesy of remembering my drink. Don't bartenders work for tips?"

Ferro's tip glass held about six bucks, two of which he'd started the night with. This idiot hadn't left him a single bill, not after all his visits to the bar. But Ferro held his tongue and said, "Was it a cranberry and vodka?"

"Not just vodka, dude, the good stuff."

Ferro took hold of the near-empty bottle of Grey Goose and splashed it into a fresh glass, dousing the potent liquor with a hint of cranberry juice.

The man took hold of the drink and walked away. No thanks, no tip.

Ferro checked his watch, wondering how much more of this he had to endure.

"Hey, you."

Oh great, another demanding, drunken jerk.

Ferro didn't respond; he was tired of being treated like wallpaper.

"Hey, boy, I'm talking to you."

Ferro looked hard at the guy, his dark eyes squinting with displeasure. This guy, with his aging party-boy looks and abhorrent behavior, had made more than an impression on Ferro.

He'd also been making headway with both Hilda and Nancy all night long. Ferro had watched with a mix of bemusement and disgust as he'd danced with both women—often at the same time—sidling up to the wife of the host with reckless disregard for Curtis's feelings. And Hilda had been enjoying every moment of his attention, wagging her sizeable breasts practically in his face; her dress left little to the imagination. Actually, it barely held her breasts. The man's tongue was practically wagging; that was, until Nancy had joined the dance (seduction?), and flaunted her brazen youth in front of the sleaze ball. He'd quickly moved from stepmother to daughter. Now he was thirsty.

"I'm sorry, what'll you have. Seltzer, coffee?"

"Wha's tha' suppa mean?" the guy asked, his slurry voice betraying his inability to hold his booze.

"Just looking out for you, uh, sir—you know, a good bartender not only serves his customer drinks but also knows when they've maybe had one or two too many."

"You saying I'm drunk? Who the fuck're you, telling me I can't have a drink…"

"Claude," Nancy said, suddenly joining the discussion. She wasn't in much better shape, but at least she could still talk, if not walk straight. How about that, an eighteen-year-old girl who could hold her liquor. *Could make a father real proud*, Ferro thought. "Claude, just give Mr. Reynolds his drink, he's one of Daddy's big contractors, and you don't say no to people like him."

No arguing with his employer. Still, he wondered if Nancy would say no to the man.

"See that, you listen to her. She knows what side of the butter her bread is spread on," the man said, cackling. "Hey, I made a rhyme, fucking funny one, too. Gimme a scotch on the rocks."

Then Nancy interjected, "And when you're done, clear away all these dirty plates. Really, Claude, this place is a mess."

She should know from messes.

Ferro did as instructed, first with the drinks, then with the recently discarded plates, before watching as the two fools made their way back to the dance floor, their bodies crushed against the others to the point that Reynolds lost about half his drink down the front of Nancy's dress. Ferro would have laughed had the pig not begun to suck up the spilled booze with his tongue. Nancy laughed heartily, to the point where Hilda grew disgusted by the display and made her way over to the bar.

"Get you something, Mrs. Curtis?"

"Well, if I thought it would do any good, I'd say you could spill a drink on me and then help me clean it up." She grinned at him, her hands gliding suggestively down her curvy hips.

"Considering this is my first day on the job and your husband is standing about ten feet away, no, I could think of other things I should be doing. So, another drink? You like them with the little umbrellas, right?"

"Why if I didn't know better, Claude, I'd say you've been paying a lot of attention to me," she said.

"Just looking out for the boss's wife, making sure she's happy."

"Not as happy as I could be," she said, leaning in toward him.

Fortunately Ferro was spared any further come-ons, as Curtis came by and dragged his wife away from the bar area. She was less than pleased to be manhandled, and her screaming at him made for snarky entertainment for the rest of the assembled guests. When the drunk Bob Reynolds began to get too fresh with Nancy, Curtis had to get rough with him, too, and soon the party was deteriorating into what Nancy would describe as a "typical Curtis mess." At last, though, the toxic atmosphere became too much, with the family bickering about motives, opportunities, accusations, and soon the guests left before the party turned into a locked-room murder mystery.

Finally, at eleven o'clock a fatigued Ferro had brought the rest of the glasses into the kitchen, where poor put-upon Doris was busily cleaning them and putting them away in the cabinet. Keeping her company was a small screen television, and it was tuned to the evening news. About ten minutes into the broadcast, Ferro's ears perked up at the mention of, of all things, his company's name.

"Can you turn that up?" he asked Doris.

"In business news tonight," began the stiff-haired anchor, "Olivetti Enterprises of San Francisco successfully and surprisingly defeated its global archenemy Dunbar Industries in its heated takeover fight for the financially troubled tech company Vodell. Richard Dunbar, the company's CEO, vowed that the fight is far from over, noting that nothing has been signed. Ferro Olivetti, the always elusive billionaire president of Olivetti Enterprises, could not be reached for comment."

Ferro stood there, shocked to hear this story on the news and not from Lawrence directly. Not that Lawrence had any way to contact him, it was just…Ferro felt helpless, stuck in this crazy house in Queens while one of the most important deals of his life was winding up. As happy as he was about the result, Ferro had to admit to remorse over missing the kill. How he would have received first the conceding call from Vodell's Ms. Wilde and the subsequent angry rant from Dunbar. Few things in life were so satisfying. Instead, Ferro was serving drinks, sucking up to drunks and crazy people who would be shocked if they knew the truth about their new employee.

"Well, well," Ferro heard behind him, "Seems your former boss is a billionaire. Do you think he favors women with a penchant for leopard skin? We move fast, like a cat, but for the right price we don't mind being captured."

Hilda Curtis was grinning at him.

Ferro, afraid his true identity was written across his face, was uncertain how to respond to such a come-on. Doris just looked away in bemusement, as she always did. He was spared from having to answer when a screeching sound interrupted their little scene.

"Claude! Claude, get in here right now!"

That was Curtis bellowing at him, and Ferro took full advantage of his boss's need to escape from the coming clutches of his horny wife. When he returned to the living room, he saw Nancy in tears, one of the straps of her dress undone and nearly both breasts on display. Bob Reynolds, the drunk contractor, was splayed out on the sofa, rubbing a sore chin. Ferro didn't need to be told what had transpired.

"Sir?" Ferro said.

"Take Mr. Reynolds home."

"But Daddy," a tipsy Nancy wailed.

"Quiet, little girl!" Curtis demanded. "Claude—take him home. Now."

He'd just scored perhaps the biggest takeover of his professional career. And his reward? Act the subservient employee and drive home a belligerent drunk who saw nothing wrong with groping the teen-aged daughter of his host.

Ferro let out a heavy sigh. What was the point of all this? Where was this journey taking him? Would there be any satisfaction at the end of the thirty days, or just this empty feeling he'd felt since he'd arrived in New York?

Home was too far away at this point.

Rome, even more so.

Surely this wasn't what his father had intended.

CHAPTER TWELVE

THE TOWN CAR HANDLED PRETTY WELL, and Ferro was glad to give the bulky vehicle a test drive before he had to assume his regular duty behind the wheel and drive Curtis wherever it was he needed to go. Accustomed as he was to be riding in the back, he couldn't remember a time when he'd actually sat up front in his own stretch limo, much less been behind its wheel. He might have enjoyed this ride tonight—getting a chance to get some air and get away from the Curtis family—had he not had to babysit the drunken idiot who sat slouched in the back seat.

"I want Nancy. Damn you, drive me back, that slut wanted all of me. And trust me, there's a lot of me."

Ferro continued to drive, easily ignoring Reynolds. He had locked all the doors from the controls on the driver's side door, but hadn't yet raised the partition that could separate them. Ferro was keeping a wary eye on him through the rearview window, making sure he didn't pull anything tricky. Ferro loved a fun drunk, like his spoiled, trust-fund friend, Steve; this guy was anything but. Part of him wondered when the guy would be sick, and as much as he would enjoy the man's misery, he knew the clean-up would be his responsibility.

The sooner he was done with this guy, the better. Ferro stepped on the accelerator, and the car pulled ahead of several slower ones on the Grand Central. With the aid of the car's GPS system, an otherwise clueless Ferro was able to figure out their destination. Reynolds certainly was no help in that department.

Before too long, the GPS instructed Ferro to take an off ramp, and he did so, turning onto a narrow, darkened road. Reynolds took that moment to awaken from his drunken stupor. He wasn't happy to find himself in the back seat, being driven home and, for that matter, all alone.

"I want Nancy. Damn you. Drive me back, I wanna hook up with that hot little chick. She was begging for it. You know what it is, right?"

"Sorry, sir," Ferro said curtly, swallowing the bile that accompanied having to use such a respectful tone with this idiot. "Mr. Curtis's instructions, and as his employee, it's those I must follow."

"Screw Curtis," he said. "Turn this boat around! I want to screw Curtis's daughter."

Ferro just kept driving, the car obviously moving forward.

"Hey, paisan, you fucking deaf or something? I said go back, that bitch was itching for some from me." Then he grinned. "Wouldn't be the first time, she's one hot slut."

Ferro wasn't such a fan of Nancy's, but still he couldn't help but defend her honor. "Sir, I'd keep quiet if I were you. Nancy is Mr. Curtis's daughter, and he's quite obviously very protective of her. He didn't hesitate in having you removed from the party, did he?"

"Who the hell do you think you're talking to? Sounding so educated, so important. You're a fricking driver, don't even have the uniform to be called a chauffeur."

Chauffeur came out sounding like "chofer." Ferro wasn't sure that was the booze talking or the guy's idiocy. Ferro just continued to push on the accelerator and propel them down the darkened street toward Reynolds's home.

"You know, I can have you fired, you punk. Just one phone call from me, and Curtis will send your ass packing," he said, fumbling in this pocket for his cell phone. He finally got hold of it, but it went flying out of his hands when Ferro brought the car to an abrupt stop. Reynolds himself slipped off his seat and fell to the floor in the rear. He hadn't been wearing his seatbelt and he wound up scraping his head on the rough carpet. He barely had time to say "oww" when the back door opened, and Ferro was grabbing hold of him.

Stretching muscles he hadn't used in days, Ferro threw his passenger up against a tree, and not gently. Reynolds breath escaped his mouth with a big "ugh," and then he doubled over to toss the contents of his stomach onto the road's shoulder. Ferro waited out the sickening sounds, but didn't turn his back on the man. No telling what he might do. Instead, he watched the man as he struggled to recover from the violent heaving of his body. When at last it seemed like Reynolds had nothing left to purge, Ferro side-stepped the filth and grinded his fist against the man's chest, holding him up and slightly bruising his sternum.

"You start acting like a gentleman or you'll find yourself walking home," he said. "And who knows, if you behave yourself the rest of the way maybe I won't tell Mr. Curtis about your previous dalliances with his daughter—or the coarse language you used to describe her. He gets wind, your contracting days are over. Heck, maybe even your life."

Ferro's eyes were like those of a tiger, sharp and piercing and meaning business; he knew his message was getting across. Reynolds just nodded his head in acquiescence, like a freshly sobered drunk. When Ferro released him, he stumbled back into the rear of the car. Two seconds later he looked like he was sleeping, or maybe just finally passed out from the booze. Ferro wondered if the jerk would even remember any of this in the morning.

About to close the door, that's when Ferro noticed the cell phone lying on the floor of the limo. He bent down to retrieve it and place it in Reynolds's pocket. A second thought came to him, and before he knew it, he was dialing a number from memory, simultaneously checking his watch to wonder if he was calling too late. One o'clock New York time meant only ten West Coast time. Ferro wondered if he had guessed right, and on the third ring his theory was proven correct.

"Still burning the midnight oil?" he said.

"Ferro!"

"Yes, it's me. Hello, Lawrence. I took a chance and called the office first, and lo and behold, there you are."

"As if I'd be anywhere else given today's news. Yes, Ferro, I'm here, but while it's hardly midnight, something tells me I'll be here way past then. Perhaps I should just order breakfast now."

"No, everything can wait. I think you should go home and get some rest. You've earned it," Ferro said. "Look, I can't talk long, Lawrence, I just wanted to check in and say a job well done to you and the staff at Olivetti. In my required absence, you have more than proved yourselves as the best in the business."

"I appreciate that, Ferro, but ultimately it's all your doing. Wilde loved your proposal, the fact that it allowed her to leave Vodell with dignity. She chose you over Dunbar because of who you are. She mentioned your father, Ferro. She said that wherever you are, it's out of obligation to your father. Is that right, Ferro? Is that what all this is about?"

"Vodell didn't solely make its decision based on some wild goose chase of mine."

"Well, it's your money, it's your gamble," Lawrence said. "She recognized that, too."

"We're all in this together, and we all have our part to do. Especially now."

"Ferro, please tell me where you are."

"I wish I could tell you," Ferro said, truly meaning it. He stole a look at the sleeping Reynolds, at the Town Car parked alongside the road on a night where the moon gave off few shadows, he wasn't even sure Lawrence would understand it even if Ferro could have explained it all. Some things in life you just had to accept as is. Ms. Wilde of Vodell knew as much as she needed to understand the man behind the company. Lawrence, for now, just had to follow orders.

"You know I'm not at liberty to say."

"But you're somewhere that you can watch the news, keep up with what's going on?"

"I haven't entered a monastery, if that's what you're asking."

"Ferro Olivetti, a monk? No, that notion hadn't crossed my mind."

Ferro grinned. It was good to hear his aide's voice, to know that even in the face of adversity and late-night hours at the office Lawrence could still drum up some humor. This lifeline to his real world was a boost to Ferro, and it made him believe he could finish out his quest now without further worries. Vodell was his, Lawrence had things under control, and now all Ferro had to do was play chauffeur for the remainder of the month and try and figure out just what it all meant. Whether he could discover the elusive thing his father had enigmatically suggested was missing from his life.

"Look, Lawrence, as a thank you for everyone's hard work, I want you to give a bonus of five thousand dollars to each of my employees."

"Certainly, Ferro, that's very generous. And what reason am I to give?"

"Just tell them it's from my father's will."

There was silence on the other line before Lawrence said, "Uh, Ferro, is that what all this is about? Your father's dying? Are you having some sort of personal meltdown?"

A night ago, fending off a homeless woman with a toy gun in the midst of Central Park, Ferro might have said yes. But right now, with a newfound job and money and a roof over his head, nothing could be further from the truth. "Actually, Lawrence, I haven't felt this good in some time. I think my father would be proud. But for now, I need to get back. I'll be in touch. Good night, Lawrence."

"Good night, Ferro."

"And, Lawrence…go home," Ferro added, only to be met with a dial tone, Even had Lawrence heard his boss' request, Ferro doubted the man would have heeded it. Sleep was not important to a man like Lawrence, dedication was.

Ferro closed the phone, but not before deleting the entry of his placed call so there would be no record of it. Then he stuffed it in Reynolds's pocket, and as he did so he found the bleary-eyed drunk staring right at him.

"Who are you, really?" Reynolds asked.

Ferro opted not to answer; he just got back behind the wheel of the car and pulled away from the curb. Checking the rearview mirror, Ferro glanced at Reynolds, who had his head buried back in the seat cushion. Ferro had to hope he was sleeping; he also hoped the man would forget this entire ride, from his threat to get him fired to the mysterious phone call he'd placed. The last thing Ferro needed was for his cover to be blown.

*   *   *

Ferro returned to the Curtis residence to find the house darkened, for which he was glad. He hoped everyone was either passed out or dead asleep, and that his presence didn't disturb anyone. Even though he'd known the family less than a day he was already tired of their antics and their continual verbal abuse of each other. They were among the rudest, crudest people he'd ever encountered, and he was looking forward to having a moment's peace to himself as he settled in for what would be his most comfortable night yet in New York.

Turned out not to be the case.

Climbing up the stairs and flicking the switch on the wall inside his bedroom, his eyes widened, and not just from the sudden shock of light but from what else he saw. Before he could really even react, he heard:

"It took you long enough to get back, what'd you do, take a wrong turn? That's not a very good quality in a chauffeur. Hopefully you're better at, uh, other things."

The person behind the sultry-sounding voice was none other than Hilda Curtis. In her hand she held a sizable martini glass, and it was bordering on empty. She was lying beneath the covers of his bed, and from where Ferro stood, he couldn't be sure if she was wearing anything under those blankets.

"Claude, my dear, I was beginning to think you'd made off with the family limo and we'd never see you again," she said, and then quickly drained what remained of the drink. With her remaining free hand, she reached inside the shapely glass and popped the lone olive into her mouth. She chewed, and she chewed some more, the contours of her mouth transforming into a wicked smile. Her intent was clear: she'd rather be eating him. "Glad to see I was wrong about that, what a waste it would have been to leave me all by my lonesome in your bed. A woman has needs, you know, and a specimen like you is perfect for fulfilling those long-neglected desires. Claude, you must take me—right now, and if can, all night long."

"Uh, Mrs. Curtis…"

"Ooh, that's sounds so like something out of that Mrs. Robinson movie, except for the fact that I'm considerably younger than that cougar."

"Yes, nearly young enough to be Mr. Curtis's daughter."

"Oh, trust me, I've got more than enough seasoning under my belt, more so than Nancy," she said. "And speaking of under the belt."

With that comment left dangling between them, Hilda moved lynx-like across the bedspread and grabbed hold of Ferro's belt, pulling him in tight against the edge of the bed. Though surprised by her quick motion, he was at least able to take in the fact she wasn't, in fact, naked; a sheer negligee hung from her lithe body, though it hid very little. With her kneeling on the bed, her ample bosom was just inches from his face.

"Mrs. Curtis, really, this is …"

"This is just what I need," she said. "Which means you must call me Hilda."

Poor thing, such a hideous name. Calling her by such an unattractive-sounding name just didn't add to the ambiance of the unfolding seduction. She was no Cassandra, and she certainly was no…Ferro's thoughts for some reason went directly to the dark-haired beauty he'd seen just the other night, sleeping on the sofa of her friend Vita's apartment. She'd been the definition of beautiful, more so when she slept so soundly, her hair splayed against the pillow, calling to him, transfixing him to the spot. He shook his head to clear the image. Now why would that stranger pop into his mind?

Ferro's mind returned to the present scene just as Hilda was working the buttons of his shirt. Three of them undone, she slid her hand beneath the fabric, her fingers toying with his chest hair while simultaneously seeking out his nipples. Stepping back to escape her grasp, he felt her nail scrape roughly against his skin.

Before he could inspect the damage, there came a knock on his bedroom door.

"Jesus, now what?" he said, more to himself than to Hilda. "Yes?"

"Claude?"

Ferro exchanged a look of sudden shock with Hilda. He watched as the woman of the house scrambled off the bed, looking for the perfect place to hide. It was clear she didn't want to be caught in the chauffeur's bed. No doubt that's why the others had been fired, and Nancy would no doubt love to stick it to her stepmother. He was certain she'd done it before, wouldn't hesitate to do it again. Before Ferro knew it, Hilda had slid beneath his bed, and he waited for a beat for her to get comfortable and for him to catch his breath.

Nancy knocked once again before Ferro could get back over to it.

"I'm coming."

"Not yet, I hope."

Was there something in the water that made these two so horny?

Ferro opened the door a crack, hoping to get her to go away quickly, but his efforts were to no avail. Give her an inch, she'd take a foot. Which just meant seconds later she had pushed her way inside his room and was now gently shutting the door behind her. For the second time in mere minutes Ferro found himself staring at a woman's body draped in nothing but the sheerest of nightgowns. On Nancy it didn't look as good—her body just hadn't shed its baby fat yet.

She didn't appear aware of her own physical limitations when she announced, "Surprise."

"Ms. Curtis, this really is not appropriate."

"I've changed my mind. You can call me Nancy now."

"Earlier you insisted on the more formal address."

"Oh, pooh! Don't listen to that naive little girl from before, the Nancy I become at night is a woman looking for fun and is a lot more daring."

"That's great, Nancy, it's good to experiment when you're young. But me, you know, I'm really awfully tired. It's been a long day."

Nancy's face grew pouty. "Are you telling me you don't want me?"

"I thought we covered this when I was washing down the limo."

"Oh that, phooey. That was just for my father's benefit. He was probably listening, he's nosy about everything. Actually, my father doesn't trust anyone, much less his daughter."

Or his wife, Ferro added as an afterthought.

"Now that everyone has gone to sleep and we're alone, why there's no telling what we can get up to. Though we can't be as loud as I like, just last week when Daddy was away in San Francisco getting his rocks off, this house was shaking." She sidled right up to Ferro, grinding her body against his. "But even quieter, I know what I'm doing. So, let's see what else we can get up, shall we?"

"Really, Nancy, I can't."

"You know, I was so glad when Daddy asked you to take that idiot Reynolds home. He thought he was going to score with me tonight, but all along I was just doing it to tease you. Get you worked up, jealous, right? I knew once you got back and I made my way to your room, well, then the real party would begin."

Ferro was doing his best to keep his hands off her and realized in doing so he had backed up against the closet door to his bedroom. There was nowhere else to go; he was trapped. Nancy moved in tight against him again, her fingers continuing the work started by Hilda.

"What's this, a little fresh blood on your shirt?" she asked.

Ferro looked down to see what she was talking about. Yup, Hilda had scratched his chest to the point where it had drawn a little bubble of blood, enough to stain his shirt. Nancy began to undo the next couple of buttons, her lips touching the graze on his chest.

"I'll make it all better," she said.

This was really going too far. Ferro took hold of her wrists to keep her from making any other sudden moves. Honestly, how much more rejection could she endure? Couldn't she get the message that Ferro wasn't interested and maybe Hilda, hiding beneath the bed, would receive it as well.

"I can't begin to tell you how much I want you."

"Good," Ferro said, "keep it that way. Don't tell me."

Nancy laughed; her chubby body jiggled at the motion.

A sharp knock once again (twice again?) came at his door. Ferro looked up, and Nancy looked over, and he imagined Hilda too had to turn her head toward the door. With the three of them already inside the bedroom, there was really little question in Ferro's mind about who was knocking. God, was Doris drinking the water, too? Still, he had to ask who was there.

Otherwise the jig could be up for all of them, and Ferro for one didn't relish getting fired before he'd even driven Curtis once.

"Who. Is. It." Ferro treated each word like its own declarative sentence.

"Claude, it is Mr. Curtis. I need to speak with you."

Nancy gazed up at Ferro and succinctly said, "Oh, shit. He'll kill me—and you—if he finds me here. Dressed like this. Daddy may be many things, but stupid is not one of them."

Ferro disagreed, but decided this wasn't the time.

Nancy dropped to the floor and made to scramble under the bed, but before she could get a leg under Ferro grabbed her arm and pulled her up. "No, no, you mustn't, you can't hide there. It could be filthy, right, dusty under the bed? You could sneeze and then where would we be? He'd hear you. Quick, inside the closet."

Ferro shoved the plump girl inside and quickly closed the door just in time. Curtis wasn't the kind of man to stand on ceremony in his own house, he'd knocked, and he'd announced himself, but damn if he was going to wait to be invited into the room. Ferro turned in time to see Curtis closing the door behind him. Okay, no sheer negligee this time, thank God, just the sixty-ish man with his balding head gleaming and his body wrapped inside an expensive flowery silk robe that could have come from the Orient. A strange choice, Ferro thought.

"Ah, Claude. I heard you pull in a while ago," he said. "Thought this was as good a time as any to have ourselves a little chat."

"With all due respect, Mr. Curtis, could this wait until tomorrow? It's been a really long day, and it's already inching toward morning."

"No, this can't wait," Curtis said. "I'm your boss, and you do as I say. Period."

Clearing having this little talk at this late hour wasn't subject to debate. Ferro wasn't used to having someone use such a word on him; he was used to saying it. Still, he had to remind himself that he was the employee and as such subject to his boss's whims, no matter the hour. Didn't Ferro himself expect the same of his people? How else to explain Lawrence always being ready, willing, and suited, no matter the time. For a fleeting second, Ferro wondered if his employees thought of Ferro as a callous, uncaring, and unforgiving boss? Was Ferro just like Curtis? The thought horrified him.

As Curtis sat on the edge of the bed, he indicated for Ferro to join him. A simple pat on the bed, that's the only motion he had. "Let's sit. Take a load off."

Hesitantly, Ferro moved closer and pressed his body down on the bed's edge. Combined with Curtis's weight, he wondered if Hilda was still breathing under there.

"Claude, I like to feel that you are more than just an employee."

"That's very kind of you, sir."

"When I'm interested in someone, I like to get to know them."

"Indeed, sir," Ferro said, wondering just what the hell was going on. Interested?

That's when he felt Curtis's hand land on his knee; he squeezed it gently. "Intimately," the man said, his voice barely above a whisper.

"Mr. Curtis," Ferro started to say, and then stopped. Was there anything he could say that didn't sound ridiculous, inappropriate, or worse, would get him fired? Never before in his life had he felt so uncomfortable, and so utterly trapped. There were three people in his room, all related, and in the course of thirty minutes all of them had tried to seduce him. The apple not falling far from the tree suddenly looked like an orchard littered with discarded fruit.

"Claude, you mustn't be nervous," Curtis said, his hand sliding up Ferro's leg. His other hand came to the final two buttons of Ferro's shirt, and with surprising agility the older man had them undone and was peeling Ferro's shirt off his shoulders.

Ferro pulled back instinctively as Curtis's hand brushed against his chest. The man seemed pleased at getting a nice feel of Ferro's taut, developed pecs, his face a mix of tortured lust and shameful guilt.

"Mr. Curtis, look, I appreciate the opportunity you've provided for me, giving me the job on such short notice and… well, I like you, too. I like your whole family," he said, knowing the so-called whole family could hear him. His mind was racing, looking for the perfect way out of this situation. "Being thought of as part of your family, well, for a man in my condition it's just such a welcome feeling."

Curtis's eyes blazed at him.

"Condition? Wanna explain that one?"

"I have a hard time talking about it. My doctor says it's all going to be cleared up."

Ferro felt his boss move just slightly away from him.

"Oh, sir, you have nothing to fear, it's nothing contagious… anymore. But I do need to abstain for a considerable period, just to make sure everything is back to normal function."

Curtis stood from the bed quickly, sliding his hands into the deep pockets of his robe. They might have buried deeper had the material allowed for it. Probably he wished all of him could disappear into the folds of the material, as though this hadn't happened, he wasn't here. Ferro could almost see the man cringing inside his own skin. *Now you know how I feel*, he thought.

"Claude, we'll talk some other time, get this matter cleared up. I think it's time we turned in. Uh, separately, of course," he said, his voice and mannerisms suddenly clunky and awkward. "We've got a big day ahead of us tomorrow, get some rest."

Faster than he'd undone the buttons of Ferro's shirt, he was gone from the bedroom.

That's when Nancy emerged from the closet, her hands covering her mouth to keep her laughter from bursting forth. "Oh my God. Guess I'm not the only one coming out of the closet."

"You didn't know?" Ferro asked.

"Hardly. Though you're gorgeous enough to turn even the Pope gay," she said. "But I'm glad you didn't choose him over me, gives a girl hope, you know?"

Wasting no more time, Nancy pulled Ferro's shirt off his shoulders and began sucking his neck, her mouth drifting down to his nipples. With more force than he intended, Ferro pushed the girl away and stood up, taking a few steps backward to get some distance between them.

Nancy was not amused. "Listen to me, Claude, I don't give up so easily. You may have scorned me tonight, but you'll be mine, and you'll love it. And as to whatever's wrong with you, like you mentioned to Daddy, it's either a total lie and I'll expose it—or I'll fix what ails you. I'm damn good in bed. I'll have you seeing stars when you're inside me."

"Actually, Nancy, what you can do for me is leave."

"You're throwing me out of my own home? Nobody does that—especially the hired help. Who do you think you are? You'll pay for this."

"Your father is my boss," Ferro said, "and I think it's pretty clear that he will look out for me. If you know what I mean."

Nancy bore a look of utter surprise at his insolence. She thought she could have control over Claude. After all, what kind of help talked back to the people paying him? Problem was, this wasn't Claude talking, it was the real Ferro, and he was tired, tired of these come-ons and this ridiculous family. He had no trouble diving from the highest deck, and as far as he was concerned Nancy was in over her head. Better for her to return to the shallow end.

"Just get out of my room, please, Ms. Curtis. You are only making things worse."

"Like I said, you'll pay. Either with your job, or your cock. Eventually. You'll see."

As Nancy stormed off, Ferro closed the door and turned the lock, finally glad to be free of the crazy Curtis clan. But of course, he wasn't alone, there was still one of them inside, like a nest of rats he couldn't get rid of. Hilda slid out from underneath the bed, and she was not only laughing, she was applauding.

"Oh, I haven't had such fun in years."

"Look, Hilda, I'm really not in the mood for what you want."

"Oh, relax, Claude, you're safe—for now. After everything that's gone in this room tonight, the last thing I'd do is try and seduce you again. Besides, I don't think I'd be able to get the image out of my mind of you and old man Curtis going at it. I know firsthand he likes them young. I just never knew he liked them with penises, too."

Hilda patted Ferro's cheek, and then she too made her exit.

As for Ferro, he was more than ready to call it a night. But the events of the last hour had left him drained and thirsty. Padding down to the kitchen— thankfully being stopped by none of the Curtis family, all of them tucked inside their respective bedrooms—he opened the large refrigerator and withdrew a bottle of chilled water. He sucked it down in one gulp, relishing the cold, clean taste. He almost felt refreshed, though he knew only a shower would truly cleanse him of this night.

As he set the bottle down on the counter, he noticed a small Maltese dog staring up at him. He hadn't previously known the family had a dog; they must have kept him locked up during the party to not intrude. Ferro considered the idea that maybe the dog was a stray and had somehow found its way into the house. But then the dog began humping his leg.

"Nope, definitely related," Ferro said aloud.

Morning couldn't come soon enough.

CHAPTER THIRTEEN

WAITING FOR MORNING TURNED OUT TO be a mixed blessing. Sure, he was one day closer to completing his father's wish, but that didn't mean it was going to get any easier. In the safety of his attic room, Ferro knew he could handle anything, Reality, though, was setting in, in what was his first full day as Stan Curtis's chauffeur and all-around punching bag.

"What the hell are you waiting for? Drive! That's why I hired you!"

It had been that way as soon as they'd pulled out of the turnabout and merged with the rest of the traffic.

"Sir, it's a red light."

"Excuses don't interest me. Just make it change to green!" Curtis bellowed, holding his cell phone with one hand and waving the other in Ferro's general direction like a magic wand. "Anyone can sit in traffic, but I'm not anyone! There's business to take care of, deals to seal, and I can't do it all over the phone. Ever hear of the personal touch?"

Ferro felt bad for those on the receiving end of such attention from Curtis.

"Damn idiots, I hire," Curtis muttered.

That last bit was spoken into the receiver of the phone, but its impact was felt directly in the front seat.

Okay, so far, the first morning of his new job was off to a less than stellar start. *Maybe Curtis wasn't really a morning person,* Ferro opined. Even as the thought passed through Ferro's brain, he knew it was utter bullshit. He'd seen this guy in action now several times, and after each incident he'd been left with the same impression: Curtis was just an asshole, happy only when making other people miserable. And given the events of last night and from his family's sudden perspective, he was a closeted asshole.

Ferro had said nothing about last night and neither had Curtis. They had each played their roles this morning, Ferro donning his chauffeur outfit for the first time and holding open the rear door as Curtis came barreling out of his home, ready to attack the day's work. That had been a few short minutes ago, and now, with the light changing to green and the Town Car finally surging into the daily rush, Curtis went back to screaming into his cell phone instead of at Ferro.

"Yeah, I'm back—of course, I'm back. I never went any-where, I just had to pass along some instructions to my new hire. Hired a chauffeur who lets things like traffic get in his way, can you imagine? Yeah, forget that, you better just focus on that apartment building out in Bayside. I want those repairs done quickly and cheaply," Curtis was saying into his phone. He paused, only to follow up the silence on his end with, "Oh, you don't say. Well, that's very interesting. Yes, I'll discuss it with him. And in the meantime, you can do two things for me: keep your hands on the job—and off my daughter!"

Curtis tossed the phone onto the seat beside him, appar-ently done with his call. So much for niceties like "goodbye."

At least Ferro now knew who he'd been on the phone with. Reynolds, the horny drunk from the party. He wondered what the old goat had to say. He didn't have to wait long.

"Oh, Claude?"

"Sir?" Ferro said, angling his neck to give the appearance of listening to his boss.

"Mr. Reynolds wasn't exactly pleased with the service last night."

"I'm sorry, I'm not sure I understand."

"He says you were rude."

"If rude is pulling over to the side of the road so he can puke his guts out on the shoulder instead of inside your car—which by the way, I washed inside and out yesterday afternoon—then by all means consider me rude."

"Hmmph," Curtis said.

Ferro hoped that was all.

It wasn't.

"He also said you borrowed his phone, made an interesting call."

"I was merely passing the time while Mr. Reynolds recovered from his, uh, purging. Honestly, I didn't think it would be a problem, most people's cell phone plans have unlimited data, it's not like it cost him anything. I wanted to assure a friend of mine that I had made it to New York safely and that I had found gainful employment. Once I'm up on my own two feet I can secure my own phone, and it will never happen again. I apologize if I stepped out of line."

"Uh-huh, sounds good," Curtis said dubiously. "Except, how exactly does that explain your talk of stocks and buyouts and bonuses?"

"I'm not sure I follow, Mr. Curtis."

"Reynolds says he overheard something about you offering up employees' bonuses."

"Mr. Reynolds does not recollect the conversation correctly," Ferro said, trying to talk his way out of his first jam. He'd thought he was safe last night, that Reynolds was too drunk or passed out to remember his even having made a call, that's why he had deleted the entry. "At the party Mr. Reynolds was standing beside me while we watched a news report on the television about my previous boss, Mr. Olivetti, who had just sealed some important deal. Perhaps that's what he was referring to?"

"Hmm," Curtis said, his third non-word answer. "You've got an answer for everything, don't you, Claude?"

"Not answers, sir. Just the truth."

This time Curtis didn't respond. He just gave Ferro a long, lingering look, and then when Ferro raised an eyebrow in question, Curtis suddenly looked away. Perhaps Curtis himself didn't remember what he'd done last night, feeling up Ferro, had he too been very drunk? He didn't think so, that's why Curtis looked away now. So, Ferro spent the next few uncomfortably silent minutes pushing toward the Manhattan skyline, fighting against oncoming cars, cabs and Long Island commuters who changed lanes like some people changed their minds. For a second Ferro thought about the kind of driving he preferred—airplanes, with the sky all to himself. This traffic was for the birds.

At last, they inched their way through the E-Z Pass toll at the entrance to the Midtown Tunnel, and before long Ferro was driving the car into the tunnel's engorged mouth, where cars were being swallowed into its encroaching darkness with regularity. Between the industrial-like yellow lights of the tunnel and the tinted windows of the Town Car, the inside of the car noticeably dimmed. Ferro gazed back, saw his boss stirring from his silence.

"Uh, Claude?" he suddenly said, his voice a near whisper.

"Sir?"

"About what transpired last night…"

Ferro said nothing at first, he just concentrated on the road ahead of him. "Sir, I'm sure I have no idea what you're talking about. I drove Mr. Reynolds home, then returned to your house, where I parked the car and promptly fell asleep in my room. My dreams were plentiful, as they tend to be when in new surroundings, peopled with everyone I've met, so I'm not even sure what's real and my mind imagined."

There was a noticeable pause from the back seat. Then came a declarative and final, "Good. Glad we understand each other, Claude. Keep up the good work, you'll go far with me."

Ferro chose not to comment on the unintended double entendre.

Curtis dug into his briefcase and tossed a small brown envelope through the divider that separated boss from employee, driver from passenger. It landed with a gentle thud on the front seat.

"Sir, what's this?"

"An early paycheck. Get yourself a phone or whatever else you need."

"Appreciated, Mr. Curtis."

"Discretion is important to me, Claude."

"Noted, sir," Ferro said. "Next stop, your office."

"About fricking time, some days I think I'll never make it in. Why other people can't just take the train with the great unwashed, I'll never know," Curtis said, his voice returning to full strength—and full attitude. Ferro had to grin; as much as he disliked this guy, he certainly allowed his emotions to dictate his moods, and his words. All of which made a man like Curtis easier to figure out than most.

Who knows, Ferro thought, *this job could be interesting yet.*

Curtis Real Estate Agency was located on Madison Avenue and Fifty-Fourth Street, on the fourth floor of an old-style office tower that rose up twenty-five floors toward a blue sky that today rivaled any lush spring day the city could conjure. Several companies occupied the numerous floors in the building, with the lobby offering up an extensive electronic directory of lawyers, accountants, advertising agencies, and, of course, real estate agencies. With Curtis quickly leading the way, Ferro followed him into the elevator, bypassing the security guard with an easy, acknowledged nod.

A minute later the elevator arrived at their floor, and Curtis stepped off with Ferro striding directly behind him. He was reminded of his return weeks ago to Olivetti Enterprises, how he'd stopped to say hello to the lobby guard, the woman who worked reception on his floor. No such treatment here from

Curtis, he just barreled forth. Ferro did the same, but suddenly his feet failed him, and he nearly tripped. That's because his wide eyes had immediately fallen on one particular employee who forced them open. She was busy with the copy machine, but even with her back to him she was easily recognizable. Ferro's beauty radar was legendary. But his expression betrayed him. What the hell was she doing here?

"Since you're here, Claude, you may as well meet the team," Curtis was saying. "You never know when I might call upon you to drive one of my agents somewhere."

Ferro thought this to himself: I've already met one member of your staff.

Still, the fact that the woman from Vita's apartment was here gave him pause. What if she exposed him for the fraud that he was? Not that she knew anything about him, just what he'd told Vita and what he'd told Vita had all been a lie. He was Claude Reneau, that's all. He had nothing to fear.

Curtis began to bellow through the open office, "Hey everyone, get your butts over here. Someone you need to meet."

Ferro realized there was no escape. He was trapped. Even if she didn't say anything, she was bound to remember him. Their meeting, their confrontation, had been memorable.

Just then a woman came scurrying up to Curtis, telling him there was a problem with one of his penthouse listings in the "new building." Curtis went dashing off in a huff, for the moment saving Ferro from possible embarrassment. Who knows, perhaps he could escape this situation after all. Curtis may just forget the introductions in light of the fire he had to put out. Hadn't things been falling his way in the last twenty-four hours? The Vodell deal going through, securing the job with Curtis, gaining a roof over his head, and now, in his pocket, some good old-fashioned cash. So why should he worry about a woman he barely knew, who barely knew him. He stole a look back at her, dressed in a nicely tailored business suit, a far cry from the sleepwear he easily recalled.

He still liked what he saw.

"Claude!"

Ferro picked up the pace and trailed after his booming boss, allowing himself to hide in the sanctity of Cutis's office without having attracted much attention. Safe, for now.

*   *   *

Ferro might have escaped the introductions at the Curtis Real Estate employees.

But that doesn't mean they didn't notice him.

"Okay, I've died and gone to heaven, and girlfriend, God is just as I've always suspected in my fantasies: an Italian stud with looks to spare, and one hundred percent yummy."

"I don't know if we should call you disgusting or just blasphemous."

"Honey, right now, you can call me Mrs. Whatever-His-Name-Is."

"Hey, Timothy, you wanna close your mouth, you're dripping all over the floor."

"Give me something to close my mouth around and I will."

"Okay, I think I've heard more than enough. Couldn't I call that sexual harassment?"

Bouts of laughter then pealed throughout those who were assembled near the small enclave of cubicles; they were all grinning at each other and enjoying the rare light mood in the office. Leave it to Timothy, who was as flamboyant as they came, and was always a good source of entertainment. He always said what the rest of them were thinking. But the frivolity would be short-lived. Another woman joined them, her arms carrying a thick stack of portfolios. She'd been busy at the copying machine, but that didn't mean she hadn't heard what they were saying.

"You better not let Mr. Curtis hear all this girly gossip," she said. "You know he hasn't been in the best of moods since he returned from San Francisco."

"Curtis hasn't been in a good mood since he was born. Momma's twat was too tight, squeezed his head something awful."

"Timothy! That's disgusting!" the woman said.

Another woman interjected and warned, "Timothy, keep up that kind of talk in the office and Mr. Curtis will fire your ass as soon as look at it."

"And trust me, he looks at it," Timothy said.

"Oh my God, here we go again."

It was a typical day in the bullpen of the Curtis Real Estate Agency, with three of the main agents bantering back and forth like it was a new Olympic sport, and the last of them taking on the role of responsible coach—or perhaps judge was more appropriate.

Timothy put his hands on his hips and frowned. "Diane, you always know how to spoil all the fun. Girl, you gotta lighten up."

Dark-haired, serious-minded, and the senior agent within the rag-tag bunch, Diane Mancini tossed her junior co-worker a sneering jab. "That's because I have work on the brain, you know, what we're supposed to be doing here. Making money, not spreading rumors. And while the work isn't always fun, it does pay the bills, right?"

"What do you know about bills? You live with your parents."

Diane visibly flinched at that remark. "Whoa, even for you, Timothy, that one hits below the belt."

He was of course ready with another retort, but fortunately one of the other girls reached over and placed a protective hand over his mouth. No more (so he thought) witty rejoinders. "Don't even think it," came her friendly warning.

As Diane settled inside her cubicle, the pile of papers sounding like a heavy sigh as they hit the desk, she looked over at her three co-workers—friends, really—and wondered why she hadn't learned to take a joke. Even one of Timothy's, lame and suggestive as they were. Maybe it was because she knew Curtis liked to run a tight ship, and that in his absence last week he had placed a lot of responsibility on her. He may be back, but that didn't lessen the fact that she was more senior than any of the others, and with that should come an air of respect. If she was to be the de facto boss when he was away, then she had to maintain a level of professional conduct among the other agents even when he was here. Didn't she? Then how come she always felt stressed out and the rest of them could laugh off even the worst tragedy? What would it hurt to indulge them a bit? What would it hurt to laugh once in a while?

"Okay," she said. "I'll bite. Obviously, I missed something that got Timothy panties in a bunch. What happened?"

"It was nothing," said a woman named Jennifer Robbins.

Jennifer was the most stylish of them all, a late thirties African-American woman who had run from her impoverished past, re-educated herself, got her realtor's license, and landed herself a job with Curtis Real Estate nearly two years ago. She was good, dependable, and the one to quickly side with Diane when the gossip got too much out of hand.

"Nothing?" Timothy said, "My God, did you see him?"

"Who?" Diane asked.

Timothy Nolan, late twenties, gym-fit and small-boned, what many would call "boyish" and "cute," was practically leaping out of his seat. "Mr. Curtis's new driver. Okay, since yum is my new word of the week, this guy…first of all, his uniform fit perfectly, like it was painted on his tight body rather than clothed. And he was slim and muscled and that dark hair. Oh, did I forget to say he was Italian?"

"I think that's where this thing started," said the fourth member of their team. She was Sandra Wells, the oldest of the bunch but the one more likely to engage in dirty-talk behavior with Timothy. Like siding with Timothy kept her young at heart. She'd worked long enough to know that if you were going to get through eight, nine, ten-hour days, you needed a little levity to break the tension. Especially when you had a cretinous boss like Curtis. "And yes, the guy definitely fit into the yummy category, Timothy's right about that."

"Well, I'm sorry I missed him," Diane said, her voice taking on noticeable lack of interest. "Like I said, I was working, trying to get this listing ready. The office is hardly the place to go looking for a relationship—much less a one-nighter that puts your job in jeopardy." That last part was directed solely at Timothy. "Which reminds me, Timothy, can you take a look at the Xerox machine? Some paper jammed, and I don't think I got it all out of the machine. The next person who goes to use it will find it not working."

"Why do I have to fix it? Do these hands look like they do manual labor?"

That was a good point. Timothy joined them all once a week for manicures.

"Maybe your yummy new Italian chauffeur prefers guys who know how to use their hands," Sandra interjected, a wide smile brightening her dour face. "Imagine his reaction seeing you getting those hands dirty with copier toner. Pulling out the paper that's stuck. Maybe break a sweat."

"Ooh, like we've started shooting the opening scene of a porno, let me at that pesky Xerox machine," Timothy said, and then went bounding off to the corner of the office to see about the oft-malfunctioning beast. He would tame it, or it would tame him. Either way, he was happy.

"God, he's a handful sometimes," Jennifer said.

This time, Diane allowed herself a laugh.

"Finally something I agree with."

Everyone got back to work, answering and typing emails and placing phone calls to prospective clients and those already signed on board who were eagerly awaiting new listings or closing dates or estimates. Before long the childish antics were forgotten, and Curtis Real Estate was busy going about its intended business of making money.

Diane was consumed with one particular account: a

penthouse she'd been trying to get her new client interested in taking, but they were haggling over the price, which he thought in this economy should be much lower. He wasn't happy with Diane's inability to get the cost down, so much so that the man had requested to speak privately—and exclusively—with Curtis. He had questioned whether Diane really knew how to close such a big deal. Now, as she worked on some less important clients (meaning cheaper deals), Diane awaited the dropping of the other shoe. She knew Curtis would be calling their client and dealing with the problem—which meant she had to deal with the consequences.

A half hour later, Diane's intercom buzzed. It was Mr. Curtis's secretary, asking for her to join him in his office. As she got up from her chair, she watched the lingering glances of her co-workers. They knew the drill, it was never a good thing to be "summoned."

"I'll be fine," she said to them, and then with trepidation in her every step, she made her way down the hallway and approached the exclusive quarters of the owner, president, and, as he was called after hours at drink sessions too numerous to count, "bully." He loved to throw around his voice and his power and watch as his employees huddled in fear. Diane steeled herself from his coming onslaught.

She knocked once, heard, "Come in," and then did as instructed.

Curtis was seated behind his desk, screaming into the phone at some poor lackey. He wasn't alone in the office. His new driver was still there, and while he had his back turned to her—seemingly looking at the listings posted on his walls— she couldn't help but agree with Timothy's assessment. Nice body, tight butt, nice everything. She felt a stirring she hadn't felt in some time. There was no denying how attractive he was and it didn't hurt to just loook. Just then he turned around and that's when Diane let out a small gasp of surprise.

Wait a minute. He looked familiar.

Him!

The man from Vita's apartment. And now here he was, her boss's driver?

How was that even possible? The world was small, but not that small. For a second, she remembered the homeless man from the other day, the way he had seemingly stalked her from the subway to her home, and she shivered at the thought that this man too was doing something similar. Before she had a chance to get her wits about her, Curtis was off the phone and looking right at her.

"Diane, what the hell's the matter with you? I've been on the phone with Mr. Richardson for the past thirty minutes and he's not at all happy with your work." Curtis suddenly stopped talking, realizing that it wasn't just he and Diane alone in the office. He turned toward the driver and said, "Uh, Claude, why don't you take the car back to the house, the Mrs. may need you to run her around town a bit. I'll be tied up at work all day anyway, just come back later to pick me up. And get that phone, so you can be reached at a moment's notice. Thank you, that will be all."

"Certainly, sir," the driver said.

As he made his way toward the door, he stopped before Diane. "We have met before, I believe," he said, and Diane knew it was true, that voice and his mannerisms were the same as they had been that strange night at Vita's apartment.

"Yes, I'm afraid so," she replied.

The man looked ready to say something else, but then apparently realized his place. He'd already been dismissed, he should clear out before he incurred the wrath of his employer, Diane thought. Apparently, he agreed. He merely nodded at her, and then left the office, gently closing the door behind him.

"Please, Ms. Mancini, have a seat. Let's chat about the importance of million-dollar deals," Curtis said.

Diane stole a look back at the closed office door and wished she could somehow be on the other side of it, even if it meant being closer to the mysterious stranger who one night was scaring the crap out of her inside her friend's apartment and another day sending eager chills throughout her body. She was a mess, a mixture of emotions, and concentration had suddenly gone out the window. She couldn't wait to call Vita and tell her. For now, though, she would have to take the brunt of Curtis's wrath.

"Mr. Curtis, Mr. Richardson is being wholly uncooperative. He expects miracles."

"So, make the miracle happen."

"Sir, with all due respect, that's not how real life works."

*   *   *

As work days went, it wasn't her finest but it wasn't her worst. She was glad, though, that it was finally coming to an end. Nearly everyone else had left already. Just Diane and Jennifer remained; Mr. Curtis had gone early, and both Sandy and Timothy had vacated the offices to take a stool at some gay bar they both liked. There they would drool over men maybe neither of them could have, and in the end, they would go home empty-handed but filled with plenty of fantasies to get them through the night.

"If all else fails, I can think about Mr. Yummy-Driver-Man," Timothy had said as they headed for the elevator.

Two more hours had passed, and darkness had fallen on the city. Diane was still in her cubicle, putting the final touches on two apartment sales she'd been pursuing lately. After the dressing down by Curtis, she had redoubled her efforts on several projects and had barely come up to breathe, much less take time for lunch or anything of a personal nature. Only Timothy's continual references to Claude offered up any kind of distraction, not that she welcomed it. Or did she? She'd certainly thought of him, in both his chauffeur's uniform and padding around Vita's apartment in his boxers. Now, finally, she was shutting down her computer—not to mention the lingering images in her mind—and thinking about going home.

"Won't your parents be mad? Usually, you're home in time for dinner with them," Jennifer said, looking up from her own computer.

"I'm how old? I think they can handle one night without their grown daughter. Besides, I've been staying at Vita's place, a little closer to the city, and it doesn't have anyone there who nags."

"Okay, geez, don't bite me head off."

"I'm sorry, Jennifer, I'm just tired."

"Then go home—to your parents, let them take care of you. I bet they have a nice piece of leftover lasagna heating in the oven. Man, you don't know how lucky you are to get home-cooked meals all the time. Tonight I think I'm having reheated ramen noodles."

"Yes, but the downside of such a good meal is I get indigestion from my mother sitting next to me, asking me when I'm going to start dating again."

"What's wrong with that? Diane, really, when are you going to make that big leap? It's got to happen sometime," Jennifer said, her tone playful and not at all looking for answers.

Still, Diane deflected the question like someone had thrown her a punch. "Look, Jen, I'll close up the office. Why not go celebrate and pick up some Chinese and a good bottle of wine? You did good today. Didn't you finally rent out the Broderick penthouse—and for a six-month commitment? That's great work, and Mr. Curtis is going to be pleased. That in addition to the other rentals and sales you've accomplished this week, I bet you'll be employee of the month."

"Oh, good. Lunch with the boss, what a reward," Jennifer said. "But thanks, Diane, I appreciate your encouragement. Maybe I will treat myself. Wine sounds nice right about now, a couple glasses. I'll see you tomorrow. Don't stay too late."

"I won't."

Jennifer cleared out, and at last Diane was alone in the office. She felt she could let out the tension that had been building inside her all day. With a heavy sigh, she leaned back in her chair and stretched her arms upward. With the overhead lights off and just a small bit of light emanating from her desk lamp, the mood was such Diane felt she could fall asleep. She could just see it, falling asleep at her desk, only to be awakened in the morning by the cawing sounds of Timothy—who was always in the office first. A second rude awakening in two days; she wasn't sure she could handle that.

And that's what got her thinking about Claude again.

Suddenly Diane was picking up the phone and dialing a number from memory.

"Vita, that you?"

"Who else would it be, you called my home. What's up, chickie? You coming over again?"

"No, uh, not tonight. Listen, you won't believe what happened today—who I ran into."

"Ooh, this sounds juicy. Do tell."

"Remember the guy we threw out of your apartment?"

"Ooh, yeah, Claude. He was pure yumminess."

Was something going on with that word lately? First Timothy, now Vita.

"He was here—at my office."

"Looking for a place to live?"

"No—he's Mr. Curtis's new chauffeur."

"Get out!"

"No, I'm totally serious. And the weird thing is, he remembered me."

"Well, of course he would remember you—men always remember the pretty ones. He and I could be the last two people on earth, and he would look at me and say it's nice to meet me. He liked you a lot more than me, that's for sure. Despite his lame claim to be gay. He was full of it, that one. So, did you talk to him?"

"No!"

"Don't get so defensive, girl. If he's working for your boss, you'll no doubt be seeing a lot of him," she said. "Which, come to think of it, that wouldn't be so bad. I wouldn't mind another chance at seeing him, and this time I mean all of him. Right down to his…"

Diane quickly interrupted her friend. "Vita, are you ever serious?"

With a quick retort that would linger far longer than she liked, Vita said back, "Diane, I think the question is: are you ever not?"

They ended their conversation a couple minutes later. Diane gathered her belongings and finally closed the office for the night. Emerging from the elevator, she said goodnight to the evening security guard, who gave her a polite nod.

A second later she heard him call her name.

"Oh, Ms. Mancini, I didn't realize you were still in the office. I would have called to let you know you have a delivery."

"I wasn't expecting anything," she said.

"That doesn't mean something didn't arrive for you anyway," the guard said.

Diane marched back to the desk to sign for her package, placing her briefcase on the desk between the building telephone and a beautiful bouquet of flowers.

"What was left for me?" she asked.

The guard just pointed to the flowers—roses, specifically, pink and vibrant in color.

"I think you must be mistaken," Diane said. No one had sent her flowers in…she did not have time to recall when it was too long ago. But when the guard indicated the card, she indeed saw her first name printed on the front. Cautious, hesitant, and maybe even a little scared, she withdrew the card and read the printed message:

"MY SINCEREST APOLOGIES FOR WAKING

SUCH A SLEEPING BEAUTY. TILL WE SEE EACH OTHER AGAIN. I HOPE IT IS SOON."

There was no signature. It didn't require one. Claude.

*   *   *

Curtis was at a business dinner, and Ferro was just waiting for the call to announce its end, so he could pick up his boss and return him to his home in Queens. Which meant Ferro had at least two hours to himself. He'd already purchased his new phone, which meant he was feeling settled in this new life of his. With the remaining cash, he'd entered a flower shop and asked about deliveries. They could handle his request with ease.

Now, at eight-thirty that night, Ferro sat in the driver's seat of the Town Car opposite the building that housed Curtis Real Estate. He'd been waiting for a good hour, and still he'd seen no sign of Diane. Surely, she hadn't left the office early. That didn't seem her speed. He looked upwards, noticed a dim light coming from the fourth floor of the building. Was that hers? How long was she planning to work? And why hadn't the guard in the lobby called up to announce that she had a delivery?

At last, the light was doused, and Ferro waited eagerly from the building. Five minutes later Diane appeared, and Ferro felt disappointment settle in his stomach. Because she held only her briefcase. No flowers. He watched as she headed down the busy sidewalk, no doubt headed to the subway or perhaps to meet friends—a man?—for drinks or dinner. Ferro couldn't be sure. How could he? He knew nothing about her, except for the fact that she intrigued him to no end. Was it something in her eyes, a vulnerable quality that called to him, that revealed someone who was uneasy about expressing her feelings?

Ferro left the car, walked back inside the lobby. The bouquet of flowers, still resting on the guard's station.

"Ah, the lady did not take them with her."

The guard shook his head. "She said she'd take them up to her office tomorrow. Guess she didn't want to carry them home."

"Did she read the card?"

"Yes."

"Thank you," Ferro said, slipping the guard five-dollar tip as thanks for the info. Then he stepped back onto the streets of Manhattan.

It was a perfect night, with twinkling stars and a light wind. Couples walked past him, holding hands, their bodies close as laughter fell from their mouths, smiles giving the city a brighter sense. He breathed deeply, feeling the air settle inside his lungs. A broad smile crossed his face. He might be alone, lost in a city where he knew no one, where he faced a future as uncertain as he'd ever felt, but that didn't mean he had nothing to smile about.

"You, Diane, are a total mystery to me," he said to the wind. "But, alas, my life is a series of mysteries already, and I am here to solve them all."

Then, for the first time since his arrival in New York, really since he'd first heard his father's strange request all those weeks ago in Rome, Ferro Olivetti was thinking thirty days wasn't going to be long enough.

PART THREE

FERRO'S PURSUIT

FOR TWO DAYS, Ferro heard nothing from Diane Mancini—not over the coincidence about finding each other again in this city of eight million people, and not about the roses he had had delivered to the offices of Curtis Real Estate, not over anything. Maybe she was busy, he tried to assure himself as he went about his own hectic schedule, driving not only Curtis wherever but Hilda and on two occasions Nancy as well, who was spending more of her father's hard-earned cash while doing a fine job of avoiding eye contract with "Claude." Still, whatever duty he performed, in the back of his mind he was thinking of the young and beautiful Diane Mancini.

The Town Car was just pulling into the circular drive of the Tudor mansion in Forest Hills; it was only three-thirty in the afternoon, but Curtis had wanted to get back before the rush hour, claiming he could catch up on paperwork at home. Ferro had been told he could spend a few hours helping Hilda with some of her home projects. He considered what those could possibly be, and no matter what he came up with he dreaded not only the work but the company.

"Oh, shit," Curtis said from the back seat of the car.

"Problem, sir?"

"Yes, I forgot my briefcase at the office. Damn, I've got some important documents in there that need my attention."

"Should I turn the car around?"

"What, are you crazy? Go all the way back to Manhattan and deal with all that traffic? Not a chance. My time is worth more than that, and so is yours, Claude."

Ferro jumped at the chance to have a moment's peace and suggested he drive back alone and retrieve the briefcase. It would spare him time with Hilda; in fact, get him away from the entire family. And perhaps give him a chance again to run into Diane.

"No, I need you here, Claude, just in case something comes up," Curtis said. "Wait, I have a better solution."

With that he picked up the phone and punched in a quick number and was on the phone with his office in seconds. He placed the call on speakerphone.

"Curtis Real Estate," a female voice said.

"Jennifer, this is Mr. Curtis, I need.."

"Uh, no, sir, this is Diane. Jennifer's gone off site to check on a rental property."

"Fine, whatever, doesn't matter who it is. Listen, Diane, I forgot my briefcase. It's on my desk, you can't miss it. Bring it to my house, pronto."

"But, Mr. Curtis…"

Her plea fell on deaf ears, and for a moment Ferro felt bad for her. This was when it was difficult working for a man like Curtis. When he wanted something, nothing else mattered, including feelings. Especially feelings. "The only 'but' I wanna know about it is yours in a taxi cab. Comprendo, Ms. Mancini?"

"Mr. Curtis, I have to leave the office early today. For a funeral. A distant relative died and I promised my parents I would attend. I cleared it yesterday with your secretary, she said she told you. I was just heading out of the office in a few minutes."

He cut her off. "You can go from here. The guy's already dead, he can wait a few more minutes. No more excuses."

He hung up the phone, where he found Claude looking back at him from the front seat.

"Something interest you there, Claude?"

"Not at all," he said, lying. Despite the circumstances, he was excited at the prospect of Diane coming to the house to return the briefcase, but he didn't want his boss to know it. "It's just she seemed upset over her deceased relative. Perhaps some sympathy."

"Claude?"

"Yes, sir?"

"You're a driver, not a therapist."

"Fine, sir. I'll just await your instructions," Ferro said through clenched teeth. Not for the first time did Ferro wonder what he would do with a man like Curtis once his thirty days were up. He could buy and sell this bully twenty times over, close his business and ruin his life. But, of course, that would leave the rest of his employees out in the cold, and hadn't they suffered enough? He would come up with something else, but all that could wait. Hilda could not, apparently.

"Talk to the wife, she'll have plenty of instructions for you," Curtis said, and then got out of the Town Car and went directly inside the house.

Ferro parked the car around the side of the house. Retreating toward the back entrance, he discovered Hilda kneeling down, her hands busy in the garden. She smiled up at him, wiggling her sizable butt as she did so.

"How about you toss on some more casual clothes, Claude. I'd love for you to get dirty with me," she said, her eyes leering at him. "In the garden."

"Let me see what Mr. Curtis wishes of me," he said, hoping she wasn't already aware of her husband's directive.

"He wishes for you to help me, he already told me you're mine for the afternoon, and I believe he already told you, too. You're not trying to make me mad, are you, Claude? I would hate to tell Stan about your insubordination. You might not like the result. Now go get changed like I said, and do it, quickly, because I want to see that cute ass of yours next to me in the garden," she said. "My begonias are pretty impatiens."

She then laughed at her flowery joke.

Ferro was able to buy twenty minutes, in which he changed into jeans and a pullover sweater (new purchases, both), grabbed a quick sandwich and a glass of water. Then, knowing he could no longer avoid the situation, he steeled himself for a game of double entendre with the neglected and horny missus. Returning outside to the bright afternoon sun, Ferro settled in to help plant a fresh bed of flowers. He'd never done much gardening, as his landscaping was always done by either his mother back home in Rome or by professionals at his villa in Napa. He wasn't all that adept at it, and thankfully after two minutes a yellow cab pulled up into the driveway and a young woman stepped out, distracting Ferro from his work. He couldn't help but stare at the lovely figure of Diane Mancini. She'd arrived, briefcase in hand.

"Hello? Earth to Claude. It's me, Hilda. Remember me?"

"Oh, what, yes, sorry."

Hilda nudged his elbow. "So, that's your type, huh? Pretty and boring."

Ferro dismissed the woman's bitchiness as jealousy, but not before he wondered what she was more envious of, his attentions toward Diane or Diane herself. He got up from his knees, wiping dirt from his jeans, saying, "That's Ms. Mancini from the office, she's come with Mr. Curtis's briefcase. Let me go bring it into the house."

"Claude, Doris can handle that."

He brazenly ignored her. This was his chance, and Hilda's petty concerns could wait.

As Ferro made his way around the front of the house, he was quickly cut off by Curtis, come to retrieve the briefcase himself. He blustered past Ferro and snatched the leather attaché from his employee with nary a thank you, ready to return inside the house when he noticed that Diane was still standing in place. But she wasn't looking at her boss anymore. Ferro was happy to note she was looking right at him.

"Diane, did you require something else?" Curtis asked.

Diane must have realized she was staring. "Oh, no, sorry, Mr. Curtis. I need to be on my way for that funeral."

"Yes, of course, I had forgotten," Curtis said with a rare case of concern. Perhaps Ferro's words had sunk in and found the small heart deep inside his chest. His brow furrowed, as though he were unfamiliar with the kindness he was experiencing. Then Ferro saw the man turn toward him. "Claude, good that you're here, you're just the man I'm looking for. Take Ms. Mancini wherever she needs."

"It will be my pleasure, sir," Ferro said, stepping forward.

"Oh, no, I couldn't possibly," Diane started to protest.

"Nonsense, you did me this big favor," Curtis said, "the least I can do is loan you my driver for a couple of hours."

By now Hilda had wandered over to the small party on the front lawn, where she expressed dissatisfaction over the changes in plans. "Curtis, Claude is busy helping me with my begonias. I need him to stay."

"You, woman, can just shut your mouth and dig yourself. Why not a grave?"

Ah, the kinder, gentler Curtis was just a passing blip.

He stormed into the house and slammed the door.

Hilda stormed off as well.

Which left Ferro alone with Diane, finally. A few moments of awkward silence fell in the space between them, the void filled only with unspoken words hidden behind their eyes. Neither seemed ready to give voice to whatever thoughts bounced around in their minds.

Finally, Diane said, "Look…uh…"

"It's Claude," he said.

But you should call me Ferro, he thought.

"Claude, yes, sorry, look, you don't have to do this. I can get myself where I'm going."

"We'll hear none of that. Of course I will take you wherever. Mr. Curtis insisted."

"Hilda didn't seem very happy to lose your services."

"Hilda is never happy. It's a family trait."

Diane actually let down her guard a moment, trying to stifle a laugh. It didn't work, and instead a small smile crossing her face gave way to a tiny laugh. *Progress*, Ferro thought, returning the smile with one of his own. It beamed in the sunlight, highlighting his dimples.

"Let me bring the car around, and we'll be off."

*   *   *

The funeral was scheduled for late afternoon in a neighborhood in Queens called Woodhaven, "located along Jamaica Avenue," Diane had instructed Ferro. She had given him the directions, but he had asked her to keep an eye out if he made a mistake, offering up his unfamiliarity with New York as his all-too-true excuse.

"The GPS sometimes sends me off in directions too complicated to follow," he said, "and I'm still learning my way around New York."

"Funny job for you, then, being a chauffeur?"

"I am a man of many talents, and a quick study," Ferro had replied, "and what I may lack in talent I make up for in drive. Or should I say driving."

It was a small enough pun, but the wordplay managed to engage her, break her from the cool efficiency she portrayed. When Diane laughed—a sound Ferro could hear repeatedly— he stole a glance in the rearview mirror, marveling at his luck to be finally alone with this lovely creature. To think that an absent-minded gesture like leaving a briefcase behind would turn the fates to his advantage—he could not have predicted such a thing, certainly not planned for it. Like much of this journey, it seemed reliant on the fates, and right now the fates were smiling as widely as Diane.

Again, he returned the smile.

"Uh, Claude, do you mind keeping your eyes on the road?" Diane suddenly asked, folding her arms across her body as she spoke.

A defensive move, Ferro surmised, but why? Had the two of them not a moment ago exchanged laughter, and wasn't laughter a first step toward friendship? Like a shared experience meant to forge a bond between two people. You would think. Now that icy barrier had returned, and Ferro could almost see the mist coming from her breath.

He went back to concentrating on his driving, cruising southbound down the wide, busy lanes of Woodhaven Boulevard. Seeking out a new way to gain back her trust, or at least to keep the conversation going, Ferro came up surprisingly empty. Opening lines and the ability to charm any woman were two of his great strengths, and never before had he felt so flustered in the presence of a woman. It's not that he was intimidated by her; in fact, he couldn't explain at all why he was so uncomfortable around her. He shifted in his seat, took one more look back. He noticed this time that she was looking at him.

He sensed another opening for conversation, and this time he went with his gut. "Ms. Mancini, I'm really sorry about what happened between us at your friend's apartment. Vita was just doing me a favor by letting me stay there. Being a bit down on my luck that day, she really helped me out. But I certainly didn't mean to startle you, or let you think I was some creep."

"I think I was more surprised to see you at Curtis's office," she said.

"A big coincidence," Ferro said.

"More like a strange one," she replied.

Ferro nodded, looking forward, still driving but still wanting to talk. "Did you like the flowers?"

"Oh, uh, yes," she said, suddenly looking down, but simultaneously adjusting her hair. "I'm sorry, I should have thanked you the other day. But you shouldn't have sent them, it was wholly unnecessary. And if you don't mind my saying so, just a tad inappropriate."

"Merely a peace offering. I know I scared you."

"Startled," she corrected him all too quickly. "I don't scare easily."

"Pink, I believe, is the color of forgiveness. That is why I chose those roses," he said.

"I'm not sure that's true," Diane responded.

Ferro shrugged. "But it sounds nice, a rose of forgiveness. Will you?"

"Will I what?"

"Forgive me, Ms. Mancini," he said, pouring on his Italian accent for added effect.

Ferro couldn't hear anything in reply and was hesitant to look back. Traffic was thick here, so he best stay focused. No need to cause a fender bender now. He suspected, though, that she was smiling back there, something she appeared to enjoy doing, and perhaps hadn't had much recently to smile over. At last, she said, "Well, if you're going to be working for Mr. Curtis, and we're going to run into each other, I suppose it would be okay if you called me Diane."

"Thank you, Diane. And I am…" He hesitated, wishing he could tell her to call him Ferro.

"Yes, I know, your name is Claude," she said.

"So, may I ask about this funeral? Who died?"

"Awful as it sounds to speak ill of the dead, a miserable old relative finally kicked the bucket. Ninety-one. A cousin of my father's, one who had turned his back on the family. He never listened to what was expected of him, just did whatever pleased him, until he ended up lonely, alone, and happy only when other people were unhappy."

"Yes, the miserable ones do tend to live the longest."

"Mr. Curtis will probably live to one hundred and fifty," Diane said, and then instantly put a hand to her mouth. "Claude, you didn't hear that."

"I am a driver, Ms. Mancini, and I hear nothing but the horns from angry drivers."

An understanding settled between them. What happened in the Town Car stayed in the Town Car. Still, Ferro was struck by her words, not just the meaning as it related to his own recent experiences with family, with death, with responsibility, but also the passion he heard in her voice. She was not a woman to be wronged. He sensed a larger betrayal could not be won back with even ten dozen pink roses.

"Why go to the funeral?"

"I guess out of some sort of obligation."

"May I ask. Would you mind if I joined you?"

"You're kidding. Why would you want to do that?"

"I too take family seriously. You and I, Ms. Mancini, are not unalike."

"Diane, remember?" she stated.

"My apologies. Diane," Ferro said, a grin spreading across his face.

"What about Mr. Curtis? Don't you need to get back to him? Or Hilda?"

"He'll call if he needs me, and trust me, I welcome the chance to escape from Hilda. She has hands that, how do you say, wander?" Ferro said. "Besides, Mr. Curtis knows I am helping one of his trusted employees. And at his own request. He won't care how long I am gone. And speaking of, I wonder, too, if you would, after the funeral, permit me to buy you coffee?"

"Oh, Claude, I'm not sure that would be right."

"It is just coffee. It would please me very much to be able to talk with you. I am new to this city, and part of me wonders what I am doing here. I seek only advice on the city and its challenges."

"Why not," Diane said. "As you said, it's just coffee."

So that's what it took to melt some of her ice, the promise of a hot, steaming cup of java. Ferro for one couldn't wait for this funeral to be over, the sooner they buried this guy the sooner the living could resume one of life's more beautiful experiences: the exchange of words and ideas by a man and woman just discovering each other. In other words, a date.

*   *   *

The funeral, such as it was, was one for the ages. With Diane and Ferro sitting in a rear pew at St. Thomas the Apostle Church, the ceremony began with the priest tripping as he approached the casket, nearly knocking it over, and it ended with not one single person volunteering to offer up a eulogy. In between, the priest—who was suffering from a bad head cold—offered up prayers and sneezes with near regularity, giving the entire funeral an odd, comical touch. It didn't help that there were so few people in attendance, which only reinforced the old priest's illness. His coughs and sneezes echoed long in the caverns of the ornate church.

It also didn't help that the priest couldn't remember the name of the deceased.

"Franco Cantorini," prompted someone from the front row, after seeing the priest shuffle through his paperwork to find the name with no avail.

"Yes, yes, we mourn the death of Ms. Francis Franco Cantolini," he said distantly. "She will be missed."

Ferro, leaning over to Diane, whispered into her ear. "Not only does he not know the deceased, he's just changed him to a her. Now, that's a way to go."

"Sshh," Diane said, suppressing a giggle.

It was her relative, distant as he was, and she should feel bad. But she also suspected that all the bad things the man had done in his life had led to this moment: a send-off worthy of a sitcom. And a lesson for those few in attendance: live your life generously and in death that generosity will be repaid.

After a torturous thirty minutes, the funeral mass was coming to an end as inevitable as death. As the priest said, "He is joining his beloved wife who died last year, and who was worth her weight in gold. Him, maybe silver."

A deafening sneeze rang through the church.

"Before we conclude, is there anyone here who would want to say a few words on the life of…?"

"Cantorini! Franco Cantorini," chimed the same person who'd spoken up at the start of the mass. Apparently, he was the only person here actually familiar with the deceased.

"Yes, yes, of course, Mr. Franco Cantorini," the priest said, addressing the lone man in the front row. "Perhaps you would like to speak of him?"

"Only ill," the man said.

No one else dared to speak up, and so the bumbling priest issued his benedictions before the closed casket, and suddenly the mass was over and poor, neglected, unloved Mr. Franco Cantorini was on his way to his final resting place. Diane did not offer up a decision on where that might be.

As they emerged into the fading light of day, they did their best to hold off on their laughter, knowing it was both cruel yet appropriate. Diane mentioned that had her cousin been witness to his own funeral, he would have been yelling up and down the aisles, clearly not happy with the way the world sent him off. Ferro offered her a handkerchief and she took it, wiping her eyes either from tears or laughter or sadness, and then in a seemingly mock version of the priest, she sneezed loudly into the silk fabric. Just then the priest came up beside her and offered her a gentle embrace.

"There, there, he's in a better place."

They all watched as the casket was loaded into the back of the gleaming black hearse, and with that the priest retreated into the church, and Ferro and Diane made their way down the narrow street to where the car was parked. It didn't appear anyone was headed for the burial other than the employees of the funeral home.

"Oh my God, can you believe what we just witnessed?"

"I believe the word you are looking for is surreal," he said. "Some experience. Should I thank you for sharing it all with me?"

"Claude, you just made it worse! I couldn't keep a straight face."

"Laughter reminds us that we are alive."

"Yes, and poor cousin Franco was certainly not laughing."

As they talked, Ferro opened the rear door of the car and waited for Diane to settle in before they found a spot for their coffee date. But she hesitated instead, giving him a strange look.

"What is it?"

"I feel funny, sitting in the back. I mean, you're not my driver. I should sit up front."

"And as Mr. Curtis's employee, I believe you have earned the right to sit in the back and enjoy the service I provide. Otherwise, it would feel disrespectful, not just to my boss and to the job, but mostly to you, a lovely lady who deserves to be spoiled."

"That's very sweet, Claude. I'll tell you what, let's forego the ride and find a coffee shop nearby. Jamaica Avenue is only a block away from the church, surely there must be a few places we could choose from."

"That sounds like a plan."

They walked up to the busy avenue, where the elevated subway trains rumbled past them with surprising speed and noise loud enough to drown out the most annoying car alarm. Horns honked from the traffic, people yelled across the street and spoke into cell phones and listened to music that was plugged into their ears. All of it served as white noise to the two people who walked silently but companionably until they came to a small corner coffee shop called "Eddie's." Holding the door open, Claude escorted Diane inside before settling into a nearby booth. The diner was not fancy at all, which probably meant the coffee was spectacular. Places like this, old mom-and-pop operations that had been around for decades, they knew what mattered most to its customers: quality, service, not style and high prices.

Before they could even order, a waitress arrived with menus and two fresh, steaming cups of coffee.

"Wow, what service," Ferro said.

"Even folks who don't drink coffee come here for our coffee," the woman said. "It's real, honest, and it doesn't cost ten bucks," she said, indicating with her whittled-down pencil the place directly across the street. It was a Starbucks, of course. Ferro took a quick sip of the coffee and smiled up at the waitress.

"Perfect."

"I'll give you a couple of minutes to decide what you want," she said, and then left the two of them alone.

That was the other thing about a place like this: they didn't like to rush their customers, especially when it looked as though the customers were in no hurry to leave. Unbeknownst to them, Ferro and Diane had come in with such a look.

As they drank their coffee, Ferro found his date staring at him.

"Is there something on your mind?" he asked.

"It's nothing. It's just, well, it's funny. You don't look like a chauffeur."

"I pull it off much better when I'm in uniform."

"And you also like to defuse situations with humor," she said. "Claude, you're more than a little mysterious. All this time we've spent together, I still only know your first name."

"Reneau," he said. "I am Claude Michel Reneau."

"French, really? You sound so Italian to me—and trust me, with a name like Mancini and with parents like I've got, you get to know Italian. Though sometimes the accent comes with a smack to the side of the head."

"Ah yes, I am familiar with the concept. My mother is Italian," Ferro said.

"Aha, an explanation that comes with even more mystery," she said. "Okay, I'll let it go—for now. So, tell me, Claude Reneau, what is it about you that gives you that air of mystery? Wait, let me guess. You're on the run from the law."

Ferro laughed lightly, recalling briefly his mishap days ago with the NYPD. "No, I've never had any trouble with the law."

"You don't sound very convincing on that issue, Claude."

"Oh, it was nothing. Just a misunderstanding with the local police when I arrived in New York last week. It was all cleared up in a matter of hours, and none of us were any worse for wear, as they say. As to the specific details, it is a long story, and one that is unexciting. I would prefer instead to talk about you."

"Speaking of unexciting," she said, retreating a bit into the safety of her coffee cup. She practically buried her face inside the cup to avoid any further discussion on the subject.

"I hardly think that's the case."

"Oh, I've got a smooth talker sitting here with me, don't I?" she stated. "As you say, Claude, it's a long story."

"It may take all night for us to tell each other our long stories," Ferro said, not at all opposed to the idea.

Their conversation was interrupted with the arrival of the waitress with a quick refill. As fast as she had appeared, she was gone again. But the quiet disruption had brought their talk to a halt, and for a few lingering moments nothing was said between them. Instead, Ferro was locked in a study of her eyes; they were dark, like drops of chocolate and just as appetizing. Before he knew it, a grin was spreading across his face, and a strange sense of calm overtook the nerves that had been bouncing around inside him. Like an electric charge given a new spark. His dormant instincts were reborn with Ferro stretching his hand across the table, as if to take hold of hers. Immediately she pulled back.

"What is wrong?" Ferro asked. "Something I said?"

"More like what you didn't say," Diane responded.

"I'm not sure I understand."

"You were so quiet suddenly, and you were just staring at me. I suppose, I don't know, I felt as though you were looking right through me."

"More like looking into you, into your soul," Ferro said, his voice filled with the first taste of true honesty he felt between them. There was no evidence that this was a line of his; in fact, it had sounded as foreign to Ferro as it had been to Diane. "Each time I have seen you, it has been either in the dark of the night, across a crowded office, or through the lens of a rearview mirror, Now, though, I am getting my first real look at you, face to face, neither of us distracted by Vita or Curtis's boorish behavior. It's just you and me."

"That's the problem," Diane said. "I'm not accustomed to there being a 'you and me.'"

"You make that sound like something bad."

"Claude, I hardly know you. A part of me cannot believe I'm even sitting here with you. Don't get me wrong, you've been a perfect gentleman, and I appreciate that more than I can say. It's just I get a sense that…" She hesitated, as though she swallowed the words that nearly came off her tongue.

"What do you wish to say? Please, Diane, finish your thought."

"I'm just not sure who I'm sitting across from."

"Again, I don't understand what you are asking. I am Claude Reneau, and I am new to New York. And you and I have accidentally met—twice, in a city where you wouldn't normally see the same person again in your lifetime. What else is there to know?"

"You have a poetic way about you, Claude."

"My Italian mother," he said.

"What about your Italian wife?" she asked.

Ferro paused, and for a fleeting moment the image of Anna Maria came to him. The past was sneaking in, just when he didn't want it. Closing his eyes, he pushed yesterday away and then reopened them, where today was all he wanted to focus on. "There is no wife, I assure you."

"Aha, you flinched. More mystery, Claude?" she asked. "Afraid of marriage, are you?"

"Not at all, it's just I am young and love my life as it is, the fun and the freedom."

Diane nodded silently as she picked up her coffee cup, draining its contents with sudden finality. "I'm afraid we're going to have to terminate this little get-together of ours. I just don't think I'm the right personality to help you perpetuate your 'fun.' Why don't you finish up, and we can get out of here. I can take the subway, I'm not that far from my home."

"Hey, come on, Diane? What did I say? We can't proceed to a second date if we don't learn to communicate during the first. I would very much like to see you again."

"This. Is. Not. A. Date." Diane could not have sounded more emphatic in her protest.

"You said that so harshly. What's wrong with the idea of a date?"

"Nothing's wrong with the concept," she said. "But an actual date taking place, much less between you and me, is just not in the cards. Besides, I've been on my share of dates, and this surely doesn't qualify."

"Why must people persist in defining what a date is? A date can be anything you make it to be, anything you want it to be," Ferro said, his smile wide and his tone trying to keep things light and friendly. "Tell me—when was your last date? What did you do? A frame of reference would be helpful—so I know what counts as a date and what is just coffee."

"Claude, this just isn't the time to get into my past. It's a…"

"Long story, yes, you've said it."

"It's late."

Ferro sensed another shift coming in the conversation. Despite his attempts at levity, Diane had grown suddenly serious, and he didn't think he was going to get her back. He hadn't seen this torment, this despair on her face before—not even a funeral had brought out her somber side, and now here it was between them, like a fifth wheel on a limo.

"When you start to speak of your life, do you know your voice always trails off?" he said. "You want to talk, clearly, but something stops you from continuing. Please, Diane, tell me something about you, anything. I am only trying to be your friend."

"My husband…he….there I go, trailing off, as you say," she said, steeling herself, looking as though she were actually going to open up. "David was his name, and he was killed in the Afghan War. Over two years ago, but it's not been any easier now than it was then."

"I am truly sorry," Ferro said, feeling guilty for having pushed her so far. That's when he noticed the gold band on her finger—but not on the marriage hand. The effect was like Diane lived in some middle place, the nexus between a past life with her husband and the possibility, the promise, of a future. A ring to keep alive the connection she had with David, but there was this willingness to try to move on. "And perhaps you and I are not so different—I too suffered a recent loss. My father."

"Oh, Claude, I had no idea. I'm so sorry."

Ferro nodded politely. "He was seventy-eight and not in the best of health. His passing was not unexpected, but no less devastating."

"The reality and finality of death—nothing can prepare you for it, expected or not."

"I still mourn my precious Papa," Ferro said, "and I suppose this new life of mine is a direct result of that. You cannot let life pass you by, it's not what your loved ones would wish for you."

"Celebrate them by living?"

Ferro nodded. "You are very wise, Ms. Diane Mancini," he said, and this time when he reached out to hold her hand, she didn't pull it back. He felt the softness of his skin, the pulsing blood rushing through her veins. Gentle but alive, the touch helped seal a certain, unexplained bond between them.

For the next hour, they sat and drank more coffee, and they shared a slice of apple pie, and as they talked, they experienced more than a fair share of laughter and smiles. Discovering things they had in common—they were only children and both had a mutual dislike for Curtis—digressing when they stumbled upon an idea or theory that separated them. The pros and cons of living with parents, music and movies—neither of them realized the passage of time. The waitress snuck the check down on the table, perhaps a not-so-subtle suggestion that the booth might be needed for customers with more than coffee on the brain.

As Ferro reached for the check, Diane insisted on paying her part.

"Where I come from, it's not a date when both people pay," Ferro said.

"How many times do I have to tell you, Claude—this is not a date," Diane said, but her words held less definition than earlier, as though they had weakened over time, lost their power. "I have to tell you—I don't know why, but I feel so comfortable talking to you. You're a good listener, with a sympathetic ear."

"I am glad you feel that way."

"After David died, I retreated into myself and let my parents baby me, try to soothe my wounded heart. They mean well, but they can be cloying and…I don't want this to sound unappreciative, but the pitying looks—and not just from them but from Vita and other friends—they can almost be worse than the memories. Sometimes I feel so suffocated. You didn't treat me that way. You let me talk, and you supported without judging. You let me breathe. Thank you, Claude."

"It's been my pleasure," he said. "I'm glad we ran into each other like we did. Curtis should leave his briefcase at the office more often."

"Speaking of Curtis, I think it's time you got back there."

"He hasn't called for me, and besides, I can easily explain that you were required to attend the burial and the reception afterwards. I of course felt bad about leaving you there, so instead I stuck right by your side. Now, though, I will drive you home," he said. "It's the proper thing to do, even though this is not a date."

As they left the diner, Ferro slipped the kind waitress a ten-dollar tip and thanked her for her wonderful service.

"I hardly had to do anything," she said to Ferro.

"Exactly," Ferro said with a smile.

"Wow, all the good ones aren't taken, are they," the waitress said.

"Perhaps not yet," Ferro said, looking at Diane standing on the street corner. "Not yet."

CHAPTER FIFTEEN

DIANE MANCINI FELT AS THOUGH she'd been transported back in time to high school, going out on her first prom date with the cutest boy who ever roamed the halls, feeling giddy and excited at the mere thought of him. She remembered his confident swagger—and his blond hair and natural blue eyes, not at all the kind of boy her parents would have approved of. He'd been too perfect, too all-American and preppy, and didn't possess that hot-blooded Italian bent that ran through the fiery-tempered Mancini family. "Like putting a white sauce over spaghetti," was how her mother had put it that one (and only) night as the pasty-complexioned kid named Peter had posed with Diane for photographs the night of the big dance. Even David, her late husband, had been graced with light-brown hair and a large toothy grin; he had hailed from a Midwest that bred apple-cheeked, corn-fed kids. He'd owned up to a bit of Spanish blood in him from a distant relative, or so her mother had managed to get out of him one night at dinner. "We're getting hotter," had been Sophia Mancini's reply to her daughter's choice of mate. "But still no spicy meatball."

Now, what would her mother have to say about one Claude Reneau?

Was he French, was he Italian? Was he for real?

Actually, that last question, that was purely Diane's thought.

As for her mother's thumbs up or down appraisal, Diane supposed she was about to find out.

Claude had just driven off in the Town Car after having dropped her off in front of her parents' modest house; she could still see the taillights as the car turned the corner. Standing on the sidewalk, her gaze lingering until even the glow of the lights had faded from her eyes, she replayed the final moments of a night which Claude had insisted calling a date. A date, she mused, the word foreign on her lips, like a forgotten kiss. She couldn't wait to get upstairs and call Vita, fill her in on everything and get her honest opinion. Of course, with Vita, her comments had to be taken with a grain of salt. She was the one who'd picked him up at the bar and brought him home, only to see her desires quashed faster than a Viagra placebo.

Not that Diane was taken with Claude. How could she be, spending a few hours in someone's company hardly qualified as enough time to evaluate them— or yourself for that matter. Still, she reconsidered, feeling as though her shoulders were the war zone for an angel and a devil. Claude had been nothing but charming all night, none more so than their final, fleeting moments.

"I thank you for the most pleasant night of my new life," he had said.

"Thank you, too, Claude. For driving me, escorting me around and braving that horrible funeral. But most of all for the lovely conversation."

"I would enjoy continuing our conversation—soon. Perhaps Tuesday? I have been promised the day off by Mr. Curtis. He has meetings all day with a client and won't be needing me. May I see you?"

Even as he'd broached the idea, she had known her answer. She'd thought of nothing else in the car ride back from their, uh, date.

Yes, she thought.

"Yes, I would like that," she actually said, emitting a laugh that surprised herself, and the night too, echoing as it did down the narrow Queens street. Such a place wasn't used to Diane having much to laugh or smile about, not for too long. She followed up her answer with the real surprise of the night, though. She'd leaned in and kissed his rough cheek. "It's a date."

Sure, sure, deny it all you want, Mancini, she thought now, you're not the least bit intrigued by this man. Want to buy a bridge to go along with that denial? Yup, deny it all you want, that quick peck on the cheek and the promise of a date had only sent her heart aflutter and her body drifting down the path of her front door with all the effects of that school girl returning home from the big prom with the cute boy. She recalled her mother had been waiting at the door that night, too, pressing her for every detail. The funny thing about life is, the situations may change slightly, you may think you've grown up, gotten past being the child, but human behavior never does. Mother Mancini always saw to that.

"Who was that?" Sophia Mancini asked matter-of-factly, the door open for all the world to see—and hear. Her voice was loud, but her evening housecoat was louder still. Bright orange fabric with a flowery design that seemed like an afterthought. She had a closet full of them.

"That was Mr. Curtis' driver. He's new."

"Hmm. Not new enough if you know him that well. You make it a habit of kissing the driver? Most people just leave a tip."

"Mother, don't be gross."

"Does he have a name?"

Diane rolled her eyes with exasperation. "Mother, everyone has a name."

"Such a fresh mouth," she said, and then when she still didn't get the answer she wanted, wagged her finger at her daughter. "What? You kiss a man on my stoop, and I'm not allowed to ask his name? You're lucky it was me spying…uh, looking out the window, and not your father."

From inside the living room, where the television blared, her father looked up and told his wife to be quiet. "I hear my name? What are you saying, I just hear noise, and I can't hear my show. You give her the third degree every night, like she's on parole or something. Just leave the poor girl alone. If she's finally getting out, that's a good thing. You're harassing her like some shrew—how does that help things?"

Sophia dismissed her husband's comments with an easy wave of the hand. "Don't listen to him, he's always been soft when it comes to you. Me, I'm just a concerned mother looking out for her only daughter—I mean, what about that nice bank executive you helped get a new apartment, what's his name, Stanley. Oh yes, Stanley Fulbright, he's a nice man, handsome enough, and he's got a good job," she said, barely pausing for breath, much less punctuation. "You turn down any number of dates and invitations to parties from him, but suddenly now you're kissing chauffeurs goodnight? You want to explain that one to your poor mother?"

"Mother, for the last time, Stanley Fulbright is not my type," she said. "And he's not yours either. Not—what did you say—spicy enough? He's from Arkansas, for goodness' sake. And as for what Claude does for a living, I don't care that he's a chauffeur. I don't care what any man does for a living, only that he's honest about it, and honest with me."

Why was she defending herself?

Why was she defending Claude?

"Besides—using your favorite word—he's really a very nice man and did me a huge favor tonight. I liked spending time with him."

Diane's voice didn't just trail off, it stopped. Her mouth closed like a gator on its prey, intent to not let anything in—or out. She was still caught up in the moment of their surprise goodbye, and who was benefiting from this rare moment of truth but her mother? Diane kept things close to the vest, for her own protection. From men, from her mother. Some days she didn't know which she hated more.

Her mother, though, was beaming like a triumphant boxer. "So, at least I got a name out of you. Claude. Okay, I'll bite. What is he? Sounds French? At least we're getting closer to the Italian border with this one."

"Oh, Mother, why do I even bother with you?"

"What are you getting so up in arms about? I can't be curious about a man you've been out with? I send you to your cousin's funeral, and you turn it into the first date you've had since you moved back in with us. You should have invited your new friend inside, we have plenty of leftover pasta and salad. Which reminds me, there's a plate in the oven, I just need to reheat it for you."

"I'm not hungry, thanks."

Another look of protest hit her mother's inquiring face. Diane had had enough. She said her goodnights and then went upstairs to her bedroom, but not before she heard one last remark from her mother. Thankfully it was directed not at her daughter but at the man sitting in the recliner, trying to watch his show and drown out the little drama playing out before him. A quick smack to the back of his head, and then Diane heard her mother say, "You're supposed to take my side. The girl needs our support."

"Your kind of support could strangle an anaconda," he said.

Silently sending down a sorry to her father, Diane at last found refuge inside the bedroom of her youth. When she'd first returned to her parents' house last year, she had worried that she would feel too grown up, too mature for such simple surroundings. Imagining her feet dangling off the full-size bed. Instead, she'd been comforted by the medals, the trophies, the awards from her days of riding horses and swimming in meets after school, from all the activities and memories that comprised who she'd once been. Back when she was innocent and didn't know the troubles that awaited unsuspecting people. The room was a cocoon, and its purpose was only to keep her comfortable, safe. That it had done.

She wondered, and not for the first time this year, much less this week, when the butterfly inside her would once again spread its wings and fly toward something new, something exciting.

Maybe tonight had been that first flight.

But as she shed her professional skin and changed into comfortable clothes, she looked at the woman in the mirror and said, "Diane Mancini, don't you dare get ahead of yourself. It was only coffee." A stranger gazed back at her. What was different? She knew immediately but couldn't give voice to it. Still, despite her mother's intrusive behavior and nagging brand of caring, Diane Mancini was still wearing one last remnant from the day.

A smile.

That smile wavered just a bit when her door opened and her mother entered with a tray, the plate full of freshly reheated spaghetti and meatballs. Sophia set it down on the small desk, and then plopped herself down on the bed.

"I'm sorry, I know I get carried away, but it's only because I care. You know why, I know why, only your father doesn't, and it stays that way." Then her mother proved how much she earned that title, as she drew a comforting hand across her daughter's face. "So pretty, such a lovely woman you are. But right now, I've got to know. Forget your new man for the moment, we'll get back to him all in good time. Tell me every detail about the funeral," she said. "Is that miserable bastard really dead?"

Diane supposed that's what was wrong with her life. For the first time in at least as year, she had something to hope to, to cling to. But in her room, where it was supposed to be safe, death still overshadowed everything. To her, in an ironic twist, for too long it seemed romance was the thing that had died.

Did Claude represent a rebirth?

She couldn't wait to find out.

Though next Tuesday seemed so far away.

*   *   *

Impatience had never been one of Ferro's admired traits, and in the guise of Claude he was no less patient when it came to getting what he wanted, especially when it came to things beyond his control. One of those was the passage of time. But the clock turned eventually, he worked, and he slept. He set his mind to other matters, and he tried his best to downplay his upcoming date, even while mentally striking through each day of the calendar until the desired day's arrival.

After nearly a week of being at Stan Curtis's beck and call, of finding his way around the busy, confusingly numbered streets of Queens and Manhattan, Ferro had been promised, if not the entire day off, a fair portion of it. As for Diane Mancini, she had rearranged her scheduled appointments so they all took place in the morning, which allowed for the two of them to escape their mutual boss and spend a few afternoon hours together. So, things were set, right? Yes, and no. Leave it to a selfish man like Curtis, and, in effect, his entire horrible family, to disrupt such carefully cultivated plans.

"Fine, you can go, Claude—but with one caveat," Curtis warned while Ferro waited inside the man's office, his chauffeur's cap in his hand, feeling like a servant waiting for instructions. Small wonder, that's just what he was. "I expect you to have your cell phone on at all times, just in case I need you to come back and drive me somewhere. In real estate, you snooze, you sleep on the street. For now, I expect you back by eight tonight so you can take me and Nancy home."

"Nancy, sir?"

"Yes, you remember my daughter, of course?"

"Certainly, sir, that's not what I meant. I just didn't know she was in the city today."

"When is she not? Shopping for hours, spending my money, getting away from her stepmother, it's the thing spoiled teenagers do these days, and she is nothing but spoiled." Ferro wondered how the girl had gotten that way? He didn't dare give voice to his thoughts. Curtis continued. "As long as she stays out of my hair, though, I don't care what she does. But I do have to pay her bills, so I'll be working late to bring my profit level back up. There's a few deals I need to work my charms on."

That shouldn't take too long, Ferro thought.

"Thank you, sir. I appreciate the time to myself."

Curtis was busy shuffling through some papers on his desk, like he couldn't be bothered. "I don't know why you need the time off—who the heck could you know in this city after just a few days? You can barely find Manhattan with my car, now you're going to go out and find friends? Ha, good luck."

"Just trying to get myself acclimated, sir," Ferro said. "You know, I really haven't had a chance to myself since arriving in the city and taking the job with you. Not that I'm not grateful to you for the opportunity, as well as the roof over my head. The afternoon will be of great help in terms of getting settled."

"Whatever. Be gone with you," Curtis said with a wave of his arm.

Ferro wanted to smack the guy, just once. Just to put him in his place for the way he treated people, servants, co-workers, family. Hell, everyone. It amazed him still that Curtis did not remember him from the airplane, but then again, why should he? Why would he equate a man in first class with someone working as a chauffeur? Wasn't there always a divider between them, manmade or otherwise?

Holding in his feelings, Ferro started to head out of Curtis's office when he was met at the doorway by none other than Diane. He nodded to her, said, "Ms. Mancini, a fine day to you," and she did so back, saying, "Hello, Claude, nice to see you," neither of them indicating that their relationship went anywhere beyond mere acquaintances. Given Curtis's personality, he might not take kindly to any sort of fraternization between employees. Still, Ferro lingered near the open door, listening in, his heart deflating as he heard their exchange.

"Oh, Mancini, glad you came by. I've got a couple potential listings—very lucrative for us if it works out, but there's no guarantee of that. The client is a real people-oriented person, said he'll go with the agent he feels a rapport with. Idiot, that's what he is. Who the hell cares if you get along with the person, it's business, just seal the deal. But he's prickly, and I don't want to lose it. So, I need you to check on the properties, make sure they're something we want the Curtis name on. Trust between clients goes both ways, right? Quality, that's my motto."

He hadn't bothered to look up and see that Diane's face had transformed from smile to frown. Clearly, he didn't remember she had taken the afternoon off. "Can't you send Jennifer, or maybe Timothy? Our clients always enjoy working with either of them."

"Timothy? That fruit? I don't think so," Curtis stated harshly. "I called you in, I told the property manager to expect you. Add both of those things up, what do you get?"

"Me," Diane said, resignedly.

"It's good for someone in real estate to be good at math," he said snidely.

Diane went to leave when Curtis called her back.

"Usually you're all over these listings, what's with the sudden resistance?"

"I had scheduled the afternoon off, sir."

"Excuse me, since when? "

"It's on your calendar."

"Well, take it off, mine and yours. What do you think I'm running, some flex-hour crap? Curtis Real Estate is a serious business, not a place to come and go as you please, Ms. Mancini, so I suggest you start wrapping your mind around that unless you want to find yourself looking for another job.

Last week it was a funeral and now . . . don't even tell me, I don't think I need to know. You want personal time? That's why weekends were invented."

"I worked all last weekend, sir. Trying to finalize that penthouse deal."

"Key word—trying. And it's still not done two days later, is it? Lotta good that did. I've got to wonder, Ms. Mancini, where your mind is lately. First, you're late picking me up at the airport, you almost kill some guy on the road, you're lucky it wasn't his funeral you were attending. Just get to those listings and report back, dammit. Pronto!"

Ferro quickly moved on down the hallway, not waiting to see Diane's reaction to her new set of instructions. Instead, he went down the elevator and emerged into the sunlight of a beautiful spring day, the kind made for two potential lovers who wanted only to stroll along the broad avenues hand-in-hand, savor the warm temperature, and spend time with each other. A day filled with dreams that would apparently have to wait for sleep. Standing beside the parked limo, still dressed in his uniform, he wondered what he might do with his free afternoon.

As Diane herself stepped out of the building, a sudden thought came to him.

"Car, madam?"

"Oh, Claude—how sweet of you to think to use the car for our day," she said, leaving Ferro wondering if she had meant to use the word date. *American women are funny, so insecure*, he thought, and then instantly regretted it. That was Ferro talking, not Claude, and he really shouldn't be so quick to judge Diane. He knew so little about her. But he was looking forward to learning more, perhaps everything.

"Diane, I know."

"No, no, you don't. You see, I'm afraid our plans were just spoiled, and I'll give you three guesses who spoiled them—and the first two don't count."

"I don't understand this guessing game," Ferro admitted.

"Sorry, just a dumb old game, a silly phrase meaning you don't have to guess, you know it was Mr. Curtis. I can't spend the day with you, Claude. Mr. Curtis is making me work some potential big client. I've got to check out a few different properties."

"I know," he repeated. "I overheard. Mr. Curtis is a hard man not to hear. I've decided I'm going to drive you to those properties."

"I couldn't possibly ask you to do that."

"You're not asking. I am insisting," Ferro said with a smile that brightened the day and her mood. "Besides, it's not like I'm dressed for casually strolling through Central Park."

"What kind of society lady would that make me, having my chauffeur escorting her," she said with a laugh. "We would both stick out."

"So, your carriage awaits," Ferro said.

With that, he opened the rear door of the gleaming Town Car—which he'd spent all morning cleaning and waxing—and watched as she settled herself comfortably on the soft, leather seat in the back. As Ferro gently closed the door and rounded the far end of the car, he noticed a familiar person crossing the street against traffic, her middle finger gesturing at the drivers who were honking at her. Whether it was for getting in their way or for her suggestive dress, he couldn't be sure. Still, he tried to avoid her and just didn't make it into his seat in time. Of course he would run into Nancy Curtis. That's the way this day was going.

"Claude, wait, I want to talk to my father," she said, trying to run down the sidewalk to the car, her body dragged down by far too many shopping bags. Not to mention a cigarette in her hands.

"Your father is upstairs."

"Haha, good try. Geez, how can I buy that kind of loyalty— from any man, much less you. But who cares, Daddy can't avoid me that easily," Nancy said, taking it upon herself to open the back door. When she saw that it wasn't her father but instead some "employee,"—as she stated with rather a lack of feeling for Diane—she backed out and tossed Ferro a confused look. "Where's Daddy?"

"As I told you, he's upstairs. He's very busy. And not expecting you till much later."

"So what," she said. "He'll see me anytime. He has to. Besides, I decided he should take me to lunch. Somewhere fancy where the rich people will stare at me and wonder who I am. Probably piss off management with my dress."

"Or lack thereof," Ferro said.

"Exactly. See, that's the point!"

"But I think it will have to wait. Like I said, he's busy."

"Who cares what you think. And if he can't, he can then pay me off and send me off to an expensive lunch by myself. Not like he's never blown me off before," she said, her nose scrunching up like she'd just smelled something foul. "What's she doing back there?"

"An errand. An important one for Curtis Real Estate."

"Whatever," Nancy said, sounding all too much like her father. "Work bores me."

God forbid that she should have to earn a living, Ferro thought.

As Nancy finally left them alone and made her way into the building, Ferro got behind the wheel and quickly pulled out into traffic, briefly wondering if this was such a good idea. The only thing larger than Nancy's breasts was her mouth, and she knew how to use it (and them). She would surely report his activities—and Diane's—to her precious Daddy the moment she arrived inside his office. There was nothing he could do about it now, in for a penny, in for a pound.

"I'm sorry you have to spend your day off this way," Diane said from the back.

"It's no problem," Ferro said. "Seeing as how difficult it was for you to even say the word 'date' the other day, the fact that you actually agreed to go out on one—and with me, of all people—was a major accomplishment. I for one don't plan on wasting it, Curtis or not."

"Running into his horrible daughter, that couldn't have been good."

"She is rather horrible, isn't she?"

"All that money, and none of the class."

"Money seldom buys people what they truly need," Ferro said, surprising even himself with such a comment.

As for Nancy, Ferro dismissed his initial concerns easily enough. She thrived on causing trouble, and there was not one thing Ferro could do to stop her. He remembered the way she'd seduced her way into his bedroom, then realized that not even that would keep Nancy Curtis from getting her way. She'd use the pope if she could. Still, Ferro half expected his cell phone to ring, a bellowing Curtis on the other end. But nothing happened, not now, and as it turned out, blissfully, not for the next several hours either.

*   *   *

The storm clouds that were Stan Curtis and his daughter, Nancy notwithstanding, it was a picture-perfect day that Ferro could not have scripted any better. Crisp temperatures and an easy breeze spread over an endless sky of azure blue, the sun reflecting off the glass and gleam of Manhattan skyscrapers, the blossoming greenery of the park their near-constant companion as they traveled up and down the East Side. It was like something out of nature's scrapbook. What made it all the more special was the fact that Ferro and Diane had dispensed with the viewing of the properties within two hours—thanks to his getting her around town faster with the aid of the Town Car.

Photos of the co-ops and rentals were taken, notes were made about things both good and bad about the buildings that were interested in signing with Curtis Realty, friendly exchanges between the garrulous client and Diane helped, and finally Diane announced after the final property that she was ready for a distraction from work.

"How about a late lunch?" Ferro suggested, noting the time had crept past three.

"Sounds good. I'm famished. I think all I caught for breakfast was a bagel—if I can even remember back that far."

"Someday, I will treat you to a meal you deserve, surrounded by a staff who will bring you whatever you wish," he said, "But for now, I know the perfect temporary place."

"Claude, why do you think you need to spoil me?" she asked.

"The question is, Diane, why do you think you don't need to be spoiled?"

They both chewed on that morsel as they headed toward their lunch destination.

He drove the Town Car to the edge of Central Park South and Fifth Avenue, counting his blessings after finding an ideal parking space not far from the once-renowned Plaza Hotel and Grand Army Plaza. From there he excised his date from the rear of the car, and as easily and gracefully as she exited, he tossed inside the car his chauffeur's hat and overcoat. From the trunk he gathered a convenient casual windbreaker, and presto, he was transformed from employee to, well, just a man at her side.

Linking his arm with hers, receiving back a cautious smile as he did so, the two of them made their way into the park, bypassing street corner artists and food vendors. Diane wondered aloud what was wrong with those vendors, but Ferro just forged ahead, knowing exactly where he wanted to go. He was practically pulling her with his enthusiasm. For Ferro, he felt as free as he had since arrived in New York. Olivetti Enterprises was as far removed from his life as it had ever been, and truth be known he hadn't even given it a thought since he and Diane had launched their burgeoning romance. He felt a flutter only when he thought of her, and now that she was in his presence he was like a kid in a candy store. He couldn't wait to taste the sweetness of her kiss again. Diane to him was not like his usual conquests, she wasn't the kind of woman to easily seduce, to toss aside once he could claim her as his. She was no one-night casino bet. Certainly, he wanted her, desired her; but he also wanted to think of her as someone beyond an easy lay, to not just wake up one morning with her but many. How was that possible, after such a short amount of time? Could it be he wanted more than that? Could it be that Ferro Olivetti was a changed man? It hardly seemed possible.

"Claude, where are you taking me?"

"Just one more moment," he said as they rounded a bend on the path. "Here."

Here was the section of the park Ferro had come to relate with. The same pond he'd seen last week where father and son had launched ships on a windy day, where a certain individual named Angelo had helped Ferro out in a moment of true need. He'd said he was there every day, selling those delicious hot dogs. Ferro wanted to see the man again, to thank him, to patronize his business. Except when they came to the cart—in the same location—Ferro was met with the face of a young man, probably no more than twenty. Yet there was something familiar about him, almost like looking at a photograph of Alberto Olivetti and his son, Ferro.

"Can I help you, sir?" the boy asked.

"Where is Angelo?" Ferro asked.

"Oh, my Papa, he is not well today. I am Giancarlo, his son."

As suspected, Ferro thought with a grin. He extended his hand in greeting. "Hello, Giancarlo. I am Claude, and this is my friend, Diane. Your father did me a great favor recently, and so I have to come to repay his generosity. We will have four hot dogs with all the fixings, and two sodas."

"Coming right up, Claude."

The boy worked quickly, like he'd been taught by a master, and Ferro supposed he had been, and suddenly the meal was ready. Ferro dug into his pockets for his cash and came up with a fifty-dollar bill.

"Keep the change," Ferro said.

"Thank you, sir, that's kind of you."

As Ferro and Diane made their way over to a nearby bench to enjoy their meal, Diane's face bore that of a woman with a question or two. "You want to tell me what that was all about?"

"Another time," he said. "Let us just enjoy the food, the company, the sunshine."

"Ooh, another mystery from my mysterious man."

Ferro's silence offered up no solutions to those mysteries.

So, they dined, each of them savoring the spicy hot dogs and the tart sauerkraut, washing down the acidic but somehow complementary tastes with the bubbly soda. When they finished, Ferro once again took Diane by the arm and they left the park, wandering down Fifth Avenue until they reached Rockefeller Center. They watched the skaters on the ice rink getting in their final pirouettes of the season. March would soon give way to April, winter was waning, and, as they said, hope springs eternal. Ferro hoped so, too.

They walked east after that, then uptown, winding their way along Madison Avenue, stopping to look in windows of certain fancy shops, going in others to sample some chocolate confection or run their hands across lovely silk items. The weather remained as ideal as possible, giving their date a polish that no one could rub off. All in all, for a second date—which Ferro claimed it was despite Diane's laughing protests that it was their first—it was as close to perfect as you could get. So then, where were the rain clouds? Nothing went so smoothly, life didn't work that way, there was always a storm brewing. Like with Olivetti Enterprises, Dunbar always hovering in the background. Like with Claude and Diane, Stan Curtis wielding his own kind of corrupt power over them.

Ferro's phone rang; it may as well have been the sound of thunder.

They both knew it could only be one person, and he wasted no time with pleasantries.

"Claude, get your ass back here this instant!"

"Mr. Curtis?"

"Of course this is Mr. Curtis. Who the fuck do you think it is, genius?" he asked. "Christ, the idiots I hire."

"Give me thirty minutes, I'll be there."

"Make it fifteen or you're fired," Curtis said. Then the call was disconnected.

"I need to get back," Ferro said, and then remembered that the Town Car was still parked near the park. It would take him fifteen minutes just to get over there and retrieve it. Or he could walk to the offices of Curtis Real Estate, ten blocks north from here. He just hoped Curtis wasn't expecting him to drive somewhere. That might present a problem, and as he'd been quick to learn, Curtis did not deal well with problems. Ferro stuck out his hand to hail a taxi.

"Claude, it's actually quicker to walk."

"It's here, let's take it. Come on, get inside," Ferro said, opening the door of a yellow cab that had conveniently pulled over. "We'll get the receipt, you can make that bastard pay. That's what expense accounts are for."

The ride went very quickly, and minutes later they emerged back out onto Madison Avenue. Ferro stopped Diane at the entrance to the building.

"I don't think you should arrive back at the same time as me," he said. "I'll go first, since I was the one he summoned. But before I do, Diane, I want to say how much I enjoyed today, these few stolen hours with you. You have made my transition to New York so much easier, I cannot express my gratitude enough. We got off on the wrong foot at Vita's apartment, but that's why we have two feet. A chance to see how we do balancing our lives."

"Claude," she started to say, only to be interrupted by the sudden touch of his lips upon hers. The kiss was sweet and tender, and neither of them pulled away from this unexpected contact, this pleasing touch. At last, though, Ferro drew back, a smile widening his face. Diane attempted another word, only this time she was shushed by the touch of his finger on those same, supple lips.

"Say nothing, let the memory be like this: silent but powerful."

Ferro entered the building alone, but for the first time since arriving in New York, not lonely. For he knew that outside on the sidewalk was a lovely woman who in a short amount of time—really, too short a time—had come to mean the world to him. He wondered what the real Ferro, the playboy who used the world's most luxurious sights for his conquests, would have made of this situation. Then he decided that the emotions swirling inside him were his and his alone. That wasn't Claude Reneau kissing her, that wasn't Claude Reneau saying those words. You could change the name, the facade, you could change everything but the man who lived inside him. No, the man behind that kiss had been Ferro Olivetti.

It was good timing, this re-emergence of Ferro Olivetti.

He had a feeling he would need all his wits, all his confidence, all his power, when it came to confronting Stan Curtis. What did the bastard want anyway, and did it have anything to do with Diane, or worse, with Nancy? He supposed there was no time like the present to find out.

The elevator opened and Ferro realized he'd have to face his fate.

CHAPTER SIXTEEN

THE MOMENT FERRO ARRIVED AT Curtis' office and saw who else was in attendance, he knew a trap had been set for him. And while she was of barely legal age, it didn't mean she wasn't an expert at manipulation, Look how she treated her father, always getting what she wanted. And Ferro had to assume that right now, she wanted to make trouble for "Claude." She was positioned on the windowsill, innocently sucking on a lollypop. As deceptive a picture as she could paint, save for that wicked grin she wore better than any of her clothes. She plastered it on her face the moment Ferro was escorted inside the office.

Oh yes, Nancy Curtis had an agenda, that's for sure.

"Mr. Curtis, Claude is here," said Molly, his poor, put-upon secretary.

"About g-d time," Curtis said, looking up from his desk. "Get in here, Claude."

Ferro wasn't going to be intimidated, not by him, and certainly not by his loser of a daughter. He was Ferro Olivetti, he reminded himself, and people like this were mere appetizers in the quest for a larger meal. Easily dispensed with, not entirely satisfying. So, he walked in with his chest puffed up, his confidence at all-time high since he'd decided to come to New York on this crazy quest of his. Still, he wasn't going to make the first overture, he wanted to see how this played out. If anything, Ferro Olivetti was good on his feet, he could handle any situation. He, Ferro thought, as though he were discussing a stranger. *I*, he revised, *I can deal with any crisis, and triumph.* It was his nature, no matter what you called him.

Curtis looked at his watch. "I said fifteen minutes. It's been seventeen."

"I'm here now, Mr. Curtis, so perhaps we can just address whatever it is you wish from me? You gave me the afternoon off, and now you call me back with urgency, even anger? I don't believe I've done anything to warrant such treatment."

"You have a job and a roof over your head thanks to me, so I'll treat you anyway I want," he said, wiping newly formed sweat on his brow.

Ferro reminded himself he was dealing with a bully. One who backed down when pushed. Where was that flight attendant and her bad potato routine when you needed her? "Sir, you're lucky I was close enough to get here so quickly."

"I'm lucky?" he said incredulously, turning toward his daughter, "You hear this guy, Peaches? Thinks part of his job is talking back to the man who employs him and who pays him." He laughed before looking back. "Hey Claude, you wanna know what luck is? Luck is you still being able to breathe."

"I don't understand."

Even though Ferro did. The best defense is knowing your enemy's move.

"Oh, I think you do. You think I don't know what's going on under my nose?"

Ferro stole a glance at Nancy, who was grinning like she'd just swallowed the Cheshire Cat. Clearly Nancy had spilled the beans about Ferro and Diane being together, and that he'd used his afternoon off to escort her around the city on her errands—and used the company car to boot. The question was, what possible motive did Nancy have for treating him like this? Because he'd rejected her sexual advances that first night?

Because she was a nasty piece of work who on a daily basis only saw the worst in people? Hell, if that's how she operated, Ferro was done for; she'd gladly out him for her own benefit.

"Look, Mr. Curtis, I was just doing Ms. Mancini a favor, that's all. I was going that way anyway."

Confusion set about Curtis's florid face. "Shut up, Claude. I don't know what you're talking about, this has nothing to do with Ms. Mancini. Frankly, what Ms. Mancini and you have between you, I could care less about. It's my daughter's well-being that concerns me, and what she told me disgusts me. Are you aware of just how old she is? Not even eighteen. Claude, how dare you take advantage of a girl of her age! And under my roof of all places."

Ferro was thrown by this unexpected accusation. "Sir, how dare I what?"

"Nancy told me everything. You're just a filthy pig. That's the last time I take any advice from Fred Evans. Guy's just a professional student; maybe he should get out in the world and see how people really are, stop being so damn trusting."

"Mr. Curtis, I'm still not sure what you're talking about. I've done nothing wrong."

"Nothing? You call going to her bedroom nothing? You call trying to seduce my little girl nothing?"

"That's not true," Ferro said, even though he knew his protests were futile. "I've never seen the inside of Nancy's bedroom—much less the outside. I'm not even sure which room is hers."

"Oh, so I'm to believe my innocent little Peach is lying, right?"

Ferro wanted to remind this jerk that his precious daughter was anything but innocent or little. That she had to be peeled off that drunk idiot from the party last week, and that any advances were all her doing. So if any word described her best, well, liar was a pretty good place to start.

"I didn't say that, sir. There was a moment, but she came on to me, just as…"

"My baby? Coming on to you?"

"She was waiting for me in my room—nearly naked."

Okay, wrong thing to say. Curtis cut him off with a thunderous, screaming bellow. Spittle came suddenly flying out of his mouth like a geyser erupting. "Get out of here, get out this instant. You are a disgusting, sick pig. I knew I never should have hired you; no references, no class, no money, and now no job!"

"Sir?"

Curtis paused, as though savoring the words on his tongue. Then, at last he spoke them, and though the words were filled with bile, there was also a certain satisfaction behind them. "You, Claude, are fired."

"Mr. Curtis, please, there's been a horrible misunderstanding here. If I can explain."

Ferro's pleas fell on deaf ears.

"Just get the hell out of my office," he yelled.

Ferro felt anger swelling inside him. He was one of the most powerful men in the business world, and he had never been spoken to like this before. He'd never even dared speak to another person like this. As Claude, he was powerless. As Ferro, he couldn't expose himself, not without going against his father's will. He was without money, power, prestige; Ferro was without his arsenal, which left him vulnerable and exposed. In the back of his mind he heard his father's soothing voice, instructing him, influencing him, and ultimately calming him down. So, Ferro took a deep breath and realized a man like Curtis would one day get his comeuppance. He was not unlike Dunbar back in San Francisco, a toothless shark whose bite wounds were only superficial. Its victims lived to fight another day.

Deciding to hold his tongue and not inflame the situation any further, Ferro turned abruptly to leave. But he did so with the knowledge that he would never forget this moment, this feeling, or this notion of complete humiliation. Not even those lonely nights in Central Park, the feeling of isolation he felt in the jail cell, could do justice to this situation. If this was how people were treated in the real world, Ferro would happily return to his ivory tower.

On his way out of the office, he bumped into the one bright spot in his life: Diane. She didn't stop, she'd obviously heard the entire exchange (everyone had, Curtis hadn't exactly been quiet) and had a few things on her mind.

"Please, Mr. Curtis, you can't fire Claude. What could he possibly have done that was so wrong? To fire him? He just started working for you, and he's been at your beck and call every hour. What makes you think you can talk to him like that?"

Curtis was already mad, and Diane had just made him madder. "Don't tell me how to talk, Ms. Mancini. This is none of your business. Don't make matters worse, or you'll find yourself on the same line Claude's going to be—the unemployment line! Now get the hell out of my office and get back to work."

Diane's face held a look of fury. "How dare you talk to me, like I'm some…well, let's just say I've never been spoken to in such a rude manner before."

"Yes you have," Ferro interjected. "Every day, by this buffoon."

"Claude!" Diane stated. "I'm trying to save your job, and that's not going to help. Look, Mr. Curtis, be reasonable."

"Ms. Mancini, if I didn't know better, I'd think you had a thing for Claude. You see that, Claude? Look at the way she defends you, she's getting all hot and bothered under the collar. Just what have you two been up to in my limo anyway? Is that what you were doing this afternoon? Yes, Nancy told me she saw Ms. Mancini in the back seat—and that the two of you drove off together. A quickie in the car, or did you drive to a hotel? Ms. Mancini, you were supposed to be checking out those properties I handed to you."

"I did, Mr. Curtis. You're being unreasonable."

"Think I'm being unreasonable now? How about trying this on for size: Good riddance to the both of you—damn bitch, you're always talking back, always ready with an excuse about why you can't do something. You haven't been able to close a single deal lately, maybe now I know why. You've been busy with your legs up in the air."

That was enough for Diane, whose fiery Italian temper had reached its boiling point. She turned and spat fierce venom back at her boss. "You know what, Mr. Curtis? You want to get down in the gutter with me, that's fine by me. I know how to defend myself, I've been doing it all my life. Diane Mancini is no pushover and she—I—will not be spoken to in such a disgusting, vile manner. So, Mr. Curtis, let this be my last act as one of your employees by telling you to your face what everyone around you wants to say—go fuck yourself!"

Ferro couldn't help it, he grinned proudly.

Diane, her chest heaving from the outpouring of emotion, was actually smiling too. It felt good to get that off her chest.

Even Nancy Curtis was showing her row of teeth, yellowed and crooked as they were. The lollypop she'd been sucking had dropped from her mouth, sticky now from the carpet which had caught it. Ferro sized her up, deciding that this confrontation was better than she could have scripted.

Ferro took hold of Diane's arm before she used it to physically lash out at her boss. Ex-boss. "I think we've more than worn out our welcome here. Shall we gather your stuff and be on our way? I feel a great itch all over my body, hives from being in such company," he said.

They started off, only to have Ferro stop. He had one more thing to say. Turning back to Curtis, he was unable to resist anymore. "You know, someone really should have thrown you off that airplane from San Francisco. I wish it had been me, but I'm sure the flight attendant you were so rude to had first dibs. The potato she served you wasn't bad—you were, rotten to the core. Then and now."

"Why you bastard … how do you know about that. Wait a minute."

"Oh, and Mr. Curtis, I know other things, too," Ferro said, his threat implicit. "And I'm not alone in that knowledge. Have a pleasant day. Though of course if you do, that means others have no doubt suffered. For them, I'm sorry, just as sorry as I was to sit right across from you on that flight."

And with that, Ferro pulled from inside his coat pocket the stupid boarding pass he'd picked up from the floor of the plane. As he flung it at the blustering man, he knew he had no further need for it. Just as he had no further need for the man himself. He would remember him, that was for sure, and for that Stan Curtis would live to regret.

As Ferro and Diane departed the office, he detected a confused, worried expression lingering on Curtis's face. He still had had no idea that Ferro was the man sitting next to him for six hours cross country, he was that absorbed, that clueless. He knew it now, and he also knew that Ferro had information—facts—about him that if exposed, might not ruin him but certainly would cause him a great deal of embarrassment. Probably cost him a fair amount of money in the divorce, too.

It was good to be rid of such a person from his life. With his toxic personality, it would be nice to no longer have his poison seep beneath Ferro's or Diane's skin. Their skin could be used for much better purposes, and if any good was to come out of this situation, it was the burgeoning, blossoming relationship between the two of them. The future, uncertain as it was, at least had them forging ahead together.

*   *   *

Diane made her quiet, hasty exit from the offices of Curtis Real Estate minutes later. Ferro watched from afar as she bade tearful goodbyes to her shocked coworkers in the bullpen—Jennifer, Timothy, Sandra, all of whom had heard the exchange, none of whom believed it had actually happened. Diane Mancini was the best agent in the office, and if she was expendable, then the rest of them barely had a prayer. They all hugged her separately and then as one big group. They wished her well, said they would be in touch. No doubt they secretly envied Diane for getting out from under Curtis's iron fist. Finally, with a small box filled with her belongings in her arms, she was ready to go. Ferro grabbed the box, relieving her of the weight of the box but not the emotion she carried with it, and together they made their way down the short hallway to the elevators.

Diane stole one last look back and took a deep breath for strength before pressing the down button for the last time. She looked sad to leave her coworkers: Jennifer who was busy now on the phone, Sandra typing away at her computer, poor deluded Timothy running a fresh cup of coffee down to his boss in an attempt to show how much of a team player he was. Timothy hadn't even made one lewd comment about Claude, especially given the fact he was at Diane's side nearly the entire time. The doors opened, and she stepped in, Ferro guiding her step.

"I still don't know what the hell just happened in there," Diane said.

"It's for the best," Ferro said. "We both reached our limit with the man, that's all. The contrast of a man like that with the beautiful afternoon we shared, I suppose the transition was too much for us, and we snapped. I for one am glad."

"I know you're right, and in the end it's the right thing for me. I feel free. But I also feel scared. It all happened so quickly, I barely knew what I was saying. All I know is I just rushed in there to stop all that screaming, that you had gotten in trouble for escorting me around. Then I sensed there was more to the story than just you taking the company car for a spin—with me in it."

"Actually, it had nothing to do with you—and in a way, everything."

"And I thought you were done with mysteries."

"No mystery."

"Riddles then," she said, feeling exasperated. "Whatever, when it comes to you, Claude, there is this air of intrigue. Wanna explain why?"

By now they had left the building, and as they stood on the sidewalk, they both realized neither knew in which direction to walk. This episode hadn't exactly been planned. They didn't know where they were going. They just started walking, going with the flow of pedestrian traffic, more intent on their conversation than their unknown destination.

"I suppose I'm partially at fault—for letting it happen, for not mentioning it to Curtis earlier. I just trusted her too much, not guessing she would use it to her advantage."

"Who? What are you talking about?"

"Nancy, that horrid daughter of his—whom he charmlessly refers to as Peaches—she came on to me the first night I was living under their roof. I mean, not twelve hours earlier I had never heard of them, and they had never met me, and next thing I know that precocious child is trying to undo the buttons on my shirt—for starters. After I drove home a client of Mr. Curtis's, Nancy was waiting in my upstairs bedroom, and she wasn't exactly wearing much. Her intent was pretty clear. I politely declined her offer, which she wasn't pleased about. Of course now she told her father a different story, that I came to her room and tried to force myself on her. She just likes to make trouble." Ferro paused, deciding for now to leave out the other details of that night, with Hilda and Mr. Curtis as well. "I've learned Nancy's quite accomplished at making trouble."

"But why expose you now? If her attempted seduction happened a week ago, why didn't she retaliate then? Right after you rejected her."

Ferro considered this before saying, "I can only guess because she saw me with you."

"Oh, Claude, it's my fault."

"Hardly your fault," Ferro assured her. "Nancy would have snapped at some point, found some other way to get back at me," Ferro said, letting out a small laugh. "She was just lying in wait, like an animal waiting for its prey to show some weakness. A classic business move, move in for is at its most vulnerable."

"For a chauffeur, you sure know a lot about business machinations."

Ferro shrugged away her comment, knowing she hadn't intended it as an insult. Diane, he knew, was no snob. "Common sense, really," he said, then, wanting to change the subject, continued: "I could have easily proven Nancy wrong in front of her father, that it wasn't me who came on to her but the other way around. I had a witness."

"Who?"

"Believe it or not, that Vegas-style wife of his."

"Hilda?"

"The one and only. Seems she was hiding under the bed."

"Why would she do that?"

"Oh, because just moments before Nancy arrived, Hilda had just tried to do to me what Nancy was trying to do to me."

"You had two women in one night trying to sleep with you?"

"Yes."

"What is it about you, Claude? Is it that accent?"

"Vita seemed to like it," Ferro said.

"So why haven't you tried to seduce me?"

"If you think about it, Diane, I have done none of the seducing," he said, with a great smile. "I guess, ultimately, that makes me a gentleman. I don't kiss and tell."

"Claude, I think there's something more you're not telling me." She paused. "Like always. Why do I trust you, even though you refuse to answer my questions?"

"All in good time."

"I think now is the perfect time. I just lost my job for you, at least give me something to cling my hopes to. Are you the real deal, or is the chauffeur outfit just another guise? Tell me something you've never told anyone else."

"How about I tell you everything that happened that night." Ferro looked at Diane, worried he was losing her, that the pressure of her sudden unemployment would cause her to retreat into the frightened shell she had worn only just last week. She nodded at him, waiting to hear more, and so he proceeded. "Okay, it's actually pretty funny. So, I told you his wife, Hilda, was hiding under the bed, and then the ill-named Peaches suddenly has to go hide in the closet because someone else came knocking at my door, and again, they were trying to put the moves on me."

"Hilda. Nancy, who else could it have…NO!"

Ferro was grinning wide, ear to ear. "Yup, the bellowing blowhard, pardon the pun, Curtis himself. Sat me down on the bed, told me how intrigued he was by me, and then he placed his hand on my lap. His intention was clear, all the way through his robe."

"I can't believe it, Curtis—gay. That ought to send Timothy's tongue wagging."

"Gee, thanks for that image," Ferro said, and then laughed. "Who knows what Curtis is, gay or maybe just a power-hungry jerk who likes to assert himself, see how far it will take him. Perhaps he doesn't know himself, or maybe he does and doesn't like it. That's what makes him so miserable. What I do know is this: He wasn't getting any further with me than were Hilda or Nancy. In fact, only one member of the family got any real action from me."

"Doris? "

"No. The family dog. Humped me right there in the kitchen later that night."

Diane and Ferro shared a laugh loud enough to draw the attention of fellow pedestrians. They ignored the funny looks as they crossed the avenue. They had reached 57th Street and Fifth Avenue, not far from where they had enjoyed their perfect afternoon of sunshine and hot dogs. The memory was obviously fresh in their minds as they both gazed toward the park.

"A lot has happened in so fast a time," Ferro said.

"Are you talking about today, or since you first saw me at Vita's apartment? You know, even if you turned down the entire Curtis household, you'll still not a saint. After all, you were practically leering at me."

"I did not come on to you, Diane—and men like me don't leer." Seriously, he said, "You, Diane, I liked you from the moment I saw you. It's no one's fault I wanted to know more. That situation is so very different."

"You scared the hell out of me that night," she said.

"I know, and I have apologized dozens of times. So, when are you going to forget it? Or are you always going to remind me of how we truly met, even when we're old and gray?"

A loaded comment like that could take a tentative relationship like theirs and either strengthen it or bring it to a sudden, screeching half. With Diane's fragile status, it was the latter. Her expression wavered as she put a bit more distance between them, both physically and figuratively. Her voice took on a business-like tone.

"Look, Claude, I realize we've had a wonderful day, but it's time to end it."

"It was just a joke, Diane. Please. A day at a time, that's my motto right now."

"Look, this is all taking me by surprise—and don't get me wrong, you've been nothing but a gentleman with me and I…I, it's just been a long time since I've looked at a man, much less let him take me out."

"And kiss you," he reminded her.

"My emotions are a wreck right now. Guess I'm feeling a bit sensitive right now. I mean, I did just lose my job—and so did you. I don't even know where we're going. What do we do now? And you, Claude! Mr. Curtis's house was where you were living. Now you need a roof over your head, food to eat. My God, did he even pay you yet?"

"I have some money from him, yes," Ferro said.

"But a place to stay?"

"I'll worry about that later. After I find something to eat. Dirty water hot dogs are fine in a pinch, but they don't fill you up like a real meal."

"Then how about dinner? Can I at least invite you to my parents' for dinner? It's the least I can do for how you've helped me."

Without hesitation, Ferro quickly and happily accepted her surprising invitation—before her nerves made her take it back. "Sounds good to me."

"Oh my God, what have I done?"

"I'm sure it will be fine. You are not allowed to bring friends home?"

"I am. I just don't. I'd like them to remain my friends."

"They are just parents. How bad could it be?

"Ha. You say that now, wait till you face the Italian Inquisition. My mother is like a dog with a bone. You'll be that bone, and she won't leave a scrap on it. On you."

Ferro just smiled, images of the villa in Rome coming to him. "Sounds like home already."

CHAPTER SEVENTEEN

THE THING ABOUT THIS STRANGE QUEST of his was, Ferro had no plan or agenda. He took each situation as it came and turned it as much to his advantage as he could. A run-in with thugs had given him a place to stay his first night, albeit a jail cell. A chance encounter with Vita at a bar had led him to meet Diane. Nearly getting run down by a truck had turned into a job, short-lived as it was, but it had managed to house him, feed him, and put money in his pocket. Now, getting fired had led to this, an invitation for dinner at the Mancini house. He supposed this moment was going to be different from all those others; he suspected he was about to meet his greatest challenge yet. And he doubted he had the power to alter its outcome.

Mother Mancini would be in total control.

The truth of the matter was, Ferro had little experience meeting the parents of the woman he was seeing. Not since back in Rome, when Anna Maria's family and his were practically already related, the marriage between their children all but certain, but that was years ago, and Ferro was a much-changed man now. His lifestyle didn't exactly afford him the chance to shake hands with a father, receive a welcoming peck on the cheek from a protective mother. When you lived the jet-set life and the women came and went as quickly as airplanes from runways, the ritual of being brought home to meet the family had escaped him. So, it was only fitting that on this first attempt he would get caught in the mother's trap, ensnared, at times squirming like a cornered animal. It didn't help that Ferro's presence proved a surprise all its own.

"What, you couldn't call your poor mother and tell her to set a fourth plate? That you were bringing home company?"

That was Ferro's initial introduction to Sophia Mancini, and had those words been spoken in Italian, he could almost swear it was his mother.

"Would you rather we turn around and leave?" Diane responded quickly.

Ferro would never speak to his mother that way. He supposed things were different between mothers and daughters; they spoke words but probably said more with their expressions. If Ferro talked that way, he'd get hit upside the head.

But Diane's response was perfect, as her mother easily fell for the line. "No, no," she said, grabbing hold of Ferro's arm, practically dragging him into their humble household. "Some notice would be nice, I would have worn a better dress, maybe put on more make-up."

"Like you need a third coating," came a deep baritone voice from the living room.

"My father," Diane explained, even though she didn't need to.

"Ignore him, he hasn't seen me without my war paint in twenty years. If he had, he'd be the first one at the drug store counter stocking up," Sophia said with a laugh, her arm still linked with Ferro's. "So, you're the mysterious Claude Reneau my Diane has been telling me about lately. Though truth be told, she really hasn't said much beyond your name. Guess that means I get to ask a lot of questions. My daughter, she's secretive. I'm an open book—and so are my guests."

"Your daughter is a cautious—and intelligent—woman, Mrs. Mancini."

"Uh, such manners. I am Sophia."

"My own mother taught respect, Mrs. Mancini," Ferro said. "And it is a pleasure to meet you."

"You have such a delicious accent, where is that from? Somewhere in Italy, but I'm not certain of the region," cooed Sophia. "I can see—and now hear—why my daughter seems so enamored of you. Please, I insist you call me Sophia."

Ferro exchanged a fleeting look at Diane. He mouthed the word "enamored," which only caused Diane to simultaneously shrug and giggle. Women had such strange rituals.

"I couldn't possibly. You are Diane's mother, and as such you are Mrs. Mancini."

"Your mother raised you right," she said.

"A dear woman, very forceful. A lot like you."

Sophia blushed. "I'll take that as the compliment it was intended as. You're quite the charmer, aren't you, Mr. Claude Reneau? But I'm sure you're more than a just a combination of handsome smile and smooth words—time will tell. For now, I hope you've got plenty of room for pasta. We've got more than enough."

"Of course, and thank you. It smells delicious," he said. "It has been far too long since I've had a home-cooked meal."

"Uh, Mom, can we let Claude catch his breath? The subway ride from the city was bad enough, let the interrogation wait."

They were all still standing in the vestibule of the house, barely out of reach of the night. At this point, either could lay claim to Diane and Ferro, and maybe the cool outside and its cover of darkness had its benefits. In the light of the house, he felt exposed, as though they could read the truth hidden behind his eyes. Ferro reminded himself he had to be careful. Mrs. Mancini was a sharp lady, and her questions could trip up a pathological liar.

With Sophia still clinging to his side, Diane led Ferro into the living room. To Ferro it was like stepping back in time to a room from another decade, perhaps the fifties if the décor had anything to say about it. Slipcovers over furniture, a faint musty smell in the air. Still, the home was charming and comfortable and seemed to perfectly reflect the personalities of the people who dwelled within its walls.

Ferro was introduced to Diane's father, who shook his hand and said, "Sal Mancini, how are you?"

"Fine, sir. A pleasure. Thank you for welcoming me into your home."

"See what I mean, Sal," Mrs. Mancini said, "he's real polite, I like him already."

"Mother!"

"What's wrong with that? You want I should say I don't like him?"

"I think we need some wine," Mr. Mancini said.

"Amen," Diane replied.

"Speaking of that, Claude, you wouldn't by any chance be Catholic, would you?"

Diane looked horrified, as though she was questioning her decision to bring him into the folds of her family. "Mother! Can you be any more annoying?"

"Listen to the way my daughter talks to me," Sophia said, nervously making the sign of the cross. "Lord, save me."

"Amen," Diane repeated.

A grinning Ferro was spared from answering the initial question about his religion—for now. His mother went to mass religiously. He was rather lapsed about the whole church thing. He had a sense he was in for a long night filled with questions even more probing than that, and he had to stay sharp. He steeled himself for the Inquisition. Silently he started looking around, wondering where Mr. Mancini had gone off to, since he sure could use that glass of wine right about now.

*　　*　　*

Polite conversation ensued over a tray of fruit, cheeses, and crackers, not to mention a bottle of Pinot Grigio. All during this exchange Ferro kept wondering the real reason Diane was subjecting herself to such torture. They could have easily gone to some restaurant, just the two of them, to commiserate over their lost jobs and uncertain future. Instead, they were sitting in the living room and drinking cheap wine while discussing what was for dinner, how her mother's balky knees were, what was the neighborhood gossip. Silly topics, meaningless, but still it finally dawned on Ferro that the topics were all dictated by Diane, and that she was carefully, systematically avoiding all talk of dates, romance, and, most importantly, work. He knew this was just a stalling tactic, the truth would win out in the end. Sophia Mancini was just too good in her role as the Italian mother,

Soon enough the four of them retreated to the dining room, where they settled into their assigned seats, the firm hand of Sophia Mancini behind it all. Ferro found he was sitting to the woman's left, directly across from Diane. With a heaping plate piled high with spaghetti passed around and a soupcon of thick red sauce and meatballs the size of baseballs to follow, they all filled their plates and began to eat.

And just as the meal had begun, so too did the real questions.

"Claude, where do you live?" Sophia began.

"I'm originally from Rome, but I've spent the last many years in California."

"Oh. What part?"

"San Francisco. Napa. The northern coast."

"And so, what brings you to New York?"

"A new adventure, I suppose. A new job, too."

"Yes, I've heard about that one. As a driver, I understand."

"It is honest work, Mother," Diane interjected.

"I'm not judging, dear. Merely curious."

For the first time since arriving, Ferro began to feel uncomfortable in his own skin. Or perhaps Claude's skin was more appropriate. It was clear to him that Mrs. Mancini was going to ask whatever she wanted, and if Ferro showed any signs of hesitancy in his answers, she just might begin to suspect something wasn't on the up and up. She'd easily move in for the kill. Just as he couldn't reveal his true self to Curtis, he couldn't do it to Diane, not now and maybe not ever. How could he explain his duplicity? *My God*, he thought to himself, *what have I gotten myself into? When did a lie become better than the truth?*

"Claude?"

He realized a question had been directed his way. His mind had wandered to the point where he hadn't heard it.

"I'm sorry, I was just thinking about how delicious these meatballs are," he offered up quickly, taking a healthy bite of one to justify his words.

"Hmm," Sophia said skeptically. "I asked you, do you intend on staying in New York?"

"It's hard to say. I mean, I'm enjoying myself here and I've met some wonderful people. Your daughter is very special. I just wonder if the fast-paced lifestyle of this city is really my speed. Back in California we're so laid back I think every driver sits in the back seat." He laughed at his little joke, but he was the only one.

Diane, glass in hand and taking a generous sip of her wine, said, "Claude, you never said anything about wanting to return to San Francisco, When were you planning on telling me?"

"Oh, no, you misunderstand," Ferro said. "It's an idea in the back of my mind, but to actually return? That is not in my plans for a while."

"A man has to be where he can do the best for himself—and in turn, for his family," said a suddenly vocal Mr. Mancini. He then returned to twirling spaghetti on his fork.

"Getting back to your job as someone's driver," Sophia said, wiping sauce from her face, getting ready to dig into the real heart of the matter.

"Mother, you make Claude's job sound so menial. A job is a job."

"Yes, and a job I no longer have," Ferro said, impulsively.

"What do you mean you don't have the job anymore? Diane? You knew about this?"

"Oh Lord, here it comes," Diane said. "Look, Mom, Dad, there's something you need to hear, and it is better you hear it from me. Yes, it's true that Claude is no longer employed by Mr. Curtis. There was a big misunderstanding today, and the result was, well, Mr. Curtis fired Claude. That man is nothing less than a pig."

"Diane Therese Mancini, you will not speak of someone like that at my table, much less a man generous enough to employ you. Honestly, I raised you better than to pass such judgment against other people."

"Oh, Mother, that's so not true. You've invited Claude to dine with us, but all you can do is look down your nose at him. You have such disdain for what he does for a living, and all he's been is polite and complimentary. Sounds like a case of the pot calling the kettle black, if you ask me."

"Diane!" her mother exclaimed.

"Okay, you two, that's enough," Mr. Mancini said, attempting to quiet the table.

But Diane was angry, Ferro could see, and he had a feeling her defense of him was only going to land her in deeper trouble. Like it had this afternoon. "Well, mother, Mr. Curtis is a pig, and thankfully he doesn't employ me anymore. So as far as I'm concerned, I can call them like I see them."

"WHAT?" Mr. Mancini suddenly yelled, his fork dropping from his hand.

The table was quieted by his booming voice, the only sound the crack of the fork against the good China Mrs. Mancini had insisted on setting out.

"Daddy, it's not a big deal. I'm fine, great actually. I've wanted to leave the agency for so long anyway, I'd gone as far as I could and really, who can work under such toxic circumstances? Always yelling, screaming. Israel and Iran have quieter conversations than we do in the office. Look, I'll find a better job, don't worry."

"Don't worry, she says. Listen to her, sounds like she's got it all figured out," Sophia said, her sarcasm evident. "It's easy when your parents give you all you need, pay your rent, and provide a roof over your head. Let you come and go, and bring whomever home for dinner without notice."

"Your mother's right, Diane, the time to get a better job is when you still have the previous one. Did you quit, or did Mr. Curtis fire you too?"

"I quit. I just couldn't take it anymore."

Just then Sophia eyed Ferro with a suspicious look. "My daughter doesn't just quit, she doesn't make those kinds of impulsive decisions. At least, she never used to. Did you have something to do with Diane losing her job? I'm not sure I'm following along—she meets you, a man without any decent prospects. What are you, thirty-two years old? You don't have a steady job, much less income, a house, a car, any grasp of the future. And here you cost my daughter her well-paying and respectable job, the best thing that's happened to her since… well, never mind since when. There's something about you, Mr. Claude Reneau, that just isn't right. I can't put a finger on it, but a mother can always tell. You never did answer my question about being Catholic, you managed to evade that question pretty well, didn't you? What else aren't you telling us?"

"Oh Lord," Diane said, shaking her head. She just looked helplessly, hopelessly, over at Ferro. Her eyes tried to convey her sorrow at what he'd just been subjected to.

"For Christ's sake, Sophia, can we just finish our meal in peace?" asked Mr. Mancini.

"Yes, not in pieces," Diane concurred.

Sophia harrumphed before going back to her meal, but she was clearly unhappy about being shut down by her husband. The noisy scraping of her fork against the plate was the only other sound she made during the remainder of dinner. As for Ferro, he finished dinner as quickly as he could, thanked his hostess for a most delicious meal, and after a quick cup of coffee he was making his excuses, he didn't want to take up much more of their time, they'd already been more than kind. Neither Mancini parent stopped him from leaving, Just as quickly as the evening had begun, it had ended, and none too soon for any of them. Disaster Pie could have been served for dessert.

As Diane escorted Ferro to the outside stoop, she said, "I'm so sorry, Claude, for putting you through that debacle. I don't know what I was thinking. You're the first man I've brought home since a bad night with some guy named Stanley, and this was after David. I thought I could handle it. Or perhaps I thought my mother could handle it. Obviously, we were both wrong. I'm sorry it ruined your evening. Our evening."

"Yes, well, I don't think I can get back to California fast enough for them."

Diane actually laughed. "They mean well, really they do. They're very protective of me," she said. "I can only dream of being on my own again."

"Why only dream? You are a beautiful, capable woman, and you should be able to take control of your own life. Not be subjected to…what did you call it? The Inquisition?"

"Certainly, the Spanish had it easier than me, I think," she said. "Claude, it's a long story as to why I live at home, one which I don't care to get into right now."

"All in good time. I'm not going anywhere," he said, although he wondered about his own choice of words. They were meant to soothe her fragile self, offer up some kind of commitment, but really, how much could he truly offer? With each passing day, California and his previous life were that much closer in sight and given the ups and downs of his journey so far, he couldn't wait to return. Only one bright spot existed in this whole mess, and she was staring him right in face. With more than two weeks remaining, there were matters to attend to. "We have more pressing matters anyway, starting with what are we going to do about jobs?"

"Let's talk tomorrow, we'll figure something out. Who knows, maybe I'll strike it rich, and I can hire you as my chauffeur."

He smiled at her. "I would drive to the ends of the earth for you," Ferro said, his voice soft as they stood on the stoop. The night was quiet, the Queens neighborhood tucked in till morning. Only a rare barking dog broke up the silence that hung between them. "For now, we have to remain realistic. Tonight, we can sleep with our most desired dreams, and tomorrow we can face our reality. Though I have to admit, the prospect of the two of us finding work together has its merits. We could look together for some new venture."

"Working together? Doing what?"

He shrugged. "Time will tell. For now, I think I should let you get your rest, and I should get out from under the Mancini roof. It's been an eventful day. Certainly, an eventful evening."

"Where will you stay?"

"There was a motel we passed, up on Queens Boulevard, right near the subway. It looked decent enough, at least for this one night. I'll be okay, I've been in worse situations. Remember, I had to live at the Curtis household. How bad could a flea-bitten motel be? I'll sleep, dreaming of wondrous possibilities, perhaps of luxurious hotels and a high thread count in the sheets."

Diane smiled, and the effect was transfixing. Ferro allowed instinct to take command of his body as he leaned in and kissed her delicately. She held the kiss, their lips as one, sealing a new-found bond between them. It was one of thanks, of support, but also a promise. As they parted, his hand reached up and gently touched her face, catching her smile in the gleam of the moonlight.

"Sweet dreams, Diane."

"Goodnight, Claude."

As he walked off into the quiet night, Ferro wondered what her soft voice might sound like when speaking the name Ferro, wondering too if he'd ever get the chance to hear such a sweet, lingering echo. There was the immediate future for Diane and Claude, but an uncertain one for an unlikely, and improbable, couple named Diane and Ferro.

*   *   *

Sleep came easily to Ferro, despite the uncomfortable bed and rough sheets, both a direct contrast to what he'd envisioned. Sounds emanating through the walls didn't help matters, but perhaps it was the exhaustion of the day, the high emotions, and the draining effect of losing the job and dinner with the Mancinis that allowed him to drift off within minutes. Sometime in the night, his dreams found him, rushing back to him like a long-lost friend. The images were comforting now, knowing his father was forever gone but how wonderful it was to see him again, even in sepia-toned images that existed only in his mind.

"Ferro, come my boy, the move is yours to make."

"Papa, I'm thinking."

"There is a time for thinking, and then there is a time for action."

"It's just a silly game."

"That is where you are wrong. Games are anything but silly. They teach you skills you will use in your everyday life. They build your character and establish what lengths you are willing to go to achieve your goals. Now, my boy, make your move."

Young Ferro gazed up at his father, but the face that looked back at him was not the strong ox he had known growing up but instead the weathered, withered body of an old man. His body mere skin and bones, the flesh that had made him so virile now a remnant. It was the same man he'd seen that final day back in Rome, just before death had claimed him. Ferro wanted to scream out, but he suddenly had no voice, and the room he was in had no exit, no escape. There was only one thing for him to do, to take his queen and move her with the precision of a master craftsman. Make a safe move to ensure the continuation of the game, or should it be a risky move that might spell doom for her—and as a consequence, for young Ferro.

The impulse to please his father overtook his instinct for survival, and suddenly Ferro had taken hold of his queen and moved her five squares forward, until she was within striking distance of his father's waiting bishop. Depending on what his father did next, Ferro could have his queen in enemy territory with the next move. He'd already thought that far ahead. Secretly he was pleased, but he would not reveal his intentions, his expression would not betray him. The early stages of Ferro's legendary poker face.

Just then a knight on horseback came riding across the board in triumph, seemingly on its own, guided more so by his father's mind than his hand. With one fell swoop, Ferro's queen was crushed, brutally eliminated from the tense game. Two moves later it was checkmate. Young Ferro was once again defeated.

But instead of the little boy sitting opposite his father in the sunny room inside the Olivetti villa, it was a grown-up Ferro having to face the failure of thinking two steps ahead, realizing that he was doomed from his eager first step. Knowing his impulsive decision proved to be his downfall. And claiming victory was not his father—not the young, vital man nor the dying soul—but another face altogether.

It was his own face, but as he went to reach across the table and touch it, the face dissolved and Ferro was now faced with a new enemy, Dunbar, and he was laughing, loudly, the eerie sound echoing in the room.

Ferro bolted awake, his body springing up from the tight confines of the hard bed. Sweat drenched his body. He got up, turned the air conditioner up, then sat up in the ratty old chair the motel provided. From a side table, he noticed a clock indicating the time was three forty-four. Never a good hour, no matter what you were doing, and a worse time for a dream to segue into nightmare. What the hell was Dunbar doing in a dream that had previously served as a message from his father, whether from far across the ocean or from somewhere beyond? Ferro sighed, wondering what all this meant. He didn't see himself getting any more sleep, not in these uncomfortable quarters, the noise of the nearby highway suddenly filling his ears to where he could no longer drown it out. A man and woman laughing, carrying on.

He thought again about the dream.

He thought he'd been done with those dreams.

Obviously, his father was not done with him.

Obviously, his father's will wasn't yet completed. There was more to come. It hadn't yet been thirty days, and the truth of his quest hadn't yet revealed itself to him. And now there was an added complication, despite the completion of the Vodell deal, for some reason Dunbar was worming his way back into Ferro's life. That couldn't be good.

*　　*　　*

"What happened after I left?"

"They spent half the night trying to convince me to not see you again."

"It's nice to see you didn't listen to them."

"They could have gone on for hours—my mother especially. She says I shouldn't trust you."

Ferro decided to ignore that comment, for now. "How'd you get away?"

"The phone rang. Vita called, my constant rescuer. Of course, I then spent most of the conversation defending you again—this time to her. She said I was nuts to get involved with you, especially after I told her about the both of us getting fired. She was like, 'until you met him, your life was fine, normal. You had a job.'"

"What did you tell her in response?"

"I said that maybe I was finally tired of being normal and playing it safe, maybe that's been my problem this past year-plus. Time to take a leap of faith, as they say. Take that big risk. Sounds crazy."

"I don't think so."

"And knowing that, having Claude, is what gives me the courage to take that leap."

Ferro sat across from her in a booth inside a diner along the busy Queens Boulevard, just down the street from the flea-bag motel where he'd stayed. Her words reminded him of his dream from the night before, and a slight chill ripped through his body. She was saying the exact thing his father had said. Only when you take a chance does life really happen. Winning and losing do not define everything.

"Are you okay?" she asked.

Ferro sook off the strange sensation. "Yes. I just didn't sleep well."

"That motel doesn't have the best reputation. Did they make you pay by the hour?"

They laughed, then quietly sipped their coffee. The silence between them was comfortable, natural. To Ferro, it also felt nice. Like this was the person he was supposed to be with at this point in his life, in the midst of this quest. His journey was nearly half over, and while it had certainly presented its own unique set of challenges, the fact that it had led up to this moment seemed entirely worth it. Diane Mancini was funny, alluring, intriguing, tinged with a sadness that made him want to embrace her. No woman since Anna Maria had made him feel that way. He didn't want to think about her now, but having dreamed of his father, of Rome, all that he'd lost, he supposed it was only natural. But Diane was not Anna Maria. He wanted to know everything he could about Diane. With Anna Maria, knowing too much meant knowing they were not destined for each other.

"Tell me what you're thinking," Ferro impulsively said.

"Isn't that the woman's line? You know, the one men hate to answer."

"Sounds to me like you hate to answer it, too. Evading my question with a question."

Leaning forward, excitement written across her face, Diane said, "I've been thinking all night and all morning about what we should do, and I think I've come up with the perfect solution. Why don't we open our own agency?"

Ferro looked at her, amused by her enthusiasm. But said nothing.

"What? Why the heck not? I have some money saved, enough to get us started."

"Trust me, Diane, I'm not downplaying your idea. In fact, I'm all for self-employment. If you can make it work without bankrupting yourself early in the process. A start-up business can be very costly, and I wouldn't want you to risk everything on a whim and a dream. We need time to think about this, to really assess whether it's strategically sound for you to invest your own savings into a proposed business that might not turn a profit for quite a while."

Diane looked taken aback at the force behind his words. "Wow, from chauffeur to business tycoon in one day. That's impressive, Claude."

She was joking, of course, but for Ferro it was hitting just too close to the truth. He knew the real Ferro could simply give her the money she needed, and she could be open for business faster than the check could clear. His current predicament prevented him from doing so, and that left him frustrated. Even so, he knew she would refuse his offer if the truth were known. Diane Mancini was nothing if not proud.

"Look, I'm just saying it's a risk."

"What good is money if you can't spend it? Between my savings and the life insurance I got from David's death, I think I've got enough to get us going for the first few months." She was smiling broadly, despite Ferro's caution. "I know, I know, it's not a lot but it's enough. And like I said, I'm in the mood for risk-taking. Living with my parents was not my idea, dealing with the death of my husband was not in the cards, getting fired from Curtis Real Estate was not ideal. But add it all up, and the universe is telling me something. You can't sit by and wait for things to happen. You have to make things happen. Come on, drink up," she said, downing the remains of her coffee in one gulp. "I've got another idea."

Ferro was still drinking as Diane was rushing up to the counter to pay their bill, and when he joined her, they were all settled up.

"Ready?" she asked.

"Care to tell me where we're going?"

"To the city."

"What's your plan?"

"I'll fill you in as we go," she said, pulling eagerly on his arm. "Come on, the subway awaits us, there is no time to spare. No more cabs. Remember, unnecessary expenditures lead to cash flow problems, and that only hinders development and expansion, not to mention draining all our start-up costs."

"Wow, now who sounds like the business tycoon?" he asked.

As though fueled doubly by coffee and enthusiasm, they clambered down the stairs to wait on the platform and managed to hop aboard the first car of the Manhattan-bound R train minutes later. It rattled its way along the tracks, giving Diane time to outline her plan. They fortunately had seats together, their bodies in proximity, touching.

"First," she said, "let's go check out that vacant store near Curtis's office—I pass by it every day, it still remains for lease, and maybe if we act fast, we can get it for a good price. Our money is better than no money, so we can negotiate down. Remember the spot? We walked past it just yesterday. There are so many store-front real estate agencies opening, it's much easier to get walk-in traffic as opposed to having to venture into an intimidating office building. Curtis survives on ads and client referrals. Walk-in is better, more personal. It's more like a travel agency, but what you're booking is your home, your future. If we can secure the lease on that property, Claude, think how that would really screw over Mr. Curtis. Imagine people heading into his office, only to see our listings right there in the window, photos, descriptions, prices—everything." Diane took a moment to breathe, grabbing Ferro's hand as she did so. "My God, I've wanted to do this for a long time but I never had the…hell, the balls to really go for it. You, Claude, you helped make it happen."

She gave him a fast, impulsive kiss that lingered far longer in their minds than it did on their lips

Still, Ferro had to react somehow. "If that's my reward, how can I help further?"

Diane playfully hit him on the arm.

"Men. You're all the same."

Ferro wondered what that sentiment really meant and was determined to not be like every other man.

When the train arrived at 59th Street and Lexington Avenue, Diane took hold of Ferro's arm and pulled him off the train, led him topside, and then within ten minutes they were standing in front of the storefront on Madison. The sign, FOR LEASE, was still posted, followed by a phone number, area code 917. Local cell service. Diane quickly took out her cell phone, punching in the numbers as fast as she could. As she spoke on the phone, her voice soft but professional, Ferro couldn't help but take in the aura surrounding this blossoming beauty. He'd seen some miserable people since coming to New York—the thugs on the Lower East Side, the entire Curtis family, the crazy lady in the park—but he'd seen the good, too. Angelo the hot dog vendor, Fred Evans who'd helped him secure a job, even Vita with her drinks and her come-ons and noticing the fact he'd dined on olives, but who had somehow set in motion this crazy relationship that was burgeoning between him and Diane. And, of course, then there was Diane herself, who had given Ferro a reason to get up in the morning, knowing he would see her, not to mention a desire to fall asleep at night, if only to see her in his dreams.

Diane hung up the phone, breaking him from his reverie, and said, "The super is just a couple blocks away; he's coming by to open up the storefront to let us have a look. Turns out, I know the guy, he also manages the upstairs offices, which include Curtis's office. So maybe we'll get some kind of concession on the rent, good neighbors and all. And once we're up and running, we'll charge a half commission, this way we'll attract good agents to help push our properties, and the prospective tenants will be better off, too. Who in this city can't deal with even a slight break when it comes to housing? Rents are out of control."

Ferro preferred to own. And pay cash. Too bad Claude could do neither.

"Oh, Claude, this will be fantastic, our needs are simple. A few desks, telephones, computers, supplies. Well, listings, too, but that will happen with a bit of hard work. Eventually some cash flow to offset the cost of running some Internet ads, but otherwise we should get lots of walk-in traffic. Come lunchtime, Madison Avenue is awash with people. Word will start to get around." She took a deep breath. "I think that's all I can think of right now."

Ferro was holding her tight, laughing with her. He gazed deep into her eyes, locking in on them before saying, "You're something else, you know that? But I think you forgot about one important detail: the actual real estate listings. Apartments to rent, apartments that need to be sold. Are you sure you can secure enough to get started?"

"I did mention them, Claude, and of course I can secure them—I've got contacts aplenty, and I'll work my tail off to get more. Without Mr. Curtis breathing down my neck all day long, I've got the freedom to be my own boss and the time to just work. No more worrying about when his bellowing would start."

"He does bellow. And not just at you, but at your co-workers. I've got an even better idea," Ferro said. "Your friends—Jennifer and Sandra and, what's his name? Tim?"

"Timothy."

"Why not get the three of them to join your agency—but not just as employees. Offer them something better. You could do something as simple as give them fifteen percent of the company, which would enable us to retain the remaining fifty-five percent. Controlling interest. If they can put up some start-up money, that might take some of the pressure off your money."

"Oh my God, I didn't even think about that. Of course!"

"You didn't have any non-compete clause in your contract, did you?"

"Contract? With Curtis? If he could do as he pleases, well, so can I."

"That's the spirit."

"If I steal his entire staff, it'll give Curtis a heart attack!"

Just then a thick-set man in overalls came trundling out of the building, a large set of keys dangling from his rough-hewn hands. Diane said hello to him, introduced "Claude," and then eagerly pressed her hands together. The man's name was Manuel, and he picked out a key and inserted it into the lock. Diane was about to step into the world of her dreams,

As such, Ferro let Diane cross the threshold first.

As she surveyed the empty store, Ferro watched as her eyes widened with possibilities. Though the walls were blank and the floor just wood and nails and a few swirling bunnies of dust, it was almost as though they could hear the sounds of the potential office coming to life, the future just within reach. Diane spun around, her arms wide, but not as wide as her smile. Finally, she turned to Ferro and said, "Am I dreaming, or can this really be happening?"

Ferro took her in his embrace. "With you, of course this can happen. Don't you know, you can make anything happen?"

Beginning with making my heart flutter, he silently added.

CHAPTER EIGHTEEN

BY THE END OF THE WEEK, Diane Mancini's dream was that much closer to fruition, with Ferro a near-constant presence at her side, encouraging her, enjoying every single moment of her infectious energy. With a one-year lease signed quickly and a deposit put down, Ferro and Diane acquired the keys and spent the next few days cleaning up the space just to make it habitable; the fine touches that would make it an operable business could come later, once they had some more money pouring in. No sense running through her entire savings in such short time. In the meantime, Ferro visited several area Housing Works thrift shops and ended up with three desks and chairs, mismatched all, but more than serviceable, and in time the office was beginning to take shape. They had covered the front display window with brown paper to keep out the eyes of any curious onlookers, and also as a way to build up interest from the steady stream of people who passed the storefront daily. Diane had said nothing yet to her former co-workers, and they didn't even know it was she behind that brown paper barrier. She wanted the business ready, up, and running before she even approached them with "Claude's" idea.

Over the course of that week, as night fell and exhaustion came over them, Diane would return to her parents' home and, as a way to conserve their money (Ferro was using his limited funds from working for Mr. Curtis), Ferro would remain overnight in the office, working late in to the night on the fresh coat of paint he slapped against the walls. It seemed as though every morning Diane arrived with provisions—coffee, croissants, muffins—Ferro had accomplished more than was humanly possible given the number of hours passed. Did he sleep, she asked? He also looked as refreshed as ever, confessing he was using a shower at a nearby hotel gym that he managed to gain easy access to. Everything was working, including the phone lines and the computers/Internet access, which Optimum had installed Friday afternoon. As the office was taking shape, Diane began hustling for clients, listings, all that was required for the successful running of the business. Ferro claimed no knowledge of the real estate business, and so was happy to oversee the back-office stuff—as manager, it was his job to ensure everything worked properly.

By Friday night, the end of an exhausting week, Ferro and Diane turned the lock on the door and gazed at their masterwork.

"My God, it's actually beginning to look like a real office."

"I think it's ready to go first thing Monday morning," Ferro said. "Just do some last-minute touch-ups over the weekend, and then you are good to go."

"Oh, Claude, I could never have done this without you."

"You have done everything. It was your vision and your dream. I was just around to help you will them into existence," he said, and then as a surprise he withdrew from their new square office refrigerator a chilled bottle of champagne. Cristalino, it was called. "It's not Dom Perignon, but in our economic pinch, it'll have to do."

"Oh, Claude, you think of everything."

He popped the cork and poured two plastic tumblers full of the golden bubbly, then handed her the first glass. He raised his own, and together the two of them toasted their future success. Linking arms, they drank from each other's respective glasses, the bubbles nipping happily at the tips of their noses, dancing on their tongues. Diane giggled like a schoolgirl, and Ferro couldn't resist her any longer. He kissed her, deeply and passionately, their embrace as passionate as any they had experienced, and she responded in kind. As he touched the soft fabric of her blouse, feeling the curve of her breast, Diane suddenly pulled back.

"What is it?" Ferro asked, his voice a whisper.

"Claude, I…," she said, her voice wavering, as though she were afraid to give voice to all she was feeling. But as she drank the surprisingly tasty champagne and looked around her new office, her mood brightened. "Truthfully, I feel like dancing."

He pulled back, uncertain what she meant. "Here? Now? Not exactly the ideal setting."

"No, no, you impossibly silly man," she said, taking a deep sip of the champagne. "Let's go out on the town tonight—I feel like celebrating. We've worked so hard all week, and I think we've earned it. I know just the perfect place to go. We'll have a blast. It's been forever and a month since I've gone dancing, and after the stress of the past week, it will be good to move our bodies."

Ferro turned and gazed upon their former construction-site-cum-office. "What do you call what we did all week? I got more of a work-out here than in a gym."

"What we did was work," she said with a big exhale. "Right now, I'm talking about fun."

Ferro liked the sound of that. It reminded him of the man he was just weeks ago, before all the business with his father. Perhaps he could relive a part of the party he missed and in the process give Diane a bit of insight into the real Claude… the real Ferro. He raised his glass of champagne. "In that case, to fun," he said.

"To fun," Diane toasted back. "God, it's been so long. I can't wait!"

Ferro had to admit, he liked the sound of a night of indulgence. His desire for Diane had only strengthened since they'd met, and now that they'd been working side by side all week and into the evening hours, there had been numerous times he'd wanted to take her into his arms, kiss her, caress her, and make powerful, passionate love to her. Yet he'd managed to control himself, not wanting to ruin their moments together, wanting so much for their first time together to be as special for him as it was for her. It had been too long since he'd enjoyed feelings…dare he call it love, alongside sex. With other women, like Cassandra, it had been a release, but with a woman such as Diane, the depth of feelings for her stretched beyond anything he'd ever known. He wanted to hold her close, never let her go, the opposite of a release. Instead, he wanted to protect her and love her, have her love him. Perhaps tonight, dancing closely, their bodies tight against each other, faces sweaty and lit with the fire of alcohol, their time had come.

Ferro looked forward to the promise of their night out, and the possibilities that existed when the moon gave way to morning, when possibility transformed into probability.

*   *   *

Returning home to shower and change, Diane said she would meet him at the club at ten o'clock. The Whiskey Bar was at 47th Street and Broadway, so don't be late, she'd warned. "The thought never entered my mind," he said. "Don't you be."

"I don't see that happening," she responded before bounding off to prepare for their night of rest and relaxation, and for forgetting about all they had done the past week, all that was still to come in the days and weeks ahead.

Diane was true to her word, as several hours later they were dressed in finer clothes, Ferro in a trendy pair of jeans and an untucked button-down shirt and a black blazer. His face held the stubble of three days, and his shock of black hair was stylishly combed. Diane had on a sleek, strapless black dress with sparkling crystals scattered all over—she claimed not to have worn it in two years, and if so, then she hadn't changed a bit in all that time, not the way the dress seemed positively painted on her slim frame. Her hair was curled and bouncy, the perfect complement to the toothy smile that kept her face bright.

Descending the steps to the basement nightclub of the W Hotel, Ferro commented on how close they were to the bar where he'd first met Vita.

"I realized that after I suggested the place," Diane said. "And truth be known about that night, I was supposed to be meeting Vita there. I just got held up at work by Mr. Curtis, and so Vita ended up there by herself. Though not for long, apparently."

"So, I might have met you under different circumstances."

"Trust me, if I saw you at Blue Fin, I would have thought you were some hustler, looking for a quick hook-up—something I would not have been interested in."

"Me? A cheap hustler?"

"Who said anything about cheap," Diane said. "But you must admit, Claude, you have the look. That dangerous look that women fall over themselves trying to have. You aren't the love 'em and leave 'em type, are you?"

Ferro blanched. *My God*, he thought, *it was almost like she could see through the facade of Claude to the real man buried beneath*. Guilt found its way to his face as he thought about Cassandra and the cavalier way he treated her, dispensed with her.

"No, I am not that kind of man," he said, wanting to believe it.

"Good, I'd hate to see those beautiful eyes of yours catching another woman's attention," she said.

Ferro couldn't remember another occasion when she'd been so handy with compliments. She usually held herself in reserve, even when excited, and her words now felt good, like she was getting to know all of him, the inside, the outside, the true

Ferro. The changed Ferro. Even if it was still necessary for her to call him Claude, he had to hold out hope that one day he would hear his name on her lips, perhaps in the softness of the night, their bodies linked.

As they entered the club, the pulse of the music bounced off the walls. Diane secured them a spot in the corner, where small black cushions surrounded tiny cocktail tables that were low to the floor. Ferro went to the bar, ordered drinks, and then brought them back to their little corner of the world. The glasses were like balloons, small openings, wide bodies, and the amber liquid inside swirled against the sides, cascading back down into its natural sea.

"What's this?" Diane asked. "I'm not much of a drinker, I'll probably get drunk with three sips."

"Good," Ferro said. "Take four."

"Funny," she said, but then she took hold of the glass at its delicate base and drank. "This is delicious. What is it?"

"Grand Marnier," Ferro said. "Nectar of the Gods."

"Okay, it's now going to be my drink. You are definitely filled with mystery, aren't you, Claude? "

"How do you mean?"

"You just have an air about you—you work menial jobs, like chauffeuring and carpentry and painting, yet you seem to be so worldly at the same time. You not only appreciate the finer things in life, you seem to know a lot about them. This drink, for instance. How did you know I would like it. How did you even know about it? You're like a walking contradiction."

"Come," he said, "Let me be a dancing contradiction."

"Wait, let's finish our drinks and then we don't have to worry about keeping our eyes on the table. I want to dance till dawn, if we can."

"Yes, that's good, keep drinking."

"Why? Are you trying to get me drunk?

"Of course. How else can a contradiction like me get to take full advantage of such a complex and lovely woman?"

Diane smiled nervously. "Don't say that. It's not a funny subject."

"I'm sorry, it was just a joke—a bad one," Ferro said.

Still, he had a sense that even as jokes went, he'd gone too far. The mood between them had shifted, coolness descending amidst the heat of the room. As couples around them engaged in laughter and body-thumping dances, Ferro realized just how much he didn't know about this woman who had become not only integral to his life but its most important factor. Far more than any quest his father had sent him on, more so than any concerns back in California regarding Olivetti Enterprises. To him, those were things, possessions, and if the past couple of weeks had taught him anything, it was that you could live without those things and still enjoy life, Diane was a person, and a wounded one at that, and as such needed to be treated differently, kindly. He'd seen the wounds in her eyes just now, and from where he sat, he knew those fears wouldn't subside easily.

"Come on, we came here to dance, let's dance."

Diane adjusted her smile and, after a moment's hesitation, took his hand, and before the next song could start, they were already moving to the gentle rhythm of the music. Electric, fluorescent beams of red, gold, and green blinked and buzzed against the walls and the floor and the pulsing dancers, and as the DJ spun his tunes the crowd grooved to the pounding beat. As the night wore on, the dance floor became even more crowded, and finally after nearly two straight hours of shaking their booties, Diane announced that she was done.

"My body can't take one more swivel of the hips."

"Let's get out of here."

"I'm tired, it's time to go home."

"No, let there be one last surprise."

"Claude Reneau, what do you have up your sleeve?"

"You'll have to wait and see."

They made their way out in to the cool night. Times Square was lit so brightly it might have been noontime instead of after midnight, but as the two of them made their way east, the city darkened all around them. Ferro held her tight, keeping her warm, as he urged her forward. After she stumbled, Ferro laughed and said, "I think you're drunk."

"Hardly. I had that one drink—two hours ago. I worked that off, as well as my mother's baked ziti, from all that dancing. These shoes are not intended for long walks. Hey, where are we going, anyway?"

"I told you, it's a surprise."

But when they crossed a near deserted Fifth Avenue and continued eastward, Diane's eyes brightened up. "I know, let's go to our office, Claude, I want to see it one last time tonight. At this hour, even on a Friday night, Madison Avenue is like a ghost town. The passing cabs are like tumbleweeds. We'll be alone, and we can gaze at our work without intrusion."

"Just my plan," he said.

"Look at that, we're so in sync."

"Next we'll be finishing…"

"…each other's sentences."

Ferro stopped to kiss Diane, right there on the corner of Madison Avenue and Fifty-First Street, in the shadow the majestic St. Patrick's cathedral, its spires reaching high into the dark sky. Ferro felt his heart climb even higher.

"Claude, how is it possible that I think I'm falling in love with you," Diane said as they pulled apart from the embrace.

Her confession surprised him, and Ferro didn't know how to react. He enjoyed their time together, but love? What did he know of love? It had been so long since he'd uttered that word, much less felt the emotion behind it. And even back then, with Anna Maria, how could he even know that what he'd felt was love? Could what he and Diane have really be what poets called love? He struggled to find the words himself, but something held him back, and he wasn't sure why. They were simple words, the important one all but four letters? How often did he say he loved something: his airplane, the taste of a fine wine, the scent of a woman. But to a woman herself, he'd only ever spoken them once before, and in return he'd received back a broken heart. Now, in this most romantic of moments, the words failed him.

"Now I know you're drunk," he said, defensively.

Diane smacked his arm. "Gee, thanks."

"Diane, don't get me wrong. I've never met anyone like you. You are such a change for me, a great wonderful change. It's just I too need time to deal with our feelings, with what's happening between us. But know this, and I mean it from the bottom of my heart, I wouldn't change the past couple of weeks with you for all the sand in Silicon Valley."

As those words slipped out from his tongue, he hoped they weren't a prediction, a sense of something looming in his future. Because to him they sounded so temporary, as though that sand could easily slip through his fingers and be taken by unforgiving winds.

"Come on," he said, "Let's go see our future."

She smiled, and Ferro guessed that he had somehow rescued the situation.

As suspected, Madison Avenue was nearly deserted, just a few random people ambling by, keeping to themselves and ignoring the beautiful, happy-looking couple who stood proudly outside the darkened storefront. Brown paper still covered the display windows, and above the door was a thick tarp.

"What's that?" she asked. "I didn't notice that before."

"That's because I took care of it after you left to change. It's your surprise," Ferro said, and with a quick, easy motion he took hold of the rope that dangled from above, and seconds later the tarp fell to the sidewalk. What it revealed left Diane speechless.

A simple sign, but powerful all the same: MANCINI & RENEAU REALTY.

"See, our realty office is now a reality," Ferro said.

Her hand covering her mouth, words still failing her, Diane

let the tears flow down her cheeks. She kept shaking her head until finally words returned to her.

"I still can't believe it."

For the next ten minutes, it was all Diane could do just to stare at the sign and simultaneously offer up sweet kisses Ferro's way. He accepted them all, happily. Finally, he coaxed her inside their office, where one last surprise awaited them. Ferro withdrew from the small refrigerator a fresh bottle of champagne and filled their tumblers. Then he lit a single candle on one of the desks, and ushered Diane to the floor, where he'd set up a bed of blankets.

"Diane," Ferro said, taking her in his strong arms, holding her. The light of the candle flickered off the walls, their bodies creating large shadows against the wall, as though indicating that this moment was larger than life, bigger than both of them combined. "Diane, I want to make love to you, right here, and right now."

He gazed deeply into her beautiful eyes, saw his own reflection in them. But what he also saw was a return of that inner fear that seemed to take hold of her whenever someone threatened to get too close. He knew right then that as wonderful the setting, no matter the mood that swirled around them, that this was not the moment for them. Love was expressed, but it would not be made.

With tears beginning to stream down her cheeks, Diane simply said, "Claude. I just can't. I'm not ready, and I don't know if I'll ever be."

"Can you tell me why?"

"It's something…it it's not something I've ever talked about."

"Not even with your mother?"

"Some of it, yes, But, not everything," she said, her lips quivering. "My mother, she asks many questions but sometimes she knows when to be quiet and just listen."

"And Vita? Surely you confided to her? "

"Vita knows everything. But no one else. Until now."

It was clear that whatever had happened, Diane had suffered for it. And even more than telling him that she was falling in love with him, what she was about to reveal was obviously the harder task.

"I wish you would tell me," Ferro said, his voice so quiet that not even the walls could hear. It was just the two of them, here in this building and perhaps even in this world. They were alone, and even secrets could not harm them. "Diane, what happened to you?"

*　　*　　*

Wasn't her life supposed to be something out of a storybook, filled with the fulfillment of all her dreams? An ideal life that her parents had promised her as a child each and every bedtime as they closed the book of fairy tales she so loved. The heroines and princesses in all those tales certainly faced adversity in the course of their lives but ultimately, they triumphed and, as young Diane Mancini been assured, they lived "happily ever after." However, for the adult Diane Mancini, her own fairy tale had barely begun before it was over.

With the candle still flickering and Ferro and Diane settled on the softness of blankets on the floor, she began her tale with the ominous sounding, "Death came to visit me one day, just over a two years ago, and it hasn't seemed to leave my side since then. It makes decisions for me, it holds me back, it keeps my fears in check and my hopes stashed away in a box. It taunts me, and no more so than when I went in search of the reason why. What does death want from me, why does it hold me so?"

"Diane, I didn't mean to push you on this," Ferro said. "If you're not ready, just say so."

"No, this is perfect—well, as perfect as it can get, I suppose. Here I sit amidst the pieces of the future, and so it's only fitting I say goodbye to the past right here, and right now." She paused, taking a deep breath for strength, for fortitude, and then began in earnest. "After I heard, you know, that David had been killed in action while on some stupid mission in Afghanistan—Bagram, I couldn't ever forget that name—I just can't explain how dead inside I felt. A numbness spread over my body, in my heart and my mind, in my arms and legs, as though inwardly I'd been paralyzed, but somehow could still move, talk, walk, work, function. I thought David was going to be at my side all my life, that in our old age our children would take care of us, just the way nature intended. That's the way it's supposed to be written. But no, there was no happily ever after, not for me."

"We all deal with death, every day. It's the part of life that makes no sense, why our beginnings must have ends," Ferro said. "It's how we react to it that truly tests our character."

"It was different with me," she said. "I don't know, I guess I wanted to know more about how David died, whether he was really the hero his commander had said in his official letter, or if it had just been some dumb accident, a freak of nature. So, after the guys in his unit came back, I wanted to know everything about how it happened, what David might have said before he died, assuming he'd even had a chance. I made dozens of calls, and most of the guys said nice things about David, but they weren't exactly forthcoming with details. I think men who share the horrors of battle feel they can't share anything with those of us on the outside; that we won't understand.

"Anyway, I finally found a man who said he was with David when he'd been shot. His words hit me like a slap in the face. I was awakened, and I was focused—because this man, Charlie, had promised to tell me everything he knew. He said he recalled David talking about me, always about me. It was like I'd found a missing link, the one man who could connect me to my beloved David. Maybe help me finally say goodbye properly. I told him I needed to see him, to hear about it in person, and so Charlie invited me to visit him. He lived in

Philadelphia, not terribly far away. So, I requested time off from my job and made my way to the city of Brotherly Love. I thought that was appropriate, Charlie had been one of David's brothers-in-combat, what better place to hear of his heroics, of his—even in death—undying love for me."

"What did you find out?"

Diane steeled herself for the rest of her story, and in so doing Ferro just wanted to reach out and embrace her. But he knew that to get through this, she needed to say focused, she didn't need the complications of another man's arms around her, not now.

"What I learned was that the atrocities people inflict on each other are not limited to war. It can happen anywhere, at any time," she said, letting a tear fall down her cheek. She didn't bother to wipe it away.

Ferro reached out a finger, where he caught the tear before it fell to the floor. The drop was like an elixir, a powerful potion that took them back to a time Diane would sooner forget, a time that she had to face in order to move on.

"Charlie Stubbs was his name, and he was nothing but a liar," she said. "No, that's not right, he was plenty more than a liar. He was a beast who preyed on the vulnerable."

*   *   *

She had never before been to Philadelphia, though it was such a quick ride down the New Jersey turnpike. The address Charlie had given her was in a section of town called "Center City," which Diane later learned meant the heart of the city, but not always the best part of town. She parked her car, a Ford Taurus that wasn't exactly brand new but that managed to stick out among the older models and rusted-out vehicles found on the side street she'd been directed to. As far as she could tell, these row houses were nothing more than tenements. She quickly found her way to the right address.

Climbing the few crumbling steps to the front entrance, Diane looked apprehensively to her right, then to her left. Could this really be the home of one of our vets, even a recent one? What kind of life had this man had before the service, and now after? Diane took a deep breath and knocked. Seconds later the door opened to reveal a man of medium height and stocky build, not exactly the model solider she had imagined, and he was seedy looking, dressed in stained khakis and the kind of T-shirt some people called "wife-beaters." Perhaps she should have taken that as a sign to leave right there and then, make some excuse, and be done with this foolish endeavor. But she'd come this far, and besides, she wasn't necessarily here for herself. This trip was about bringing to a close the notion of lost dreams, ones that had once existed between herself and David. That's when she noticed the can of beer in the man's hand.

"Charlie Stubbs?" Diane asked hesitantly.

"Yeah, that's me. The famous Diane Mancini. Wow, David always said you were pretty, but you know how guys talk, especially in the military. They talk of their girls being swimsuit models, but usually they end up looking like a beached whale. But you're a knockout."

"Oh, uh, thank you. I suppose."

"Come on in," Charlie said, eagerly. "Yeah, definitely you should come inside."

Filled with renewed apprehension, Diane stepped inside against her better judgment. The apartment, if you wanted to call it that, hadn't been cleaned for some time, and was probably better suited to housing a family of rats than human inhabitants. Trash littered the floor, and boxes of empty take-out covered the surfaces of both a dining room and living room table. Empty beer cans were the only attempt at decoration. Thinking of leaving, she turned to find that Charlie had maneuvered behind her and had clicked the lock shut.

"How about a beer, bon?"

"Oh, uh, no thank you. I don't drink. Please, Charlie, I don't have a lot of time. I just came to hear what you have to say about David. He was in your unit, right? That's what you said over the phone."

"Oh yeah, I knew him. Good guy, always liked sharing a beer with him. Why don't you join me, you know, like in memory of him? Be just like when I was over there with him, fighting those damned rag heads. Nighttime would arrive and we'd knock back a few brewskies. Yup, Davey sure liked to kick back and relax. Here, let me get a fresh one."

Meaning get himself a fresh one. Diane still declined his offer.

She knew something was definitely wrong. David never went by any other name, and he was much more responsible than to "kick back" with a bunch of beers. Except what did she really know of the situation "over there." Tours of duty could change a man, could kill him even while still alive.

"Charlie, I appreciate your, uh, hospitality, but I just want to hear about David, about how he died. How it happened, did he say anything before…you know."

In response she heard the pop of the top of a can. Wrapping her arms around her, she gently sat on the edge of a ratty sofa and waited as he returned from the kitchen. His fleshy lips were sucking down on the cold can in his hands. She was beginning to think this was a huge mistake, that this drunken fool knew nothing about what had happened to David. She wondered if he even knew him. Davey.

"About David?"

"Not much to tell, happened like it happened to too many people I saw over there," he began, "We were pulling a raid on some house, the suspected headquarters of some terrorists, Potential suicide bombers—you know, the bad guys. So, the whole unit moves ahead on David's command, and we've got our rifles out, ready to shoot first, ask questions. Hell, we never asked questions, stupid fucks couldn't understand us anyway. So, we go in, guns blazing, when some nutcase comes screaming at us from behind a hiding place. He starts letting loose with an AR-16. Bullets started flying everywhere. We had no chance, all of us ducked for cover—all of us except David, who stood his ground like the officer he was and returned fire. He took one in the chest and next thing you know, he's down and he's done. For good. Nothing anyone could do; he was gone before he dropped." Charlie

sucked down the rest of his beer, perhaps in an effort to bury the bloody image he'd just brought to reality. Dull the pain. "Yup, that's how it happened, that's all I know. He saved our lives, that's for damn sure. Once he hit the ground, hell, the rest of the unit started shooting. Raghead didn't have a chance. He was pulp before we were done."

Diane's eyes were filled with tears, and she wasn't sure why. Whether hearing of the heroism displayed by her husband, or for the clinical way Charlie had told his story—as though it were fiction, some fabrication that had no meaning beyond simple storytelling. Perhaps these guys were taught to maintain an emotional distance. Diane, she couldn't be so cold.

"Hey, hon, why don't you forget about that guy. He knew what he was doing, serving his country, saving us all. We should honor a man like that—by sharing a beer together. Come on, I know one won't kill you. Hell, thousands can't kill you," he said, as though he had tried, was still trying. "We can talk about something in the present, you know, like us."

"No, no, thank you," she said, still fighting back the tears. "I've got to go now."

"Go? What are you in such a hurry for? You just fucking got here," he said, his voice growing angrier with each uttered word. "I want my money's worth."

"Money? I have no money." Diane had no idea what he was talking about, surely the man did not expect to be paid for the information. What kind of a monster was he?

"Money. Just an expression, hon. You know, like, I tell you what you want to hear, and then I get a little payback in return. Come on," he said, sidling up beside her on the battered sofa. "What's the rush, babe? Not like you got someone waiting at home for ya. Maybe you can stay over, you know, keep a vet company? I get you home safe after that—what do you say, I ain't got no job, nothing to do for the next few days. Look, you and me, we could have ourselves a real fun time. Got plenty of beer."

Diane looked at the man's pock-marked face, at the wanton expression, the emptiness beyond his eyes. That's when she noticed he was dangling a small cellophane bag in front of her. White powder filled half the bag. My God, *she thought,* not only is this guy a drunk he's high on drugs—cocaine. *She had to get out of here, but smoothly, without getting him any madder.*

"Mr. Stubbs, I appreciate your telling me what happened, but I really must go."

"Babe, relax, we could do this whole bag, really make us feel good. Keep the party going all night, make a real night of it. Maybe the whole weekend."

"Hearing your story about David, I'm sorry, I'm really very upset now. I must go."

Diane rose from the sofa, only to have Charlie grab her hand in an effort to keep her from leaving. "Where the hell do you think you're going? What, I ain't good enough for you? Shit, women are all alike. You try and be nice, offer up a drink, and all you get in return in some prissy attitude. It never works when you ask nice. So, I guess I gotta stop asking."

By now he had pulled Diane close, and she could smell his alcohol-laden breath on her face. She turned away in disgust, which only angered him further.

"Look, he's dead, ain't he? Worm food by now. Me, I'm alive, and I'm ready to get it on. You can just stay here, keep me company, right? Just for tonight?"

"No, I've told you, I've got to get back. Please, let me go. I have to leave."

A sick grin washed over his face, the rejection egging him on, the beer altering his personality. "You want to leave, baby? Fine by me, but first you gotta give me a little kiss, you know, as thanks, Come on, hon, I was the last man to see your hubby go down, he told me to look after his babe, make sure she was happy. That's me, I can make you real happy."

"Leave me alone," *Diane said, trying to push him away.*

The man wasn't taking no for an answer. He went to kiss her, missed as she squirmed in his arms. She felt his hands pull her body tight against him, and she shuddered from his touch. He didn't take the hint. In fact, her resistance only served to fuel him on. He grabbed hold of her blouse and ripped it, tearing the fabric, exposing her body, her breasts.

The man heaved with pleasure. "Yeah, that's what I want. Show me what you've got."

"Please, please, let me go."

His breath was hot against her neck. He nuzzled her, hands groping her chest, "Sure, I'll let you go, just as soon as you give me a kiss."

"No, stop it. Please, I only came for…"

"Oh, I know what you came for, little lady," he said, and then with one fluid motion he grabbed hold of her and threw her down on the sofa. Diane screamed as he came for her, his body falling on top of her. She could feel the pressure of his erection as he ground himself into her, nearly suffocating her in the smelly old sofa cushions. Diane couldn't believe this was happening. My God, what did this man want? Was he going to rape her? Was he that drunk and high he didn't know what he was doing, or had this been his plan all along? He'd lured her here for this. She had to stop him.

As he continued to struggle against her protests, Diane searched for something nearby to smash against him, anything to get him off her. What she found was the beer can; it certainly wasn't heavy enough to knock him out, but as she reached for it, she discovered it was nearly full. She grabbed it and instantly began pouring it over the man's head.

"What the…" he said, scrambling to his feet as the cold liquid doused him.

Diane took advantage of the sudden freedom and ran for the door, tears streaming down her face. She somehow got the lock undone and opened the door, fully expecting Charlie to make one last lunge for her. Instead, she noticed he hadn't moved from his spot in the middle of the living room, beer staining his clothes, his face, almost like he too was crying, a pungent mix of salty tears and dripping beer.

"Fucking bitch, you don't know what it's been like."

Diane closed the door behind her and ran down the street to her car. As she left Center City and began the trek back to New York, she wondered what kind of life Charlie Stubbs would have, how much had he been affected by the horrors he witnessed over in in the Middle East? Not that it excused his behavior, but for the first time, and certainly not the last, Diane thought that maybe her David had gotten the better of the deal. With what the atrocities they faced in war, what kind of life was this to come back to?

*   *   *

Ferro blinked away his own set of tears as he held Diane in his arms. He said nothing, waiting only for Diane to resume her story.

"I honestly thought he was going to rape me, maybe even kill me. He was so out of control, and so obviously miserable. When I left his apartment, I didn't even want to return home, I was embarrassed at what had happened. I mean, how could I willingly enter a strange man's apartment. Didn't I have any common sense? I could only imagine what my mother would have to say if I told her."

"You wanted answers about David, it's perfectly natural," Ferro said. "Diane, I'm sorry I pushed you to tell me that. Had I known the pain you experienced well, I would not have put you through that. I don't know what else to say. Just…I'm so sorry."

She wiped away the tears. "After that encounter, something inside me clicked, changed me. A kind of paranoia took over—I felt that any man who looked at me wanted to rape me or do worse. I felt all sorts of eyes on me while I rode the subway or walked home, thinking someone would pounce out of the darkness and attack me. That's when I decided to move back in with my parents. They could protect me, the adult reverting to childish fears."

"Whatever happened to Charlie?"

"I got an email one day from someone else in David's unit. Charlie Stubbs overdosed one night about six months ago. He was a sad, pathetic man, and I can only imagine the horrible life he must have had. He needed help, I know that now. Still, what he did to me, his pain wasn't an excuse to cause more. I'll never forget his touch, I'll never get his image or his stink out of my mind."

Ferro held her tight, rocking her like a baby. "It's okay, it's all over, and you've turned the page, started a new life. You told me, and I cannot begin to express how much that means to me. And how proud I am of you; how brave you are. Tomorrow morning, the sun comes up, and you know what? You'll have a brand new life ahead of you. A bright new life."

"You think it's that easy?" she asked.

"Yes, I do. Mornings mean change, mornings mean possibility," Ferro said.

"That sounds like it's almost possible."

He kissed her again but said nothing, waiting only until she fell asleep.

Amidst the tumble of blankets, Ferro eased her down and watched as she settled in for the night. Ferro slid in beside her, held her lithe body tight, protecting her from the past, promising only wonderful things for their future, their tomorrow. Ferro knew what he had to do. She'd opened herself up to him, emotionally, and soon it would be his turn. Not just about his own past, the wound he still felt over Anna Maria's betrayal, but about his real identity. But not just yet, his father's will continued to hover over him. There was still much to be done.

So it was on this night, on the floor of their new offices, that Ferro and Diane slept, their lives becoming as entangled as the blankets that covered them. But as much as some secrets were exposed, others lay buried, deep under the covers, deeper still, in their souls. For now, all the blankets could do was protect them against the cold and other predators of the night.

CHAPTER NINETEEN

IT WAS AN HOUR MADE FOR THE WICKED, when shadows hid motives, when moonlight illuminated the activities of those who thrived in the underbelly of society. While all good people slept away the troubles of the day in the arms of their loved ones, one man accustomed to sharing space with bitterness planned to stay awake long into the wee hours of the morning, busy plotting his next move, his next step—his next conquest. Sleep had never been his friend, and so he often used these fading nighttime hours to his advantage, to prey upon the weak. Inside his San Francisco apartment, which overlooked Ghirardelli Square and the lush, picturesque Bay, Richard Dunbar impatiently paced the floor, waiting for his expected guest to arrive.

At forty-three minutes after the midnight hour, Dunbar's bell rang once. He'd instructed the doorman downstairs to not announce his guest, just to let him up. Check his ID, but then let him up. Dunbar hated the sound of the bell, the way it echoed through the apartment. It reminded him of the many times he'd awaited late-night visitors, their arrival leaving him hollow, their departure shaming him. Scrambling across the floor now, an anxious, nervous Dunbar opened the door and let his guest inside quickly.

"You're late."

"You told me to wait until he'd left the office. That only happened a half hour ago."

"Damned persistent he is," Dunbar said. "Not like anyone I have on staff."

The guest said nothing.

Dunbar escorted the trench coat-clad man into the living room, where he proceeded to pour two fingers of Glenlivet scotch into a glass of cut crystal. He plopped one ice cube into the precious liquid, swirled the glass around, and breathed in the potent aroma. He sighed easily, his nerves calmed at the first sip. He stared back at his guest, who was gazing at him expectantly.

"It's been a long day, surveillance takes patience, Mr. Dunbar," the man said, his handle-bar mustache twitching from his own bouncing set of nerves. He looked as uncomfortable in this home as he felt. "Sure does look inviting, you know, that drink."

Dunbar frowned. "This stuff doesn't come cheap."

The man waved a manila folder at his client. "Neither does this."

"Fine," a resigned Dunbar said, realizing how much he hated depending on sleazy operators like these. Damn private investigators, sometimes they were more opportunistic than the people they were hired to follow. "Make it yourself, I'll take that file off your hands."

Dunbar took hold of the thick manila envelope and moved to the soft comfort of the leather sofa. There were already two indentations in the thick leather, remnants from earlier. For a second he stole a look back toward the bedroom, hoping all was quiet, and that it stayed that way. Setting his drink aside, Dunbar withdrew the contents and immediately began poring through the collected documents, agendas, photographs, all of it neatly put together by date, time, person. He had to admit it, the guy did good work. So what's a little lost Glenlivet.

By now the private investigator had rejoined Dunbar, though he remained standing.

"You'll see, it's a very complete accounting of all you asked for."

"Yes, yes, so I can see. Mr. Carpenter, this is good work, very good work indeed. I'm impressed," Dunbar said with admiration that surprised even himself. More so than depending upon other people, he hated to admit when they were good at their job. Gave them an inflated sense of self, which, truth be known, he could puncture with one quick insult. For the moment, though, setting all the paperwork aside, Dunbar refrained from his normal course of action. "So, you say Olivetti left his office only a half hour ago?"

"No, not Olivetti. His number one, that guy named Lawrence Henderson."

"I know him. A yes man if ever there was one," Dunbar said.

Carpenter just nodded. Agreeing would cost too much.

"Keeps all sorts of late hours, he does," the investigator said, "and doesn't seem to have anything in the way of a personal life. I've been trailing him for over a week. He's never deviated from his pattern. Guy should get laid, that might help loosen the tie."

"Hmmph," Dunbar said, who only shed his tie at the end of the day, when he could hide behind the privacy of his own abode. Then, with a sneer, said, "Probably a big closet case, Henderson, I bet has a secret crush on Olivetti. Speaking of which, what do you have about my mysterious opponent?"

"From what I've been able to figure out from employees and other folks in the building and neighbors near his villa, Ferro Olivetti has been AWOL for nearly three weeks. I spoke with this real looker of a woman, Cassandra something, she was Olivetti's last known paramour. Her photo is in the batch, somewhere. Can't miss her, boobs out to here. Seems she met Olivetti on his big European vacation a couple months back, but the last she saw of him was the night he got word about his dying father. That's when he dumped her and left her out to dry. So, she was only too willing to talk to me. Guy should watch where he puts his pecker." The investigator paused to laugh. "Guess we all should."

Dunbar looked back down at the paperwork. "So, Olivetti's mysterious disappearance coincided with his father's dying?"

"It's beginning to add up that way. I haven't been able to talk to Olivetti's driver yet, not that he would talk, probably," Carpenter said, but it was clear there was something in his voice, hesitancy that gave doubt to his statement. "You know, there's something strange about this Olivetti fellow."

"Like what?"

"Well, finding a good picture of him has proven to be quite difficult—a Google search doesn't provide much. I mean, we know what the guy looks like, the ladies seem to like what he's got, but even though he seems to have skipped town, sometimes I think I see him."

"What the hell does that mean?"

"I don't know. A couple of times last week, I spotted Olivetti's limo outside the office building, and so I kept watch on it. See that group of photos? Yeah, those."

Dunbar picked up a series of 20 eight-by-ten black-and-white photographs, beginning to flip through them as Carpenter recounted what he'd witnessed. "Guy comes out of the building, he's slick looking, just as you imagine Ferro Olivetti to look. You know, designer labels, fancy shades, the works. Following behind him is his trusty aide, Lawrence. But it's what happened next that made me wonder what was going on. The Ferro-guy gets in the back, as expected. But it's Lawrence who gets behind the wheel and drives away."

"So what?"

"From what I've learned, Mr. Olivetti has a personal chauffeur who drives him everywhere. Neighbors gave him up, guy by the name of Claude Reneau. Haven't been able to dig up much on him."

Dunbar started to grin. "I see an opening. Get me as much info as you can about this Reneau character. It could be the most important clue yet as to what happened to Olivetti. I mean, the guy hasn't been seen in weeks, but somehow he was able to close the Vodell deal? Something is fishy, and I've got the hook. And the bait."

"You suspect some kind of foul play with Olivetti?"

"Doubtful," Dunbar said. "Ferro doesn't let anyone get too close to him, not enough to mess with him. But I'm beginning to wonder: what if Olivetti had some kind of nervous breakdown after his father's death, and the company—Lawrence and this Ferro stand-in—are trying to fool the business community into thinking that everything is normal with Olivetti Enterprises. What if he's holed up in some institution, bouncing off the padded walls? If word got out, Olivetti stock would take a tumble, might even spoil the Vodell deal he stole from under me. The paperwork hasn't been signed; they just have a gentleman's agreement in place so far. In any case, Ferro Olivetti is ripe for the picking."

Carpenter departed ten minutes later, his drink drained and his new assignment clear. As Dunbar looked out the huge window, the mist was beginning to descend upon the Golden Gate Bridge and the City by the Bay. You could hide in mist that thick, but eventually it would burn off and reveal all your secrets. Dunbar better take advantage when he could.

"Olivetti, I've got you now," he said, taking a last sip of his Glenlivet. "If what I suspect is true, and I can help spread the word, then in one week's time your company will cease to exist. A shell of a corporation, it will just be a part of Dunbar Industries. It will be like Ferro Olivetti never even existed."

Excitement bubbling over, he went to attend to his beloved orchids, which he kept at home in addition to using as decoration in his office. He loved their lingering scent, the air of danger they represented. He snipped the head off a particularly weak looking one, once so full of life. Now the head of the flower lay discarded on the floor, dead, forgotten. Dunbar stared out the window, saw his own devilish smile in the ghostly reflection.

That's when he heard a voice coming from the bedroom.

"Hey, I didn't fly all the way across the country again to watch you pace the floor."

Dunbar grinned wildly. He was feeling powerful, more so than he had earlier.

He looked forward to a new game of dominance.

"Coming, Stan."

*   *   *

For Ferro Olivetti, the fortunes of his past in no way measured up to the last week or so of his life, and he couldn't imagine a more perfect scenario than the one playing out before his very eyes. He and Diane, growing closer every day, their business freshly launched. For Ferro it was like nothing could possibly go wrong. He'd won as his father had asked, to recreate himself, all the while taking pride in his ability to start again from scratch.

Time was about to catch up to him.

A week in the life of Mancini & Reneau Realty had quickly passed, and in that time Ferro and Diane had seen it go from empty storefront in bad need of some fixing up to a tastefully— although eclectically—furnished office bustling with bountiful promise; and as luck would have it, with customers, too. For a company with little word of mouth and, at the moment, zero ad budget, business was near booming. Being on the ground level, walk-in traffic was encouraging and managed to keep the sales folk on the floor busy. Jennifer and Sandra were talking up the new office with their established contacts, having just joined the new business a few days ago. When they'd given notice, Curtis had, of course, thrown them out right away.

"You want to leave, go now," he'd bellowed in his characteristic way. "Watch that stupid business downstairs fail faster than you can say unemployment."

The lone hold-out from Curtis's office had been an uncertain Timothy, who didn't have any money of his own to put into the start-up business. He also managed a surprising amount of sympathy for his boss. "Think of poor Mr. Curtis, too, sure he's mean but that's just a front. There's something sweet beneath his gruff veneer."

"Timothy, you're hopeless."

He sighed and said, "Hopeless romantic is more like it."

"Okay, ick," Jennifer had said.

"Yeah, TMI," Sandra said.

Diane and Ferro shuddered at the very thought of an unlikely pairing of Timothy and Curtis together when told of the conversation; of course, they knew a few more things about Curtis's predilections than either of the two women, much less Timothy, and wouldn't they all be surprised? Some jobs were changed, some jobs remained the same, none of them holding it against Timothy, the Samantha to their Carrie, Miranda, and Charlotte. He was still one of them, at lunch and at after-work drinks, where gossip was as intoxicating as anything the bartender could whip up. But that was then, this was now—a busy office on Monday morning, their second full week of operation.

Diane had just arrived after a nerve-wracking hour-plus subway ride that seemed to take days, but still she maintained a sunny demeanor. There was something about being your own boss that was refreshing; stress still existed; it was just a different kind. No more worrying about the fluctuating moods of your supervisor. She found Ferro waiting inside her office, as she had every morning since they'd opened their doors. She gave him a quick kiss out of sight of everyone else, then, in addition to her morning coffee and bagel, Diane removed from her purse a small, exquisitely wrapped gift.

"I'm so glad you're here, Claude. I've bought you something," she said.

"Bought, or brought?" Ferro asked.

"Bought, Claude. As in, I spent money and purchased you a gift—as a thank you. Here, please, with my eternal gratitude."

"Diane, you really shouldn't have gone to the trouble. You know I don't need anything. Just seeing that beautiful smile on your face every morning is reward enough. Besides, we've only just opened the doors, there are bills still mounting. There shouldn't be any unnecessary expenditures."

"Buying you this gift, that's what puts the smile on my face," she said, then mockingly added, "Besides, the more I get to know you the more you sound less and less like a handyman and more like you've been digesting business books—or maybe even wrote one. That kind of experience, you should have a better compensation package."

"Now who sounds like they've been reading 'The One Minute Manager'?" Ferro said, this last part as he leaned against her desk, hoping for a second, enticing kiss. She did as he'd hoped, and when they parted, he saw the small, rectangular wrapped present before him. She nodded toward the gift.

"Diane, really, I appreciate the thought."

"Gessh, you're impossible. You have got to be the only person I know who doesn't want a surprise—and you're also the only person whom I want to give one to. And see, it's already wrapped so there's no returning it now. Guess you'll just have to open it," she said with an easy, playful shrug. "It's nothing big, really, just a token of my..."

"Affection?" he asked, hopefully.

"Appreciation," she said, smacking his cheek lightly.

Ferro slid a finger beneath the tape and unwrapped the gift. He lifted the lid and found himself looking at a smart-looking, blue and gold watch made from Swatch. He gazed back at Diane with an inquiring look on his face.

"There's more, go ahead, look at the bottom of the box."

He dug under the tissue paper, where he came up with two tickets to watch the Blue Angel's air show over Jones Beach on Saturday afternoon. "The watch is so you'll know when to pick me up for our date."

"What's this? Diane Mancini initiating a romantic night for the two of us?"

She pushed him away. "No more kisses for you, wise guy."

"Diane, I appreciate the thought, but we really do need to watch our costs."

"Do you know how much you and I netted in the last week? Over five thousand dollars."

"Really, that much?" Ferro said, his voice a mixture of surprise and bemusement. He'd once spent more than that just on lunch.

Diane studied the informed skepticism on his face. "I know it doesn't sound like a lot of money, but we've been doubling our clients each day, so pretty soon we'll be able to open up more branches, become an even bigger presence in the New York real estate market—certainly bigger than Curtis ever dreamed of being."

"If that keeps up, not only will we be able to buy out Curtis, but we might just give the Rockefellers a run for their money," Ferro said, getting a sarcastic laugh out of her. She laughed a lot more these days, and smiled too, much more so than when he'd first seen her at Curtis's office, in the back seat of the Town Car, or during their first date at the coffee shop after the funeral. She'd been a bundle of nerves then, and only now had she begun to relax, to enjoy herself. Work could be fun, you just had to be in the right business. The money-making business, Ferro thought.

"Let me ask you something, Diane," Ferro said, his voice suddenly serious. "If you had only one penny in your possession, and you doubled it each day for forty days, how much do you think it would come to?"

"I'm not sure what you're getting at."

"Think about it. You have one penny the first day, two pennies the second, four pennies the third, eight pennies the fourth day, sixteen, thirty-two, sixty four, and so on."

"Okay, I get the scenario. But I still don't know what you're getting at."

"You said we were doubling our money every day," he said. "By using my lesser dollar amount model—but still using the same equation—how much do you think you'd have by the fortieth day?"

"Thousands of dollars, I guess."

"How about if I told you the total comes to over ten billion. Not ten billion pennies—but ten billion dollars."

"That's ridiculous. You're pulling my leg with your fancy math," Diane said, her brow creased.

"You wouldn't want to bet your share of the partnership on that, would you?"

"Against yours?"

"Yes, absolutely."

"No, I don't think I'm going to take any chances with you, Claude. Once again, you've got me thinking I'm working with a CPA or something. Let me guess, Harvard Business School, summa cum laude. Decided you didn't want to follow in daddy's footsteps, and you rebelled, much to his displeasure."

"First of all, it was magna cum laude," Ferro said, a grin crossing his face. "And no, my father was quite proud of my pursuits. He appreciated that I could be my own man, even if sometimes I strayed too far from his ideals."

"You know, Claude, you don't often talk of your family. Your father. I'm sorry if I touched on a difficult subject. Just as mothers and daughters have a strange bond, fathers and sons have their own code. Were you close, you and your Dad?"

"Very," Ferro said, his voice suddenly heavy. How had they gotten on this subject? In all the time he and Diane had spent together, he had carefully avoided talk of himself, his past, his family, it had always been about fulfilling Diane's dream. "There is much to tell you, Diane, but now is not the time. We have just begun the work week, and as my example has proven, there is much work to be done."

"Claude, I'm not sure I understand what you're trying to say to me. Is there a lesson in your mathematical equation?"

"All I'm saying is, nobody doubles their business every day. There will be lean times ahead, and so it's better to conserve our cash reserves and not go spending them on frivolous—if sweetly intended—gifts. At the moment, caution is the better part of valor."

Diane sat back in her chair, feeling slightly dejected. "I give a gift, and I feel guilty. You sure have a strange way about you, Claude Reneau. I just wanted to let you know how much you've helped me—changed me."

"It goes both ways," Ferro said, "and I love you for the gesture."

Hearing those words—three little words that hung in the air like a heavy storm—a flustered Diane reached for something, anything. The phone, her computer mouse, the discarded wrapping paper, to help distract her from what she'd just heard. Expressing love, even in such a passing fashion, was a lot to absorb. She swallowed the knot of emotion in her throat, then said, "Come on, like you said, there's work to be done today," she said, and then pointed to his new watch. "The clock is ticking."

"You passed, Ms. Mancini. A+."

As Ferro departed her office with a wide grin, he couldn't help but realize how right Diane was. Time was slipping by so quickly, so suddenly, he was nearly at the end of the thirty days he'd promised his father. Funny that the first two weeks had passed so slowly, making him endure the struggle, the pain, the unfamiliarity, and the hunger. Now that he was more settled and had a plan set in motion, the days were slipping by. Soon, the month would be over, and so too would his life as Claude Reneau. Then what? Then who was he? As simple as this life was, Ferro knew it was just a matter of time before things got a whole lot more complicated.

He would need to come up with an explanation sooner rather than later.

*   *   *

One of the safety rules set up by the staff at Mancini & Reneau Realty was that no agent went to visit a new off-site location without someone else to accompany them, and it was usually Ferro who accompanied the agent—whether Sandra, Jennifer, or Diane. Since he was designated the office "floater," without any specifically assigned duties, he was more than happy to assist where needed.

As it turned out, this morning, a Thursday, it was Diane who requested he join her.

"I need to get to 94th and Riverside stat, meet with a client at their apartment. They want to sell quickly, and I think I can do it for them. A young couple was in here just the other day looking for just this kind of place," she said. "Hello, Claude, are you paying attention to me?"

Ferro was sitting at Sandra's desk, staring at the calendar on the desk. He had been marking out days, realizing three weeks had already passed. He was down to his last nine days in New York, and as such, he found himself wondering how he was going to explain himself once it was all over. When it came time to return to being CEO of Olivetti Enterprises.

"Claude?"

He was concentrating on what it would be like to be Ferro again, so he didn't hear the name he'd been calling himself for the last weeks. "Hmm?" he asked, turning around to find Diane standing over him. "Oh, yes, sorry. Sure, ready when you are."

Diane already had her coat on, her purse and her shoulder bag at the ready. Ferro needed to hunt down his jacket, which he felt like he'd been wearing for the better part of a month. When Diane saw him put it on, she frowned.

"I think we need to buy you some new clothes," she said.

"What did I say about buying me stuff?" he stated.

"Claude, if you're going to accompany us to our meetings, you need to look a bit more professional. You give off this casual air, and the client may not take us seriously if they think they've hooked up with a bunch of slackers. So, consider the clothes another business expenditure—besides, how are you going to buy any clothes when you're not accepting any salary? Come on, we'll stop at a men's shop on our way back to the office. My treat—and no resistance. Got it?"

"Your name comes first on the business," he said.

"Don't you forget it." But her voice was anything but firm.

Smiling, the two of them were preparing to leave the office when the front door opened. The bell above it jangled to announce they had a visitor, a potential customer. Over the course of the past week and a half the bell had rung so many times the sound was growing old, but it was still a good way to get the agents' attention. Though right now it was the perfect warning bell, considering their surprise guest.

"So, this is the little office that could," spoke Curtis, bemusement written across his face.

"Is there something we can help you with, Mr. Curtis?" Diane asked, trying to maintain a polite facade despite the seething she felt inside her. In truth, she detested the sight of him, his corpulent face, his overhanging belly, the sneer he thought went with everything.

"Just thought I'd check out the…competition."

"Worried?" Claude said.

Curtis tossed Ferro a look of utter disdain. "You. A chauffeur, my ass, This is all your fault, filling Ms. Mancini and the others with delusions of grandeur, thinking they can do better without me. My life has been a mess since the moment we met—and that goes back to that time on the plane. What fun you must have had at my expense."

"'Had' indicates that we are no longer laughing at your expense," Ferro said.

"Damn nuisance, you and this damn business. You'll fail within a month."

"If you really thought that," Ferro said, "you wouldn't be here."

"Speaking of which, Mr. Curtis, what do you want?" Diane asked.

"Just wanted to give you fair warning," he said.

"About what?"

"This kid-sized company of yours, there's no way it can survive the cutthroat, moneyed real estate world of Manhattan," he said, with more than a snicker. "It won't be tomorrow or the next day, but I'll see to it personally that Mancini and…whatever other name is on this business, Reneau? Fancy French name. This realty office will fail. Thinking you can steal my clients by setting up shop downstairs from my office? You'll be ruined, all of you, and none of you will work in real estate again—you, especially, Claude Reneau or whoever the hell you really are."

Ferro stepped forward until he was face to face with Curtis. The man backed away just slightly.

"What's the matter, Curtis," he said, his voice a whisper so no one else could overhear. This was between them. "Don't want to get too close to me now, huh? Why is that? Just like your sleazy wife and vile daughter, one can hardly forget that you too wanted to get in my pants. You want me to expose that, Curtis? What will Hilda think then? You think your prenup will cover fraud? Your marriage is a sham, just like your entire life. So, before you go threatening Ms. Mancini and her employees, I suggest you take a good hard look at what's really important to you. Because you don't want to mess with me. I could destroy you without having to lift a finger. One phone call, you're done." He paused, and then with adrenaline coursing through his veins, said, "You're right about one thing, though. This is all my doing, and I wouldn't change a thing about how it's happened. I had faith that Ms. Mancini could run her own business and no longer have to be under your miserable thumb. The fact that our new venture has made you miserable in the process, well, I just consider that a bonus."

"You're just a fucking driver, what the hell do you know."

"I know much more than you could possibly realize," Ferro said, feeling like his old self, as though he were on the phone with Dunbar and shooting down his challenges. "If you knew who I really was, you'd think again about trying to cross me. So, remember this: No matter where I am, what I'm doing, know that I'll be watching your every move. And if you so much as make a move against this office, I will retaliate."

By now Diane had moved in next to Ferro, wanting to hear what was transpiring. Seeing her beside him, Ferro suddenly clammed up, afraid to reveal anything further. He'd already said too much.

As for Curtis, his face had grown tomato red with a mix of anger and embarrassment, and finally he slinked off, but not before impotently slamming the door behind him. Before leaving he turned and issued one last warning: "I'll take you all down—starting with you."

Of course he was pointing at Ferro.

Ferro just laughed at the pathetic man and watched him disappear into the foot traffic outside.

"My hero," Diane said, grabbing hold of his hand. "What did you say to him to get him so riled?"

"Forget it. Forget him. Let's go, you don't want to be late for your appointment."

But Ferro knew this meeting with new clients was just a delaying tactic. Diane wasn't the type of woman to let anything go. Considering the lengths she'd gone to find out the truth about the death of her husband, Ferro wondered what she would do once Ferro disappeared from her life. She'd demand answers, and sooner or later she would get them. Ferro had to consider whether it was time for her to learn the truth.

*   *   *

Two hours later, Diane and Ferro had finished viewing the luxury apartment on Riverside Drive, and as a beautiful, spring day played out before them, they opted to enjoy a late lunch outdoors. Grabbing gourmet sandwiches and Cokes from a nearby deli, they wandered into Riverside Park and found an empty bench and began eating. Joggers jogged by; skaters skated by. Dogs barked. Kids played ball. Life swirled all around them. They ignored it all, content to be in each other's company.

"Claude, that confrontation you had with Curtis? What did you say?"

"I just told him not to underestimate you."

"Me? Thanks for the vote of confidence, but as you know, he's been in business a long time and, as such, has lots of contacts. He could do a lot of damage to my reputation, knock us down before we've even gotten started. But that's for another day. Right now, I'm more interested in what you said to him: 'No matter where I am,' that's what I heard. Which makes it sound like you're leaving town. Is that the case? Like at dinner that night with my parents, are you planning a return to San Francisco?"

Ferro set down his sandwich, wondering if he had the stomach for either the food or the current conversation. He turned to her and said, "Diane, I realize you know so little about me, that I do not enjoy discussing my previous life. All you need to know is that I am a man who lives for each day, but I also don't take them for granted either. Who knows where any of us will be a day, week, a year from now."

"Smooth, Claude, but a total nonanswer. With Mr. Curtis, you weren't speaking metaphorically. Your voice, your intonation, already had you somewhere other than here in New York. Please, be honest with me, are you planning on leaving New York? Is it your previous life in California? Is it something there— someone there?"

Ferro leaned in, pressed his lips against Diane's. "Can we just enjoy the moment? "

"That's not what I was hoping to hear."

"Think of it this way. If I were to leave, wouldn't that make your parents happy? They didn't exactly take to me that night.

Might have fed me to the dogs, if you'd had any. And I'm not sure what you've told them about my involvement with your new venture, but I can't imagine it would go over well. You've been the driving force, and you put all the money into it. I've just been the hired help. They might just think it was my idea to have you invest your savings into this start-up business."

"Well, you've got me there, I can't disagree," she said. "My parents—my father mostly—would go crazy if they found out I invested all of my savings in my own company. Particularly going into business with you. My mother is already starting to ask too many questions, wondering why I'm spending so many hours at my new job. A girl like me needs to date, have fun. She keeps pushing that stuffy accountant Stanley at me. Anyone to keep the likes of you away from me, that's my mother's name for you. The Likes of You."

"Just assure her that I'll be gone soon."

Ferro resumed eating his sandwich, taking large bites, keeping him from talking.

"See, there you go again—mysterious and cryptic," she said. "Claude, I can't stand thinking about you leaving. It's like we're in a countdown to the end of our life." She paused, her mood suddenly optimistic. "Who knows, maybe we can open a branch in San Francisco. You could run it, and I could come and visit and we could…"

"I think you need to start a bit more slowly, Diane."

"I'm just excited. When I go to sleep at night, I can't help but dream, and my dreams these days are big. I know you're right, Claude, in the light of day, reality has a way of invading all you hope for."

Just then Ferro dropped his sandwich, mayonnaise and tomatoes staining his suit jacket. What made him lose control wasn't merely Diane's questions, but rather inside his jacket pocket his cell phone had vibrated. Only two people had the number, and he was sitting with one of them. Which meant Lawrence was calling, and that could only mean one thing.

Trouble was brewing far away. But he couldn't possibly answer it now; that would only make Diane start to ask even more questions. So, he deflected the conversation back to his suit.

"Looks like we'll have to get that new jacket now," Ferro said.

Diane looked dubious. "I think you did that on purpose, to change the topic."

Sort of, he thought. "Shall we go shopping?"

"Maybe I'll buy you a tie, too," Diane said, "that way I can strangle you with it."

The idea was that Ferro could not look stuffy—that was not the image Mancini & Reneau Realty wanted to project. They were running a trendy boutique realty office, and so as they finished their lunch and wound their way down the Upper West Side, Diane pulled him inside the Urban Outfitters on 72nd and Broadway and immediately began pulling items off the racks, holding them up against Ferro. An antsy Ferro waited out a few suggestions, and then finally he was able to pull himself free and head to one of the dressing rooms.

"I want to see you in every item," Diane said, her voice trailing behind him.

"All at once?" Ferro added.

"Funny boy," she said. "I'm going to go look for more stuff."

"Fine, thanks," Ferro said, glad to have a moment's peace. Since his phone had buzzed nearly thirty minutes ago, his mind had conjured too many scenarios to count, none of them good. Lawrence had been instructed to call only in the case of a "dire emergency."

Quickly taking out the cell phone, he saw the missed call status. Lawrence. He pressed send and in seconds it was ringing thousands of miles away.

"Ferro, is that you? Oh, thank God."

"Yes, Lawrence, it's me. I don't have much time. Just tell me what's happening?"

"Bad news, the biggest. Dunbar's been furious about losing Vodell and he's been looking for a way to retaliate. So, he's made a serious move to take control of Olivetti Enterprises. He's made a tender offer of sixty-five dollars a share to anyone with a sizeable chunk of our stock."

"Clever, isn't he? But he can't afford to do that forever. Not everyone will sell to him. Let's counter his offer with seventy dollars a share. Knock that son-of-a-bitch out before he's even started."

"Ferro, we're already stretched to the limit. Most of our money is tied up with the Vodell deal, you know that. Dipping into our reserves would put the company in serious financial jeopardy, and if word gets out, that might make our investors panic even more than they are. Ferro, rumors are circulating about you here on the West Coast—where are you, why haven't you been seen. People are wondering what's wrong with Ferro Olivetti. Even your friend Steve called, wondering if he should sell to Dunbar. I think Dunbar is behind the rumors."

"Steve would never sell. As for the rumors, they're just rumors, Lawrence."

"You say that, I know it. But people think rumors are just a smokescreen for the truth—which they envision being worse than the actual truth. Ferro, I know what you're doing is important to you, but I really think you need to come home and resume your role as CEO. It's time."

"It's not time. I cannot do it."

"Ferro, don't be foolish. This is Olivetti Enterprises we're talking about."

"Nothing is more important than what I'm doing right now, I wouldn't still be away if it wasn't. Look, Lawrence, just hold off our investors for another week, ten days at the most. This is almost over."

"Ferro, I've been fending off questions for the past three weeks the best I can, but if you remain AWOL much longer. well, I just can't be held responsible for how the business community responds. They may just side with Dunbar—he's not without influence, you know."

"Lawrence, just handle it."

"Dunbar petitioned a judge, it's his first move in his take-over attempt. The hearing is set for tomorrow. That's why you've got to get back here."

"So, block it. Ask for a continuance."

"I tried. Can't do it. You may have been able to avoid the Vodell hearing, but the judge is gonna start to get suspicious."

"Damn. Same judge?"

"Probably sits in Dunbar's pocket," Lawrence said. "Ferro, this is serious, you could lose everything you've built."

Ferro thought about the situation. Leave New York, save his company. Stay with Diane, lose the respect of his treasured father. Dammit, why did these two items have to be mutually exclusive? Hadn't his father understood what was truly important to Ferro, that without his company, without his fortune, he was just another…what? Mere mortal? A failure. A man with nothing to cling to? Just who was he doing all of this for? Himself? A wave of selfishness washed over Ferro. He felt as though his father was suddenly beside him, an angel sitting on one shoulder. Was there a devil on the other shoulder? And if so, who was it—Dunbar, or maybe even Ferro himself?

"Claude, what's taking you so long in there?"

"Listen, Lawrence, I've got to go. I'll call you later."

Ferro quickly hung up the phone and then tossed on one of the cool blazers Diane had picked out. He wiped the sweat from his brow and emerged from the dressing room as though nothing was amiss.

"I like it," she said, "We'll buy it. Now, what do you think of this tie?" Diane asked.

The tie was simple, colored red, white, and blue, with an inspiring pattern of Lady Liberty. As though its presence signified something special between them, a sense of freedom they had unleashed in each other.

"It's the perfect complement to the blazer, and the most

wonderful remembrance of my times in New York," he said, his smile wide. "You should pick out all of my clothes."

"I'd love to," Diane said, even though her voice betrayed her truer thought. Because both seemed to realize at this exact moment how unlikely a wish that was. Only days separated them from an awkward present to an uncertain future, and neither felt like speaking about it. Ferro felt horrible for how he had led Diane on, knowing he couldn't promise her anything beyond his thirty days. How did he allow her to convince him to put his name on her business? It wasn't even his name anyway, and soon he would be gone, absorbed by the ether, transported back to a different time, a different life. When that day came, Claude Reneau as she knew him would cease to exist.

CHAPTER TWENTY

A NEW DAY, A NEW ADVENTURE. Ferro had decided to make the most of these last few days in New York, and to not waste a moment of them without Diane. A special day had been planned, and Ferro had taken it one step further. He surprised her on her doorstep that Saturday afternoon, flowers in his arms, a smile on his face. And a car waiting to whisk them away.

Diane's first comment?

"Claude, I thought we were cutting back on business expenditures."

"You are," Ferro stated agreeably, "but I never agreed to such a thing. I must retain a level of flexibility. It enables me to make executive decisions behind your back. Besides, this ride isn't exactly costing us much beyond the price of gas—not cheap, I grant you, but doable under current budget constraints. I believe, though, if you look closely enough, you'll recognize the car. And perhaps even the driver.

The day was gorgeous, a lush and beautiful sky filled with fluffy white clouds set against a backdrop of the most alluring blue. Ideal weather conditions for flying, and while they themselves would not be venturing into the sky, that wouldn't stop their hearts from zooming upwards.

"Mademoiselle, your chariot awaits," he said with a wave of his arm.

"That's Mr. Curtis's Town Car!" she exclaimed.

"Yes, it is," he said. "Now, come on, get in before your mother gets sight of me and whisks you back inside and ties you up. Anything to keep me from you, is that not so?"

"I think you're exaggerating," she said, "but with my mother, why give her an opening."

Giggling like a school girl, Diane jumped into the rear seat, and Ferro quickly joined her. He addressed the driver. "Timothy, we're ready whenever you are."

"Timothy! " Diane said. "What are you doing?"

"It's okay, Diane. Mr. Curtis has taken a shine to me lately since you girls all went out on your own. Guess he doesn't want to lose anyone else. So, when I asked if I could borrow his car, he didn't even hesitate. He said he was going out of town for the weekend anyway, so he wouldn't be needing it. No questions asked, can you imagine? I think he's starting to come around, realize that you need to treat your employees better. Whatever his reasoning, it's all to your benefit. Let's go."

The car pulled away from the curb, next stop Jones Beach for their date with the Blue Angels air show. Though this April day was early in the season for the spectacular aerial show, they had been blessed with a day that hinted at a summer of promise. Starting with the picnic Ferro had packed.

They enjoyed deliciously tart mimosas during the car ride, and when they arrived at their destination Ferro took hold of a wicker basket and blanket from the trunk, much to Diane's delighted surprise. With instructions for Timothy to pick them up after the show, the car sped off, and Diane and Ferro made their way through the gathering crowd. Finding a spot on the cool sandy beach, spreading the blanket, and donning sweaters to offset the breeze blowing off the ocean, they were ready for the most enticing of dates.

Setting out caviar, soft brie cheese, and a loaf of crusty French bread, Diane couldn't hold back her excitement.

"Everyone around us is going to be so jealous," she said.

"Who is this everyone you refer to?" Ferro asked. "I don't see anyone but you."

"I think my heart just swooned."

As they feasted on their lunch, washing it down with a crisp, chilled Sauvignon Blanc from New Zealand, they waited anxiously for the arrival of the legendary Blue Angels. At last, from a distant point in the sky, they heard the airplanes first, the supersonic sound shooting across the sky with a thunderous boom. Then the planes themselves emerged from the clouds in perfect formation, and they did a quick fly-by of the beach, much to the joy of the crowd. Applause rang out, not nearly as deafening as the sound from the airplanes, but enthusiastic just the same.

Their bodies close together, Diane and Ferro settled in to watch a show filled with daring maneuvers and brilliantly executed tumbles through the air. For nearly thirty minutes the show continued, each aerial feat more impressive than the last. Ferro himself was mesmerized by the display, and he couldn't help but think of his own plane, Gambit One, sitting idly back in San Francisco, neglected all these weeks by the pilot who caressed its controls like a lover. He imagined something similar happening in the cockpits of the Blue Angels; there was nothing like being behind the controls of a plane, shooting into the sky, thrilling to the sensation. For a second Ferro was taken back a couple of months to when he'd returned from his holiday with Cassandra in tow, back before this entire quest of his had begun. He wondered briefly about where Cass might be now, and then he stole a look at Diane and realized there was no comparison. The fact that a woman of Diane's beauty and character was beside him, he couldn't contemplate a life without her. But he would have to, and soon.

Damn, he thought, *why must he always get distracted by thoughts of what might never be. Why couldn't he enjoy the moment with worrying about tomorrow?*

"What is it?" Diane asked him.

Ferro knew he'd just sent off a signal, a tinge of sadness hanging in the air between them.

"Oh, nothing. Just realizing how incredible this moment is. I wish I could just stop time and make today last forever."

Diane leaned against his body, her hand caressing his shoulders. "Is this about the possibility of you leaving? Again? Claude, I can't even begin to think about it. Surely there's something that could keep you here."

Ferro shushed her with his finger. "If you knew all about me, you wouldn't want me to stay."

"I don't believe that for a second," she said, her voice strangely confident. Ferro knew that two weeks ago a comment like that would have sent her off running, claiming she didn't want to see him again. How she had changed, grown. He feared what his departure would do to that confidence. "I know you better than you think I do, Mr. Claude Reneau. In fact, I know you so well that I can tell you this: that I love you."

Ferro leaned in for a kiss, received one in return.

He was about to say those same exact words when the Blue Angels began their final set, distracting them both, taking them out of their private moment. The sound of the soaring engines was once again deafening, and Ferro's words, hanging on the tip of his tongue, were lost to the patterns of the wind. He pulled away just slightly, not because he didn't wish to be close to Diane. His phone was vibrating again. *Shit, he thought. Lawrence had lousy timing.*

*   *   *

"I called as quickly as I could," Ferro said. "Make it fast, I only have a couple minutes."

The Blue Angels had shot off into the sky for the final time, the crowd had dispersed, and Diane and Ferro had decided to take a walk along the boardwalk. Right now, Diane had gone for some cold sodas to freshen them up, leaving Ferro alone on a wooden bench, the picnic basket and blanket at his side. He'd quickly called the phone number.

"Okay, I've been dealing with our lawyers since we spoke. Yesterday's hearing didn't go so well. Dunbar's team got the judge to issue a restraining order, stopping us from interfering with his tender offer. They've subpoenaed you to appear in court on Monday. That's as much of a continuance as I could get."

"Stall them."

"Ferro, I can't. The judge was furious that you weren't there yesterday. Comments were made—and not just from Dunbar but from the judge himself—that if you don't care enough about your own company, why should he stop someone who wants it from taking over. This is serious business, Ferro."

"I can't leave, not yet. I could be there next Wednesday, at the earliest."

"Ferro, we're out of time," Lawrence said gravely. "The judge so much as acknowledged that if you don't appear in his courtroom at eleven A.M. this Monday, he'll accede to Dunbar's request, and you'll lose control of your company by default."

"But that's impossible."

"Ferro, please. The judge must be in Dunbar's pocket. Whatever this trip of yours is all about, surely it's not worth losing everything you've worked for to a carnivore like Dunbar. You've been gone twenty-seven days—trust me, I've been marking them off on the calendar. Surely, you've accomplished what you needed to do by now, what difference will a few more days make in the grand scheme of things? You're putting your very future on the line, don't you know that?"

"More than you realize, Lawrence," Ferro said, eyeing Diane as she approached from the other side of the boardwalk. "Look, I've gotta go. I'll call you back."

"You always say that, and yet I'm always the one dialing."

Ferro closed the phone, putting it back in his pocket just as Diane neared.

"Who were you on the phone with?"

"Oh, uh, Timothy. He's stuck in traffic."

"Claude?"

"Yes?"

"What's the matter—really? The expression on your face, I can tell you weren't talking with Timothy."

"And how do you know that?"

"Because I just got off the phone with him. I told him we might need a few more hours."

Confusion crossed Ferro's face. "I'm not sure I follow."

Diane settled in next to Ferro, brushing her hand against his scruffy cheek. "Meaning I wasn't ready for the date to be over. In fact, I was thinking maybe our date could last well into the night, if you catch my meaning."

"Diane…"

"But now I don't know," she said. "I come back and join you, only to have you lie to me. Claude, please tell me what's going on. I can help, but only if I know what's really going on."

Taking a deep breath, Ferro said, "I may have to go back sooner than expected."

"Why? To what? What's going on?"

"I can't tell you."

Diane stood up, clearly annoyed. The mood from this perfect day, from the champagne and the caviar and the Blue Angels and the dreams they tossed into the sky, was all fading as fast as the afternoon sunlight. "Why do you keep so many secrets from me? How can I ever learn to trust you, Claude?" When he had nothing to offer, Diane asked, "Tell me one thing: are you in trouble with the law?"

"No, it's nothing like that." Ferro tried to find more words and they failed him.

"You know what, Claude? I think I can find my own way home. Thank you for a lovely day. I wish you the happiest of lives. wherever it finds you."

"Diane, wait."

Ferro wanted to run after her, but if he did…what then? What could he possibly say to her that would return her to his arms? How could she even begin to understand the duplicity he'd pulled on her. None of it was deliberate, he was caught in his own personal web, spun by his father, and now he had trapped others inside it. The best he could do was cut them free, maybe even himself. Of all his options, only the truth would bring them together. But the truth might also destroy them, and right now he couldn't take that risk.

*   *   *

Nighttime at Mancini & Reneau Realty on Saturday found Ferro Olivetti just as he'd been when he arrived in New York all those weeks ago. Alone, and facing an uncertain future. Since Diane had left him on the boardwalk at Jones Beach, Ferro had been pondering what had gone right, and ultimately what had gone wrong during these past weeks. He'd done as his father had asked; he'd stepped away from his life and taken stock of his place in the world. He'd done it with no money, no influence, just himself and his wits. And what had he come up with? More than anything, he wanted to spend his life with a woman named Diane Mancini, a woman he'd never even met a month ago, a woman who he now couldn't imagine a life without.

But yet here he was, without her.

The back room of Mancini & Reneau Realty wasn't as comfortable as Ferro had alleged. The sofa bed they'd bought from Housing Works had come with a thin mattress, and most nights Ferro didn't even bother to remove the cushions. He'd just crash on the sofa itself, tossing blankets over his body in an effort to bury himself from this existence. Sure, it was better than a park bench or the attic room atop the Curtis house, where he wasn't safe from stepmother, daughter, or father. That did not mean he had to be content with his lodgings. Truth be known, he was growing more antsy as his father's-imposed deadline loomed. The Dunbar threat didn't help. It was as though the closer to his thirty-day expiration date he came, the more unsettled he became.

Tonight, it felt like time had stopped, his wish granted but with consequences. No Diane. Even a check of the watch Diane had given him offered up no encouragement. The hours had yet to turn past midnight, the miserable end to a day that previously held such promise was not yet here.

Getting up from the sofa, Ferro padded his way into the main office, looking around at the darkened computers, the silent phones, the coffee maker, which always seemed to drip during the day. None of these items showed any signs of life; he was truly by himself.

"This is ridiculous," Ferro said aloud, staring around at all he'd helped build in the last two weeks. "I'm jeopardizing the company I built and doing what instead? Sleeping by myself in an empty office for a company that I don't even own. Papa, if at any time during this trip I've needed your guidance about what next to do, now is that time. A sign, a voice from above, some advice?"

Silence was his answer.

"That's not what I was looking for," he said, and realized maybe it wasn't up to his father to decide but for Ferro to figure out. He was a take-charge kind of man, and all month long he'd been letting others dictate the situation, all the while figuring that by going along for whatever ride he found himself on was just as it had been intended. His father's will, brought to fruition. But at what cost?

What to do? In this city of eight million people, he was just one more lost soul searching for the answers to life. In other words, he was helpless. He wasn't the powerful, influential, dangerous Ferro Olivetti. He was Claude Reneau. A nobody.

That's when the room brightened with the light of an idea. "Of course, Claude!"

Eagerly, Ferro returned to the back room, where he fished

for his cell phone from his jacket. He dialed Lawrence's offices, and the man picked up on the first ring.

"I have an idea," Ferro said.

"Oh, thank God."

"Lawrence, listen closely. Claude has my license, my wallet. All of my identification."

"And?"

"It's simple. Claude looks enough like me, just have him go to court for me."

"What? Now I know you've gone completely crazy. Ferro, it's too risky, too dangerous. This isn't a game we're playing— we try and deceive the courts, and we could lose more than Olivetti Enterprises, we could lose our freedom. Jail time."

Ferro had already spent a night in jail. He'd survived. "I don't see any other option, Lawrence."

"Well, I do—come back home where you belong," Lawrence said. "Look, Ferro, even if I don't fully understand what you've been up to the past month, I respect that you felt you had to do it. Out of some obligation to your father; I get it. But finding yourself at the request of your deceased father is one thing; losing everything because of it, I can't possibly think that's what he had in mind."

"Lawrence, you didn't see him—in Rome, on his deathbed. The life was draining from him, and all he could do was point to the newspapers and magazines that featured articles about me, about the way I was leading my life. My father didn't see me as some all-powerful business man. He saw me as a spoiled playboy, moving from party to party, woman to woman. I need to show him that I'm a deeper man than he thought."

"Then come home and be that businessman. Be that man, Ferro. Honestly, is there something else going on? What's really keeping you there?"

And that's when the answer hit Ferro: absolutely noth- ing. Diane had walked away from him, and he'd let her go without any attempt to rectify the situation. What more could he accomplish in the remaining days that he hadn't already accomplished? He knew what he wanted, he'd learned so much about himself, and now, maybe what he'd learned most was what mattered most in the world. Papa was from a different time with different ideals. Ferro's company, his empire, all that he'd built, that's what mattered, what drove Ferro, what awakened him in the morning and allowed to sleep contentedly at night. It might not be as fulfilling as a heart full of love, the knowing warmth of someone who loved you, but it was who he was. His father had taught him to never give up. Not in chess, not in life.

Okay, the next move was his.

And though most rules of the game of chess advised against it, Ferro knew he had to move his king. Not out of harm's way, but right in the path of danger. Bring them on, he wasn't king by mistake.

It was time to move.

"Fine, Lawrence, send the Gambit One," Ferro said. "Send my plane. And make sure there is plenty of cash on board."

"*Your* plane?"

The voice he heard wasn't Lawrence's, and it hadn't even come from the telephone. Ferro spun around in surprise, and his expression faltered when he saw the unlikely woman standing behind him. He eased the cell phone down, closing its lid on his trusted pal.

"How did you get in here?"

"A woman like me has her ways," said Hilda Curtis, gently stepping forward into the darkened room. Her fur coat and heels appeared to be all she was wearing. That, and her all-knowing grin. "See, I knew something was different about you. No day laborer has hands like you, with hardly a scar on them. Nice skin, nice manners. It started to dawn on me earlier this week when Curtis would come home, bellowing in his boorish way about how you had ruined him, helped Diane and those others start up this company. I told him he was exaggerating; you were just an out-of-work driver, a nothing. Now, I'm pleased to see that I've been wrong."

Ferro said nothing. He waited for what was to come next.

"It wasn't until I was at my hairdresser earlier today that I started to do some probing all my own," she said. "See, the thing about hair salons, we have plenty of time on our hands, and so we page through magazine after magazine, poring over the photos of the rich, the famous, the beautiful people who live lives the little people only dream about. And though the photographer didn't get a good shot, I recognized a certain quality in the man in the photo I was studying. Not his face, but rather his hands. They were smooth, creamy you might say. Like they'd never done a hard day's work in their life. Combine those with the scruff of his cheeks, and I began to see a resemblance. So, how am I doing, Mr. Olivetti?"

"I don't know what you're talking about. My name is…"

"Yeah, I've heard your song and dance routine. Claude Something-or-Other. Some faux French name. Trust me, I don't believe you. I barely did when I met you. The name didn't exactly fall trippingly off your tongue." She smiled at that, her own tongue sliding against her ruby red lips.

"What do you want?"

"Oh, that's simple enough," Hilda said, shedding herself of her fur. As suspected, the woman he thought of as Curtis's Vegas wife was wearing nothing but her birthday suit. Her breasts were full, with surprisingly large nipples, enticingly erect. Where her legs met hips was a neatly trimmed triangle of hair, barely hiding her pleasure zone. With her heels clacking against the floor, she sidled up beside Fero, running her hands over his chest. "You take care of me like I want, and I'll keep your little secret. Besides, from what I read, you're quite the cocksman."

With that she grabbed hold of his shirt, and unlike her previous seduction attempt, she didn't bother with the niceties of unbuttoning it. She tore the material of his shirt, exposing his strong, muscled chest to the fresh, cool air of the room. His nipples jutted out from beneath his chest hair. She grazed her ruby nails against his skin.

Quickly, Ferro pulled her wrists back to keep her from making any further contact, but she resisted, managing to steal a nibble of a kiss on his ear lobe as her body pushed against his. Despite his feelings, he found himself responding. It had been too long since he'd been with a woman, any woman, and the day had begun with such promise that who should have been with him right now was Diane. Instead, the temptation that was Hilda Curtis was here, now, ready, and willing. The Ferro of old would have taken her in an instant. And wasn't that who he really was, Ferro Olivetti? She whispered to him, "Come on, Ferro. You know you want me. Satisfy me like Curtis never could, and never will."

He pushed her down, roughly, onto the sofa.

"What do you really want? Money?"

She laughed. "Hardly. I'll have more than I need once I'm free of Curtis, and that's going to happen sooner rather than later. Come on, Ferro, from all I've read of your exploits, you're quite the lover. You bed anyone and everyone. Who knows, Ferro," she said, clearing enjoying the sound of his real name on her tongue, "you just might realize that Hilda Curtis is more than enough woman for you. So much so you won't need anyone else. That naive Diane included."

Time no longer stood still; zones crossed and melded, they came together.

Which meant of course that Diane chose that moment to appear at her own office.

"Claude!"

The fates were clearly working against Ferro, so it stood to reason that Diane would walk in on this situation. Ferro turned at the sound of her voice, saw her standing in the doorway. He stole a look back at Hilda, her naked self more than exposed on the sofa, and realized he was half undressed himself.

"Diane, it's not like…"

"Forget it, Claude. My God, all this time I've been allowing myself to fall in love with you, and you've done nothing but make a fool of me. I trusted you, I told you the painful things that happened to me, and this is how you treat me in return? My parents were right to not believe in you, you've done nothing but lie to me since you came into my life. Now it's time for you to leave my life. Get out of her right now, and take that piece of trash with you. Claude, I never want to see you ever again."

As a disappointed Hilda gathered up her fur and strode out of the back room, she turned to Diane and said, "You may want to ask him his real name. It's a doozy."

When Hilda was gone, Ferro looked back at Diane. "Will you let me explain?"

"I don't really care who you are," Diane said through falling tears. "All I know is that the Claude Reneau I knew is gone, dead, and in his place is a complete stranger. You're no better than Charlie Stubbs, leading me on only to take advantage of me. Please, leave me alone. Go back to where you came from, and never contact me again."

Ferro knew there was nothing left to say. Diane was right, he'd ruined everything and nothing could salvage this situation. Though he had to admit the Stubbs comment hurt so deep inside his heart, he doubted it would ever heal. Not even bothering to take any of his belongings, Ferro shuffled out of the office and into the darkened night of Manhattan. It would be his last night in New York. He'd tried to make a new life for himself, he'd tried to see beyond his privileged world and make room in his heart for a passion he'd never even dreamed possible. And in all of this he had failed.

All Ferro Olivetti could do now was wait for the arrival of his plane to whisk him away from this unmitigated disaster. Papa was wrong, he'd been wrong all along, and this past month had been fruitless, a waste of time and energy. Of money. It had risked all that Ferro owned, all that Ferro was. Ferro Olivetti was who he was, and everyone would have to deal with that. His friends certainly, and now, for certain, his enemies.

The night air felt good. It cleared his lungs.

He felt good, he was back.

He looked down at his watch, the one Diane had given him. The hour had just turned to midnight, the new day had begun. Taking hold of the strap, he removed the watch from his wrist and tossed it into the trash. He felt nothing except a hollow echo in his heart.

He'd made it twenty-eight days. Two shy of his goal.

But what did it matter?

Forget this foolish venture, this so-called quest.

Forget everything.

Forget everyone.

Papa. Diane.

Only Ferro Olivetti mattered now.

PART FOUR

FERRO'S REVELATION

CHAPTER TWENTY-ONE

A NEW DAY DAWNED, perhaps a new era, and with it came new possibilities. Making matters even better was the fact that the old Ferro Olivetti was back where he belonged. The hills of San Francisco looked golden, the bridge that spanned from land to land as majestic as ever. This City by the Bay was an endless gateway to the West, a welcome landing pad for those tired from the frenetic pace of the East. And as much as Ferro was glad to be back, no one was more pleased than Lawrence.

"My God, are you a sight for sore eyes."

"Thanks, Lawrence, it's good to see you, too," said a tired and distracted Ferro. The world looked different to him, as though he'd just woken from a deep sleep, where he had dreamed of another life, another existence. "Now isn't the time for pleasantries, I'm afraid. I believe we have a court battle ahead of us, and after that, a war to win. If that means destroying our opponent, then so be it. In fact, I prefer it that way. Come on, time is wasting, and I, for one, cannot wait."

As he spoke that last phrase, Diane immediately came to his mind; it was one she had used often when setting up her business. On his wrist he felt the emptiness from the watch she'd given him that was no longer there, and instead he swallowed all thoughts of his life in New York and forged ahead from the tarmac to the waiting limousine.

The flight across the country had been interminable. Never before had Ferro been up in the sky and wanted so desperately to be part of the living on the ground. His pilot who had brought the Gambit One to him had asked him if he wanted to take over, a request Ferro had surprisingly denied. Assisting only with the take-off, feeling that rush as they hit the air, he'd then retreated to the main cabin and tried his best to sleep. He'd finally given up, rejoined the pilot just as they were an hour outside of San Francisco. Ferro then took hold of the controls, as though by doing so he was also taking back control of his life—the one he knew.

Now, returned safely to terra firma and with Lawrence trailing frantically behind him, Ferro approached the waiting limo and shook hands heartily with Claude. "Nice to see a friendly face. Claude, how are you?" The name Claude on his tongue sounded foreign, strange, even though he'd been answering to it for what seemed years. Back on his own turf it was good to be Ferro again.

"Fine, sir. Glad to have you back home," said his trusty chauffeur.

"Indeed."

Ferro couldn't have agreed more.

He piled into the rear of the limo, Lawrence scrambling right behind him. Doors closed, Claude resumed his post, started the engine, and in seconds the sleek limousine that spoke of privilege and money pulled away from the airstrip and began the trek back into San Francisco. Ferro, back in comfortable surroundings, wasted little time jumping back in.

"Give me the latest on Dunbar."

"You're not going to like it," Lawrence said.

"I usually don't. That doesn't mean I don't want to hear it."

"I'll show you, instead."

Lawrence handed over yesterday's edition of the *San Francisco Examiner*, where on the front page of the business section a headline read, "Is this Ferro Olivetti?" and the accompanying photograph showed a man dressed all in black, standing beside a limousine. And it was not just any man, but clearly, to Ferro at least, the man was Claude Reneau, and he was leaning not just against any limousine but the very one they were riding in right now. The photo had been taken outside Ferro's Napa estate. "Someone's been following Claude?" Ferro inquired.

"It would appear that way. In fact, I think I've been followed a few times myself."

"Dunbar trying to dig up dirt? Probably hired some sleazy investigator."

"With all due respect, Ferro, I think Dunbar has succeeded. The article suggests the exact same thing you had mentioned to me on Saturday—about possibly having Claude appear as you in court."

"Damn fool, Lawrence! Dunbar's managed to bug your phone."

"But how could he do that? We have the tightest security."

Ferro said nothing more, his mind reeling at the implications of such a security breach. So, Dunbar wanted to play dirty by trying to make a fool of Ferro Olivetti? Suggest he was hiding in plain sight as a driver? Fine, Ferro thought, two could play that game. And with Ferro engaged as his opponent, Dunbar might not like the end result. In fact, Ferro would make sure he didn't. A grin emerged onto Ferro's face. Ferro only lost games to his father, no one else.

"You have an idea, Ferro?"

"Better than that," Ferro said darkly, his tone ominous, threatening. "By the time I'm done with Dunbar, he'll wish he was never born, much less taken on the futile attempt at ruining me. Claude? I trust you still have my wallet?"

"Of course, sir."

"Excellent. I knew I could count on you."

Lawrence looked confused. "Uh, you want to clue me in?"

It was good to be home.

*   *   *

San Francisco Superior Court, 11 A.M. A small entourage emerged from the rear of the sleek black limousine, and immediately the press began to hound the three men. Wearing dark suits and sunglasses, they did their best to hide their faces as they bypassed the throng of cameras and microphones, making no comment to the members of the press corps despite being bombarded with questions. Entering the hallowed halls of the city court building, they made their way down to their assigned courtroom. With Lawrence in the lead, he opened the doors and took up his post behind the defense table. The striking-looking man in the designer black suit followed close behind, taking up in the chair beside Lawrence. The third man, also in black, sat in the last row, behind a group of onlookers.

Just then the doors opened again, and in came a bustling Richard Dunbar, flanked by two attorneys who looked like they ate sharks for breakfast. Expensive suits, power ties, purposeful strides, confident looks. Dunbar himself waddled back and forth like a penguin; he didn't look so healthy, his color pale and wan. Still, it didn't diminish the fire in his eyes.

Suddenly the bailiff appeared from behind a closed door near the judge's chambers and announced that the hearing of *Dunbar v. Olivetti* would commence, "the Honorable Judge Alan Kaufman presiding."

A stern-faced, hunched-over figure emerged from the antechamber, slowly clambering up to his elevated seat of judgment. He banged his gavel and looked out at the assembled guests. "Well, it seems we have a larger turnout than we had last week—including at the defense table. Perhaps the recent interest from the news media has influenced this case. Mr. Henderson," the judge said, indicating Lawrence. "It's good to see your client at your side."

"Hmmph," came a guttural noise from the prosecution side.

"Mr. Dunbar, you wish to add to my opening remarks?"

Dunbar just shook his head.

"Good. It's better to let your lawyers speak for you. Even when trying to editorialize," Judge Kaufman said with authority. When he received no further commentary, he readdressed the two sides. "Fine. Let's get on with things. Any new motions on this hearing?"

Just then Dunbar's lead attorney stood up.

"Mr. Sharp?"

"Your honor, Mr. Dunbar has come here with the utmost respect for the legal system and has done everything by the book during this process. He has filed the appropriate paperwork, been present at each step of the way, assisted the legal process with every turn. His desired acquisition of Olivetti Enterprises, though, has been met with all sorts of stalling tactics and delays. We believe another ruse is being perpetrated here today, which not only mocks this system we hold dear, but wastes our time and, most importantly, the court's time."

Kaufman looked annoyed. "Mr. Sharp, want to cut through your legalese and spit it out? We have people here who do not hold fancy law degrees."

"Certainly, Your Honor. We believe that the person seated at the defense table is not the actual Ferro Olivetti. We believe him to be an imposter."

Kaufman's eyes slid down his nose. "Well, I have to admit, that's a new one, even for someone who's been on the bench for over thirty years. It's not only unusual, but also a serious accusation, Mr. Sharp."

"It's also the truth," Dunbar added, rising from his seat. "That man over there is nothing more than a chauffeur—Olivetti's chauffeur, and he's trying to pull the wool over the eyes of the system. It's common knowledge in the tabloids that Olivetti likes having a stand-in for various purposes, and so he purposely chose a man to work for him who has features similar to his own. Don't let the fancy suit fool you."

"Mr. Dunbar, what did I tell you about addressing the court? Let your lawyers handle this."

Dunbar sat down, but he didn't apologize for his outburst.

"Mr. Henderson, seems we have a bit of a situation here," Judge Kaufman stated, a hint of a smile on his face. "Is there any credence to the prosecution's accusation?"

"None whatsoever, sir. It's ludicrous to even suggest such a thing."

"Well, gentleman, I find myself in a peculiar situation. Since it was I who granted last week's continuance given Mr. Olivetti's inability to appear, I suppose it's up to me to figure out this peculiar mess. Though I'm beginning to understand the placement of this weekend's confounding article about Mr. Olivetti's whereabouts and the accompanying photograph of his, uh, driver." The judge drank from his water, maybe because he was thirsty or maybe because he was trying to figure out the right approach to this case. Then he looked down at the man sitting beside Lawrence and said, "Sir, can you confirm your identity as Ferro Olivetti?"

"Yes, your honor," Ferro said, rising from his seat.

"You can show proof of your identity? "

"Of course, your honor."

"Please approach the bench."

The man rose, walked around the table, and came before Judge Kaufman. From his pocket he withdrew a thick leather wallet and handed over the driver's license. The judge gazed at the photo, then back at the man standing before him. Then he looked a second time, squinting as though that enabled him to see deeper into the man's skin, perhaps down to his soul.

"Mr. Olivetti, why would the prosecution suggest that you may be an imposter?"

"I couldn't say, your honor."

"And your driver, what's this about his being a a stand-in for you?"

The man shrugged. "Mr. Claude Reneau, sir, yes, he is my

driver, and he's a trusted employee. No, a friend, who has on occasion stood in for me for photographic sessions. It's done merely as a security precaution. A man of influence and wealth cannot be too careful in today's world. If you would like to discuss it with him, he's sitting in the back row."

The judge peered to the back as a gentleman stood up. He was dressed all in black, and out of respect for the court he was holding his cap rather than wearing it.

"If I may add, your Honor, I apologize for not being here for last week's hearing—I was attending to some family business that required me to be out of town for longer than I wished. My father passed away just a couple of months ago, and so there were urgent matters that I needed to attend to, as per his will."

"Yes, well, the court accepts your apology, Mr. Olivetti— and it also offers its condolences on the loss of your father. I read about that, and I understood that you were very close," the judge said with sympathy. "You may sit down while I secure an apology to both you and to the court from Mr. Dunbar and his illustrious barristers."

Ferro returned to the table, where Lawrence patted him on the shoulder.

"Mr. Dunbar," the judge began, "in light of today's strange turn of events, I am hereby dismissing this case and returning full operating privileges of Olivetti Enterprises to its CEO, Ferro Olivetti. How you thought such an accusation could work in your favor, I couldn't say. Just don't try it again. I would caution you to check your facts before presenting them to the court as such. We are adjourned."

Another bang of the gavel, and the judge was gone.

So too was Dunbar's takeover attempt.

On his way out of the courtroom, Ferro made his way over to the prosecution's table. Dunbar looked up, giving him a look of defiance.

Ferro tossed a small electronic device at the man—the bug the old man had put in Lawrence's phone. He wasn't surprised to find it, which is why he had been cautious in what he told Lawrence on the occasions they spoke. Ferro knew that if Vodell went through during his absence, Dunbar would try to retaliate. He'd been ready for it. "Sometimes you have to be careful what you overhear, Dunbar. It could just backfire."

Ferro and Lawrence left the courtroom, laughing with victory. Claude followed behind.

When they returned to the limo and it sped away from the courthouse, Lawrence turned to Ferro and said, "I can't believe he thought we would actually pull something like that. But, my God, Ferro, when I heard you suggest it, I thought you were out of your mind."

"What you fail to realize, Lawrence, is the fact that I assumed Dunbar had your phone tapped. Why else would I suggest something so foolish? He took the bait, and we caught him." Then to Claude, who was driving but listening and smiling along with them all, said, "You looked great in front of Villa Olivetti in that photograph we staged. I'm so glad we had it sent to the papers anonymously. Some reporters love a tip." Ferro paused to take in the celebration before switching into business mode. "Now, let's get back to the office, I have a lot to get done, including looking into a small investment I made while I was away. Lawrence, did you know how cutthroat the real estate business is?"

*   *   *

"Mancini…uh, Mancini & Reneau Realty, may I help you?"

The pause in the name of the business caught him by surprise and he stumbled on his own words. "Uh, yes, Ms. Diane Mancini, please."

He sensed hesitation on the other end of the phone before the woman said, "Claude, is that you?"

Ferro assumed his voice would be recognized. It was rather distinctive, his accent heavy. "Yes, it's me, Claude. Is this Jennifer … or Sandra?"

"It's Sandra. And I'm sorry, Claude, but Diane's not taking calls."

"All calls, or just my calls?"

"Asked and answered," Sandra said tightly. Another phone could be heard ringing in the background. "Look, Claude, don't get me wrong, I think you're a great guy and none of this—the office, Diane's dream, our escape from Curtis— none of it would have happened without you. But right now, I've got to respect Diane's need for some space, you know, to think about all that's happened since she told me what went down with Mrs. Curtis. Look, it's real busy here and we're short-staffed and I've gotta take that call. Give it a couple more days, try back, okay?"

"I appreciate your support, Sandra," Ferro said.

"Like I said, just give her some time, let her figure things out."

Before Ferro could say another word, the connection was cut. Secure in his office tower at Olivetti Enterprises, Ferro replaced the receiver and gazed about the expansive suite and its expensive décor. A far cry from where he'd been staying the last couple of weeks, and while it was certainly luxurious and comfortable, there was something cold about the surroundings, as though it lacked a soul. It just didn't feel like home. A funny concept to Ferro—the back room of a ground floor office had felt more like his residence than this office, more than his home in Napa, which he'd yet to see since returning to the West Coast two days ago. Rattling around the large house by himself, it just held no appeal.

Actually, nothing gave Ferro much pleasure lately. Not his work, truth be known not even his sweet victory in court. Each time he accomplished something—closed a deal or felt good about a meeting's result—the first thing he'd wanted to do was pick up the phone and tell Diane every detail. Which he supposed was a better impulse than the one that was bubbling beneath the surface—hopping into the *Gambit One* and flying back to New York. Ferro Olivetti was a man used to getting his way. He knew how to fight for what he wanted, and he knew how to win.

But Diane Mancini wasn't a corporation. She wasn't some faceless opponent.

What was she then?

Easy, he thought. *She was the love of his life.*

Sure, he could think it. But could he say it? Could a man with Ferro's pride open himself up like that, again, especially given the precarious nature of his and Diane's relationship? His wound from Anna Maria had taken years to heal, only to see it reopened when he saw her—and her little girl—at his father's funeral.

Suddenly inspiration struck, and Ferro picked up the phone again, this time punching out a series of numbers he'd memorized. He waited while the connection was made, and then heard a voice both familiar and scary.

"Mancini residence."

"Oh, uh, Mrs. Mancini, this is Fer." He stopped and corrected himself. "This is Claude Reneau," he said, hating the hesitancy in his own voice. Even to him he sounded weak. "I would like to speak with Diane."

"You got some nerve calling here."

"Mrs. Mancini, please listen to me. There's been a horrible misunderstanding, and I just need to explain what the truth is," he said. "It's really important that I speak to Diane now. She needs to hear."

Sophia Mancini cut him off, not that he was surprised. "She needs what? What she needs is to not have you bothering her anymore. Look, Mr. Reneau, how many times must you be told to stay away? Diane doesn't want to talk to you, she doesn't want to hear from you, or ever see you again. She told me what happened, she told me everything. You've betrayed her, and that's unforgivable. If you really want to do her a favor, you'll forget all about her. Don't call again, or I'll file harassment charges against you."

Then she hung up on him.

Ferro recognized the reality. Diane was lucky to have such supportive friends and family. But they were wrong, they all were, even Diane. Especially Diane. If they all knew the truth, not just about what had happened between him and Hilda, but about his true identity and why he'd needed to keep such a tight hold on his secrets, they might see things differently. He knew they would see his side of the situation.

A frustrated Ferro grabbed hold of his phone and ripped it from his desk, angrily throwing it across the large room. He didn't care where it landed or what damage it did. What did any of it matter? They were trinkets inside his office. In the grand scheme of things they didn't matter. Glass shattered, shards sprinkling to the carpet.

The commotion he'd caused brought a quick knock to his door, Lawrence's head popped into the office. "Everything okay in here, boss?"

Ferro, standing in the middle of the room, hand on his hips and feeling completely helpless, waved his friend inside. He knew he couldn't concentrate on any major projects, so he just said, "Bring me everything that needs my signature. Also, I need a check for fifty thousand dollars. It should be made out to a man named Fred Evans."

"Did I hear you right? Fifty thousand?"

"Yes, Lawrence, I trust I have that much in petty cash. And Lawrence, please stop questioning everything I do and say. I ask, you do. Isn't that how this relationship works?"

Admonished, Lawrence withdrew from the office, simply saying, "I'll be right back, sir."

Ferro felt bad about taking his frustration out on Lawrence. He knew it was wrong, but he also knew that he'd never felt this way before. These were emotions that pinged inside him, nicking his nerves, his arteries to the point he might, meta-phorically at least, drown in his own blood. Even when he was at his most down during the New York trip, such as that night he'd spent in the park, he'd known things would get better, he'd always been in control. The situation with Diane was different—because it was not just his life, it was hers, and she was strong enough to prevent any person from telling her how she was going to live it.

Retreating behind his desk, Ferro grabbed a pen and on his personal stationery started to compose a quick note. It read: "Dear Fred. Use the enclosed check to complete your education, then contact me to discuss your future plans. Olivetti Enterprises is always looking for not just book-smart individuals, but also men of strong moral character. You are both. With best wishes, Ferro Olivetti, Olivetti Enterprises. (Alias: Claude Reneau!) P.S. Thanks for the bagels and coffee that early morning when you nearly ran me over with your truck."

Ferro smiled, both at the letter's contents and at the memory of that chance meeting that one morning. It was when his fortunes in New York had truly turned. Fred's kindness had led him to getting the job with Curtis, which in turn had introduced him, properly at least, to the wonder that was Diane Mancini.

"My God," Ferro said aloud. "Do all roads lead to Diane?"

"Who's Diane?"

Looking up from his desk, Ferro realized Lawrence had returned with all the paperwork he'd requested. A curious expression waited for an explanation.

"It's nothing, Lawrence."

"I mean, calls have come in from Cassandra, from Dora. I'm sure there have been others, there always are. Poor Estelle has been fielding calls virtually since word broke about your court victory. The word is out on the street that Ferro Olivetti is back in town, and so that's got the ladies of the bay back on the prowl. But Diane—that's a new one."

"I told you, Lawrence, forget it. Did you bring the check for Mr. Evans?"

"As requested."

Ferro signed the check, then handed over the letter he'd written, now sealed inside a crisp white envelope. "This is to accompany the check—the address is on the front. Overnight delivery, hear me? And Lawrence, stop asking questions. I've got too much on my mind and cannot deal with inane questions. I'm out of here." Ferro breezed past his trusted associate, but not before he caught sight of the damage his telephone had done. In addition to several photographs and their frames lying cracked on the floor, some pieces of his prized chess set had joined the rubble. He noticed one piece in particular, broken in two pieces. He had no time to mourn the death of the game he had so enjoyed with his father. There was a message hidden in the disarray.

The queen stared up at him, her head separated from her body.

He knew what he had to do

He rushed out of the office, a man on a mission.

*　　*　　*

"Hello, Mother?

"Ferro, darling."

Finally, the soothing voice of a woman who would not hang up on him.

It was nearly midnight in California, late morning the next day in Rome. Both Ferro and his mother were in their respective villas, separated, as always, by thousands of miles but by nothing else. Their lifelong bond was as strong as ever, and just hearing the unconditional love that poured out of her nearly healed Ferro's wounded heart.

He was sitting out on his back patio on this perfect night, gazing at the bright stars that littered the sky like diamonds. A month ago been he'd been partying here with friends, anticipating a night of love-making with Cassandra, when a phone call had disrupted not just the celebration but his entire life. It was appropriate that he be here now, bringing the events of his life full circle. Even a glass of champagne accompanied him, the bottle not much further away.

"How are you, Mama?"

"I'm well, Ferro. Getting along, with the help of your aunt and uncle. I haven't had the easiest of times, but I go to church daily to pray, and I visit with your father most mornings after mass."

"I'm sorry I haven't been there for you."

"Oh, but Ferro, you are always there for me. In my heart, you are always with me."

"Papa's loss, it is sinking in. But I still miss him terribly. So many times, I've wanted to pick up the phone and ask his advice."

"Yes, my dear, I feel the same, and seeing the empty side of the bed makes it that much more real. Still, your father may not be around any longer, but all he has taught you, all the lessons imparted, nothing can change that," she said. "Ferro, I need to ask—did you do as your father's requested? The thirty days away?"

Ferro took a sip from his champagne. It suddenly tasted bitter.

"I'm afraid I have failed him," Ferro said.

"I sincerely doubt you could ever fail him, Ferro," she said, her voice comforting, like always. "Not hearing from you for so long, I assumed you had gone away to do as he'd asked."

"I did," Ferro said. "I fell short of the thirty days."

"Oh, Ferro, my dear sweet boy," she said, "I'm not so certain your father meant that time to be taken so literally. He wanted you to reassess your life, to take a new chance and find out what was truly most important in this world. Let me ask you this: how long were you away?"

"Twenty-eight days, Mama, nearly twenty-nine," he said, embarrassed to admit just how close he'd come to succeeding.

"What made you return to your regular life?"

"Work, I'm afraid—just the very thing Papa warned me against. Having my work consume my life wasn't fulfilling enough, I know now that's what he was getting at. That it was all about the money, the power, what I could buy, and what I could destroy. But I had to return to my business or lose everything. Given the situation, I didn't feel I had any choice. It's not just my livelihood but that of the people who work for me, who trust that I will keep this company afloat. And now I have to live with the fact that I've disappointed my father, dishonored his last request."

"Oh, Ferro, you must not be so hard on yourself," she said. "Your father would never have wanted you to make a sacrifice such as your company. The fact that you did your best to honor his wishes says much more about your character than actually having completed all thirty days. He would not have had it any other way."

"Papa was the wisest man I ever knew.

"Yes, that he was, teaching by example was his method," Helena said. "Ferro, let me ask you this. During your time away, did anything of note happen? Because you sound different, my son, calmer. There is a quality to your voice which I'm having trouble discerning. It's not something I've heard before from you. Ferro? Who is she?"

"She? Why do you assume it's a woman?"

"Because I am a woman, Ferro, and I know when a man has a woman on his mind, and in his heart. Your Papa was the same way with me. Skittish, uncertain, worrisome. Business was business, easily handled, little emotion needed to get the job done. Affairs of the heart? Ah, now those are different. A completely separate matter, not to be handled in the same way. So, I'm right, yes?"

Ferro smiled. If his father was the wisest, his mother was the most astute. "Of course you're right, Mama. But then you always are," Ferro said. "Yes, I met someone, she was so different from anyone I had ever known. She was real and genuine and filled with vibrancy and a smile that could light all of Manhattan."

"She sounds wonderful."

"No one better," Ferro said, surprised by the deep conviction in his voice.

"She's not with you now?"

"No. She's in New York—where I went to fulfill Papa's will."

"And you are home in California? Why?"

"It's complicated," he said, knowing it really wasn't. Truth, betrayal, hurt, honesty, these were the juxtaposed emotions that simply needed to be explained, and once they were all would fall into place. Hopefully they would each fall into the other's arms. "I've tried to talk to her. Something happened. it's hard to explain, but now she won't return my calls. Assuming she's even getting my messages."

"Ferro Olivetti, when trouble hit your company, what did you do?"

"Faced it down, and I triumphed," he said. "But it's not the same thing, as you said, with relationships. Papa knew when it came to things of a romantic nature, you couldn't apply the same old rules. Your heart would interfere with the operation of your brain."

"Your father—for all his smarts—could be a fool, too," Helena said, laughing at some distant memory. "Ferro, you are not a quitter, neither in business nor in love. I know you saw Anna Maria, and that you spoke to her. She broke your heart, we know that, but it's time to stop letting that keep you from moving on with your life, your future loves. If this woman is so important, then you need to fight for what you want, for what you believe, for who you love—if indeed that's how you feel."

"I haven't been able to get her out of my mind."

"Then go to her," Helena said. "No phone calls, too impersonal. You need to do this in person. Ferro, think about it. Your father never said the thirty days needed to be consecutive. Here's your chance, both to honor your father's wish to its fullest and to fix whatever happened between you and my goodness, I have not even heard her name."

"Diane. Diane Mancini," Ferro said, a smile breaking out over his face. It was the first time he'd said her name aloud since returning to San Francisco, and it felt good to hear her name. To tell it to his mother. Now if he could hear her voice.

"Italian. I like her already," Helena said. "I hope only the very best for you, Ferro."

"Thank you, Mama."

Mother and son exchanged pleasant goodbyes, and after setting the phone down and reaching for his glass of champagne, Ferro had to smile broadly at the memory of the phone call. Of his mother's soothing, all-knowing voice. He had been right to call her, to seek out her gentle counsel. Mother always did know best. Downing the remains of his glass, feeling the warmth spread through his body, Ferro rose from his chair, stretched his body. It felt good to move; he'd been indolent too long since returning home.

As he headed back inside, he grabbed for his cell phone, and he dialed quickly.

"You awake?"

A groggy Lawrence said, "Of course."

"Good. Get the Gambit One ready for take-off. I'm leaving for New York first thing in the morning."

"Oh Lord. Thirty more days of secrecy?"

"Nope," Ferro said. "If I can't achieve success sooner than that, then I have lost all that matters to me."

CHAPTER TWENTY-TWO

INSIDE THE OFFICE OF Mancini & Reneau Realty, business went about its normal course. Phones rang, and emails popped into inboxes, clients arrived for their meetings, and rarely was there a quiet moment in the front section they had named "the bullpen," just as it had been called when they worked upstairs for Mr. Curtis. Jennifer and Sandra were more than pulling their weight, building up a steady client base. If only Diane could snap out of her funk, spending her time sitting in her private office located toward the back today, just as she'd done all week. She hadn't felt a part of the bullpen, much less the team.

Right now, she was daydreaming, thinking about possibilities and lost regrets. Diane Mancini felt as though she'd reverted to her old self, just as she had been getting used to the new, impulsively confident woman who had seemingly taken control of late. Now her days consisted of the very same routine: at work by eight in the morning, home by seven at night, in bed by ten o'clock. With the weekend fast approaching, there was little chance of any variation in her schedule. In fact, her mother's hovering presence at home had already put in motion Diane's plan of action for Saturday. She was planning to spend most of the day at the office.

"But Stanley is coming down from Westchester. It's tax time, and your father is itching to get them done before the deadline. I've invited Stanley to join us for dinner that night."

"Sorry, I have plans for Saturday."

"With who?" had asked a skeptical Sophia Mancini.

"Vita. She's taking me to dinner."

"Girl's night out?"

"Definitely. No men invited."

"Stanley will be disappointed not to see you," her mother had said.

"Stanley is used to that from me," Diane had said.

The last thing Diane needed was to be in the company of a man, much less one like the simpering Stanley Fulbright. He wasn't unattractive, but there had been something about him that kept Diane at bay, and through her own transformation she could put words to it. He lacked ambition, that fiery burst of personality that told people he got what he wanted, that he never gave up. How she knew this was because of the secretive, elusive Claude Reneau—who had been the very definition of excitement; he'd had her sleeping with the anticipation of a new day and what it might hold. Of course, Diane had learned something else about Claude. As fiery as he was, as much as he pushed Diane to achieve her own goals, he'd easily given up when things had gotten tough. Not business-wise, but personally.

She knew she hadn't helped the matter by overreacting to what she'd walked in on at the office. Trust wasn't a trait that came naturally to Diane, not after what had happened to her husband, David, and subsequently to her with Charlie Stubbs in Philadelphia, the way he'd attacked her after she'd gone to him in a moment of weakness. Then the unexpected romance with the mysterious Claude had bloomed. How she had savored his kisses, their enticing blend of gentle and urgent, a heady mix that had left her weak in the knees more than once. Their dates had been wonderful, treasured moments, more so than she'd even expected because she'd allowed herself to open to him. She could talk with him, and more importantly, he would listen.

All of that was gone. Claude was gone.

A commotion in the front office broke Diane from her reverie. She realized that while she was moping inside her office, a celebration was happening out where the real work was done. Before she could rise from behind her desk, a quick knock came at her door and then it opened, Jennifer's smiling face poking in.

"Diane, huge news!"

"I gathered. Okay, I'll be right out, just give me a second."

Jennifer's expression was one of appreciative sympathy. "Trust me, it's great news, and based on the way you've been acting lately, you sure could use some. Diane—you need to move on, realize that what's going on here is a dream come true. Your dream. Sandra and I, we're just along for your ride."

"Thanks, Jen."

Gathering her wits about her, checking her appearance in the mirror, Diane joined her friends out in the main area of the office, where they were celebrating with their two new office assistants. In total, the office employed five people, and with the news Diane was about to hear it just might be able to expand faster than expected.

"Remember that penthouse you were trying to close on?" Sandra said, the moment she saw Diane.

"Yes—it was Curtis's building, I was merely doing the legwork."

"Yeah, well, it must have paid off. Carter Industries, which controls the entire building, has agreed to let Mancini & Reneau Realty handle the leasing of the entire building. We have an appointment early tomorrow morning to discuss the details. But from what I've been told, the holding company just wasn't satisfied with Curtis—I believe their rep said, 'We don't like his style.' He must have bellowed at them. In any case, his loss is our tremendous gain." The assembled gang cheered their success again, and Diane had to admit the news was great, nearly overwhelming. She felt numb. She also knew this deal would put her little start-up company on the map. Why then did the victory feel so hollow?

She wouldn't give voice to the answer.

Still, that didn't stop the image of Claude clinging to her side, insisting they celebrate by cracking open a bottle of champagne. "The good stuff," she could hear in his heavily accented English. If nothing else, Claude was imbued with expensive tastes. Not to mention having good taste. My God, a man educated by the finer things in life, sweet as the day is long, and gorgeous on the eyes. Nothing wrong with this picture.

Except for the secrets he kept so tight.

Diane wondered, and not for the first time, what he'd really been hiding. She'd spent several sleepless nights trying to figure out what his real story was, and each time she came up with a blank page. She also knew she'd never know the answer.

Seeing that Diane wasn't partaking in the celebration as she should be, Jennifer and Sandra pulled her aside and asked her what was wrong.

"Claude," Diane finally said, sighing heavily, hopelessly. "He's gone for good, isn't he?"

"Only if you want him to be," they said simultaneously.

That was the thing, girls knew so much more about men than the reverse.

*　　*　　*

Men were used to getting their way, and when they didn't all hell could break lose. Case in point, what was right now transpiring inside the office of Curtis Realty. The effects of Claude Reneau's disappearance were also being felt by its owner—and not in a good way.

"Goddammit! How could that happen?" screamed a visibly angry Curtis, his gruff voice reverberating against the walls of his office. He slammed the tele phone down, and then without another thought swept the entire contents of his desk onto the floor, the crash of heavy and delicate items finally leading to his secretary opening the door.

"Mr. Curtis! Is everything all right?"

"Does it fucking look like everything is all right?" Curtis screamed, his breath coming in heavy waves, his anger escalating. Just go back to your desk. I don't want to be disturbed."

"But I was just about to buzz you—you have company."

"I don't want to see anyone. Tell whoever to fuck off."

An amiable face poked through the door. "Sorry to disturb you, Mr. Curtis. I wouldn't interrupt, but it's important."

"Fred Evans. I should throw your ass out the window for introducing me to that pain in the ass. Claude what's his name. What the hell do you want?"

"May I come in?"

"Christ, can't a man get a moment's peace?" As much as he wasn't in the mood for company, the appearance of his sometime delivery man, Fred Evans, was not without its appeal. He was handsome enough to look at. Maybe, too, he had showed up with a special delivery, some good news in the face of the crappy info he'd just heard. "Fine, come in. But it better be good."

"Good, hell yeah it's good," Fred said, stepping aside the scattered mess on the floor. "Sorry to catch you at a bad time, but I was in the neighborhood and well, I just thought I'd let you know I've just given notice at the delivery service. I'm going to school full-time."

"What happened, you win the lottery?"

"Actually, yeah, sorta."

"Come on, out with it. What the hell are you talking about?"

"That guy, remember Claude, who I recommended for your chauffeur job?"

"Who could forget him. I fired his ass, and rightly so."

"Well, you may want to take a look at this," Fred said, and then thrust forward a plain white envelope.

Curtis unfolded the letter and quickly read its contents. Blood drained from his face, and without even feeling his body falling he dropped back to his soft leather chair, clearly in shock. "What the hell is this?"

"He wasn't a driver. I mean, he was, sure, for you. But he was only masquerading—why, I don't know. He doesn't explain that. All I know is that he was grateful to me for what I did to help him—recommending him for the job with you and such. He wrote me a check for fifty thousand dollars and told me to finish my education. And when I'm done I'm to contact him about a job."

"Him? This guy Claude. He's Olivetti? That's impossible," Curtis said.

But then perhaps it wasn't so impossible. He recalled the day he'd fired the incompetent and disloyal Claude, how the man had in turn tossed Curtis's boarding pass from his most recent trip to San Francisco. He'd searched his brain that day, trying to remember the passenger who had been seated across from him. Had it been the same man? Curtis had been so busy making the flight attendant miserable he'd missed out on noticing the man near him. That's how upset he'd been on that return flight.

And now Claude, aka Ferro Olivetti, was no doubt seeking to repay his debts. Which entailed giving money and promises to the people who had helped him. What of the people who had wronged him, turned their back on him, treated him like, like the way Curtis treated everyone? That's when the realization hit him—the penthouse deal, that huge building going up on the Upper East Side, he'd been assured the deal would go through for him to handle its full occupancy. Only the phone call he'd just received had told him otherwise. In fact, the person on the other end had been only too pleased to tell Curtis that Mancini & Reneau Realty would be handling all the luxury building's business.

"It can't be," Curtis said. "My God, that stupid wench Hilda was right."

He dismissed Fred more politely than he'd greeted him, wishing him the best, thanking him for passing along his news. But being kind was too late for a man like Curtis. He'd been bested by someone far more powerful than he would ever become. He'd tried to screw over—not the mention screw—a billionaire, one who seemingly rewarded those he trusted. And no doubt ruined those who didn't. But why, what did it all mean, why would a billionaire mask as a chauffeur?

Just then another knock came at the door. When Curtis didn't respond, the door opened.

"I told you I didn't…"

"It's not your secretary, Mr. Curtis," said Timothy, a sweet smile on his face as he closed the door behind him. "She stepped out for some coffee. When I noticed you were alone well, I just wondered if there was there anything I can do?"

"No, Timothy. Not a damn thing."

But Timothy wasn't that easily deterred; perhaps there was something about Curtis's tone or mannerism that encouraged the last remaining associate at Curtis Realty to finally make his bold move. Timothy rounded the desk and placed his hands upon Curtis's hunched shoulder. Gently he began to rub them, trying to ease the pressure, the stress.

"Mr. Curtis, pardon me for speaking up, but I think it's time you tried a new tactic,"Timothy said. "My yoga instructor slash therapist slash best gal pal slash waitress says that negative energy will ruin you faster than any food, drink, or ailment. Instead of screaming and yelling all the time, why not try a new approach? "

"Oh, and what would that be?" Curtis asked.

Timothy's hand slid further down Curtis, massaging his chest, then even lower.

"Happiness," Timothy said. "My mother always said you catch more flies with honey."

"Timothy?"

"Yes, Mr. Curtis?"

"Would you call me by my first name?"

"It would be my pleasure, Stan."

Men understood nothing about women. Perhaps men knew only what other men needed.

*   *   *

Ferro Olivetti had seen his share of obstacles of late: nearly losing the Vodell deal, his beloved father and subsequent death request, the failed hostile takeover attempt from Richard Dunbar; there had even been minor irritants like working for that blowhard Curtis and his over-sexed family, and the crazy lady from Central Park who chased him from a bench one lone night. But winning the fair heart of Diane Mancini, now that accomplishment was going to prove amongst the most difficult of challenges he'd yet to endure. And not only because he had to sway Diane from what she thought had taken place that night with Hilda Curtis, but he had to convince someone else even more.

Sophia Mancini.

A woman's mother was always the toughest of customers, Ferro knew that much. His own mother, whom he loved beyond words, had raised him to revere, respect, and fear the true leader of the household. The man could think he was in charge, but deep down even he knew the lady ruled the roost. Which is why at this very moment Ferro approached the Mancini house with as much trepidation as a novice trainer set to feed a hungry tiger.

Ferro had spent a good portion of the return flight to New York contemplating how to go about rectifying this situation. Did he go directly to the Mancini (and Reneau?) Realty office and try and explain to Diane the truth about what she'd walked in on. But Ferro knew Diane wasn't merely upset over finding the very naked Hilda in his arms—it was the underlying secrecy of their relationship, his complete lack of honesty. Now that he'd fulfilled his father's will and subsequently learned what truly mattered to him, Ferro could finally lay bare the truth behind Claude's facade. But would she understand? The billion-dollar question, that's what that is, Ferro thought with increasing uncertainty. So that's why he decided to alter his approach. It was the middle of the work day, so he was confident Diane was busy and her father at work also, leaving him plenty of time to convince Sophia Mancini that he was anything but a monster,

Quite the opposite. He had to convince her that he was the ideal man for her daughter.

After paying the taxi, Ferro—dressed in the finest of Italian suits, the open neck shirt of the most decadent silk—patted away any stray wrinkles, then made his way down the path. The day was brightly lit, with the sun riding high in the afternoon sky. A lovely spring day, rich with promise. Not surprisingly, he found Mrs. Mancini in her vegetable garden, digging up pesky weeds and seed packets at her side. He considered this a good omen. Having her outside already lessened the chance of having a door slammed in his face.

"Excuse me, Mrs. Mancini?" Ferro said, clearing his voice of any initial hesitancy.

Sophia turned, revealing a small shovel in her hands that she held like a dagger. Ferro, upon seeing the garden tool-cum weapon, took a small step backwards. Until the situation was under control, caution had a place right between them.

"You," she said. Spat might have been a more appropriate word.

"You are looking well, I see. I hope you will pardon the intrusion."

"Well? What I am looking is covered in dirt—so don't try any of your supposed charm on me, Mr. Reneau."

"I don't mean to be disingenuous," he said. "If I might have a moment of your time?"

Sophia, using the shovel to help her get to her feet, stood as tall as she could, though it was hardly intimidating in the face of the tall, muscled Ferro. But when she landed her hands on her hips, her look of defiance won the day's battle. "I thought you were gone, back home to your former life in California."

"It's true that business took me away, yes. But I have returned."

"Business. Limo driver needed in Nob Hill? Hell, you're wasting your time. How do you say 'get lost' in Italian. Or is that French, Mr. Reneau?"

"I suppose I deserve that, and more," Ferro said with a nod of his head. "I haven't exactly been very forthcoming with details about myself."

"That's a fancy way of saying you lied."

"I had my reasons."

"Doesn't everyone."

"Please, Mrs. Mancini, just five minutes of your time? Perhaps a cup of tea would help soothe any misplaced feelings?"

Sophia Mancini raised an eyebrow, eyeing him with suspicion. He knew he was being appraised, and his reaction to it could make the situation go either way. Ferro had been to many a business meeting where genial manners and a nice suit had served as an effective icebreaker to more fruitful times. He had to hope this was one more occasion where his personal acumen would enact a decisive touch.

"You look different, I'll give you that," she finally said. "You're all cleaned up, not such a desperate, messy-looking character as before. What's changed?"

"Everything," Ferro said. "And it's all because of Diane."

"Hmmph," she said, though her tone indicated she was beginning to soften. "Some tea, you say?"

"I'd be happy to prepare it," he said.

"Not in my kitchen," Sophia said.

Ferro actually laughed. "You and my mother would get along famously."

That comment seemed to seal the deal, or at least present a moment's détente. Five minutes later Ferro and Sophia were settled in the Mancini kitchen, steaming mugs of Earl Grey tea in front of them. A small plate of Italian cookies was spread out before them, with Ferro taking one and nibbling at it out of politeness.

"Okay, Mr. Reneau, the clock is ticking. When the tea gets cold, you get out."

He nodded, but he smiled too at her cleverness. As much as Ferro wanted to admit to who he really was, he wanted that news to be Diane's to hear first and not anyone else's. What he needed to accomplish here to was present information by way of disinformation, sway the mother with his serious, sincere intentions. After he'd won over fair maiden Diane, they could together, hand in hand, tell her parents the real truth about who he was, and why he'd needed to be so secretive. So, Ferro launched his prepared speech.

"I arrived in New York a confused man, at a crossroads you might say," Ferro began. "Certain, uh, circumstances had set my trip in motion, but there were serious conditions attached to them, chief among them no money, no job, no prospects. It was up to me to start over again. Call it a test of character, a battle of wills—the fulfillment of a promise is what it really amounted to. I was determined that nothing would stop me from achieving my goal." He paused, ensuring he had the full attention of his small audience. Sophia Mancini hadn't touched her tea; arms crossed over her bosom, she wore her skepticism like a second skin.

"Along the way, I learned a great deal about myself. I discovered that I was lacking something truly wonderful, and over the course of the last several weeks I'd gotten a glimmer of just what that something was." He paused to drink some tea, also to let her absorb what he'd revealed so far. "As corny as it may sound, what I was lacking was companionship, someone to share my life with. In a nutshell: someone to love. I don't even think it took two weeks; I think I fell in love the first night I laid eyes upon your daughter."

"Love? You love my daughter?"

"Very much so."

What happened next caught the attention of Sophia and Ferro both; because a third voice entered not just the room but the conversation, with a proclamation that surprised one, delighted the other.

"Oh, Claude, and I love you too."

The voice certainly wasn't Mr. Mancini, returning home from work. Of course it was Diane, but what she said made the turn of events no less shocking. Ferro spun around, nearly spilling his tea in the process. He caught the mug just before it went sliding off the table, and then once it was secure he went running up to Diane. She had appeared out of nowhere, a vision out of some hidden mist or secret door, only to reveal herself at the most opportune time. Speaking the most wonderful of words.

"I tried a dozen times to call you," Ferro said, taking Diane in his arms. "You would not take any of them, and I knew that I had to come back and see you in person. To tell you everything."

"I didn't know about the calls, not until recently. Everyone thought they were protecting me. The girls down at the office just told me you'd called the office, and now I learn that you've been calling here, too. Claude, I'm sorry I was so jealous of Hilda. And that I couldn't respect your privacy. Only after you were gone from my life did I realize how selfish I'd been. I revealed to you my story that night at the office, and if I trusted you enough to talk about…Charlie, well, I should have trusted you enough to know that one day you would return the favor. That you would reveal everything when you were ready."

"I'm ready now," Ferro said. "That's why I'm here."

"I just needed to know you cared."

"It's more than just caring," Ferro said.

"I know, I know, I heard you. I love you so much, Claude."

Ferro pulled back slightly, wishing he could hear his real name being spoken by those lips, her voice expressing her ultimate love for Ferro. Ferro Olivetti. "I treasure those words, Diane, you have no idea. But there is something more I want to hear from you, my love," he said. "But only after I tell you my story will you be able to say it."

"I don't understand," she said.

"Make that two of us," Sophia said.

"Ah, Mrs. Mancini, allow me to give you an explanation," Ferro said, then pulled out his cell phone. He punched in the pre-assigned number. After waiting for a second ring, a familiar, comforting voice answered. He spoke rapidly in Italian, nodding his head before passing the phone to Sophia. "I think you will enjoy the conversation; the two of you have much in common, and hopefully will have even more in the near future. You will learn a lot about the man who loves your daughter."

As Sophia took the phone, she said, "Hello," and then started to listen.

Distraction well in hand, Ferro grabbed hold of Diane and led her outside of the house. Rays of sunshine beamed down on them, the spring day still very much alive. Night wasn't yet ready to reveal its shadows. It was a time for the sun to bring things to light.

"Did you really come back for me?" Diane asked.

"I even flew my own plane to get here," Ferro said. "No Blue Angel, but close enough."

Diane's face scrunched with confusion. "Uh, did you say your own plane? And by you flew it, meaning?"

"As you are about to learn, Ferro rarely jokes about anything so serious."

"Ferro? Claude, I don't understand."

"Come, Diane, come with me, my love. Much truth awaits us tonight," Ferro said. "But promise me one thing, that you will never ever call me Claude again. It may be the name of a man I have great respect for, but it is a not a name I wish to be addressed as again. It's a long story, and it all began with my father's will."

She would listen with rapt attention, finally knowing Ferro's story from his point of view.

*   *   *

Standing in the lobby of the exclusive Kimberly Hotel in midtown Manhattan, Ferro Olivetti was dressed in a classic black tuxedo, his lapels perfectly ironed, the stylized "F" cufflinks of his crisp white shirt brand-new, gleaming under the golden lights. His thick black hair was swept back to reveal not just his handsome face, but a wide grin that grew broader as the sleek limousine pulled up curbside. The driver rushed from the front door to the passenger's side, where he opened it with a flourish. Out stepped Diane Mancini, looking like a model straight out of the pages of *Vogue* or *Paris Match*. Wearing a glittering gown she'd just been fitted for, her hair done up by the city's most accomplished stylist, she was the picture of womanly perfection, of class and sophistication. Add a sparkling diamond necklace and matching earrings, and a Hollywood red carpet might just turn green with envy.

As she swept into the lobby, Ferro took hold of her hand and kissed it lightly.

"You look absolutely radiant," he said.

"Thank you. I feel like a million dollars."

"Much more than million. You, Diane, are the billions of dollars I have always sought, all captured in one perfect package," Ferro said. "Now, if you'll follow me, dinner awaits."

He escorted her to the elevator, where the express lifted them high to the penthouse suite, which, when he unlocked the door, revealed the most romantic setting either of them could have conjured. A sea of scented candles flickered against gilded mirrors, giving off the impression of an endless row of glowing light. A small round table had been placed in the center of the room, draped with a white linen cloth and adorned with another candle. A bucket with the finest champagne was situated next to it. In the air you could hear the swells of a violin; a hidden stereo pumped in the dreamy strings sounds that gave the setting an added hint of old-world romanticism.

"Ferro, my goodness, you've spared nothing," Diane said.

"It is just the beginning," he said, smiling at the sound of his true name on her lips.

Just six hours ago, Ferro hadn't even been sure this night would happen. Now, having won over Diane's mother (with a major heads-up to his own mother and the two-plus hours of conversation the two women had enjoyed) and having also explained himself to Diane—his father's death and his strange request—Ferro could at last begin to relax. Everything was all right in the world. Diane Mancini was at his side.

Pouring champagne into crystal flutes, he passed one to Diane and then took hold of his own.

"What do we toast to?" he asked.

"There's only one thing," she answered. "To us, to the future."

"I could not have said it more perfectly," Ferro said, and with that they clinked glasses and drank.

They set their glasses down, and Ferro led Diane over to the plush, violet colored divan. Taking her in his arms, he placed a kiss upon her lips. She responded in earnest, and before long the champagne was forgotten as they indulged in their eager passion, their kisses taking them to new, unexpected heights. When at last they came up for a deep breath, Ferro watched as Diane gazed deep into his eyes, as though she were looking into his soul. His real soul. Ferro's soul. He was happy to reveal it to her, to share it with her.

"Ferro, I think it's going to take me awhile to get used to that name."

"We have all the time in the world."

"Tonight, Ferro, I want the world to stop."

"I can make that happen."

Ferro took hold of her again, kissing her even more deeply, his lips dancing down her silky throat, her arms digging into him, as though pulling him tighter, never wanting to let him go.

"Can dinner wait?" she asked breathlessly.

"Your wish, my command. So, if dessert is what you desire…" he said, which got her to laugh.

Leading her with his arm, Ferro brought Diane over to the king-size bed, the thick downy bedspread covered with the petals from two dozen roses. With ease he laid her down, their kisses consuming them, their bodies suddenly entwined, two into one. With a touch as gentle as the morning wind, Ferro slid the strap of her dress down her shoulder, his lips and his tongue soaking up her skin, her perfume like a taste discovered for the first time. Soon he was easing down the zipper at the back of her dress, revealing to him the lush curve of her breasts. Suckling at them, his tongue encircling her ripe nipples, he heard Diane cry out with exquisite pleasure. She urged him on, begging him to never let her go.

As her dress parted ways with her lovely body, falling to the floor in an elegant mass of chic fabric, Ferro took in the very sight before him, knowing full well he was casting his eyes on the most beautiful sight in the world.

"You are incredible. A vision that defies definition," he whispered to her. "More lovely than words could possibly describe."

"Ferro, my love, my irrepressible man, take me now. Please, make love to me like you've never made love before."

Her wish was his deepest desire.

Ferro eased off the tux of his jacket, tossing it aside. As he reached for his shirt, Diane's hands appeared, and with a grin both sexy and enticing, she ripped it open—the tux shirt was adorned with snaps, making for an easy strip. Her hands grazing at the black hair of his chest, she pulled him back down, peppering him with her eager kisses. Then, steering him onto his back, her tongue lapped up his strong, muscular chest, following the trail of hair down his taut, flat belly.

At last, she came to his pants, and with surprising agility

she worked the zipper down and soon had Ferro in just his undershorts. Those didn't stay on much longer either.

"Oh, Ferro," Diane said.

Taking her in his strong arms, Ferro knew he couldn't wait one single moment more. He prepared to enter her, to finally make passionate love to the woman who had for the past several weeks consumed his dreams, his nights, his life. Yet he hesitated.

"Ferro, is something wrong?"

He gazed into her seeking eyes, realizing that in all the times he had bedded women he had never before thought to look deep into the woman's heart. Maybe with Anna Maria, but even so, that was so long ago. He'd been a mere boy and what did a foolish youth know about love, anyway? No, those previous times had been filled with animal instincts, aggressive moves, and notable conquests. Now, today, at this very moment when moon and stars dotted an otherwise dark sky with light and hope and promise, Ferro Olivetti knew he was truly making love for the very first time.

"I love you, Diane Mancini," he said.

"And I love you, Ferro Olivetti," she answered.

With a gentle, easy move, Ferro slid deep into Diane. He heard her gasp with pleasure. Sliding out, then sliding back in, Ferro began to feel the passion overwhelm him to the point where his breathing grew constricted, as though the concept of love was doing just as the fairy tales had suggested, revealing a breathtaking moment between a man and woman brought together by destiny. It was a powerful, awe-inspiring feeling and completely foreign to him.

As their emotions drove their physical desires, Ferro and Diane engaged in long, lengthy, lovemaking, each of his eager thrusts being met by the cries of a waiting, willing partner. With his chest brushing against her breasts, her nipples alive in the night air, their kisses urgent, Diane hugged him tight, with her legs, with her arms, with her heart if that was possible.

Nails dug into his back, and as he thrust harder and deeper, she fought that much harder to keep her hold on him.

"Oh, oh, Ferro…yes…"

Ferro could feel her climax, once, twice, again. As the rushing waves of passion overtook her, Ferro knew he was not far from releasing himself. But he continued, thrust after thrust, sending more shockwaves through her system until finally the pent-up emotions spilled over to his body. He felt orgasm begin to claim him, and so he pushed that much harder, deeper inside her, and at last the sensation grew into an earth-shattering explosion of mind and body, emotion and thought, lust and, ultimately, love.

The two lovers lay entwined for what seemed forever, their slick, sweat-coated bodies seeking rejuvenation, breath seconds. Finally, Ferro slid out of her, getting up from the bed to retrieve their champagne glasses.

"Sustenance," he said.

"You think of everything, Ferro," she said.

"Oh, there's much more to come," he said.

"I hope so," Diane said, snuggling tightly against Ferro. She stroked his chest while he poured them fresh glasses of golden bubbly. When he spilled some of it on him, Diane eagerly lapped it up. Ferro kissed her, touched her, and she reached downward, finding him ready, willing, and definitely able.

"So," she said. "Can dinner wait again?"

"At this rate, we may just settle for breakfast," Ferro said, taking Diane in his arms again.

*　　*　　*

Midnight had come and gone, and now the early hours of dawn began to creep into their perfect world. The brief curve of the sun could be seen rising over the distant horizon, giving light to the discarded remnants of their late-night dinner and the empty bottles of champagne that happily littered the floor.

Lying in his strong arms, feeling safe, protected, loved, Diane breathed deeply.

"Ferro, are you asleep?"

"Not a chance," he said.

"I don't want to spoil the mood," she said. "But we can't stay like this forever, much as I would like to."

"Yes, my ever-practical Diane Mancini," he said. "What is it you wish to know?"

"What comes next—for us?"

"What would you like to come next?"

"That's not fair, you can't ask that question," she said. Her expression turning serious, she gazed up at him to better read his face, seek out answers to all she wished to know. "Well, for starters, you work in San Francisco and I work in New York. How will this work? Will I be visiting you in California? How often will you be coming to New York? Can we handle a long-distance relationship? "

"I have a better idea," Ferro said.

"What? "

"Come back home with me."

A tear suddenly spilled from her eye onto the pillow, leaving a stain that was fleeting but memorable, not unlike the words Ferro had just spoken. She'd heard them but couldn't possibly believe he meant them. It was the moment overtaking them, he did not intend for the words to mean what she thought. "I can't believe you said that. Do you honestly mean…"

"Diane, I did not fly all the way back to New York just to share one night with you."

"What about the business? About Mancini & Reneau Realty. God, we're going to have to change that name, unless we want your chauffeur to make a claim to it. The business is ours. I never would have had the guts to open it up without you. And now, it's barely been two months since I opened up the agency."

"Why not sell your shares to Jennifer and Sandra? With that new building going up on the east side, they're going to have their hands full. They'll probably have to hire some new staff, and maybe it would be wise for them to buy an already existing agency, pool their resources."

"How do you know about that building? We landed that account after you left."

Ferro grinned widely, revealing an ace up his sleeve. That is, had he been wearing any clothes. "I have many business contacts all over the world. A simple phone call was all it took. And before you get angry, I didn't necessarily do it for Mancini Realty—though I knew you could handle it perfectly, I just thought Curtis needed a bit of a comeuppance."

"Ferro Olivetti, you're full of surprises, aren't you."

"Come with me to California. There may just be one more surprise waiting for you," he said. "The biggest."

"What bigger than now, Ferro?"

His response was simple, just one word. But what it implied was greater than all the words she could speak.

"Tomorrow."

CHAPTER TWENTY-THREE

Same plane, the *Gambit One.* Same situation, asking a woman to accompany him home to his villa in Napa. What was different was two-fold. First, Diane Mancini was dramatically different than Cassandra, the last woman to step inside the cockpit of the private Gulfstream. Second, the pilot may have looked unchanged, the same, handsome visage, the same wicked grin thrilled at the prospect of taking to the clouds, but in fact Ferro Olivetti felt reborn, as though he were seeing things, life, through new eyes. The open sky that stretched out before him looked ready to welcome him, his companion, and the sleek aircraft to its azure backdrop. It would cradle them in its cushy air, glide them across the country and to their destination.

"This is Gambit One, we're reading for takeoff. Over."

The sizzling crackle over the headset alerted him to the fact his message had been received, acknowledged. A disembodied voice came back and said, "Roger that, Gambit One, you have clearance. Have a great flight, Mr. Olivetti. It's a beautiful day up there."

"They're all beautiful days from now on," Ferro spoke into his headset before dismissing the tower's response of "huh?" as a lack of imagination. He stole a look over at his passenger. "All secure? Ready to take to the sky?"

"Yes…and no," said an obviously nervous Diane Mancini. "Are you sure you know how to fly this thing?"

"Do you see any other pilot?"

"That's not exactly a comforting answer," she said.

"Haha. You have nothing to be scared about. This plane is as safe as they come, more so than the commercial jets that stuff people in like sardines. The only game of chance here is in the plane's name," Ferro said.

"I wondered about its name. Can you tell me?"

"We have a long flight. I will tell you many things about the world you are about to soar over, about the world you are soon to descend upon," he said, and then he leaned over and kissed her. "Let's take to the skies." He pushed the controls, easing them toward the runway.

Teterboro Airport in New Jersey was where Ferro had landed upon his return to New York, and now the exclusive airstrip for corporate jets and private planes was his lifting off point for the next phase of his life.

The sleek Gulfstream jet roared down the runway, building up momentum and speed until its nose jutted upwards, and its wheels left the hard ground. In seconds they were shooting into the lush blue sky, climbing and climbing still through wisps of clouds. Ferro's grip on the controls was strong, determined, but on his face was a look of utmost pleasure. He stole a look over at Diane, where he saw an equally excited look brighten hers.

"Oh, Ferro, this is magnificent, I've never seen such a view. Now I see why pilots love to fly. Being cramped in economy seats and sneaking glances out a tiny window, you're right, there's no comparison. Look at the world, spread out before us, as though no one else exists."

"Exactly my point. I am so glad to share my part of the world with you, here in the sky and home among my treasures," Ferro said. "Once we reach our cruising altitude, I can turn on the automatic pilot."

"Then what?" Diane asked, looking aghast at the idea of no one controlling the plane.

"Why, that's when I make love to you at thirty thousand feet."

"Ooh, the mile-high club, I've heard about such a thing but never imagined I'd ever experience it. Take us higher, as high as we can go," she said, emitting a small giggle.

"I will take you to great heights," he said.

"Is there anything, Ferro Olivetti, that you can't do? Anywhere can't you go?"

"Diane Mancini, right about now, I feel like I could take us to the moon."

*   *   *

Inside the luxurious bathroom aboard the Gambit One, Diane brushed her hair, and decided she also needed to touch up her make-up. As they prepared for landing, she wanted to look her absolute best. This was Ferro's world she was about to enter, and, already jittery with nerves, she had to believe first impressions meant everything to the people he surrounded himself with. She stole a look back in the mirror, where she was faced by a grinning school girl, one who still could not believe the sudden, swift upturn in her life. Just two days ago she was lamenting the loss of Claude Reneau, and now she was anticipating a pleasure-filled trip with a man who had revealed himself to be the elusive Ferro Olivetti, charming, world-class businessman, rumored billionaire, and, if that wasn't enough, he was the finest lover she had ever had. From the plush bedroom at the Kimberly Hotel to the luxuriant sofa inside the Gambit One, Ferro had not failed in his promise of taking her to new heights, both pleasurably and literally.

She thought about her parents, about the warnings they had imparted to her as she'd packed for the trip. Such trappings in this life could lead to no good, broken hearts, lost promises, and expectations not met.

"You should think before this more carefully about going away with him," Mr. Mancini had said. "He's lied to you before. What assurances has he given you that his intentions are above board now?"

As for her mother, she'd come around more so and was already putting the cart before the horse; or in her case, the ring before the question. "What if he asks you to marry him? Diane, are you truly ready for this new life? With his money, he lives differently. People will look at you and wonder if you married for love, or for money. What he can offer most people can only dream about."

"Both of you—I know you are only looking out for my best interests, just as you've done since David died. But there's no need to worry. I'm not planning on moving there, and besides, from what I've read of Ferro Olivetti, he's not the kind of man who has intentions of being held down by marriage. He's a free spirit."

"Diane, honey, in his world—nothing is free," her father instructed her.

"That's okay, Ferro can just buy it," her mother followed up with.

Now, replaying that conversation in her mind, Diane had to smile. She could hardly chide her parents for their caution, she was their only child, one who had seen her share of pain in the last couple of years. She reminded herself to call them when they landed. They had acted more nervous than she when they'd found out she was flying in a private plane. Not to mention that Ferro was the pilot. He hadn't even been able to find his way around Queens with a limo.

"Diane?" Ferro's said through the speaker system. "We're about ten miles outside San Francisco International, the tower has us ready for landing."

"Be right there," she said.

She rejoined him in the cockpit, secured her seatbelt, and then settled in to watch as the plane descended through the clouds and mist, ready to zoom across the landing strip. She steeled herself against the impact of wheels against the tarmac, but the landing was as smooth and gentle as it could be, almost like the first time she and Ferro had make love. Suddenly he pulled on the reverse thrusters and she was jerked back in her seat, the rush of sensations bouncing around inside her like their second lovemaking, more urgent and determined. Did everything he do produce such climaxes?

Ferro reduced the speed, and the airplane taxied its way to the private hangar away from the commercial airliners and terminals. As the sleek aircraft rolled to a stop, Ferro did his cross-check examinations. Then, when all was said and done, they both unbuckled themselves and prepared to deplane. Before he opened the door, Ferro turned to Diane and pressed a lingering kiss on her.

"Welcome to San Francisco. Welcome to my life, Diane Mancini."

As the door swung down, automatically exposing the steps, Ferro took hold of her hand and led her down to the tarmac. Of course, a limousine was waiting for them, a gentleman in a black chauffeur's uniform waiting with the rear door open. "Ferro, you didn't have to go to such expense. A taxi would have been fine."

"This is not a rental, Diane. This is my limo, and this man here this is my driver."

Diane nodded a polite hello, but found she couldn't get a word out. Surprise lodged in her throat by the man's appearance. "But he looks like…in that uniform."

"Diane Mancini, I'd like you to meet the real Claude Reneau."

She attempted a smile and realized it had faltered with surprise. "Hello, Claude" she said, the name sounding funny on her tongue. "Wow, okay, I've got to get used to that."

"It's my intention that you get used to a great deal," Ferro said. "Claude, shall we get Ms. Mancini settled at home?"

"Indeed, sir. As you wish. Ms. Mancini, it is a great pleasure to meet you."

As Diane and Ferro slid into the rear of the limo and Claude attended to their bags, Diane gazed admiringly at the luxury of the interior, the soft leather seats, the small screen television, the cool blast of perfectly tempered air conditioning. It made Curtis's Town Car look second-rate, like an ordinary car you found on the streets. And seeing Claude in that uniform, he looked so like Ferro had when she'd seen him inside Curtis's office. The effect was dizzying, and only slightly uncomfortable. For a passing second, she wondered if another ruse was being played on her, which of them was the real Claude, which the real Ferro?

With the gentle touch of his hand upon her arm, Diane felt familiar tingles and knew her thoughts were purely irrational. This was Ferro, she knew that touch she knew how he made her feel. "Now, can I get you something to drink?" Ferro said, unclasping a secret compartment that revealed a well-stock bar and gleaming crystal. "A Grand Marnier, perhaps?"

"Oh, Ferro, you remembered."

"With you, Diane, things are unforgettable, our memories are burned into me forever."

"Forever?" she asked. "That's a dangerous word."

"I find it rather a nice word. It holds such wonderful implications."

*   *   *

Ferro was growing impatient with the long ride. Not only was he eager to return home to Villa Olivetti and enjoy the comforts that had been denied him this past month, he also couldn't wait to see the expression on Diane's face when she took in the beauty of his Italian-style mansion. He knew she would love it and feel immediately at home within its walls, its many rooms.

Over an hour passed but at last the limo approached the entrance to the estate, the iron gates that blocked the driveway suddenly opening with a fluid motion, timed perfectly so that Claude never missed a beat, never needing to apply the car's breaks. Ferro nodded with approval, everything was working out perfectly, seamlessly. The good life was measured in small details. With Diane's hand already clasped in his, he squeezed it for good measure, then said, "Ready?"

"No going back now, is there?"

"Actually, no, there is not," Ferro said.

The limousine emerged from under a copse of trees to reveal the oversized mansion, its facade done up as an exquisite replica of the Italian Renaissance, looking all the more beautiful now during the sunset. A soft yellow glow hung over the house, as though it was awakening from a long slumber to find the world filled with possibilities, to the notion that soon, very soon, the sounds of life, of love, would once again traverse its previously empty halls, its neglected rooms.

"My God, Ferro, I've never seen a more beautiful home," Diane said, holding a hand to her chest to ease her breathing, "To think that you live here, live among such luxuries. I mean, all that room, that space. Not to mention these cultivated grounds and is that a marble fountain over there? Do I detect Cupid atop the fountain, spewing water?"

Ferro nodded, his eyes sparkling over her child-like innocence regarding his lifestyle. Hopefully that would pass soon enough, and she would take to it like a duck to water. "And an Olympic-sized pool in the back, several tennis courts, saunas, a Jacuzzi, all the amenities of home."

"Not any home I've ever known."

"Let us say we change that perception."

They got out of the limo, and Ferro guided Diane up the walkway and to the main door, which, not unlike the front gates, opened without nearly any effort. Suddenly an older gentleman appeared from behind it, nodding a greeting.

Ferro greeted him warmly, like a long-lost relative, then introduced Diane.

"Harrison, meet Ms. Diane Mancini."

"Ma'am, a pleasure," the butler, Harrison, said.

"Thank you," Diane said.

Inside, the house smelled of fresh-cut flowers, and indeed an assortment of bouquets adorned with porcelain and crystal vases in nearly every room that Ferro whisked her through. Living room, den, conservatory, formal dining room, library, and then at last the kitchen, where Diane was again introduced to another member of the house staff.

"Barbara, this is Diane Mancini."

A smart-looking woman, perhaps sixty years of age with a knowing, welcoming smile, said, "Welcome to Villa Olivetti. Nice to meet you, Ms. Diane, if there's anything you need you only need to let me, or my staff know. Mr. Ferro, it's wonderful to have you home again, things are just not the same around here without you."

"I'm glad to be home, and to see you all," Ferro said. "So, what delicacies have you been preparing for us? I'm famished, and no doubt Ms. Mancini is after the long flight and drive."

"I'm sure you'll be pleased—I've been working all day, ever since Claude called with the news of your return."

As they exited the kitchen, Ferro brought Diane back around to the foyer and announced he would give her time to get freshened up. With the butler as their lead, Ferro and Diane climbed the wide, winding staircase to the second level, Diane clutching at him, saying, "I never dreamt of a place like this. My mind was always filled with the practical things, running water and heat. Not this."

Ferro laughed. "Yes, we too have running water and heat. Come, let me show you your room."

Her smile faltered slightly. "My room?"

Leaning in, whispering into her ear so the butler could not overhear, he said, "In a house like this, it is good to keep up polite appearances. Fear not, we will share more than just the common areas downstairs."

"Ms. Mancini," Harrison announced, his face unwavering, confident, loyal. "This will be your room, which I hope you find to your satisfaction. Claude has already brought up your bags. If you need anything, there is a phone by the bedside which links directly with either myself or Barbara. Your wish, our duty. That's how we do it at Villa Olivetti."

"I've never been inside a house with a name before," she said, marveling that it might take some getting used to. "That's so kind of you, I'm sure I'll be quite happy."

Ferro kissed her on the cheek out of proprietary's sake before dashing off down the hallway. He looked back, saying, "I will meet you a bit later, in the garden. On such a lovely night, that's where we will dine. Barbara will make sure you find it." Ferro laughed. "Perhaps we'll draw you a map of the grounds, we wouldn't want you getting lost."

I'm already lost, Diane thought. *Lost in Wonderland.*

*   *   *

Two hours later, a sparkling night of dark sky and illuminating stars had fallen across the Napa Valley, and as the remnants of their glorious meal were whisked away by Barbara, Ferro took hold of Diane's hand again and led her down a garden path, lit like diamonds, looking not unlike the sky that stretched out for miles above them. Diane had commented on how big the sky was in Napa, how the buildings and skyscrapers of New York kept people from truly appreciating the expansive beauty of the heavens.

"But here, it's like you can see forever."

"Yes, forever," Ferro said. "There's that word again."

"Oh, Ferro, don't get me wrong, your home is magnificent and you've been the most perfect, tender, caring host, and I couldn't have been more welcomed by your staff, gosh, that's so hard to adjust to, having people fawn over every detail. But, I know you can't promise me anything, and I'm not even looking for any promise. I mean, I just arrived a few hours ago. And here I am, practically saying I want to move in and oh, what am I saying, I think it's the champagne is affecting my judgment. Why don't I just clam up right now?"

Ferro laughed, the sound echoing even in the expansive night. He pulled her in tight for a kiss as sweet as the flowers that bloomed all around him.

"Diane, whatever you wish, it's my fervent desire to make it come true."

"Ferro, honestly, this is all just too much. I'm just a working girl—my goodness, I have responsibilities back in New York, to the agency and to Jennifer and Sandra. Do you know they have designs of taking over Curtis's business? I think I've created monsters, ready to claim all of Manhattan as their hunting ground. They need someone to take their minds out of the clouds, but how can I when mine is there, too? I'm the responsible one of the group, they count on me. And then there's my parents."

Ferro silenced her with another kiss.

"Please, Diane, let us just walk. Talking is for later."

A pleasant silence settled over them as Ferro continued to lead Diane down the garden path. At last, they emerged onto the back end, where a gazebo stood, its white-washed columns and black-tiled roof awash in radiant candlelight. In the gentle wind, the flames flickered, casting shadows on the green lawn.

"Oh, Ferro, this is all too much."

"Sshh," he said.

Leading her up the steps and onto a wooden swing, he sat beside her as they gently rocked, staring at the sky, occasionally at each other, sneaking in a kiss when the mood struck them, which was often. They were like teenagers who suddenly found themselves out from under the watchful eye of parents, the thrill was that exciting, that enticing. But this was unlike any high school date Diane had ever been on, especially not when Ferro's butler appeared from out of the darkness, carrying more champagne and a dish of caviar on a silver tray.

As the decadent treat was placed before them, Harrison once again pulled his magic trick, disappearing from the light faster than he'd appeared. Ferro took over the honors, popping the cork on the vintage Dom Perignon, the cork's explosion echoing in the otherwise quiet of night. He poured her a glass, then one for himself.

Ferro turned to her, his expression one of the utmost seriousness.

"Diane, before I met you, every other day I used to think I loved one woman after another. They were all intoxicating to me, not unlike this champagne here, but none of them were of the right vintage. Even back when I was a foolish youth who thought he knew what love was. When I thought my entire life had been mapped out already, I really knew nothing. My heart never swelled, I never felt that zing of 'wow.' With this glass, with your eyes sparkling in its golden glow, I feel in my heart that I have found the perfect mix of bubbly personality and strong moral character. Meeting you that night at your friend Vita's apartment, seeing you again at Curtis's office, driving you to the funeral and our subsequent 'first' date—all of those were like arrows hitting my heart, all of them perfectly placed. As though shot by the Cupid statue atop my fountain out in the front yard."

"Yes. I think he struck me, too."

"I have told you about my life, about my father's will, which led me to New York and my crazy adventure. But I have yet to tell you about a woman, one who was so important to me."

"Ferro, you don't have to, not now."

"You told me of David. I would like to tell you about Anna Maria."

"Ferro, I realize there have been women in your life, probably more than I want to know about. But right now, amidst these candles and the warm breeze and your company, this delicious dessert, the last thing I want to do is introduce our ghosts from the past. They have made us who we are, but they can no longer claim any hold over us."

Ferro paused, where he allowed one telling tear to slip down his cheek. He'd never felt such understanding, such acceptance. His past transgressions, his jet set lifestyle—they had been sources of antagonism between him and his parents, hailed as empty gestures in a life lacking in substance. He'd pushed those accusations away, assigning them to a generation that no longer mattered. How wrong he'd been.

"Now I know you are truly the only woman I have ever loved.

"Ferro, my adoring and adorable Ferro," Diane said, happy tears streaming down her cheeks. "That's the first time you've said that to me, and in such a setting, and with heartfelt emotion behind it. I'm nearly speechless." Then she laughed. "See, nearly. Very little gets Diane Mancini to shut up."

"What you've done for me, the level of trust you instilled in me, there are no words. In New York, you made me a full partner in your dreams. You risked your savings, your security, all of it on a whim and an idea, trusting me with almost reckless abandon. A gesture like that, it's when I first realized that I didn't want anything separating us, not the past and not the coasts. Let me return that favor. No, that's not right, favor is hardly the right word. I want to share everything I have with you as my partner, as my love."

"Ferro, what are you asking me?'

Ferro wanted to steel his nerves for the words he was about to speak, but the truth of the matter was that they came with no hesitation. He just simply said, "Diane, I am asking you to be my wife." He got down on one knee, tradition dictating his actions. "Diane Mancini, will you please do me the honor of becoming my wife? Will you marry me?"

"Oh, Ferro, I didn't mean...oh...I feel like I've pressured you into asking me, that you weren't ready."

That's when an eager Ferro reached onto the silver platter and withdrew from beneath a silk napkin a large, gleaming diamond ring, its magic and sparkle captured perfectly by the flickering light of the candles. "As you can see, you have not pressured me into anything. My life is consumed with complex business deals, ones I spend days or weeks or months looking into, examining every angle, because to do so is prudent. It's a case of playing it safe. But that's for work, and work alone, where the brain dictates your action. Here with you, now, I know only one thing, and that's what my heart speaks. It says I want you as my wife, for forever."

"Yes, Ferro," Diane said, her hands set against her cheeks with a mix of surprise and delight, a dream-like quality rising above her, as though she would never wake from this beautiful moment. "Yes, I will marry you."

Ferro slid the ring on her delicate finger, then leaned in to kiss her soft, tear-stained lips. Then they embraced, and even without music playing in the background, they began to dance, like palms fronds in the wind, swaying to an all-consuming whirlwind they themselves had created. It was a dance that would last long into the night, from the gazebo to the garden, and finally to the bedroom, where Ferro and Diane would come together as one, not for the first time and certainly not for the last time.

The future had arrived, even though there were still matters to attend to.

As Diane slept, Ferro edged off the bed and padded his way to the window. In the distance he watched as a streak of lightning illuminated the sky. Thunder followed, rumbling across a sky soon to be lit by the morning sun bathed in gray clouds. Was the coming storm a sense of ominous things still to come, or was it just Mother Nature signaling a shift in the air? A way to clear away the dust of yesteryear and start anew?

"Papa, are you here?" Ferro asked to the darkened sky, glad to be awake, glad not to have been disturbed by dreams. "For one last game to play?"

CHAPTER TWENTY-FOUR

AFTER SPENDING A MAGICAL WEEK with Diane, a time in which they had spent countless hours talking, getting to know each other on a deeper level, telling stories about their youth, their family and their friends and even past loves, sharing intimate secrets they would never reveal to another soul and further indulging passions that showed no signs of diminishing, Ferro awoke on Monday morning a man on a brand-new mission. Or perhaps it was a remnant of his former mission, with one last move still to be made. He'd thought long and hard these past days, and at last he knew which square to choose. A visit to the lion's den was in order, and he wondered if perhaps he shouldn't arrive with an orchid plant as an offering of good will.

Diane had already had breakfast, and right now was busy in the morning room addressing envelopes.

"Good morning, my love," he said, entering the room to the delighted smile of his betrothed. A fire had been lit, taking the chill off the rainy morning. "I see you're hard at work on your invitations."

"Ferro, this is a whirlwind of a wedding. We can't possibly pull off all these details in time."

Ferro just grinned at her. "That's nonsense, my dear. You make the demand, I write the check, and those who work for us can't get it done fast enough," he said. "Besides, my Mama will be arriving from Rome later this afternoon, and she will take over every detail. You'll get used to the pace, though I suspect you're already well acquainted with it—like in your business when a great apartment comes on the market, the bids come faster than the bank can approve a mortgage."

"Promise me you'll be here when your mother arrives. I cannot meet her all on my own," she said.

Ferro cupped her chin, smiling at her. "You make it sound as though my mother is your mother."

"Not funny," she said, but still she laughed anyway. "Ferro, how can you be sure all of our guests can attend our wedding? I can't believe you've instructed Claude to take all the invitations to FedEx to have them sent out overnight," she said, "not to mention the airline tickets accompanying each invitation. First class—for everyone and their guests? Ferro, it's extravagant beyond words, but the gesture sure makes it difficult for anyone to turn us down, even with the short notice."

"Our wedding will not wait. I don't believe in sitting around and waiting for an event, I prefer to make the event happen when I…when we want. Our guests will be here, I can assure you. Who passes up an invitation to a celebration at Villa Olivetti at the height of a Napa spring? The air is fragrant with the region's bounty—speaking of which, I've arranged for you and Mama to visit Napa Crest Vineyard for a tasting, I think they will have the most perfect wines for our perfect day," he asked. "Diane, we are to be married this weekend, and my fondest wish is to have all who matter most to us be there. All who helped put the happy ending on our fairytale romance."

Ferro leaned down and plucked one of the cream-colored envelopes from the desk, securing it inside his jacket pocket.

"What are you doing with that invitation?"

"One of them needs to be hand-delivered. I have to go out. I will be back later," he said.

"More secrets, Ferro?"

"Hardly, my dear. Just consider it an overture on my part. We will see what happens," Ferro said. "It is something I need to do. My father, he would expect it from me."

Diane had learned already that when it came to the wishes of Ferro's departed father, nothing got in the way. And so, she accepted one more kiss from Ferro, and then the man was off on his mission.

An hour later, Ferro arrived in downtown San Francisco, but not at the Olivetti building. Rather, he was clear across town, and dressed like the successful businessman he was, in a suit of fine Italian cut, he had every assurance he would be able to see his intended party without difficulty. He stepped off the elevator of an office tower high above the city, glass windows offering spectacular views of the Presidio and the bay, the Golden Gate stretching out into the mist. This was Ground Zero for his enemy, Dunbar Industries. Passing through a set of glass doors, a pretty receptionist smiled up at the handsome Ferro and asked if she could help him.

"I hope so. I'd like to see Mr. Dunbar."

"Oh, well, let me see," she said, beginning to flip through an appointment book. "I trust you have an appointment?"

"Sorry, I don't."

Her pretty brow frowned. "As I'm sure you can appreciate, Mr. Dunbar is a very busy man. This is wholly unorthodox. We don't just accept visitors off the street like this. Are you certain you are supposed to be here?"

"Mr. Dunbar and I go back awhile, and it's been quite a while since we've seen each other. I was hoping to surprise him. And yes, I realize my presence is out of the normal realm of business, and under normal circumstances I wouldn't give a stranger the time of day either, much less grant his request. But if you'll kindly inform Mr. Dunbar that I, Ferro Olivetti, am here and wish just a moment of his time, I would appreciate it."

The woman blanched, perhaps realizing she was in the presence of billions. Not literally, but Ferro certainly gave off the confident appearance of a man for whom money was no object, and no was merely a two-letter word without obstacle. "Are you really Ferro. Oh, oh, certainly Mr. Olivetti. I didn't recognize you."

Of course you didn't, Ferro thought, wondering how much that would change with his marriage to Diane. She was a woman to parade around the city, to show off and to spoil. With that would come an expectation that Ferro Olivetti would not be so camera-shy. With love, you made sacrifices. He supposed he'd have to learn to smile more often for the dreaded *Paparazzi*.

The receptionist quickly dialed a number, speaking quietly to whomever he assumed was Dunbar's secretary. Moments later she replaced the receiver.

"You'll be seen," she said. "Perhaps you'd like to have a seat while you wait?"

"No thank you. I'm sure it won't be long."

Not two minutes later a flustered-looking woman came bustling down the long hallway. Ferro felt bad for her, just after nine o'clock on a Monday morning, and the woman's nerves were already frazzled. He was sure it wasn't because of the caffeine from her morning coffee. He silently apologized for having been the cause of any of her consternation, but working for a man like Dunbar, she had no doubt come to expect rough waters.

"Mr. Olivetti, if you'll follow me?"

The woman escorted Ferro through a complicated maze of hallways and offices, past conference rooms and cubicles, filled with employees who no doubt came to work with the fear of God sitting beside them. What a pressure cooker of an office, a direct contrast to the atmosphere he projected at Olivetti Enterprises. Ferro felt he could cut the tension here with a knife. He'd have to watch his back, no doubt one of those knives, perhaps a literal one, could be found on these corporate premises.

At last they came to a closed set of wooden doors. Brass handles still gleamed from a weekend polish. Dunbar hadn't had many intrusions in this young week. The woman knocked, heard a grunt, then opened both doors. "Mr. Dunbar, Mr. Olivetti to see you."

Ferro stepped inside an office he'd only before imagined. Not unlike his own sanctum, filled with expensive furniture, orchid plants dotting several surfaces. Damn, he'd forgotten his peace offering. Ferro found a hunched-over Dunbar facing out the huge plate-glass window, himself a wilting flower. As though Ferro's very appearance had taken the air out of the old man's shoulders, leaving him deflated. Defeated? Ferro had to wonder if something else had happened in the man's lonely life. Dunbar didn't turn, he didn't greet his guest. He merely said, "You've got some nerve coming here."

"Good morning. I've come with an offer, Mr. Dunbar."

The gruff old businessman suddenly turned, a scowl on his withered face. "So formal, Olivetti? I can't recall you ever calling me by anything other than Dunbar."

"Yes, well, perhaps I've been a tad disrespectful. In business, we should know that even if we're on opposite sides, we are both gentlemen."

"Spit it out, Ferro," Dunbar said, showing none of the graciousness of his guest.

"During a recent personal crisis of mine that left me vulnerable, you sought to take advantage of my company, to take it over and systematically destroy all I'd built. That's not something I can easily forgive. My father's death was not something for you to exploit. Why you wanted to destroy me, I cannot fathom. Out of retaliation for besting you in the Vodell deal? Attempting to ruin my reputation and take what is rightfully mine seems rather an extreme reaction, but in the spirit of decency, I've decided to let it go. Let bygones be bygones."

"A fine speech, but I know you. It's a ploy for something sneaky. Just spit it out: What are you setting me up for, Olivetti?"

"Not a thing, Mr. Dunbar," Ferro said, moving in closer, nearly standing beside the man. Together they shared the view of the city, one certainly big enough for both, and others. Ferro noticed the large bouquet of flowers on the windowsill. "Those are orchids, are they not?"

"Yes, what of them?"

"You care for them very nicely. I had heard you had an affection for the flowers."

"They're plants," Dunbar stated proudly. "Is there a point to all this? Are you going to make some kind of comparison between me and my prized orchids? Are you planning to snip off their heads when they show signs of weakness, of losing their lust for life? You think just because I've got more years under my belt than you that I'm vulnerable? You speak of retaliation? I'll tell you this, Olivetti, try and take over my company and I'll see you in hell."

Ferro let out a small, innocent laugh. He didn't respond directly to Dunbar's accusation. He merely gazed out the window at the impressive, towering buildings that defined the skyline of the City by the Bay.

"You know, Mr. Dunbar, you look at this brilliant city, and at all that it has to offer and you have to ask what's it represent? So many businesses, so many people just trying to get by, make a living while they realize what's truly important to them. The way I see it, there's plenty of room in this city for the two of us to happily co-exist. You can be enemies in business, but when the offices close and the real beauty of life awakens, that's what makes it all count. A wise, wonderful man taught me that."

"He was a fool."

"That 'fool' as you so cavalierly put it, was my father," Ferro Olivetti said. "And I see that I've wasted my time in coming here. There is no dealing with a man so angry at the world he cannot recognize an olive branch when he sees one. I wish your orchids good luck surviving in such an environment. And good luck to you, Mr. Dunbar—whoever broke your heart, I hope you find the special someone to help heal it. Trust me, it's possible."

"Don't talk to me of love."

"Why not, Richard? In the end, it's all that matters." When the old man did not respond, Ferro merely nodded. "I wish you only well-being and happiness."

Ferro started off and had made it to the door when Dunbar called out to him. Ferro spun around saw the old man staring at him with the most curious of expressions. He sensed the man's cold heart had hit a heat wave.

"You want to tell me what you're really doing here?"

Ferro withdrew from his jacket pocket the thick, cream-colored envelope he'd taken from Diane. He walked over and handed it to Dunbar.

"What's this?"

"An invitation. To my wedding."

"I wasn't aware you were getting married," Dunbar said, his eyes softening just the slightest. Ferro sensed the man's defensive stance beginning to dissolve, and for the first time he wondered if there really was a heart inside the old man. He must have been wounded greatly, and perhaps recently. But just as quickly as the emotion had surfaced, it was swallowed by a lifetime of hatred, of anger, and perhaps, of desperate loneliness. Dunbar tore the invitation in two, tossing the pieces into Ferro's face.

"Love is for suckers."

Ferro shook his head, began his retreat from an office so filled with everything that was wrong with the human condition. "Have it your way. You'll never learn, Dunbar, what's truly important in life. Fortunately, I have had the privilege of discovering it, and you want to know what? I learned it from the best man I will ever know in my life, a man I was lucky enough to get one last chance to see, to talk to, and ultimately, to fulfill his last wish. If Ferro Olivetti has achieved anything in his life, success, wealth, the love of the most amazing woman, I have my father to thank. Good day."

And when Ferro left, he realized deep in his heart there remained one last visit before he could truly be free of an obligation he'd never asked for. One that had forever changed his life.

*   *   *

"You're where?"

"On an airplane."

"Ferro, where are you going?"

"Trust me, Diane, I will be back before the wedding. That, I promise you."

"But your mother is coming. Claude called thirty minutes ago to say she had landed, they were on their way the villa. What do I tell her?"

"Tell her Papa needs me one last time," he said, and then laughed. "You'll be fine, both of you. My two favorite women together, I cannot imagine anything more perfect."

"You being here, that would help."

"Such nonsense, I would only be in the way of all the planning," he said. "It's perfect that I take care of this last piece of personal business before I marry the woman who changed my life. Be well, Diane, and know that I love you always."

It was fittingly appropriate that Ferro Olivetti was again seated on an airplane, settled comfortably in First Class, with thankfully no sign of any bellowing buffoon to be seen. Isn't that how this entire adventure of his had begun? More planes, more miles than he could count, he guessed he had circled the globe at least once since he'd arrived back from his European junket with Cassandra. Now it was back over the Atlantic. He didn't want to tell Diane where he was headed, not yet, for fear that she might talk him out of it. How could he possibly be back in time for the wedding? But he knew, this last trip was necessary if he was truly to put the past behind him.

Simply put, he was bound for home.

There were ghosts to finally bury.

One more discussion to be had before he could move on with his life.

With his future. With Diane.

The thought of her, her image and her enthusiasm and her love for him, her deep-set, dark eyes that stared back at him with awe, with desire, when he made love to her, all of that kept him company during taxi and takeoff and well over the Atlantic, where the plane steadily jetted them high above the clouds toward their destination. At last, they landed at Fiumicino Airport, where Ferro hailed a taxi and immediately entered the fray of Rome's circular traffic. He'd packed no bags; he would achieve what he'd come for and then turn right back around and get on the next plane back to the States.

Fifteen hours since the plane had lifted off the ground in San Francisco, Ferro Olivetti found himself entering through the iron gates of the cemetery where his father was buried. It had been a long trip, but even so that didn't mean he knew what he was going to say once he reached the grave. Rain had begun to fall in the city, and Ferro realized how unprepared he was for anything. Putting his suit jacket collar up around his neck, he ventured forward through the rows of graves, his memory guiding him to his father's final resting place.

At last, he found the row, his eyes attracted to a beautiful bouquet of flowers laid before the grave marker. Ferro knelt, oblivious to the wet grass around him, closing his eyes as he did so. Blessing himself, he kissed his fingertips and then pressed them against the gray marble headstone. He opened his eyes to find the words "Alberto Olivetti, beloved husband and father" staring back at him. Seeing such words, it was almost as though a magician had conjured the man himself, so vivid were Ferro's memories of the great man. And what he imagined was not the frail man who had issued his stern warning while waiting to die, but the vibrant, youthful father who had patiently taught him the ways of the world.

"Papa," Ferro said, "I was angry with you when last I saw you. I flew halfway across the world to be at your side while you passed into a better world, and all I wanted to do was hold you, embrace you, and help ease your pain. You had other plans, as you always did. Mama, she knew what you were going to ask of me, but for me, what you said, how you judged me, I will admit that it pained me to hear it. To listen to such disapproval come from your lips, to know those words were meant for me. I couldn't imagine why, on your deathbed, it was I who was being judged.

"Papa," Ferro said, "after your funeral, I was a mess. I thought I had disappointed you, that you had gone to your grave believing your son had failed you. I couldn't allow that to happen, and Mama, she asked if I was prepared to honor your request. To give up all my worldly possessions, to seek out a new life and rediscover what was important in life it was a crazy notion, made even more so by the complications in my life. But yet I did as you asked, I stepped away from everything, and for almost thirty days—twenty-eight to be exact—I lived a new life under a new name. And you know what happened?

"Papa," Ferro said, "I met the most wonderful woman, and I learned what I was missing. I learned finally what you wanted for me. All the money and possessions in the world, they are mere distractions for the empty hours of a life. They do not complete it. Diane, that's her name, Diane Mancini. Yes, Mama is of course happy she is Italian. They are together now, at the Villa in Napa, planning the wedding. That's right, your son Ferro is getting married, and afterwards there will be children. Mama will be a grandmother and in spirit you will be a grandfather.

"Papa," Ferro said, "you saved me. Your strange request of me, it was only to be understood after completion, when I could assess where I was before and where I was now, and whether I was a better man because of it. I am, but I am also a better man because of you. You instructed me daily, even on days when you could not be at my side. You shared your vision of the world, and in the trying times during those thirty days, when I could count on no one, I would think of you, why you had asked this of me, what I could also possibly mean. Life is a game, not unlike the games of chess we shared over the years. There are people on your team who will help you achieve your goals. There are people on the opposing side who will do everything they can do stop you.

"Papa," Ferro said, "I could never win a chess game against you, and then what do you do, you send me off to play the biggest game of chess ever, on the world's biggest stage. And this time, with no pawns, no knights, just a lone man with his thoughts and his ambitions, his dreams, and his grief over losing a father he'd thought he'd disappointed. But I feel I have won that game, the king has reached his destination, and in the process, he has found his queen. For all your wisdom, for the way you pushed me, during your lifetime and beyond, there is no way to ever repay you. But know this. I will never forget you, and I will visit you when 1 can, and when my first son is born, he will carry your name.

"Papa," Ferro said, "For a time I thought I would be the last of the Olivettis, and now I know that is not the truth. What you taught me, I will turn around and teach my own son. The name Olivetti will live on to play a game again."

At last Ferro stood. From his pocket he withdrew a small item, which he placed graveside, just next to the flowers his mother had no doubt left before she flew to the States for the wedding. Ferro gazed at the item, smiling at the memories it brought him. Carved of ivory, it was the king from the chess set his father had given him.

"I no longer need this piece, Papa," Ferro said, "because I have finally won a game against you. I will leave you with one final word, a word I never got to utter in your presence." And then he paused, smiling broadly. "Checkmate."

By now the rain was coming down hard, and he was soaked to the skin. During his speech to his father, he hadn't even noticed the fierce downpour, nor the thunder that clapped against the dark skies, the lightning which streaked over a city called Eternal.

It was time to depart for the states. Once in New York, the Gambit One awaited him, once again his destiny was back in his own hands.

*   *   *

It was a day made for dreams to come true. A picture-perfect azure sky hovered above the Olivetti estate, and a warm breeze swept across the land, breathing fresh new scents to a lawn already overcrowded with floral bouquets of the most delicate and exquisite composition. A string quartet set up inside the gazebo played quietly, its subtle interpretations of Bach and Beethoven and Verdi imbuing the setting with a taste of the old world. Champagne flowed from a specially designed fountain, the bubbles catching in the sun's brilliant gleam. Along with ideal weather conditions, a definite buzz hung in the air, as the guests mingled about, waiting for the main event.

A wedding was to take place at Villa Olivetti in just a few moments.

Except there was one problem.

"Where's Ferro?" Helena Olivetti asked.

"He said he'd be here," Lawrence assured her. "You know he's had trouble getting back from Rome because of a storm, but he assured me he would make it in time. Perhaps you should attend to the bride and help relieve her nerves. From what Ferro has told me of his future mother-in-law, she's not exactly a calming influence."

"Thank you, Lawrence, you're a good man, and I appreciate your loyalty to my son."

"What's a best man for?"

While Helena went to see about Diane, Lawrence checked his watch. The ceremony was supposed to begin in thirty minutes, and still there was no sign of Ferro, no word from him. Just then his phone issued a "bleet bleet" and Lawrence grabbed for it. The caller I.D. had him breathing easier.

"Ferro, where are you?"

"Just minutes away, Lawrence. Please, have all the guests assembled in their seats, and make sure Diane and everyone are waiting."

"Are you in a taxi? Because Claude is here, and so is the limo."

"Yes, he should be. For the wedding. Today no one works," Ferro said. "Lawrence, I can see the house from here, just another couple minutes until I arrive."

"What?"

A sound in the air caught Lawrence's attention. He gazed upwards into the sky, and that's when he saw the aircraft piercing the fluffy white clouds as it began its descent. *My God*, Lawrence thought, *what was he going to do, parachute down, or was he planning on landing that thing on the road?* He shook his head, but really, should he have been surprised? Ferro Olivetti never did anything on a small scale, and so why should his wedding be anything different? Lawrence sprung into action, handing out directives and instructions like the dutiful second-in-command he was.

"Ladies and gentleman, if you would take your seats please," an usher instructed, dressed in a classic black tuxedo, a red rose in his lapel the only hint of color on him. He was Steve Donovan, Ferro's golfing buddy and friend, who was escorted today by his girlfriend, Dora. They had hooked up shortly after Ferro's party all those months ago, and things were going great. Dora too was helping the guests, urging them to their seats. When most of the guests were seated, Steve radioed back to Lawrence, saying they were all set.

"Thanks, Steve."

Just then the air above them was filled with sounds of a droning engine, which had everyone looking up. Women held onto their hats, and men applauded over the balls it took to land that thing on something other than an airstrip. Lawrence stood alone, keeping a watchful eye on the plane as its altitude decreased, bringing it closer and closer to the ground. The plane zoomed past them, banking slightly before coming around from the north to the wide road that led up to the main entrance of Villa Olivetti. A hand came from inside the cockpit, thumb raised upwards. Lawrence breathed a sigh of relief, knowing all was good. Ferro was safe and he was purposely landing the plane. It wasn't a case of engine trouble.

Ferro just wanted to make a spectacular entrance.

And he did, as the *Gambit One* touched down upon the ground, racing up the road toward the driveway. The sound of squealing engines shook the land around them like an earthquake had hit the valley, but as quickly as the plane had appeared, it came to a halt just yards from Villa Olivetti. The door opened and out stepped Ferro Olivetti, and he was already dressed in his tuxedo, though he was missing his bow tie.

"I think I work for James Bond," Lawrence said aloud, to the laughter of several people around him.

He went running toward his employer, who greeted him with a huge embrace. "So, Lawrence, where is my bride? I believe I am to be married in moments. Though I am missing one important item. I trust you found it?"

"Have I ever disappointed you, Ferro?"

"Never, Lawrence."

*　　*　　*

With Lawrence at his side, in business and for his wedding, Ferro knew he was in good hands, and together the two friends made their way, traversing along a white carpet that had been set out for the special occasion. Approaching the trellis from which Diane would soon pass, Ferro stopped to take in the amazing sight before him. Spread out on his lawn was the most magnificent burst of colors, from the fancy dresses worn by the women to the bountiful flowers, it was as though a rainbow had come to live at his home, filling his world with Technicolor dreams.

Ferro made his way down the aisle, smiling, shaking hands, placing kisses on the cheeks of all those assembled. When he got to the front row, he kneeled and tenderly embraced his mother.

"It gives me the greatest pleasure in the world to have you here, Mama."

A resplendent-looking Helena Olivetti, a tear in her eye, said, "Such an entrance, always the showman. I am blessed to have a son like you. And soon, a daughter-in-law like Diane. Ferro, she's the most wonderful woman, we've had such a great week getting to know each other. I know you both will be very happy."

"It was Papa's doing," he said. "You do know that's why I nearly missed my wedding. I had to talk to him, one last time."

Helena looked at the sky, Ferro watching her. "He knows, and there is no way he would have let you miss this day. He's watching us today. That warm sun that you feel? It is him, beaming proudly."

Ferro kissed his mother's cheek one more time, then moved into position. Even though it needed little adjusting, Ferro smoothed down the special tie he now wore. Smiling at the memory of when Diane gave it to him, he took a quick glance at the image of Lady Liberty woven into the fabric. There was no way Ferro would get married without it. Lawrence took up beside him. The two men greeted the priest, thanked him for whatever he had to do with the fine weather.

"God knows when to provide his blessings," the elderly priest said with a twinkle in his smile.

Ferro glanced back at the waiting guests. In addition to coworkers and associates from Olivetti Enterprises, as well as several prominent businessmen from San Francisco and Silicon

Valley, Ferro was heartily pleased to see how many of Diane's friends had made the long trek across the country. He hoped they enjoyed the first-class service he'd provided. And it was not just her friends, but people who had become like family to him, too, a virtual tour of the thirty days he'd spent in New York. He smiled at Jennifer and Sandra, who sat together with their respective dates; he nodded at Fred Evans, who had traveled alone but looked handsome enough to make new friends easily; Ferro was especially pleased to see Angelo Pelligrino, the hot dog vendor from Central Park, who was accompanied by his wife and their son. A couple that took him by surprise, not just because they were together but because they were here, was Timothy and the new man in his life: one Stan Curtis. Guess love comes in all forms. Ferro recalled hearing that they had found each other, and that Curtis had even ended a long-distance relationship in his quest to find himself. As mismatched as they looked, Ferro had to admit he'd never seen Curtis happier. *Love*, Ferro mused, *is not without its mystery.*

Just then the string quartet paused, then started up again with a new song. The wedding march. The guests all stood, and Ferro looked on eagerly, waiting for his first look at his bride-to-be. The rear door of the villa opened, and the first one to step out was Diane's maid of honor. Ferro grinned at the sight of a smiling, beautifully dressed Vita Banger, remembering their initial meeting at the bar in Manhattan. It was amazing that a seemingly innocuous meeting could lead to something as wondrous as this. Ferro would be forever grateful to Vita.

Then, Ferro saw Mr. and Mrs. Mancini emerge, both of whom then put out a hand to help their daughter step down onto the grassy lawn. The same Mancinis who had once questioned his motives were now set upon moving to San Francisco to be closer to their daughter. Speaking of which, Diane was still too far away for Ferro to truly take in her beauty, but that didn't stop him from gasping at the mere hint of her presence. He had missed her terribly during his ordeal in Rome, waiting out the weather to catch a plane back to the States. It was worth the wait, he had to admit. As the music swelled, the bride and her parents grew ever closer, Ferro felt the anticipation building exponentially with each of their steps. Was this wedding really happening? This magical, perfect, ideal moment in his life, when he would soon be joined forever to the woman who inspired him, moved him, challenged him, loved him.

Beneath the veil, Ferro could see Diane's smile, and her tears. His heart had never been so full. He also felt the walk down the aisle was the longest in history, as he waited with noticeable impatience and eagerness for Diane to link arms with him. She looked radiant, her dress a mix of delicate lace and flowing silk, a dress made especially for her. For Ferro had spared no expense, not on the day, not on the dress, not on anything that pertained to giving Diane the most perfect of days. A day that would linger long in their memories, a day, he'd said, "You'll remember forever." He had a feeling the way he'd arrived would add to the memory.

As Ferro took her hand, he knew from her touch that what existed between them was truly meant to be for forever.

"You look beyond beautiful," Ferro said to Diane.

"Welcome home," she said.

"You saw my entrance?"

"Who didn't?"

"Are you mad?"

"My handsome groom, what woman would be upset that the man she loves did anything and everything he could to make it the wedding? Landing the Gambit One on the lawn? Only my Ferro."

"My father taught me to always be myself."

"And you always do as your father asks," she said. "And by the way, Ferro, you look so handsome, too. And the tie. That means so much to me."

"The tie means so much to me, too. It reminds me of you."

The priest then stepped forward. "Are we ready?"

"For our lives to begin?" Ferro asked. "I've been ready since I first set eyes on this beautiful lady."

"Oh, Ferro. I'm going to cry. Cry tears of joy."

"That's what we'll have for all our lives, endless joy."

The priest smiled, and then addressed the crowd. "Dearly gathered here in the sight of God and these witnesses to join two loving souls, Diane Mancini and Ferro Olivetti. Truly, forever, as the heavens have decreed that these two are meant to be together.

The dream always began the same way.

"Papa, Papa, please, play a game with me."

A young Ferro bounced energetically up on the bed, waking his slumbering father this Sunday morning. The smells of breakfast wafted from downstairs, and soon Papa was tossing back the covers. He knew that on a day such as today, there was no denying the wishes of his son.

"And what game is it you wish to play?"

"Chess," the small boy said.

He was all of seven years old, but intelligent beyond words. Papa laughed, tousling the boy's hair. "Come, let's head down to the den and set up the game pieces."

"I've already set them up," the boy said.

"Of course you have," Papa said.

With the boy's small hand in his, Papa padded his way out of the bedroom and down the long hallway. The boy practically pulling him down the stairs, he said, "Slow down, Ferro, there is plenty of time, we have all day. Remember, it is Sunday, and what are Sundays?"

"Family day!" the boy cried aloud.

"That's right. No work today, just lots of fun."

They made their way to the den, where on the side table was set up the game of chess, the pawns and queens and rooks carved of ivory more sculptures than game pieces. It had been a gift to the boy on his fifth birthday, and since then he had become quite adept at the game's intricate strategies, He was still searching out his first win, though.

Also placed near the game was a steaming cup of coffee for Papa, a glass of orange juice for the eager boy. Taking a grateful sip, feeling energized by the caffeine, Papa silently thanked his loving wife for her attentiveness, her thoughtfulness. She knew he would need the extra brain power to defeat their incorrigible son.

"Papa, who goes first?"

"Oh, my boy, you may go first."

The game progressed, with the boy making quick work of his father. Pieces fell like territories being crushed by the Roman Empire. Except, at the very last moment, Papa made an unexpected move and announced, "Checkmate."

"Oh, Papa, how did you know to do that?"

"As you get older, you learn many things, my son. Not chief among them, how to win at business and at life, and at love."

"Papa, will you teach me everything you know? I want to be just like you when I grow up."

"Then you must listen carefully, my boy," Papa said, "because my will is the only way."

*   *   *

Ferro Olivetti awakened from his dream, a broad smile gracing his handsome face. Mostly he was happy because he knew that the images that had floated through his sleeping mind were not just his subconscious working overtime, they were the pictures already embedded in his mind. What everyone simply called memories.

What was real now was the fragrant smell of breakfast—coffee brewing, bacon frying, not unlike in the dream. The pleasant odors permeated the house, pulling at him, to the point where he quickly grabbed his robe and slippers and made his way down to the kitchen. The vision before him was one not even a dream could hope for. Diane, looking as radiant today as the day he'd married her, smiled at him.

"Good morning, dear."

"Good morning, my love."

Just then the room was filled with the joyful sounds of three screaming, delighted children as they came running into the kitchen, all of them swirling around Ferro with reckless abandon. "Papa, papa, papa," they said in unison.

Ferro bent down and embraced them all, collectively and individually.

He looked up at Diane and smiled broadly before saying, "I love Sundays."

"And who else used to say that?"

It was the oldest child who answered, a boy named Alberto. "Grandpa did!"

ACKNOWLGEMENTS

While many authors believe that writing is a solitary craft, I have found the opposite to be true, and I wish to acknowledge the many people who assisted me in transitioning "My Secret Billionaire" from screenplay to novel, draft after draft, until we reached the final product. Special thanks go out to my editor, Joseph Pittman, for his huge contributions in curating this project.